THE SKY ROAD

Also by Ken MacLeod

THE STAR FRACTION
THE STONE CANAL
THE CASSINI DIVISION

THE SKY ROAD

Ken MacLeod

TOR®

A TOM DOHERTY ASSOCIATES BOOK
NEW YORK

THE SKY ROAD

First published in Great Britain by Orbit

This book is printed on acid-free paper.

A Tor Book
Published by Tom Doherty Associates, LLC
175 Fifth Avenue
New York, NY 10010

www.tor.com

Tor® is a registered trademark of Tom Doherty Associates, LLC.

ISBN 0-312-87335-2

First US edition: August 2000

Printed in the United States of America

0 9 8 7 6 5 4 3 2 1

For Mic

Contents

1

The Light and the Fair

So it came that Merrial found him
in the square at Carron Town

She walked through the fair in the light of a northern summer
evening, looking for me. Of the hundreds of people around her, the
thousands in the town and the thousands on the project, only I would
serve her purpose. My voice and visage, mind and body were her
target acquisition parameters.

I sat on the plinth of the statue of the Deliverer, drained a bottle of
beer and put it carefully down and looked around, screwing up my
eyes against the westering sun. The music faded for a moment, then
another band struck up, something rollicking and loud that echoed
off the tall buildings around three sides of the square and boomed out
from the open side across the shore and over the water. The still sea-
loch was miles of gold, the distant hills and islands stacks of black.
The air was warm and shaking with the music and heavy with scent
and sweat, alcohol-breath and weed-smoke. People were already
dancing, swinging and swirling among the remaining stalls of the
day's market. I caught glimpses and greetings from various of my
workmates, Jondo and Druin and Machard and the rest, as they
whirled past in the throng with somebody who might be their partner
for the hour, or for the night, or for longer.

For a moment, I felt intensely alone, and was about to jump up and
plunge in and seek out someone, anyone, who would take me even
for one dance. It was not normally this way; usually at such occasions
through the summer I had got lucky. Like most of my fellow-workers,
I was young and – of necessity – strong, and my vanity needed no flattery, and we were most of us open-handed strangers, and therefore

welcome. But I was in a serious and abstracted mood, the coming autumn's study already casting its long shadow back, and in all that evening's gaiety I had not once made a woman laugh, and my luck had fled.

She walked through that dense crowd as if it wasn't there. I saw her before she saw me. Her long black hair was caught around the temples by two narrow braids; the tumbling waves of the rest showed traces of auburn in the late sun. That golden light and ruddy shadow defined her tanned and flushed face: the large bright eyes, the high cheekbones, the curve of her cheek and jaw, the red lips. She wore a gown of plain green velvet that seemed, and probably was, made to show off her strong and well-endowed figure. Her gaze met mine, and locked. Her eyes were large and a little slanted, and they caught my glance like a trap.

There is, no doubt, some bodily basis for the crude cartoon of such moments – the arrow through the heart. A sudden demand on the sugar reserves of the cells, perhaps. It's more like a thorn than an arrow, and passes in less than a second, but it's there, that sharp, sweet stab.

A moment later she stood in front of me, looking down at me quizzically, curiously, then she came to some decision and sat down beside me on the cold black marble. The hooves of the Deliverer's horse reared above us. We stared at each other for a moment. My heart was hammering. She appeared younger, more hesitant, than she'd seemed with her first bold gaze. Her irises were golden-brown, ringed with green-blue. I could see a faint spatter of freckles beneath her tan. A fine gold chain around her neck suspended a rough mesh of gold wire containing a seer-stone the size of a pigeon's egg. It hung between her breasts, its small world flickering randomly in that gentle friction. An even thinner silver chain implied some other ornament, but it hung below where I could see. The dagger and derringer and purse on her narrow waist-belt were each so elegant and delicate as to be almost nominal. There was some powerful undertone to her scent, whether natural or artificial I didn't know.

'Well, here you are,' she said, as though we'd arranged to meet at this very place. For a couple of heartbeats I entertained the thought that this might be true, that she was someone I really did know and had unaccountably, unforgivably forgotten – but no, I had no memory of ever having met her before. At the same time I couldn't get rid of a conviction that I already knew her, and always had.

'Hello,' I said, for want of anything less banal. 'What's your name?'

'Merrial,' she said. 'And you are . . .?'

'Clovis,' I said. 'Clovis colha Gree.'

She nodded to herself, as though some datum had been confirmed, and smiled at me.

'So, colha Gree, are you going to ask me for a dance?'

I jumped to my feet, amazed. 'Yes, of course. Would you do me the honour?'

'Thank you,' she said. She took my hand in a warm, dry grasp and rose gracefully, merging that movement with her first step. It was a fast dance to a traditional air, 'The Tactical Boys'. Talking was impossible, but we communicated a great deal none the less. Another measure followed, and then a slower dance.

We finished it a long way from where we'd started – fetched up close to the outside tables of the biggest pub on the square, The Carronade. Some of the lads from work were already at one of the tables, with their local girls. My mates gave me odd looks, compounded of envy and secret amusement; their female partners were looking lasers at Merrial, for no reason I could fathom. She was attractive all right, and looking more beautiful to my eyes with every passing second, but the other girls were not obviously less blessed; and she wasn't a harlot, unless she was foolish (harlotry being a respected but regulated trade in that town, its plying not permitted in the square).

Introductions were awkwardly made.

'What will you be having, Merrial?' I asked.

She smiled up at me. She was, in truth, almost as tall as I, but my boots had high heels.

'A beer, please.'

'Fine. Will you wait here?'

I gestured to a vacant place on the nearest bench, beside Jondo and his current lass.

'I will that,' Merrial said.

Jondo shot me another odd look, a smile with one corner of his mouth turned down, and his eyebrows raised. I shrugged and went through to the bar, returning a few minutes later with a three-litre jug and a couple of tall glasses. Merrial was sitting where she'd been, ignoring the fact that she was being ignored. I put this unaccustomed rudeness down to some petty local quarrel, of which Carron

Town – and the yard and, indeed, the project – had plenty. If one of Merrial's ancestors had offended one of Jondo's (or whoever's) that was no business of mine, as yet.

The table was too wide for any intimate conversation to be carried on across it, so I sat down beside her, setting off a Newtonian collision of hips all the way along the bench as my friends and their girlfriends shuffled their bums away from us. I filled our glasses and raised mine.

'*Slàinte*,' I said.

'*Slàinte, mo chridhe*,' she said, quietly but firmly, her gaze level across the tilted rim.

And cheers, my dear, to you, I thought. Again her whole manner was neither shy nor brazen, but as though we had been together for months or years. I didn't know what to say, so I said that.

'I feel we know each other already,' I said. 'But we don't.' I laughed. 'Unless when we were both children?'

Merrial shook her head. 'I was not here as a child,' she said, in a vague tone. 'Maybe you've seen me at the project.'

'I think I would remember,' I said. She smiled, acknowledging the compliment, as I added, 'You work at the *project*?' I sounded more surprised than I should have been – there were plenty of women working on it, after all, in catering and administration.

'Aye,' she said, 'I do.' She fondled the pendant, warming a fire within it, and not only there. 'On the guidance system.'

'Oh,' I said, suddenly understanding. 'You're a – an *engineer*.'

'I am a tinker,' she said in a level tone, using the word I'd so clumsily avoided. She spoke it with a pride as obvious, and loud enough to be heard. A snigger and a giggle passed around the table. I glared past Merrial's shoulder at Jondo and Machard. They shook their heads slightly, doubtfully, then returned to their conversations.

Justice judge them. As a city man I felt myself above such rural idiocies – though realising her occupation had given even me something of a jolt. Whatever passed between us, it would be less or more serious than any fling with a local lass. I leaned inward, so that Merrial's shoulders and mine defined a social circle of our own.

'Sounds like interesting work,' I said.

She nodded. 'A lot of mathematics, a lot of' – and this time she did lower her voice – 'programming.'

4

'Ah,' I said, trying to think of some response that wouldn't reveal me to be as prejudiced as my workmates. 'Isn't it very dangerous?' I resisted the impulse to look over my shoulder, but I was suddenly, acutely aware of the massive presence of the hills around the town, their forested slopes like the bristling backs of great beasts in the greater Wood of Caledon.

'*White* logic,' Merrial explained. 'The right-hand path, you know? The path of light.' She did not sound as though the distinction mattered a lot to her.

'Reason guide you,' I responded, with reflex piety. 'But – it must be tempting. The short cuts, yeah?'

'The path of power is always a temptation,' she said, with casual familiarity. 'Especially when you're working on a guidance system!' She laughed; I confess I shuddered. She fingered her talisman. 'Enough about that. I know what I'm doing, so it isn't dangerous. At least, not as dangerous as it looks from outside.'

'Well.' Despite the electric frisson her words aroused, I was as keen as she was to change the subject. 'You could say the same about what I do.'

'And what do you do?' She asked it out of politeness; she already knew. I was sure of that, without quite knowing why.

'I work in the yard,' I said.

'On the ship?'

'Oh, not on the ship!' A self-deprecating laugh, not very sincere. 'On the platform. For the summer, I'm a welder.'

She slugged back some beer. 'And the rest of the time?'

'I'm a scholar,' I said. 'Of history. At Glaschu.'

This was a slight exaggeration. I had just attained the degree of Master of Arts, and my summer job was a frantic, frugal effort to earn enough to support myself for an attempt at a doctorate. Scholarship was my ambition, not my occupation. But I refused to call myself a student. Merrial looked at me with the sort of effortful empathy with which I'd favoured her self-disclosure. 'That sounds . . . interesting,' she said. 'What *part* of history?'

I gestured across the square, to the statue's black silhouette. Behind it, from the east, the first visible stars of the evening pricked the sky.

'The life of the Deliverer,' I said.

'And what have you learned?' She leaned closer, transparently more interested; her black brows raised a fraction, her bright dark eyes widening. Without thinking, I lit a cigarette; remembered my manners, and offered her one. She took it, grinning, and helped herself to the jug of beer, then filled my glass too. 'You wouldn't think there'd be much new to learn,' she added, looking up through her eyelashes.

I rose to the bait. 'Ah, but there is!' I told her. 'The Deliverer lived in Glasgow, you know. For a while.'

'A lot of places will tell you she lived there – for a while!' Merrial laughed.

'Aye, but we have evidence,' I said. 'I've seen papers written with her own hand, and signed. There is no controversy that it was her who wrote them. What they mean, now, that's another matter. And a great deal of other writing, printed articles that is, and material that is still in the – you know.'

'Dark storage?'

'Yeah,' I said. 'Dark storage. I wish—' Even here, even now, it was impossible to say just what I wished. But Merrial understood.

'There you go, colha Gree,' she said. 'The path of power is always a temptation!'

'Aye, it is that,' I admitted gloomily. 'You can look at them, labelled in her own hand, and you wonder what's in them, and – well.'

'Probably corrupt,' she said briskly. 'Not worth bothering with.'

'Of course corrupt—'

She shook her head, with a brief, small frown. 'In the technical sense,' she explained. 'Garbage data, unreadable.'

Garbage data? What did that mean?

'I see,' I said, seeing only that she'd just tried to explicate part of the argot of her profession; another unseasonable intimacy.

'All the same,' she went on, 'it must be strange work, history. I don't know how you can bear it, digging about in the dead past.'

I had heard variations of this sentiment from so many people, starting with my mother, that exasperation welled within me and I'm sure showed on my face. She smiled as though to assure me that she didn't hold it against me personally, and added, 'The Possessors don't work only through the black logic, you know. They can get to your mind through their words on paper, too.'

'You speak very freely,' I said. For a woman, I didn't add.

She took it as a compliment, and thus paid me one by not recognising the stiff-kneed priggishness that my remark represented.

'It's the tinker way,' she said, giving me another small shock. 'We talk as we please.'

I couldn't come back on that, so I ploughed on.

'We have to understand the Possession,' I explained self-righteously, 'to understand the Deliverance.'

'But do we understand the Deliverance?' she asked, teasing me relentlessly. 'Do you, Clovis colha Gree?'

'I can't say,' I said – which was true enough, though ecological with the truth.

'Good,' Merrial said. '*We* would not claim to understand it, and we knew the Deliverer better than most.' A sly smile. 'As you know.'

I nodded, slowly. I knew all right. Despised and feared though they sometimes are, it is not for nothing that the tinkers are known as the Deliverer's children. They worked her will long ago, in the troubled times, and the benison of that work has protected them down the generations; that and – on a more cynical view – their obscure and irreplaceable knowledge.

I had heard rumours – always disparaged by the University historians – of a firmer continuity, a darker arcana, that linked today's tinkers and the Deliverer, and that reached back to times yet more remote, when even the Possession was but a sapling, its shadow not yet covering the Earth.

Her hand covered mine, briefly.

'Don't talk about it,' she said.

So we talked about other things: her work, my work, her childhood and mine. The glasses were twice refilled. She stood up, hefting the now empty jug. 'Same again?'

I rose too, saying, 'I'll get them—'

'I insist,' she said, and was gone. I watched the sway of her hips, the way it carried over to swing her heavy skirt and ripple the torrent of hair down her back, as she passed through the crowd and disappeared through the wide door of The Carronade. My friends observed this attention with sardonic smiles.

'You're in for an interesting time, Clovis,' Jondo remarked. He stroked his long red pony-tail suggestively, making his girlfriend laugh again. 'Looks like the glamour's got you.'

Machard smirked. 'Seriously, man,' he told me, 'take care. You don't know tinks like we do. They're faithless, godless, clannish and they don't settle down. At best she'll break your heart, at worst—'

'What is the matter with you?' I hissed, leaning sideways to keep the girls out of the path of my wrath. 'Come on, guys, give the lady a chance.'

My two friends' expressions took on looks of insolent innocence.

'Ease off, Clovis,' said Machard. 'Just advice. Ignore it if you like, it's your business.'

'Too damn right it is,' I said. 'So mind your own.' I spoke the harsh words lightly – not fighting words, but firm. The two lads shrugged and went back to chatting up their lassies. I was ignored, as Merrial had been.

The late train from Inverness glided down the glen, sparks from the overhead wire flaring in the twilight, and vanished behind the first houses. A minute later I could hear the brief commotion as it stopped at the station, a few streets away. The clouds and the tops of the hills glowed pink, the same light reflecting off a solitary airship, heading west. Few lights were on in the town – half past ten in the evening was far too early for that – but the houses that spread up the side of the glen and along the shore were beginning to seem as dark as the pine forest that began where the dwellings ended. .

Farther up the great glen the side-lights and tail-lights of vehicles traced out the road's meander, and the dark green of the wooded hillsides met the bright green of the lower slopes, field joined to field, pasture to pasture all the way to where the haunches of the hills hid the view, and the land was dark. Somewhere far away, but sounding uncannily close, a wolf howled, its protracted, sinister note clearly audible above the sounds of the town and the revelry of the fair.

The square was becoming more packed and noisy by the minute. The drinking and dancing would go on for hours. Jugglers and tumblers, fire-eaters and musicians competed for attention and spare cash, with each other and with the hawkers. The markets on summer Thursdays were locally called 'the fair', but only once a month did they amount to much, with a more impressive contingent of performers than were here now, as well as travelling players, whirling mechanical rides and, of course, tinkers; the last pursuing their legitimate trade of engineering and their less reputable, but often more lucrative, craft of fortune-telling.

The train pulled away, trailing its sparks along the Carron's estuarial plain and around the Carron sea-loch's southern shore.

Merrial returned with a full jug, a bottle of whisky and a tray of small glasses. Without a word she placed the tray and the bottle in the middle of the table and sat down, this time opposite me. She filled our tall glasses, put down the jug and gestured to the whisky bottle. 'Help yourselves,' she said.

My friends became more friendly towards her after that. We all found ourselves talking together, talking shop, the inevitable gossip and grumbles of the project, about this scandal and that foreman and the other balls-up; ironically, the girls seemed to feel excluded, and fell to talking between themselves. Merrial, showing tact enough for both of us, noticed this and gradually, now that the ice was broken, returned her conversation to me. Jondo and Machard took up again their neglected tasks of seduction or flirtation. When, a couple of hours later, she asked me to see her home, their ribaldry was relatively restrained.

The square was noisier than ever; the only people heading for home, or for bed, were like ourselves workers on the project who, unlike the locals, had to work on the following day, a Friday. We walked through the dark street to the north of the square and across the bridge over the Carron River towards the suburb of New Kelso. Merrial stopped in the middle of the bridge. One arm was tight around my waist. With the other, she waved around.

'Look,' she said. 'What do you see?'

On our right the town's atomic power-station's automation hummed blackly in the dark; to our left the fish-farms, warmed by the reactor's run-off, spread down to the shore. I looked to left and right, and then behind to the main town, ahead to New Kelso, across the loch to the other small towns.

She smiled at my baffled silence.

'Look up.'

Overhead the Milky Way blazed, the aurora borealis flickered, a communications aerostat glowed pink in a sun long since set for us. The Plough hung above the hills to the north. A meteor flared briefly, my indrawn breath a sound effect for its silent passage. To the west the sky still had light in it: the sun would be up in four hours.

'I can see the stars,' I said.

'That's it,' she said, sounding pleased at my perceptiveness. 'You can. We're in the very middle of a town of ten thousand people, and you can see the Milky Way. Not as well as you could see it from the top of Glas Bhein, sure enough, but you can see it. Why?'

I shrugged, looking again back and forth. I'd never given the matter thought.

'No clouds?' I suggested brightly.

She laughed and caught my hand and tugged me forward. 'And you a scholar of history!'

'What's that got to do with it?'

She pointed to the street-lamp at the end of the bridge's parapet. Its post was about three metres high; its conical cowl's reflective inner surface sharply cut off all but the smallest upward illumination. 'Did you ever see lamps like that in pictures of the olden times?' she asked.

'Now that I come to think of it,' I said, 'no.'

'A town this size would have had lamps everywhere, blazing light into the sky. From street-lamps and windows and shop-fronts. The very air itself would glow with it. You could see just a handful of stars on the clearest night.'

I thought about the ancient pictures I'd peered at under glass. 'You know, you're right,' I said. 'That's what it looked like.'

'Some people,' Merrial went on, in a sudden gust of anger, 'lived their whole lives without once seeing the Milky Way!'

'Very sad,' I said. In fact the thought gave me a tight feeling in my chest, as if I were struggling to breathe. 'How did they stand it?'

'Aye, well, that's a question you could well ask.' She glanced up at me. 'I thought you might know.'

'I never noticed, to be honest.'

'And why don't we do it?' She gestured again at the electric twilight of the surrounding town.

'Because it would be wasteful,' I said. As soon as the words were out I realised I'd said them without thinking, and that it wasn't the answer.

Merrial laughed. 'We have power to spare!'

It was my turn to stop suddenly. We'd taken a right and were going down a path past the power-station. I knew for a fact that it could, when called upon in a rare emergency – such as when extra heating was required to clear snow from a blizzard – produce enough electricity to light up Carron Town several times over.

'You're right,' I said. 'So why don't we do it? I've seen pictures of the great cities of antiquity, and you're right, they shone. They looked . . . magnificent. Perhaps it was so bright they didn't need to see the stars – they had the city lights instead! They made their own stars!'

Merrial was slowly shaking her head.

'Maybe that was fine for them,' she said. 'But it wouldn't be for us. We all get – uneasy when we can't see the night sky. Don't you, just thinking about it?'

I took a deep breath, and let it out with a sigh. 'Aye, you're right at that!'

We walked on, her strides pacing my slower steps.

'You're a strange woman,' I said.

She smiled and held my waist more firmly and leaned her head against my shoulder. I found myself looking down at her hair, and down at the scoop neckline of her dress and the glowing stone between her breasts.

'Sure I am,' she said. 'But so are we all, that's what I'm saying. We're different from the people who came before us, or before the Deliverer's time, and nobody wonders how or why. The feeling we have about the sky is just part of it. We live longer and we breed less, we sicken little, sometimes I think even our eyes are sharper; all these changes are hard-wired into our radiation-hardened genes—'

'Our what?'

I felt the shrug of her shoulder.

'Just tinker cant, colha Gree. Don't worry. You'll pick it up.'

'Oh, I will, will I?'

'Aye. If you stay with me.'

There was only one answer to that. I turned her around and kissed her. She clasped her lips to mine and slid her hands under my open waistcoat and sent them roving around my sides and back. I could feel them through my silk shirt like hot little animals. The kiss went on for some time and ended with our tongues flickering together like fish at the bottom of a deep pool; then she leaned away and gripped my shoulders and looked at me and said, 'I reckon that means you're staying, colha Gree.'

Suddenly we were both laughing. She caught my hand and swung it and we started walking again, talking about I don't know what. Out on the edge of town we turned a corner into a little estate of dozens of single-storey wooden houses with chimneys. Some of the houses were separate, each with its own patch of garden; others, smaller, were lined up in not quite orderly rows. Even in the summer, even with electricity cables strung everywhere, a smell of woodsmoke hung in the air. Yellow light glowed from behind straw-mat blinds. A dog barked and was silenced by an irritable yell.

'Hey, come on,' Merrial said with an impish smile.

I hadn't realised how my feet had hesitated as the path had changed from cobbles to trampled gravel.

'Never been in a tinker camp before,' I apologised.

'We don't bite.' Another cheeky grin. 'Well, that is to say . . .'

'You really are a terrible woman.'

'Oh, I am that, indeed. Ferocious – so I'm told.'

'I'll hold you to that.'

'I'll hold you to more.'

She held me as she stopped in front of one of the small houses in the middle of the row, and fingered out a tiny key five centimetres long on a thong attached to her belt but hidden in a slit in the side of her skirt. The lock too seemed absurdly small, a brass circular patch on the white-painted door at eye level.

'So are you coming in, or what?'

Lust and reason warred with fear and superstition, and won. I followed her over the polished wooden threshold as she switched on the electric light. I stood for a moment, blinking in the sudden 40-watt flood. The main room was about four metres by six. Against the far wall was a wood-burning stove, banked low; above it was a broad mantelpiece on which a large clock ticked loudly. The time was half past midnight. On either side of the stove were rows of shelves with hundreds of books. In the left-hand corner a workbench jutted from the wall, with a microscope and an unholy clutter of soldering gear and bits of wire and tools. Rough, unpolished seer-stones of various sizes lay among them. The main table of the house was a huge oaken piece about a metre and a half square, with carved and castered legs. A crocheted cotton throw covered it, weighted at the centre by a seer-stone hemisphere at least thirty centimetres in diameter, so finely finished that it looked like a dome of glass. Within it, hills and clouds drifted by.

Merrial stood by the table for a moment, reached up behind her head and removed a clasp from her hair, so that the two narrow braids fell forward and framed her face. Then she lifted the chain with the talisman, and the other, finer silver chain, from around her neck and deposited them on the table.

The place smelt of woodsmoke and pot-pourri and the bunches of flowering plants stuffed into carelessly chosen containers in every available corner. The wooden walls were varnished, and hung with an incongruous variety of old prints and paintings – landscapes, ladies, foxes, cats, that sort of thing – and tacked-up picture-posters related to the project. An open door led to a tiny scullery; a curtained alcove beside it took up the rest of that end of the room. I presumed it contained the bed.

But it was to a big old leather couch in front of the stove that she drew me first. She half-leaned, half-sat on the back of it, and began unbuttoning my shirt, then explored my chest with her lips and tongue – and teeth – as I applied myself to undoing the fastenings down the back of her dress, and working my boots off. As I kicked away the right boot the *sgean dhu* clattered to the floor. By this time she had unbuckled my belt, and with a shrug and a step we both shed our outer clothes, which fell to the floor in a promiscuous coupling of their own. Merrial stood for a moment in nothing but her long silk underskirt. I clasped her in my arms, her nipples hard, her breasts warm and soft against my chest; and we kissed again.

We moved, we danced, Merrial leading, towards the curtained alcove. She pulled away the curtain to reveal a large and reassuringly solid-looking bed. I knelt in front of her and pulled down her slip and knickers, and kissed her between the legs until she pulled me gently to my feet. I managed to leave my own briefs on the floor.

We faced each other naked, like the Man and the Woman in the Garden in the story. Merrial half-turned, threw back the bedcovers and picked up from the bed a long white cotton nightgown, which she shook out and held at arm's length for a moment.

'I won't be needing *that* tonight,' she grinned, and cast it to the floor, and me to the bed.

I woke in daylight, and lay for a minute or so basking in the warm afterglow, and hot after-images, of love and sex. Rolling over and reaching out my arm, I found that I was alone in the bed. It was still warm where Merrial had slept. The air was filled with the aroma of coffee and the steady ticking of the clock—

The time! I sat up in a hurry and leaned forward to see the big

13

timepiece, and discovered with relief that it was only five o'clock. Thank Providence, we'd only slept an hour and a half. With the same movement I discovered a host of minor pains: bites on my shoulder and neck, scratches on my back and buttocks, aching muscles, raw skin . . .

The animal whose attacks had caused all this damage padded out of the scullery.

'Good morning,' she said.

I made some sort of croaking noise. Merrial smiled and handed me one of the two steaming mugs she'd carried in. She sat down on the foot of the bed, drawing her knees up to her chin to huddle inside her sark, its high neck and long sleeves and intricate whitework giving her an incongruous appearance of modesty.

I sipped the coffee gratefully, unable to take my eyes off her. She looked calmly back at me, with the smile of a contented cat.

'Good morning,' I said, finding my voice at last. 'And thank you.'

'Not just for the coffee, I hope,' said Merrial.

I was grinning so much that my cheeks, too, were aching.

'No, not just for the coffee. God, Merrial, I've never . . .'

I didn't know how to put it.

'Done it before?' she inquired innocently.

Coffee went up the back of my nose as I spluttered a laugh.

'Compared with last night, I might as well not have,' I ruefully admitted. 'You are – you're amazing!'

Her level gaze held me. She showed not the slightest embarrassment. 'Oh, you're not so bad yourself, colha Gree,' she said in a judicious tone. 'But you have a lot to learn.'

'I hope you'll teach me.'

'I'm sure I will,' she said. 'If you want to stay with me, that is.' She waved a hand, as if this were a matter yet to be decided.

'Stay with you? Oh, Merrial!' I couldn't speak.

'What?'

'Nothing could make me leave you. Ever.'

I was almost appalled at what I was saying. I had not expected to hear myself speak such words, not for a long time to come.

'How sweet of you to say that,' she said, very seriously, but smiling. 'But—'

'But nothing!' I reached sideways and put the mug on the floor and shifted myself down the bed towards her. Without looking away from

14

me, she put her mug down too, on a trunk at the end of the bed, and rocked forward to her knees to meet me. We knelt with our arms around each other.

'I love you,' I said. I must have said it before, said it a lot of times through the night, but now there was all the weight in the world behind the words.

'I love you too,' she said. She clung to me with a sudden fierceness, and laid her face on my shoulder. A wet, salt tear stung a love-bite there. She sniffed and raised her head, blinking her now even brighter eyes.

'What's wrong?' I asked.

'I'm happy,' she said.

'So am I.'

She regarded me solemnly. 'I have to say this,' she said, with another unladylike sniffle. 'Loving me will not always make you happy.'

I could not imagine what she meant, and I didn't want to. 'Why are you saying this?'

'Because I must,' she said. Her voice was strained. 'Because I have to be fair with you.'

'Aye, sure,' I said. 'Well, now you've warned me, can I get on with loving you?'

She brightened instantly, as though some arduous responsibility had been lifted from her shoulders.

'Oh yes!' she said, hugging me closer again. 'Love me as much as you like, love me for ever!' She pulled back a little, looked down, then raised her gaze again to mine.

'But not right now,' she added regretfully. 'You have to go.'

'Now?!' We had fallen out of our mutual dream into the workaday world, where we were two people who didn't, really, know each other all that well.

'Yes,' she insisted. 'You have to get back across town, get . . . washed, and ready for work and catch the bus at half past six.'

'I can catch it from here.'

'The hell you can. People will talk.'

'They'll talk anyway.'

'People around here, I mean.'

I climbed reluctantly off the bed. Merrial slipped lithely under the covers and pulled them up to her chin.

15

'What about you?' I asked, as I searched out and sorted my clothes.

'I'm an intellectual worker,' she said smugly as she snuggled down. 'We start at nine.'

She watched me dress with a sort of affectionate curiosity. 'What have you got on your belt?'

I patted the hard leather pouches and fastened the buckle. 'The tools of a tradesman,' I told her, 'and the weapons of a gentleman.'

'I see,' she said approvingly.

'So when will I see you again?' I asked, as I recovered the *sgean dhu* and stuck it back down the side of my boot.

'Tonight, eight o'clock, at the statue? Go for something to eat?'

I pretended to give this idea thoughtful consideration, then we both laughed, and she sat up again and reached out to me. We hugged and kissed goodbye. As I backed away to the door, grudging even a moment without her in my sight, a flickering from the big seer-stone caught my eye. I stopped beside the table and stooped to examine it. As I did so I noticed Merrial's two pendants: the talisman – the small seer-stone – now showing a vaguely organic tracery of green, and on the silver chain a silver piece about a centimetre in diameter which appeared to be a monogram made up of the letters 'G' and 'T' and the numeral '4'.

The table's centre-piece was all black within, except for an arrangement of points of light which might have been torches, or cities, or stars. They flashed on and off, on and off, and the bright dots spelled out one word: HELP.

I glanced over at Merrial. 'It's reached the end of its run,' I remarked.

'Reset it then,' she said sleepily from the pillow.

I brushed the stone's chill surface with my sleeve, restoring it to chaos, and with a final smile at Merrial opened the door and stepped out into the cock-crowing sunlight.

and she threw her arms around him
that same night she drew him down.

2

Ancient Time

Death follows me, she thought, as she rode into the labour-camp. There was something implacable about it, like logic: it follows, it follows . . . The thought's occurrence had nothing to do with logic; it appeared like a screensaver on the surface of her mind, whenever her mind went blank. It troubled her a little, as did another thought that drifted by in such moments: *where are the swift cavalry?*

The gate rolled shut behind her, squealing in its rusty grooves. The wind from the steppe hummed in the barbed-wire fence and whipped away the dust kicked up as she reined in the black horse. A guard hurried over; he somehow managed to make his brisk soldierly step look obsequious, even as his bearing made his dark-blue microfibre fatigues look military. He doffed a baseball cap with the Mutual Protection lettering and logo.

'Good morning, Citizen.'

That title was already an honorific. Myra Godwin-Davidova smiled and handed him the reins.

'Good morning,' she said, swinging down from the horse. She could hear her knee-joints creak. She lifted the saddlebags and slung them over her shoulder. The weight almost made her stagger, and the guard's arm twitched towards her; but she wasn't going to accept any help from that quarter. 'That will be all, thank you.'

'As you wish, Citizen.' The guard saluted and replaced his cap. She was still looking down at him, her riding-boots adding three inches to her five-foot-eleven height.

She patted the big mare's rump and watched as the guard led the beast away, then set off towards the accommodation huts. As she walked she pulled off her leather gauntlets and stuffed them awkwardly into the deep pockets of her long fur coat, and tucked a stray strand of silver hair under her sable hat. Hands mottled, veins showing, nails ridged: tough claws of an old bird, still flexible, but a better indication of her true age than her harshly lined but firm face, straight back and limber stride. Her knees hurt, but she tried not to let it show, or slow her down.

The camp perimeter was about one kilometre by two. Beyond the far fence she could see straight to the horizon, above which rose the many gantries and the few remaining tall ships of the old port. It had been a proud fleet once. How long before she would have to say, *all my ships are gone and all my men are dead?*

As if to mock her thought, a small ship screamed overhead; she caught a glimpse of it: angular, faceted, translucent, a spectral stealth-bomber shrieking skyward from Baikonur on a jet of laser-heated steam. The trail's after-image floated irritatingly in front of her as she turned her gaze resolutely back to earth.

One of the camp's factories was a couple of hundred metres away, a complex of aluminium pipework and fibre-optic cabling in a queasily organic-looking mass about fifty metres wide and twenty high, through which the control cabins and walkways of the human element were beaded and threaded like the eggs and exudate of some gargantuan insect. The name of the company that owned it, Space Merchants, was spelled out on the roof in twisty neon.

As she approached the nearest workers' housing area it struck Myra, not for the first time, that the huts were more modern and comfortable than the concrete apartment block she lived in herself. Each hut was semi-cylindrical, its rounded ends streamlined to the prevailing wind; soot-black polycarbon skin with rows of laminated-diamond windows.

This particular cluster of accommodation huts was in two rows of ten, with the rutted remains of a twenty-metre-wide paved road between them. A gang of a dozen men was engaged in repairing the road; the breeze carried a waft of sweat and tar. The men were using shovels, a gas burner under a tipping-and-spreading contraption, and a coughing diesel-engined road-roller: primitive, heavy equipment. On the sidewalk a blue-suited Mutual Protection guard lounged, picking his teeth and apparently watching a show in his eyes and hearing music or commentary in his ears.

The loom of Myra's shadow made him jump, blink and shake his head with a small shudder. He started to his feet.

'No need to get up,' Myra said unkindly. 'I just want to speak to some of the men.'

'They're on a break, Citizen,' he said, squinting up at her. 'So it's up to them, right?'

'Right,' said Myra. Physical work counted as recreation. It was the intellectual labour of design and monitoring that taxed the convicts' nerves.

She turned to the men, who waved to her and shouted greetings and explanations: she'd have to wait the few minutes it would take for them to finish spreading and rolling some freshly poured tarmac. Not offering one to the guard, she lit a Marley and let the men take their time finishing their break. She'd always insisted that her arrivals and inspections counted as work-time for the labourers.

Her spirits lifted as the Virginia and the Morocco kicked in. The labourers had their yellow suits rolled down to the waist, and were sweating even though the temperature had just climbed above freezing. Most of them were younger – let's face it, *far* younger – than herself; dark-tanned Koreans and Japanese, muscular as martial arts adepts – which, indeed, some of them were. She enjoyed watching them, the effect of smoke amplifying the underlying undertone of lust, the happy, hippy hormonal hum . . .

But that reminded her of Georgi, and her mood crashed again. Georgi was dead. Sometimes it seemed every man she'd ever fucked was dead; it was like she carried a disease: Niall MacCallum had died in a car crash, Jaime Gonzalez had died – what? – *seventy* years ago in the contra war, Jon Wilde had died in her arms on the side of the Karaganda road (on snow that turned red as his face turned white), and now Georgi Davidov had died in the consulate at Almaty, of a heart attack. (They expected *her* to believe *that*?)

There had been others, she reminded herself. Quite recent others. It wasn't every man she'd ever fucked who was doomed, it was every man she'd ever *loved*. There was only one exception she knew of. All her men were dead, except one, and he was a killer.

Even, perhaps, Georgi's killer. *Fucking heart attack, my ass!* It was one of their moves, it had to be – a move in the endgame.

A door banged open somewhere and the street suddenly swarmed with children pelting along and yelling, their languages and accents as varied as the colours of their skins. Few of the camp's bonded labour-force were women, but many of the men had women with them;

19

there was every inducement for the prisoners to bring their families along. It was humane, but politic as well: a man with a woman and children was unlikely to risk escape or revolt.

Surrounded by children calling to their fathers, poking fingers in the hot asphalt, crowding around the machines and loudly investigating, the gang knocked off at last, leaving the guard to mind the newly tarred road. Myra savoured his disgruntled look as she crushed the filter roach under her heel and stepped out into the centre of the untarred part of the street.

'Hi, guys.'

They all knew who she was, but the only ones among them she recognised were two members of the camp committee, Kim Nok-Yung and Shin Se-Ha. The former was a young Korean shipyard worker, stocky and tough; the latter a Japanese mathematician of slender build and watchful mien. Kim seized her hand, grinning broadly.

'Hello, Myra.'

'Good to see you, Nok-Yung. And you, Se-Ha.'

The Japanese man inclined his head. 'Hi.' He insisted on taking her saddlebags. The whole gang surrounded her, flashing eyes and teeth, talking to each other and to her without much regard for mutual comprehension. They shooed away the children and led her into the nearest hut. Its doorway film brushed over her, burst in a shower of droplets with an odour of antiseptic, and reformed behind her. She blinked rapidly and shrugged out of her heavy coat, throwing it on to one of a row of hooks that grew from the curving wall.

Her first deep breath was evidence enough of how effective the filter film was at keeping out the dust. At the same time, it brought a flush to her skin as her immune system rushed to investigate whatever she'd just inhaled of the nanoware endemic to the building's interior. She followed Kim into the dining-area, an airy space of flat-surfaced furnishings – some a warning red to indicate that they were for heating, others white for eating off. The chairs were padded black polycarbon plastic. Around the walls, racked on shelves or stacked on floors, were thousands of books: centuries' worth of classics and bestsellers and blockbusters and textbooks, as if blown from the four winds and fetched up against these barriers. It would have been the same in any of the huts. The next most common items of clutter were musical instruments and craft equipment and products:

20

plastic scrimshank, spaceships in bottles, elaborately carved wooden toys.

As they sat down around a table Myra felt prickly and on edge. She tugged her eyeband, a half-centimetre-wide crescent of translucent plastic, from her hair and placed it across her temples, in front of her eyes. A message drifted across her retina. 'Nanoprotect56 has detected the following known surveillance molecules in the room: Dataphage, Hackendice, Reportback, Mercury, Moldavian. Do you wish to clean up?'

She blinked when the cursor stopped on the Proceed option, took a deep breath, held it until her lungs were burning, then exhaled. The faces around the table were incurious and amused.

'Cleanup in progress,' the retinal display reported. Myra took a deep breath. It felt cool this time, as well as smooth.

'So we have privacy,' one of the Koreans said, with heavy irony.

'Ah, fuck it,' Myra said. 'Happens every time. You gotta assume they're listening.' There was bound to be something else her current release of 'ware wasn't up to catching: she imagined some tiny Turing machine ticking away, stitching sound-vibrations into a long-chain molecule in the dirt. She took a recorder – larger and less advanced than the one in her mental picture – from her pocket and laid it on the table. 'And I'm listening. So, what have you got for me?'

A quick exchange of glances around the table ended as usual with Kim Nok-Yung accepted as the spokesman. He rustled a paper from an inner pocket and ran a finger down the minutes; Matters Arising started with the routine first question.

'Any progress on POW recognition?'

Myra was touched by the note of hope with which he asked the question, the hundredth time no different from the first. She compressed her lips and shook her head. 'Sorry, guys. Red Cross and Crescent are working on it, and Amnesty. Still no dice.'

Nok-Yung shrugged. 'Oh, well. Please make the standard protest.'

'Of course.'

As they ticked their way down the list of complaints and conditions and assignments and payments, Myra noticed that the whole pattern of production in the camp had changed. The intensity of the work, and the volume of output, had gone up drastically. Twenty engines and a hundred habitat modules completed for Space Merchants in the past month! Nok-Yung and Se-Ha were subtly underlining the changes with guarded glances and shifts in tone, but they weren't commenting explicitly.

Myra looked around the table when they reached the end of the agenda. No one had complained about the speed-up. They didn't seem troubled; they had an air of suppressed excitement, almost glee, as they waited for her to speak. She checked over again the figures in her head, and realised with a jolt that at this rate most of the men here would work off their fines – or 'debts' – in months rather than years.

Another endgame move. Myra nodded slightly and smiled. 'Well, that's it,' she said. 'Don't overwork yourselves, guys. I mean it. Make sure you get in plenty of road-mending, OK?'

The prisoners just grinned at their shared secret. She reached for the saddlebags, as though just remembering something. 'I've brought some books for you.'

The men leaned inward eagerly as she unpacked. They weren't allowed any kind of interface with the net, and nothing that could be used to build one: no televisions or computers or readers or VR rigs, not even music decks. Nothing could stop Myra carrying in whatever she liked – the saddlebags were legally a diplomatic bag – but any electronic or molecular contraband would have been confiscated the moment she left. So hardbooks it had to be. The prisoners and their families had an unquenchable thirst for them. Myra's every visit brought more additions to the drift.

This time she had dozens of paperbacks with tasteful Modern Art covers and grey spines, 20th Century Classics – Harold Robbins, Stephen King, Dean Koontz and so on – which she shoved across the table to the men whose names she didn't know. For her friends Nok-Yung and Se-Ha she'd saved the best for last: hardbooks so ancient that only advanced preservation treatments kept them from crumbling to dust—

Rather like herself, she thought, as the books passed one by one from her gnarled hands: an incredibly rare, possibly unique, copy of Tucker's edition of Stirner; the Viking *Portable Nietzsche*; and a battered Thinker's Library edition of Spencer's *First Principles*.

Kim Nok-Yung looked down at them reverently, then up at her. Shin Se-Ha was in some kind of trance. Nok-Yung shook his head.

'This is too much,' he said, almost angrily. 'Myra, you can't—'

'Oh yes, I can.'

'Where did you get them?' asked Se-Ha.

22

Myra shrugged. 'From Reid, funnily enough.'

All the men were looking at her now, with sour smiles.

'From *David* Reid? The owner?' Kim waved his hand, indicating everything in sight.

'Yeah,' said Myra. 'The very same.'

There was a moment of sober silence.

'Well,' Nok-Yung said at last, 'I hope we make better use of them than he did, the bastard.'

Everybody laughed, even Myra.

'So do I,' she said.

She settled back in her chair and passed around the Marley pack and accepted the offer of coffee.

'OK, guys,' she said. 'The news. Everything's still going to hell.' She grimaced. 'Same as last week. A few shifts in the fronts, that's all. Take it from me, you ain't missing much.'

'A few shifts in *which* fronts?' asked Se-Ha suspiciously.

'Ah,' said Myra. 'If you must know – the north-eastern front is . . . active.'

Another silent exchange of glances and smiles. Myra didn't share in their pleasure, but couldn't blame them for it. The two encroaching events that filled her most with dread were, for them, each in different ways an earnest of their early liberation.

She said her goodbyes, wondering if it was for the last time, and took her now empty bags and stalked away through the restitution-camp streets, and mounted her horse and rode out of the gate, towards the city.

Thinking about Reid, trying to think calmly and destructively about Reid, she found her mind drifting back. He had not always been such a bastard. He'd been the first person to tell her she need never die. That had been eighty-three years ago, when she was twenty-two years old. She hadn't believed him . . .

Death follows me.

'You don't have to die,' he told her.

Black hair framed his face, black eyebrows his intent, brown-eyed gaze. Dave Reid was dark and handsome but not, alas, tall. He wore a denim jacket with a tin button – a badge, as the Brits called them – pinned to its lapel. The badge was red with the black hammer-and-sickle-and-4 of the International.

'What!' Myra laughed. 'I know it feels that way now, everybody our age feels like that, yeah? But it'll come to us all, man, don't kid yourself.'

She rolled back on her elbows on the grass and looked up at the blue spring sky. It was too bloody cold for this, but the sun was out and the ground was dry, and that was good enough for sunbathing in Scotland. The grassy slope behind the Boyd Orr Building was covered with groups and couples of students, drinking and smoking and talking. Probably missing lectures – it was already two in the afternoon.

'Seriously,' Dave said, in that Highland accent that carried the sound of wind on grass, of waves on shore, 'if you can live into the twenty-first century, you have a damn good chance of living for ever.'

'Says who? L. Ron Hubbard?'

Dave snorted. 'Arthur C. Clarke, actually.'

'Who?'

He frowned at her. 'You know – scientist, futurist. The man who invented the communications satellite.'

'Oh, *him*,' Myra said scornfully. 'Sci-fi. *2001* and all that.' She saw the slight flinch of hurt in David's face, and went on, 'Oh, don't get me wrong, I'm not saying it's impossible. Maybe hundreds of years from now, maybe in communism. Not in our lifetimes, though. Tough shit.'

Dave shrugged and rolled another cigarette.

'We'll see.'

'I guess. And the rate you smoke those things, you'll be lucky to be alive in the twenty-first century. You won't even get to first base.'

'Och, I'll last another twenty-four years.' He sighed, blowing smoke on to the slightly warm breeze, then smiled at her mischievously. 'Unless I become a martyr of the revolution, of course.'

'"I have a rendezvous with death, on some disputed barricade",' Myra quoted. 'Don't worry. That's another thing won't happen in our lifetimes.'

The shadow of the tall building crept over Dave's face. He shifted deftly, back into the sunlight.

'That's what you think, is it?'

'Yeah, that's what I think.' She smiled, and added, with ironic reassurance, 'Our *natural* lifetimes, that is.'

Dave hefted a satchel stuffed with copies of revolutionary newspapers and magazines. 'Then what's the point of all this? Why don't we just eat, drink and be merry?'

Myra swigged from a can of MacEwan's, lowered it and looked at him over its rim. 'That's what I *am* doing right now, lover.'

He took her point, and reached out and stroked the curve of her cheekbone. 'But still,' he persisted. 'Why bother with politics if you don't think we're going to win?'

'Dave,' she said, 'I'm not a socialist because I expect to end up running some kinda workers' state of my own some day. I do what I do because I think it's right. OK?'

'OK,' said Reid, smiling; but his smile was amused as well as affectionate, as though she were being naïve. Irritated without quite knowing why, she turned away.

The city was called Kapitsa, and it was the capital of the International Scientific and Technical Workers' Republic, which had no other city; indeed, apart from the camps, no other human habitation. The ISTWR was an independent enclave on the fringe of the Polygon – the badlands between Karaganda and Semipalatinsk, a waste-product of Kazakhstan's nuclear-testing legacy. A long time ago, Kapitsa would have looked modern, with its centre of high-rise office blocks, its inner ring of automatic factories, its periphery of dusty but tree-lined streets and estates of low-rise apartment blocks, the bustling airport just outside and the busy spaceport on the horizon, from which the great ships had loudly climbed, day after day. Now it was a rustbelt, as quaintly obsolete as the Japanese car factories or the Clyde shipyards or the wheat plains of Ukraine.

Myra, however, felt somewhat cheered as the mare took her through the light traffic of the noonday streets. The apple trees were in bloom, and every wall had its fresh-looking, colourful mural of flowers or stars or ships or crowds or children or heroes or heroines. Real ancient space-age stuff, an effect enhanced by the younger – genuinely young – people enjoying the chilly sunshine in the fashionable scanty garb, which recalled the late 1960s in its jaunty futurism. She looked at girls in skinny tights and shiny, garish minidresses and found herself wondering if they were cold . . . probably not, the clothes were only an imitation of their nylon or PVC originals, the nanofactured fabrics veined with heat-exchangers, laced with molecular machines.

The bright clothing gave the people on the street an appearance of prosperity, but Myra was all too aware that it was superficial. The clothes were cheaper than paper, easily affordable even on Social Security. Over the past few years, with the coming of the diamond ships, the heavy-booster market had gone into free fall, and unemployment had rocketed. The dole was paid by her department out of the rent from Mutual Protection, and it couldn't last. Nostalgia tourism – the old spaceport was now a World Heritage Site, for what that was worth – looked like the only promising source of employment.

Before she knew it, the horse had stopped, from habit, outside the modest ten-storey concrete office-block of the republic's government on Revolution Square. Myra sat still for a moment, gazing wryly at this week's morale-boosting poster on the official billboard: a big black-and-white blow-up of the classic Tass photo of Gagarin, grinning out from his cosmonaut helmet. She remembered the time, in her grade-school classroom on the Lower East Side, when she'd first seen this human face and had formed some synaptic connection between Gagarin's grin and Guevara's glare.

Space and socialism. What a swindle it had all been. She shook the reins, took the mare at a slow pace around to the back, stabled it, wiped the muck from her boots and ascended the stairs. The corridors to her office – at the front of the building, as befitted a People's Commissar for Social Policy and Prime Minister Pro Tem and (now that she came to think about it) Acting President – were filled with a susurrus of hurrying feet and fast-fading whispers. Myra glanced sharply at the groups she passed, but few seemed willing to return her look.

She closed the door of her office with a futile but soul-satisfying slam. Let the apparatchiks worry about her mood, if she had to worry about theirs. The last time she'd sniffed this evasive air in the corridors had been just before the first – and only – time she'd fallen out of power, back in 2046. Then, she'd suspected an imminent move from the Mutual Protection company and its protégés within the state apparatus: a *coup d'état*. Now, she suspected that Mutual Protection and its allies were into the final moves of a much wider game-plan, as wide as it could be: a *coup du monde*. Or *coup d'étoile*!

She stalked to the window, shedding her coat and hat and gloves in quick, violent movements, leaned on her knuckles on the sill and scanned her surroundings in a spasm of fang-baring territoriality. No tanks or tramping feet sounded in her city's streets, no black helicopters clattered in her country's sky. What did she expect? There were days at least to go before anything happened – and, when it did, the opening blows would be overt in larger capitals than hers; she'd be nipped by CNN sound-bites in the new order's first seconds.

She sighed and turned away, picked up her dropped clothes and hung them carefully on the appropriate branches of a chrome-plated rack. The office was as self-consciously retro-modernist as the styles on the street, if a little more sophisticated – pine walls and floor, lobate leather layers at random on both; ornaments in steel and silver, ebony and plastic, of planetary globes and interplanetary craft.

She dropped into the office chair and leaned back, letting it massage her shoulders and neck. She slid the band across her eyes, summoned a head-up display and rolled her eyes to study it. The anti-viral 'ware playing across her retinae flickered, but there was nothing untoward for it to report; here, as in all the offices, the walls had teeth. Her own software was wrapped around her, its loyalty as intimate, and as hard to subvert, as the enhanced immune-systems in her blood. It was personal, it was *a* personal, a unique configuration of software agents that scanned the world and Myra's responses to the world, and built up from that interaction a shrewd assessment of her needs and interests. It looked out information for her, and it looked after her investments. It did to the world nets what her Sterling search engine did for her Library – it selected and extracted what was relevant from the vast and choppy sea of data in which most people swam or, more often, drowned.

Having a good suite of personal 'ware was slightly more important for a modern politician than the traditional personal networks of influence and intelligence. In the decade since she'd recovered power, Myra had made sure that her networks – both kinds, virtual and actual – were strong and intertwined, strong enough to carry her if the structure of the state ever again let her down. Though even that was unlikely – her purges, though bloodless, had been as ruthless as Tito's. No official of the ISTWR would ever again have the slightest misapprehension of where their best interests lay, and no employee or agent of Mutual Protection would fancy their chances of changing that.

She'd have to consult with the rest of Sovnarkom soon enough – a meeting was scheduled for 3 p.m. – and round up some of the scurrying underlings from the corridors to prepare for it, but she wanted to get her own snapshot of the situation first.

27

Myra's personal didn't have a personality, as far as she knew, but it had a persona: a revolutionary, a stock-market speculator, an arms dealer, a spy; a free-wheeling, high-rolling, all-swindling communist-capitalist conspirator out of some Nazi nightmare. It had a name.

'Parvus,' she whispered. The retinal projectors on her eyeband summoned an image of a big man in a baggy suit and a shirt stretched across his belly like a filled sail, scudding along on gales of information. He strolled towards her, smiling, his pockets stuffed with papers, his cigarette hand waving as he prepared to tell her something. She'd never come across a recording of the original Parvus in action, but she'd given this one the appearance of one historic Trotskyist leader, and the mad-scientist mannerisms of another, whose standard speech she'd once sat through, long ago in the Student Union in Glasgow.

'Give me the big picture.'

Parvus nodded. He ran his fingers through his mop of white hair, furrowed his brow, grinned maniacally.

'*Jane's*, I think.' He flicked an inch of ash, conjured a screen. Her gaze fixed on an option; she blinked, and the room vanished from her sight; again, and Earth fell away.

Her first virtual view, spun in orbit, was from *Jane's Market Forces* – a publicly available, but prohibitively expensive, real-time survey of military deployments around the world. She was running the next-but-one release, currently in beta test. It had cost the republic's frugal defence budget nothing more than the stipend to place a patriotic Kazakh postgrad in the Stockholm International Peace Research Institute's equally cash-starved IT department. (That, and an untraceable credit line to his comms account.) Myra, long familiar with the conventional symbols and ideographs, took it all in at an abstract level: colour-coded, vectored graphs in a 3-D space, with other dimensions implied by subtle shadings and the timing of pulsations. That photic filigree hung like a complicated cloud-system over the relatively static histograms depicting the hardware and the warm bodies. The physical locations and quantities of personnel and *matériel* could provide only a basement-level understanding of the world military balance, just as the location of physical plant was only a rough cut of the state of the world market. Second by second, market and military forces shifted unpredictably, their mutual interpenetration more complex than any ideology had ever foreseen. With most of the world's official armies revolutionary or mercenary or both, and most of the conflicts settled in unarguable simulation before they started, everyone from the bankers down through the generals to the grunts on the ground would shrug and accept the virtual verdict, and change sides, reinforce or retreat in step with their software shadows – all except the Greens, and the Reds. *They* fought for real, and played for keeps.

It was like the old Civilization game, Myra sometimes thought, with a new twist: Barbarism II. Nobody was going to wipe the board, nobody was going to Alpha Centauri. They were all going down together, into the dark . . . Just as soon as enough major players decided to contest the incontestable, and put the simulations to the audit of war.

But, for the moment, the dark was full of twisting light. And in the real world, blinked up as backdrop, one front was more than virtual, and closer than she'd like. Beyond the northern border of Kazakhstan, itself hundreds of kilometres north of the ISTWR, the Sino-Soviet Union's ragged front-line advanced in flickers of real fire: guerilla skirmishes and sabotage on one side, half-hearted long-range shelling and futile carpet-bombing on the other.

The Sheenisov – the name was subtly derogatory, like Vietcong for NLF and Yank for United Nations – were the century's first authentic communist threat, who really believed in their updated version of the ideology which communistans like the ISTWR parodied in post-futurist pastiche. Based in the godforsaken back-country of recusant collective farms and worker-occupied factories, stubbornly surviving decades of counter-revolution and war, armed by partisan detachments of deserters (self-styled, inevitably, 'loyalists') from the ex-Soviet Eastern and ex-PRC Northern armies, they'd held most of Mongolia and Siberia and even parts of north-west China since the Fall Revolution back in 2045, and in the years since then they'd spread across the steppe like lichen. Myra detested and admired them in equal measure.

Of more immediate, and frustrating, concern: the Sheenisov were outside the virtual world, a torn black hole in the net. Their computers were permanently offline; their cadres didn't trade combat futures; they refused all simulated confrontation or negotiation; like the Green marginals in the West and the Khmer Vertes in the South, the Reds in the East put all to the test of practice, the critique of arms. Even *Jane's* could only guess at their current disposition.

29

But their serrated south-western edge was clear enough, and as usual it was cutting closer to her domain than it had been the last time she'd checked. Like, this time yesterday . . .

She sighed and turned her attention from the communists to tracing the darker deeds of a real international conspiracy: the space movement. Somewhere in that scored darkness, reading between those lines of light, she had to find the footprints of a larger and more ragged army, impatient to assume the world.

Her first step – acknowledged by the system with startled gratitude – was to update the information on Mutual Protection's labour-camp output. When this was integrated and plausibly projected to the company's whole global archipelago, a first-cut re-evaluation of relative military-industrial weightings sent ripples through the entire web. Just as well she was working with a personal copy, Myra thought wryly. This was information to kill for (although already, presumably, discounted by Mutual Protection itself, which must surely know she knew).

She zapped the speculative update with a flashing 'urgent' tag to the People's Commissar for Finance, and a less urgent summary to the comrade over at Defence. Then she invoked her ongoing dossier of space-movement activity, meshed in the new output figures, and sent it to all the commissars, with her own interpretation.

The 'space-movement coup' had been talked about, openly, for so long that it had become unreal – as unreal as the Revolution had been, until it had finally come to pass. Myra herself had cried wolf on the coup, once before. But now she felt herself vindicated. And, again, David Reid was involved.

Her former lover had built up Mutual Protection from a security-service subsidiary of an insurance company into a global business that dealt in restitution: criminals working to compensate the damage they'd done. Originally touted as a humane, market-driven reform and replacement of the old barbaric prison systems, its extension from common criminals to political and military prisoners after the Fall Revolution had given it an appalling, unstoppable logic of runaway expansion, in much the same way as the use of prison labour in the First Five-Year Plan had done for the original GULag.

For more than a decade now, those on the losing side of small wars and increasingly minor crimes had provided the manpower for a gigantic space-settlement boom, applying whatever skills they had – or

30

could rapidly learn – to pay off their crime-debts as quickly as possible. At the same time, the proliferation of space-movement enclaves, each of which incited a horde of beleaguering barbarians or a swarm of furious bureaucrats, had provided an endless pool of new convicts. Quite a large proportion of the prisoners, on completion of their payback time, had seized the abundant employment opportunities the space projects offered.

Mutual Protection was now the armature of a global coalition of defence companies, launch companies, space settlement programmes, political campaigns and a host of minor governments – many of them creatures of these same companies. The space-movement coalition was on the point of assembling enough forces to re-create a stable world government and to bring the former Space Defense battlesats back under UN control. Their objective, long mooted, was to roll back the environmentalist and anti-technological opposition movements, and shift enough labour and capital into Earth orbit to create a self-sustaining space presence that could ride out any of the expected catastrophes below – of which, God knew, there were plenty to choose from.

The coup itself was expected to proceed on two levels. One was a political move to take over the rump ReUN, by the votes of all the numerous ministates that could be subverted, suborned or convinced. The other was a military move, thus legitimised, to seize the old US/UN Space Defense battlesats. That, Myra reckoned, was behind the speed-up in the labour-camps. No doubt massive subversion was going on among the orbital military personnel, but by the nature of the case there wasn't much she could know about that.

She stared at the virtual screen for a long time, until the clenchings of her fists and the twitching grimaces of her face and the blinking-back of tears confused the 'ware so much that it shut off, and left her staring at the wall.

Sovnarkom – the Council of People's Commissars, or, in more conventional terminology, the Cabinet – was the appropriately small government of an almost unviably small state (population 99,854, last time anyone had bothered to count, and dropping by the day). The structures of the ISTWR were an exercise in socialist camp, modelled on those of the old Soviet republics but without the leading role of the Party. The result of that strategic omission had been a democracy as genuine as that of its inspiration had been false. Or so it had seemed, in the republic's more prosperous days.

Myra arrived early, and took the privilege of the first arrival – the chairman's seat, at the head of the long, bare table of scarred mahogany with a clunky blast-proof secretarial device in the centre. There were another dozen seats, six along either side of the table, each with its traditional mineral water and notepaper in front of it. The room was bare, windowless but lit by full-spectrum plates in the ceiling. The only decoration on the white walls was a framed photograph of the long-dead nuclear physicist after whom the city was named.

Valentina Kozlova came in, her military fatigues elegant as always, her hair untidy, her hands full of hardcopy. She was in her fifties, a still-young child of the century, young enough and lucky enough to have got the anti-ageing treatments before she got old. She smiled tensely and sat down. Then Andrei Mukhartov, cropped-blond, forty-ish and looking it – probably by intent – soberly conventional in a three-piece suit of electric-blue raw silk. Denis Gubanov, younger than the others, ostentatiously casual, needing a shave, looking as though he'd just come in from sounding out an informer in some sleazy spaceport bar. Alexander Sherman arrived last, giving his usual impression of having been pulled away from more urgent business. His fashionable pseudo-plastic jump-suit was doubtless just the job for his post, but Myra liked it even less than she liked him. He sat down and glanced around as though expecting the meeting to begin immediately, then pursed his lips and slid two sheets of paper across to Myra.

'More resignations, I'm afraid,' he said. 'Tatyana and Michael have . . .'

'Taken off for richer pastures,' Myra said. 'I heard.' She looked at the empty spaces around the depleted table, and shrugged. 'Well, according to revolutionary convention there is no such thing as an inquorate meeting, so . . .'

'We really must co-opt some new members!' Sherman said.

'Yes,' said Myra drily. 'We really must.'

Her tone made Alexander snap back, 'It's a disgrace – we have no Commissar for Law, or the Interior, or—'

'Yes, yes,' Myra interrupted. 'And half the fucking members of the Supreme Soviet have fucked off – the wrong half, as it happens. *I* couldn't find a competent commissar for *anything* among the remainder. At the rate we're going, we won't have enough of an *electorate* to make up the numbers! So what do you suggest?'

Alexander Sherman opened his mouth, closed it, and shrugged. His mutinous look convinced Myra that he'd be the next to go – as Commissar for Industry, he had the right connections already.

'OK, comrades,' Myra said, 'let's call the meeting to order.' She took off her eyeband and laid it formally on the table, and those who hadn't already done so followed suit. It was not quite a rule to do so, but it was the custom – a gesture of politeness as well as an assurance that everyone was paying attention – to set aside one's personal for the duration of the meeting. Myra could never make up her mind whether it was mutual trust, or mutual suspicion, that lay behind the custom of not doing the same with one's personal weapons. Nobody'd ever pulled a gun at a Sovnarkom meeting, but there were precedents . . .

'Recorder: on. Regular meeting of the Council, Friday 9 May 2059, Myra Godwin-Davidova presiding, five members present.' She looked around, then looked back at the recorder's steel grille. 'I move that we shelve the agenda and go straight to emergency session. Starting with the death of Citizen Davidov.'

No dissent. Seconds of silence passed.

'Don't all talk at once,' she said.

Valentina Kozlova (Defence) spoke first. 'Look, Myra – Comrade Chair – we've all spoken to you about Georgi's death. We were all very sorry to hear of it.'

Myra nodded. 'Thank you.'

'Having said that – we need to decide on our political response. Now, obviously the police in Almaty are investigating, and so far there seem to be no indications of foul play.' She shrugged. 'That, of course, is hard to prove, these days. However . . . Georgi Yefrimovich had a great deal of responsibility –' she gestured vaguely at Andrei Mukhartov, the International Affairs Commissar '– and in the circumstances, natural causes do seem likely.'

Myra sighed. 'Yes, I appreciate that. And I appreciate what all of you have said to me. Let me say for the record that personally I don't accept that Georgi's death was anything but an assassination.'

She faced down the resulting commotion.

'*However*,' she continued, 'I don't ask or expect any of you to take this as more than a suspicion. At the moment, even the question of who might benefit from it is very unclear – if Georgi was murdered, it might have been by one side or the other. Possibly some elements in the space movement saw him as an obstacle to their . . . diplomacy. Possibly some forces opposed to the space movement thought we'd think exactly that, and had him killed as a provocation. Or maybe, just maybe, his heart gave out. Whatever – it's come at a bad time for us.'

Mukhartov grunted agreement.

After a moment of gloomy silence Valentina spoke again. 'We've all studied your message,' she said. 'What's your own suggested course of action?'

'We try to stop them, of course. Damned if I want the fucking UN back on top of us, let alone one controlled by the goddam space movement and its proxies.'

Valentina leaned forward. 'For my part,' she said, 'I agree with your assessment. We have to be ready for the new situation in which the space movement controls the ReUN, and with it the Earth Defense battlesats. But –' she hesitated a moment, sighed almost imperceptibly, and continued '– I think that the death of Georgi, the understandable suspicions this has aroused, and the, ah, unexpected and unauthorised increase in labour-camp output may have given your response a . . . subjective element.' Kozlova glanced around the table. 'The coming shift in the balance of power can't be stopped by us, or by anybody. The most we've been able to do – thanks to Georgi's diplomacy – has been to help keep Kazakhstan neutral, with a tilt against the take-over. Even they wouldn't take direct action against it, though God knows Georgi tried to persuade them to. They assured us they just didn't have the clout, and I believe them. Now you seem to be suggesting that *we* throw our weight, such as it is, against it. My own view is that we'd accomplish more by staying neutral. It could work to our advantage – *if* we accommodate ourselves to new realities in good time.'

Myra unfroze her face. 'Get in on the winning side, you mean?' she suggested lightly.

'Yes, exactly,' Kozlova said. She seemed encouraged by Myra's response, or lack of response. 'After all,' she ploughed on, 'we ourselves are in a way part of the space movement, we go back a long way with it, and the Sheenisov are as much a threat to us as the barbarians

34

and reactionary governments are to some other enclaves. Frankly, I think we should put out some diplomatic feelers to the other side before the crunch, which as you correctly point out is a matter of days or weeks away. And we're not exactly in a position of strength at the moment. So there is indeed a certain urgency to our decision.'

'Interesting,' Myra murmured. 'Anyone else?'

Denis Gubanov (Internal Security) broke in sharply. 'The Chair spoke in her message of states being suborned and subverted. I don't think we should let ourselves become one of them! Whatever the rhetoric, and the propaganda of inevitability, it's obvious what's going on. Imperialism took a severe blow with the fall of the Yanks, but the blow wasn't fatal, worse luck. Monopoly capital always finds new political instruments, and the space movement, so-called, has proved an admirable vehicle.' He snorted, briefly. 'Literally – a launch vehicle! Through it, the rich desert the Earth. Why should we help them on their way?'

'More to the *point*,' said Sherman (Trade and Industry), making his disdain for Denis's rhetoric emphatically clear, 'there is the question of what we will do for a living when the camps are worked out.'

'We could always—' began Kozlova, as though about to say something in jest, then glanced at Myra and shut up.

'What?'

'Nah. Forget it. The business to hand is what we do now, about the coup.'

Myra let the argument go on. There was a case, she admitted to herself, on both sides. But Valentina had been right – there was a subjective edge to Myra's response. The space movement's central element was Mutual Protection, and Mutual Protection's central element was David Reid. If the space movement got its way he would be the most powerful man in the world.

No way was she going to let that bastard win.

3

The Ship o the Yird

An hour later, after a run across town that was bloody hard in (and on) my boots, and a hasty wash and change into my work clothes, I stood at the station bus-stop with my steel safety-helmet in one hand and my aluminium lunch-box in the other. Packing my lunch was the only non-basic service that my landlady provided, but for me that was enough to forgive her the absence of breakfast, dinner, laundry and reliable hot water.

The sun's growing heat was burning off the morning mist on the loch and between the hills. I felt as though I might at any moment rise and float away myself. My eyes felt sandy and my brain felt hot, but these discomforts did not diminish the kinder glow of elation somewhere in my chest and gut. In a strange way I could hardly bear to think about Merrial – every time I did so brought on such an explosion of joy that I quivered at the knees, and I almost feared to indulge it to excess. I wanted to keep it, hoard it, dole it out to myself when I really needed it, not gulp it all down at once. (Which is of course a mistaken notion – that particular well, like all too many others, is bottomless.

What I thought about instead was another woman – the Deliverer, under whose memorial I had met Merrial, and under whose remote and ancient protection she and her people lived. (Protected from persecution, at any rate, if not from prejudice.)

Over the past four years, History had been one of the arts I had struggled to master. It hadn't been easy, even in Glaschu, where the place fair drips with it, as they say. The baffled aversion expressed by Merrial was a common enough reaction. In a time of so many opportunities, and a place buzzing with innovative work in so many fields which could be applied to bring about manifest human

36

betterment, it seemed perverse (sometimes even to me) for a vigorous and intelligent young man to turn aside from such arts as Literature, and Music, and Kinematography, or from the sciences: Astronomy, Medicine, the many branches of Natural Theology; from the improving pursuits of Practical Philosophy and Mechanical and Civil Engineering – to turn aside from all these useful works of the intellect, not even for the understandable and, within reason, commendable attractions of business and pleasure, but to fossick about in mouldering documents and crumbling ruins, and to fill his head with bloody images and mind-numbing figures from the megadead past.

It was a distasteful and faintly disreputable fascination, with a whiff of necrophilia, even of necromancy, about it. But, whether we will or no, we're all historians, each with our own outline of history in our heads. This was a point I'd often had to make to sceptical listeners, from parents and siblings through to patronage committees and on to friends and workmates in drink-fuelled debate. We pick up the outline from parents and teachers and preachers, from songs and statues and stories.

In the beginning, God made the Big Bang, and there was light. After the first four minutes, there was matter. After billions of years, there were stars and planets, and the Earth was formed. The water above the sky separated from the water below the sky, which brought forth all manner of creeping things. Over millions of years they were shaped by God's invisible hand, Natural Selection, into great monsters of land and sea. The Earth was filled with violence, and God sent an asteroid, Katy Boundary, to destroy it. The sky was dark at noon for forty days, and almost all the living things were destroyed. Among those who survived were little beasts like mice, and they replenished the Earth, and burrowed into it and became coneys, and climbed trees and became monkeys, and climbed down and became Men –

– ape-men and cave-men, Egyptians and Babylonians, Greeks and Romans, Christians and Americans, Chinese and Russians. The Americans fell but their empire lived on as the Possession, until the Deliverer rose in the east and struck it down. Troubled times followed, and then peace.

So why disturb it – answer me that, lad!

Because the truth is more interesting and ultimately more

instructive than a farrago of fable? I had acquired the taste not just for truth but for detail; for the peculiar pleasure that comes from seeing the real relationship between events in terms of cause and effect rather than narrative convention. It's a satisfaction which I'll defend as genuinely scientific.

But what use *is it, eh?*

To that I had no ready answer, except to define the result as art, in the same way as the method could be defined as science. The argument that those who do not learn from history are doomed to repeat it failed to impress most people, convinced as they were that there was no risk whatsoever of history's more ruinous errors being repeated. So I had to reach for the argument that real history told a better story because it was a truer story; that reality had its own beauty, sterner and higher than that of myth.

The particular story I wanted to tell was of the life of the Deliverer. My proposal for a thesis on her early years as a student and academic in Glasgow, long before she became the figure known to history, was only the beginning of my own world-conquering ambition: to reconstruct, as much as one can across that gulf of time, the mind and personality and circumstance that had shaped the future that was now our past.

It might take decades of research, years of writing. Whatever else I did, this biography would define my own: a life for a Life. Perhaps it was an unconscious balking at that price, or some half-baked, self-justifying attempt to pay my dues to what my more practical-minded contemporaries called 'real work', or something more positive, a dimly felt attraction to the world of material striving and measurable success, a turning towards the future and away from the past, that led me that summer to Carron Town and the Kishorn Yard.

'Thank God it's Thursday,' said a cheerful voice behind me. I turned and grinned at Jondo, who was leaning against the bus-stop sign and eating a black pudding and fried-egg roll. Behind him a score of workers were by now queuing up. Vendors of snacks, hot drinks and newspapers worked along the line.

'It's Friday,' I pointed out.

'That's what I meant,' he said around a mouthful, hand-waving with the remainder of his breakfast. 'Force of habit.' He swallowed. 'Pay-day, at any rate.'

I nodded enthusiastically. Half my pay was telegraphed straight to my account at the Caledonian Mutual Bank; out of the remainder I had to pay for my lodgings, food and drink, and a modicum of carousing at the weekly fair. By Friday mornings I had just enough cash to get through the day. Pay was high, but so was the cost of living – the project had pulled up prices for miles around it.

Jondo was a man about my own age, his beer-gut already as impressive as his muscles. His long red hair, now as usual worn in a pony-tail, and his pale eyes and eyebrows gave him the look of a paradoxically innocent pirate; inherited perhaps from his ancestors who'd gone a-viking, and come to this land to pillage and settled down to farm, and to whom the Christian gospel had come as good news indeed, a welcome relief from heathendom's implacable codes of honour and vengeance. He spoke with the soft accent of Inverness, where – rumour had it – there were Christians still.

I tried to imagine Jondo drinking blood at some dark ceremony. The momentary absurd image must have brought a smirk to my face.

'What's so funny, Clovis?' he growled. Then he smiled, balling up the waxed paper and chucking it, wiping the grease from his hands on the oily thighs of his overalls. 'Ach, I know. A good night with your tinker lass, was it?'

'You could say that.'

'Aye, well, each to their own, I suppose,' he said, in the tone of one making a profound and original observation. 'Here's the bus.'

The bus, already half-full, drew to a halt beside us in a cloud of wood-alcohol exhaust, its brakes squealing and its flywheel shrieking. I hopped on, paid my groat to the driver and settled down in a window seat. Jondo heaved his bulk in beside me, gave me another lewd grin and a wink, released an evidently satisfying fart and went instantly to sleep.

Some passengers busied themselves with newspapers or conversation, but most dozed like Jondo or stared bleary-eyed like me. The discrepancy between the time-honoured four-day week and the project's more demanding schedules reduced Friday work to a matter of clearing up problems left over from the past week and preparing for the next. Not even the inducement of double time could make more than a handful of the labour-force encroach on the sanctity of Saturday and Sunday, although it could make most of us work overtime through the week. No amount of patient lecturing from

39

managers with clipboards and redundant hard hats could persuade us to adopt what they considered a more rational work pacing.

The bus lurched into motion. I lit a cigarette to dispel Jondo's intestinal methane and laid my temple against the welcome throbbing coolness of the window. As we crossed the Carron and passed New Kelso I gazed beyond the suburb's neat bungalows to where morning smoke rose from the tinker camp. A vivid image of Merrial asleep – the tumble of black hair, the white-sleeved arm across the pillow – lit up my mind. I wondered what my chances were of seeing her through the day. I didn't even know which office she worked in, and a desultory fantasy took shape of finding some fantastic excuse to visit them all: of working my way through the administration blocks and drawing-offices, spurning the flirtations of giggling girls and pensive older women with hunky pin-ups above their desks, until I finally walked into an engineering lab to find Merrial alone and in a day-dream of her own, about me, into which my real arrival would be a passionately welcomed incursion . . .

Probably not.

My head swung away from the window as the bus turned left on to the main road along the northern shore. I jolted upright, making sure my head didn't swing back and crack against the pane. Even at this hour in the morning the road was busy with commuter traffic and heavy trucks. The bus chugged slowly along, picking up yet more passengers in Jeantown, another village that the project had expanded, its packed buildings teetering perilously up the hillside. Out on the loch a pod of dolphins sported, their leaps drawing gasps and sighs from the less jaded or dozy of my fellow-passengers.

Then, with a great clashing of gears and screeching of flywheel as the auxiliary electric motors kicked in, the bus turned right, on to the road up into the hills between the two mountains, An Sgurr and Glas Bhein, that dominated the northern skyline of the lochside towns. To me, this afforded an inexhaustibly fascinating view of further ranges of hills and reaches of water. Everybody else on the bus ignored it completely. Someone opened a window to let out the smoke and let in some fresh air; a bee blundered in, causing a ripple of excitement and much brandishing of rolled newspapers before it bumbled out.

Above the last houses, above the meadows, the trees began: twenty-metre-tall beeches, then pine and rowan and birch, all the way up to the crags and the scree. Centuries ago these hills had been bare of all but rough pasture and heather, cropped by the infamous black-faced sheep. But these same bare hills had somehow sustained the sparse guerilla forces of Jacobite and Land Leaguer and Republican. Far below I could see the rocky peninsula known as the Island, a sheltering arm around the harbour, still with a small bunker on its top. During the First World Revolution a thirteen-year-old had written herself into local legend by bringing down a stealth fighter with a nuclear-tipped rocket-propelled grenade. In Jeantown's poky museum you can see an ancient photograph of her: the grubby, grinning cadre of a Celtic Vietcong, posed with the rocket tube slung on her shoulder, beside unrecognisable wreckage on a scarred hillside where to this day nothing will grow.

Over the top of the saddleback and down into the long, dark glen where the Pretender had evaded Cumberland's troops, where the Free Kirk had preached to the dispossessed, and where, later, the Army of the New Republic had cached their computers, the hardware of their software war against the last empire. The grim glen opened to another fertile plain of woods and fields and recently grown town, Courthill. Beyond it, at the edge of the sea-loch, lay the great scar of the Kishorn Yard. There was a trick of the eye in interpreting the sight – everything there, the cranes and the platform and the ship, were much bigger than their normal equivalents, like the Pleistocene relatives of familiar mammals.

The bus pulled up at the works gate. The stockade around the yard had been constructed more to protect the careless or reckless from wandering in than to safeguard anything it enclosed. I nudged Jondo awake and we alighted in a dangerous, fast-moving convergence of buses and cars and bikes. We strolled through the gate just as the seven-o'clock klaxon brayed. Hundreds, then thousands, of workers streamed through the gate and swarmed out across the yard. The place looked like a benign battlefield, crater-pocked, vehicle-strewn, littered with the living. I clamped the heavy helmet on my head, and with Jondo puffing along behind me, plunged in; ducking and dodging along walkways, over trenches, under cables; leaping perilous small-gauge railway tracks and over waterlogged trenches and dried-up culverts (drainage here had always been a bit hit-and-miss); past haulage vehicles and earth-movers, air-compressors and power-plants, portable cabins and toilets set down as if at random in the muck, until at length we reached the immense dry-dock that was the focus of the whole glorious affray.

The dry-dock was a giant rounded gouge out of the side of a hill where it sloped down to the sea – hundreds of metres across, tens of metres deep. Its rocky cliffs were old and weathered; it looked like some work of Nature, or of Providence – even of Justice, the smiting of the Earth by a wrathful God; but in fact it was the centuries-old work of Man. (It is their civil engineering that most impresses, of the works of the ancients, but this is perhaps because so much of it endures – greater works than these have gone to the rust and the rot.) Iron sluice-gates, on an appropriately Brobdingnagian scale, held back the sea – though pumps laboured day and night to counter the inevitable seepage and spill.

Within it towered the platform, a – someday soon – floating bastion of concrete and painted steel, and within that towered the ship. The *Sea Eagle* (*Iolair* – pronounced something like 'Yillirrih' – in the Gaelic) looked like a rocket-propelled grenade buried nose-down in the platform. Four fin-like flanges sloped from its central tower to intersect the ovoid surface of its reactor-shell and reaction-mass tank, which was forty metres across at its widest diameter. The part of it concealed by the platform tapered from this equator to the aerospike of the main jet, around which the flared nozzles of attitude jets made a scalloped array.

By now I was tramping along in the middle of my work-gang, Jondo and I having been joined by Machard, Druin, the Lewismen – Murdo One and Murdo Too – Angelo and Trike. We descended a zig-zag iron stairway, down and down again, and walked across the floor of the dock, splashing through puddles of rainwater and seawater (some of which were so long-established that they had their own ecosystems) to the door at the base of the platform's southwest leg. It was like going into a lighthouse: up and up, around and around the winding stair. The air smelt of wet metal, hot oil, damp concrete. Every surface dripped, every sound echoed.

After two minutes' climb we reached the level of the internal scaffolding where we were working. I ducked through a service door in the inner side of the leg and emerged on to a walkway facing one of the platform's turbines across a twenty-metre gap. At our current worksite, a dozen metres along the walkway, ladders, more scaffolding and planks disappeared into – in fact appeared to merge with – the unfinished structure of struts joining the support leg to the platform's engine mount.

Our contract for the month was to finish that structure. There was no flexibility in the contract: there was only a month to go before the platform was floated out. Angus Grizzlyback, the foreman, was sitting at a wooden pallet mounted on crates to form a table, on which were spread some disassembled welding-torches, a small tin of kerosene and a few now very dirty seagull quills. He stood and glowered at us, reflexively lowering his head so as not to bash his pate on the next level up. You could see the white hairs on his chest and forearms which had inspired his nickname (or, for all I know, his surname, local custom being what it was). He was nearly two metres tall and about a hundred and fifty years old.

'Ah, good afternoon, gentlemen,' he said. 'I trust you all enjoyed your long lie? Let's see if we can think of something to occupy our leisure for the rest of the day.'

He drew a sheaf of finger-marked papers from his pocket as we gathered around the pallet. His pale grey eyes, under white brows, fixed me for a second.

'And you can get started right away, colha Gree,' he added.

I nodded brightly, winced at the effect of this sudden violent motion, and went off to make the tea.

The morning meeting – twenty minutes of sitting around, drinking tea and smoking – was the routine start to the day. Work on the project was organised through a sort of ecological pyramid of contractors and sub-contractors, from the great kraken of the International Scientific Society all the way down to frantically scrabbling krill like myself. Angus Grizzlyback combined the functions of entrepreneur and foreman, which partly cut across, and partly complemented, the job of the shop steward (in our case, Jondo) who held the equivalent position in the parallel pyramid of the union.

Conversation at the meeting, in my two months' experience, revolved around rumour, the day's news and sport. At the end of it everybody would drain their mugs, fold their newspapers, stub out their cigarettes, glance at some scrap of paper or doodle of slopped tea, nod to Angus and get cracking on some complex job to which only the most recondite allusion had been made. I would clear up the mess, rinse out the mugs if we were near a tap, and listen to Angus spell out my task for the day in terms suitable for the simple-minded.

Today's agenda was dominated by a motion before the Strathcarron district council, reported in the *West Highland Free Press*, that the locality should delegate its coinage to the regional council at Inverfefforan. This dangerous proposal for centralisation found no favour around the pallet. It was forensically dissected by Angus, vulgarly derided by the Lewismen, angrily dismissed by the Carronich. I myself pointed out a recent lesson of history. A few years earlier, a similar proposal had been passed in Strathclyde. The Glasgow mark had lost all public confidence, and the scheme was abandoned when annual inflation reached a ruinous two per cent. The discussion moved on to the national football league, and my attention wandered.

You can guess where. This time, however, my thoughts were more rational, and troubling, than my previous delighted memories, eager anticipations and fond fantasies. High as my opinion was of myself, I could not shake off my impression that Merrial had expected to find me; that she had known me, or known of me; that her first glance had signified recognition. Love and lust at that sight there had been, on both sides I was sure; but I was equally, though more obscurely, sure that this was not the first sight. I had recognised her too, but had no idea from where; with her it was conscious from the beginning, unconcealed but unexplained.

For a moment – I admit with shame – I considered the notion that we might have *known each other in a previous life*, whatever that may mean. On an instant I dismissed the idea as the foolish, womanish, oriental superstition that it is. Metempsychosis (though undoubtedly within the power of Omnipotence) has no place in the natural and rational religion.

So I lounged, elbows on the rough wood of the crude table, and sipped tea and smoked leaf while my companions argued about finance or football, and tried to apply my infinitesimal portion of Reason to a problem on which my passions were fully, and turbulently, engaged. The rational conclusion was that if we recognised each other we must have met before, not in an imagined previous life, but previously in this.

There were a number of possibilities on my side of the equation. (Merrial's I set aside – there were any number of ways in which she, from her privileged vantage, could have observed me, unobserved herself, and investigated me, undetected.) Was it conceivable that one of the hundreds of faces I saw nearly every day had been hers, unnoticed at the time? It seemed unlikely: hers was the kind of face I couldn't help but notice. I'd have given her a second look, and more, in a crowd of thousands.

Had I seen her, then, in another context, perhaps not even in the flesh? In, for example, some poster or moving picture about the project (all of which, for understandable reasons of recruitment, lied about its complement of pretty girls)? The same objections applied – I'd remember the film, I'd *have* the poster.

By further elimination I quickly returned to the first explanation that had struck me: that we had met, or at least seen each other, in our earlier years; in childhood. Merrial, I now recalled with renewed interest, had not explicitly disavowed the possibility – only discounted it, saying that she wasn't from around here.

Neither, of course, was I. There was no reason why I couldn't have seen her. I couldn't remember any such encounter, but I already knew that our childhood memories are as vagrant as our childhood selves, and as elusive; and as capable of innocent, shameless deceit.

The brute-force approach suggested itself: interrogate my parents, brothers and sisters; ransack family photographs . . . not yet. Already, the conscious thought that I sought the memory would have released the insensible agency in my mind that I privately thought of as the Librarian. That part of me would do the rest, and bring back the record if it were to be found at all – no doubt at some time as unexpected as it would be inopportune, but welcome nonetheless.

'– the torch parts?' said Angus.

I realised I had missed something. Angus sighed.

'You understand how to fit them, test and adjust?'

'Sure,' I said, nodding with more confidence than I felt.

'Fine, fine,' said Angus, standing up and briskly brushing the palms of his hands together. 'Let's get on with it, gentlemen.'

The others were grinning at me.

'Some night that must have been,' said Murdo Too, setting off another round of ribald teasing. I took it in good part but was relieved when they'd all clambered away into the support structure, leaving me to get on with my job without benefit of Angus's unheard instructions. A couple of hours passed quite pleasantly, if dangerously, and at the morning tea-break Angus was happy enough with the results to turn me loose on some sheet metal a dozen metres inward and ten up. I perched in the din-filled open space of the support structure, with nothing visible while I worked but what my own torch's jet illuminated, and with little else on my mind.

About twelve o'clock I decided to knock off for lunch. I throttled down the torch and lifted my mask. As I gathered up the bits of kit to carry back I heard Merrial's voice. I blinked and looked down. There she was, looking up from under a safety-helmet.

'Hi, Clovis!' she shouted, waving a lunch-box.

I waved back and returned to the scaffolding, dropped my tools and grabbed my lunch-box and descended to the dock's floor so quickly that my boots made the stairwell ring. By the time I'd reached the bottom, Merrial had walked over and was waiting for me. She was wearing the standard boiler-suit and boots, an outfit which – with her tied-back hair – gave her a boyish look. Her hug and kiss of greeting were sweet and warm; the rims of our helmets clanged, and we pulled apart, laughing.

'This is a fine surprise,' I said.

She caught my hand. 'Come on,' she said. 'I know a good place.'

We set off across the dock, to the predictable whistles and cat-calls of my mates, high above. Around the vast perimeter of the platform we went, and out into the daylight on the seaward side. Just left of the huge sea-doors Merrial turned towards the cliff, where a series of shelves and foot-holds formed a dangerous-looking natural stairway, which she skipped up on to and nimbly ascended. I followed, not looking down, until she stopped on a wider, grassy, heathery shelf a good thirty metres up.

We sat down. Merrial leaned back against the rockface, and I, unthinking, did the same – then jerked forward as I discovered again the scratches and bruises on my back. With our legs stretched out, our feet were almost at the edge. I felt more uneasy on that solid rock than I ever had at greater heights on the platform. Across the top of the gates, across the sea-loch, the Torridonian battlements of Applecross challenged the sky. The scale of those ancient mountains dwarfed the ship itself to a metal sculpture some eccentric artist had made in his back garden in his spare time.

'My place,' Merrial said.

'Some place,' I acknowledged. 'It's you who should be working on the platform, with a head for heights like this.'

'I'll keep to my cosy lab and my long lies, thanks.'

We opened our boxes and spread out and shared the contents, then got stuck in, both ravenous. For a few minutes we ate, without saying much, then Merrial topped up the mugs, lit herself a cigarette, passed one to me and leaned back against the rock.

'Clovis, I have something to ask you—'

She stopped. She was looking straight ahead, as though she wanted to talk without looking at me.

'What is it?'

'Something you can maybe tell me. Something you might not be supposed to. It's to do with the ship.'

This was getting more serious than love.

'You want to know about welding?' I asked, trying to be flippant.

She laughed. 'No, about history.'

'Oh.' I waved a hand. 'Any time. But there must be plenty better qualified than I, all I know about in any depth is—'

She watched me as the penny dropped.

'The life of the Deliverer?'

'That's the one,' she agreed cheerily.

'You're serious?'

'I'm serious,' she said. She wasn't looking away from me now, she was looking at me with a fixity and intensity of gaze I found alarming.

'All right,' I said, my mind treading water. 'You seriously want to know something about the Deliverer? I can tell you anything you want. But what has that to do with the ship, for God's sake?'

She took a deep breath, gazing away from me again at the tall ship. 'It's a fine ship there, colha Gree, and proud I am to be working on it. But consider this: it'll be the first ship to have lifted from the Yird for many a hundred year. The first since the Deliverance. We don't know much of what happened then, but we do know there were people and machines in space before the Deliverance, and we've heard never a word from them since. There's no doubt they're all dead. Why do you think that is?'

47

'There was a war,' I said patiently, 'and a revolution. The Second World Revolution, or the Deliverance, as we call it. The folk outside the Yird had followed the path of power, and they fell with the Possession. Starved of supplies, or killed each other, most like.'

'So the story goes,' she said, in the tone of one tired of disputing it. 'But what if it's wrong? What if whatever cleared the near heaven of folk and machines and deils alike is *still there*?'

'Ah,' I said, glancing involuntarily up at the clear blue sky. 'But it stands to Reason, the people in charge of the project will have considered this. Why don't you take it up with them?'

'They've considered it all right,' she said, 'and rejected it. There's no evidence of anything up there that could do the ship any harm. There's no evidence that the loss of the space habitations was anything but what you've said.'

'So why do you think I might know anything about this –' I waved my hand dismissively '– *supposed* danger?'

'Because . . .' At this point, I swear, she looked around and leaned closer, almost whispering in my ear. 'There has long been a tinker tradition, or rumour, or hint – you know how it is with the old folk – that whatever *did* destroy the space settlements and satellites and so on might still be there, and that it was . . . the Deliverer's own doing.'

My mouth must have fallen open. I could feel it go instantly dry, and I felt a moment of giddiness and nausea. My fingers dug into the tough grass as the world spun dangerously. I looked at her, sickened, yet fascinated despite myself. The natural religion has no sin of blasphemy, but this was blasphemy as near as dammit. 'That's deep water, Merrial.'

'You're telling *me*!' she snorted. 'I've had trouble enough for even suggesting it. Everybody thinks the Deliverer was a perfect soldier of God, like Khomeini or somebody like that! Oh, among my own folk there's a more realistic attitude, they'll admit she had faults, but that's just among ourselves. In public you won't find a tink saying a word against her.'

I smiled wryly. 'Except you.'

'This is not public, colha Gree.' She ran a finger down the side of my face and across my lips.

'You must be very confident of that,' I said. 'To tell me.'

'I'm confident all right,' she said. 'I'm sure of you.'

To distract myself from the turmoil of mixed feelings this assurance induced, I asked her, 'So what is it that I can tell you?'

'What you know,' she said. 'I've always thought the scholars might know more about the Deliverer than they're letting on.'

I laughed. 'There are no secrets among scholars, they're not like the tinkers. All we find out is published. If it doesn't square with what most folk believe, that's their problem; but most folk don't read scholarly works, anyway. And – well, I suppose they are like the tinkers in this – they have a more realistic attitude among themselves. It's true, the Deliverer was no perfect saint. But I've seen nothing to suggest that she ever did anything as dire as . . . as you said.'

She made a grimace of disappointment. 'Oh, well. Maybe it was too much to hope that something like that would be written down on paper.' She plucked a pink clover and began tugging out the scrolled petals one by one and sucking them; passed one to me. I took it between my teeth, releasing the tiny drop of nectar on to my tongue.

'On paper,' I said thoughtfully. 'There could be other information where we can't reach it.'

'In the dark storage?'

'Aye, well, like I said last night – it's there, but we can't reach it.'

'I could reach it,' Merrial said casually.

'Oh, you could, could you?'

'Yes,' she said. 'I can get hold of equipment to take data out of the dark storage and put it in safe storage.'

'Safe storage?' I asked, too astonished to query more deeply at that moment.

'You know,' she said. 'The seer-stones.'

'And how would you know that?'

Again the remote gaze. 'I've seen it done. By . . . engineers taking short cuts.'

'There's a good reason why the left-hand path is avoided,' I said.

'"Necessity is its own law",' she said, as though quoting, but the expression came from no sage I'd ever read. 'Anyway, Clovis, it's not as dangerous as you may think.'

Curiosity drove me like prurience. 'How do they do it safely? Draw pentagrams with salt, or what?'

'No,' she said, quite seriously. 'They make lines with wire – isolated circuits, you know? That's what confines anything that might be waiting to get out. There are other simple precautions, for the visuals –' she made a cutting motion with her hand in response to my baffled look '– but ninety-nine times out of a hundred there's nothing to worry about anyway. Just words and pictures.' She chuckled darkly. 'Sometimes *strange* words and pictures, I'll give you that.'

'And the hundredth time?'

'You meet a demon,' she said, very quietly but emphatically. 'Most times, you can shut it down before it does any damage.'

'And the other times?' I persisted.

'It gets loose and eats your soul.'

I stared at her. 'You mean that's actually *true*?'

She laughed at me. 'Of course not. It makes your equipment burst into flames or explode with a loud bang, though.'

'I can see how that might be a hazard.'

She reached over and touched my lips. 'Shush, man, don't go on like an old woman. Most of the stuff in the dark storage is useless to us, or evil in a different way from what you think. Evil ideas from the old times, they can make you sick, and make you want to share them, so they spread like a disease.'

She leaned back again and closed her eyes, enjoying the sun like a cat. 'I reckon you and I are strong enough and healthy enough in our minds to be safe from that sort of thing.' She opened her eyes again and gave me a challenging look.

The path of power is always a temptation, as Merrial had so lightly said last night. Until now, it had never seriously tempted me; I knew the dangers, and knew no way of getting to the undoubted rewards. Now such a way was being offered; it might reduce by years the time required for researching my thesis, it might even give me a head start on the Life. The lust for the lost knowledge made my head throb.

The question was out before I knew what I was saying. 'Do you want me to help you to do it?'

Her eyes widened and brightened. '*Could* you? That would be just – wonderful!'

She was looking at me with so much admiration and respect that I could not imagine not doing what it would take to deserve it. But even in my besotted eagerness to please her, my genuine concern about the problem she thought she'd uncovered, and my own desire for the knowledge and for the adventure of obtaining it – even with all that, my whole training and my natural caution came rushing back, and I wavered.

'Oh, God,' I said. 'I'll have to think about it.'

'Can you get your thinking about it over by eight tonight?' Merrial asked drily.

'Maybe. And what if I say no?'

She held me in her level gaze. 'I won't think any the less of you. It won't change a thing about that.'

'Sure?' I said, not anxiously but mischievously. I had already decided. She had seduced me into a frame of mind that feared neither God nor men nor devils. 'Then what will you do?'

She shook her head. 'I'll find some other way, or at the worst just register my protest in the record, and go on with my work as I'm told.'

'That sounds like a more sensible course in the first place.'

'It is that,' she said. 'But I'd rather have the satisfaction of knowing the ship is safe, one way or another, than of saying "I told you so" afterwards.'

I couldn't argue with that, and I didn't want to. What she said must have had some deeper effect on me, because when we descended the perilous steps down from the heathery eyrie, each of us one stumble away from the welcoming arms of Darwin, I wasn't afraid at all.

My room was narrow and long, under the slope of the roof. After the heat of the day it was full of the smell of old varnish and warm rust and the sound of creaking wood. The westward-facing skylight let in enough light to see by, and enough air to breathe.

I came in from work and threw off my overalls and shirt, tossed my temporarily heavy purse on the bed, and uncapped a chilled bottle of beer I'd bought at the bus-stop. I opened the skylight to its fullest extent and sat myself under it on the room's one tall chair, and leaned my elbow on the window's frame as though sitting at a bar. Beside my forearm tiny red arachnids moved about on the grey and yellow lichen like dots in front of my eyes.

Merrial and I would meet again in two hours. Plenty of time to wash and shave and dress, to consider and reconsider. I was almost tempted to have a brief sleep, but decided against it, attractive though the barely straightened bedding seemed at this moment. After soaking up the beer I'd get a good jolt of coffee. I lit my fifth cigarette of the day and gazed out over the rooftops towards the loch, my parched body gratefully absorbing the drink, my tired brain riding the rush of the leaf.

Merrial's disturbing but alluring proposition had preoccupied me all afternoon, and although my decision was made I had plenty of doubts and fears. I would not be the first to mine the dark archives in the interests of history, or of engineering for that matter; it was neither a crime nor a sin, but it had always been impressed upon me that it was a dangerous folly. And, to be sure, I could think of no good reason for doing it, other than the ones which motivated myself and Merrial; no doubt everyone who had taken that path had felt the same about *their* reasons. Rationally, it was obvious why the dangers were better publicised than the benefits – those who found only madness and death in the black logic could not but be noticed, whereas those who found knowledge or wealth or pleasure discreetly kept their sinister source to themselves.

What hypocrisies, I wondered, did the tinkers practise, if they themselves would on occasion turn their hand to the leftward path? Until Merrial had mentioned it, I'd suspected no such thing: but then, with the tinkers' virtual monopoly of an understanding of the white logic, it was in their interests to publicly disparage the black. Optical and mechanical computing, and more especially the delicate interface between them – the seer-stones set like gems in the shining brass of the calculating machinery – were their speciality and secret skill. What would happen if people outside their guild were to start exploring the left-hand path in earnest, as a public enterprise rather than a private vice, heaven only knew. A new Possession, perhaps; in which case the tinkers might have to engineer a new Deliverance. It was not a reassuring thought.

I stubbed out the cigarette and sent the butt tumbling down the slate roof-tiles to the dry gutter. The sounds of people going home, of engines and hooves and feet, rose from the street below. I turned back into the room and finished the beer, then undressed and went into the sluice-shower and washed myself down. The water ran cold just before I got the last soap-suds off; I gritted my teeth and persisted, then leapt out and dried myself off while the electric kettle boiled. I filled a ewer with a mixture of cold and hot water and shaved carefully, then set some coffee to brew while I got dressed: in the same trousers and waistcoat as I'd worn the previous night, but I thought the occasion deserved a clean shirt.

The bed was close enough to the table for the two items of furniture to form a somewhat unergonomic desk. I sat down with the coffee and looked at the stack of books and papers I'd brought with me to read over the summer. I reached over and hauled a volume from the stack, cursed and got up and found a rag and wiped dust and cobwebs from all the books, washed my hands and sat down again. Sipping the cooling coffee, turning over the pages, I tried to focus my mind on the matters they contained.

When I was awakened for a third time by my forehead hitting the table I gave up and poured another coffee and turned my mind to my real worry, the one I didn't want to think about: what if Merrial were simply using me? That she had sought me out in the first place because she wanted me to do a job for her?

I walked up and down the room's narrow length, turning the question over almost as often as I turned around. After several iterations I decided that I couldn't have been fooled about her feelings, that her passion was real – and that if she'd been intent on manipulating me, she would have done it more subtly—

But then, perhaps that itself was evidence of how subtly she'd done it. At that point I stopped. To suspect manipulation that subtle – an apparently clumsy and obvious approach disguising one devious and elegant – was to undermine the very confidence in my own judgement on which all such discriminations must perforce rely.

So I forgot my suspicions, and looked once more at the books, and at a quarter before eight went out into the evening to meet her, and my fate.

4

Paper Tigers

Three flags hung behind the coffin: the Soviet, red with gold hammer and sickle; the Kazakhstani, blue with yellow sun and eagle; and the ISTWR, yellow with black trefoil.

About two hundred people were crammed into the hall of the crematorium. The funeral was the nearest thing to a State occasion the republic had had since the Sputnik centenary. The entire depleted apparat was there, and a good proportion of the workers, peasants and intelligentsia was probably watching on television. The distinguished foreign guests included the Kazakhstani consul, the head of the Western United States Interests Section, and David Reid, who was wedged between a couple of Mutual Protection greps. Myra sat with the rest of Sovnarkom in the front row, dry-eyed, as one of Georgi's old comrades – another Afganets – delivered the eulogy.

'Major Georgi Yefrimovich Davidov was born in Alma-Ata in 1956. At school, in the Pioneers and the Komsomol, he soon distinguished himself as an exemplary individual – studious, civic-minded, with great athletic prowess. After obtaining a degree at the University of Kazakhstan, where he joined the Communist Party of the Soviet Union, he completed his national service and chose a military career. In 1979 he qualified as a helicopter pilot, and later that same year was among the first of the limited contingent of the Soviet armed forces to fulfil their internationalist duty to the peoples of Afghanistan.'

A ripple of dissidence, expressed with indrawn breaths, or sighs, or shifting of feet, went through the room. Myra herself sniffed, compressed her lips, looked down. All those nights he'd woken her by grabbing her, holding her, talking away his nightmares; all those mornings when he'd said not a word, given no indication that he remembered any interruption to his sleep, or to hers.

The speaker raised his voice a little and continued undaunted.

'His service earned him promotion and the honour of Hero of the Soviet Union. In 1985 he applied for transfer to the space programme, and after training at Baikonur he won the proud title of Cosmonaut of the Soviet Union. However, many decades were to pass before he was able to fulfil this part of his destiny.'

By which time it was a fucking milk-run, and there was no fucking Soviet Union, so get on with it—

'During the turbulent years of the late 1980s, Major Davidov took some political stands about which his friends and comrades may honestly differ –'

Nice one, he was a fucking Yeltsinite, get on with it—

'– but which testify to his true Soviet and Kazakh patriotism and the seriousness with which he took his civic duty and the Leninist ideals of the armed forces, which in his view proscribed the use of violence against the people.'

Myra was not the only one who had to choke back a laugh.

'After the Republic of Kazakhstan became independent, Major Davidov's expertise in the areas of nuclear weaponry and questions of nuclear disarmament gave him a new field for his great political skill and personal charm . . .'

Myra bit her lip.

He was in front of her in the taxi queue outside the airport at Alma-Ata. Tall, even taller than she was, very dark; swept-back black hair, eyebrows almost as thick as his black moustache; relaxed in a stiff olive-green uniform; smoking a Marlboro and glancing occasionally at a counterfeit Rolex.

Myra, just arrived, lost and anxious, could not take her eyes off him. But it was the yellow plastic bag at his feet that gave her the nerve to speak. Printed on it in red were a picture of a parrot and the words:

THE PET SHOP
992 Pollockshaws Road
Glasgow G41 2HA

She leaned forward, into his field of vision.
'You've flown in from Glasgow?' she asked, in Russian.

55

He turned, startled out of some trance, and looked at her with a bemused expression which rapidly became a smile.

'Ah, the bag.' He poked it with his foot, revealing that the carrier was bulging with cartons of cigarettes and bottles of Johnny Walker Black Label. 'You're a stranger here, then.'

'Oh?'

'These plastic bags have nothing to do with Glasgow. They're used by every shop from here to China, God knows why.' He laughed, showing strong teeth stained with nicotine. 'Have you been to Glasgow?'

'Yes,' said Myra. 'I lived there for several years, back in the seventies.'

Something cooled in his look. 'What were you doing?'

'I was writing a thesis,' Myra said, 'on the economy of the Soviet Union.'

He guffawed. 'You got permission to do *that*?'

'It wasn't a problem—' she began, then stopped. She realised that he'd taken her for a former-Soviet citizen. Former *nomenklatura*, if she'd had clearance for such dangerous research.

'I'm not a Russian, I'm from the United States!'

He raised his eyebrows.

'Your accent is very good,' he said, in English. His accent was very good. They talked until they reached the top of the queue, and then went on talking, because they shared a taxi into town, and went on talking . . .

Would she ever have spoken to him, Myra wondered, if it hadn't been for that yellow bag? And if she hadn't spoken to him, would she ever have seen him again? Perhaps; but perhaps not, or not at such a moment, when they were both free, and on the rebound from other lovers, and in that case . . .

She wouldn't be here, for one thing, and Georgi wouldn't be in that coffin, and . . . the consequences went on and on, escalating until she didn't know whether to laugh or cry. For want of a nail the kingdom was lost – and the result of that triviality, the fictitious Pollockshaws pet-shop address on the plastic bag, had gained her a republic, and imposed on others losses she could not bear to contemplate. Or so it might seem, if anyone ever learned enough about her to see her hand in history.

But then again, maybe not, maybe old Engels and Plekhanov had been right after all about the role of the individual in history: maybe it did all come out in the wash – at the end of the French Revolution *someone*, but, of course, ha-ha, 'not necessarily that particular Corsican', would have stepped into the tall boots which circumstances, like a good valet, had laid out for a man on horseback.

She'd never found that theory particularly convincing, and it gave her small comfort now to even consider it. No, she was stuck, as were they all, with her actions and their consequences.

'– in recent years Georgi Yefrimovich played a leading part in the diplomatic service of the ISTWR, in which duty he met his death.' The eulogist paused for a moment to direct a stabbing glance at the distinguished foreign guests. 'He is survived by his former wife and loyal friend, Myra Godwin-Davidova, their children and grandchildren –'

Too many to read out, and none of them here, get on with it—

Messages were, however, read out from all of the absent offspring, other relatives, old friends. The eulogist laid down his sheaf of papers at last, and raised his hand. The crematorium filled with the oddly quiet and modest sound of Kazakhstan's national anthem. The coffin rolled silently through the unobtrusive hatch. Everyone stood up and sang, or mimed along to, the Internationale. And that was that. Another good materialist gone to ash.

Myra turned and walked out of the crematorium, and row by row, from the front, they fell in and walked out behind her.

Her hands were shaking as she fumbled with her black fur hat and tried to light a cigarette in the driveway. Out on the street, cars were being moved into position to carry the dignitaries off to the post-funeral luncheon function. Somebody steadied her hand, helped her with the cigarette. She lit up and looked up, to see David Reid. Dark brows, dark eyes, white hair down to the upturned collar of his astrakhan coat. He looked less than half his age, with only the white hair – itself an affectation – indicating anything different; none of her give-away flaws. She was pretty sure his joints didn't creak, or his bones ache. They had better fixes in the West. His minders hung about a few steps away, their gaze grepping the surroundings. People were milling around, drifting towards the waiting cars.

'Are you all right?' Reid asked.

'I'm fine, Dave.'

He scuffed a foot on the gravel, scratched the back of his neck.

'We didn't do it, Myra.'

'Yeah, well . . .' She shrugged. 'I read the autopsy. I believe it.'

You'd be dead if I didn't, she disdained to add. She believed the autopsy; she had no choice. She believed Reid, too. She still had her doubts about the verdict: natural causes – it might be one of those dark episodes where she could never be sure of the truth, like Stalin's hand in the Kirov affair, or in the death of Robert Harte . . . But Reid took the point she wanted him to take. He seemed to relax slightly, and lit a cigarette himself. His gaze flicked from the burning tip to the crematorium chimney, then to her.

'Ah, shit. It seems such a waste.'

Myra nodded. She knew what he meant. Burning dead people, burying them in *a fucking hole in the ground* – it was already beginning to seem barbaric.

'He didn't even want cryo,' she said. 'Let alone that Californian computer-scan scam.'

'Why not?' Reid asked. 'He could've afforded it.'

'Oh, sure,' Myra said. 'Just didn't believe in it, is all.'

Reid smiled thinly. 'Neither do I.'

'Oh?'

He spread his hands. 'I just sell the policies.'

'Is there *any* pie you don't have a finger in?'

Reid rubbed the side of his nose with his finger. 'Diversification, Myra. Name of the game. Spread the risks. Learned that in insurance, way back when.' He reached out, waiting for her unspoken permission to take her arm. 'We need to talk business.'

'Car,' she said, catching his elbow firmly and turning about on the crunching gravel. They walked side by side to the armoured limousine. Myra, out of the corner of her eye, watched people watching. Good: let it be clear that she no longer suspected Reid. Not publicly, not politically, not even – at a certain level – privately. Just personally, just in her jealous old bones. But there was more to it than making a diplomatic display; there was still a genuine affection between them, attenuated though it was by the years, exasperated though it was by their antagonism. Reid had never been a man to let enmity get in the way of friendship.

Myra glanced at her watch as the car door shut with a well-engineered clunk. They had about five minutes to talk in private as the big black

Zhil rolled through Kapitsa's city centre to its only posh hotel, the Sheraton. She settled back in the leather seat and eyed Reid cautiously.

'OK,' she said. 'Get on with it.'

Reid reached for the massive ashtray, stubbed out one cigarette and lit up another. Myra did the same. Their smoky sighs met in a front of mutual disruption. Reid scratched his eyebrow, looked away, looked back.

'Well,' he said. 'I want to make you an offer. We know you still have some of your old –' he hesitated; even here, there were words one did not say '– strategic assets, and we'd like to buy them off you.'

He could be bluffing.

'I have no—' she began. Reid tilted his head back and puffed a tiny jet of smoke that, after a few centimetres, curled back on itself in a miniature mushroom-cloud.

'Don't waste time denying it,' he said.

'All right,' said Myra. She swallowed a rising nausea, steadied herself against a dizzy, chill darkening of her sight. It was like being caught with a guilty secret, but one which she had not known she held. But, she knew too well, if she had not known it was because she had never tried, and never wanted, to find out.

'Suppose we do. We wouldn't sell them to anyone, let alone you. We're against your coup—'

It was Reid's turn to feign ignorance, Myra's to show impatience.

'We wouldn't *use* them,' he said. 'Good God, what do you take us for? We just want them . . . off the board, so to speak. Out of the game. And quite frankly, the only way we can be sure of that is to have control of them ourselves.'

Myra shook her head. 'No way. No deal.'

Reid raised his hand. 'Let me tell you what we have to offer, before you reject it. We can buy you out, free and clear. Give everybody in this state, every one of your citizens, enough money to settle any- where and live more than comfortably. Think about it. The camps are going to be wound down, and *whoever* wins the next round is going to move against you. Your assets aren't going to be much use when Space Defense gets back in business.'

'That's a threat, I take it?'

'Not at all. Statement of fact. Sell them now or lose them later, it's up to you.'

59

'Lose them – or use them!'

Reid gave her a 'we are not amused' look.

'I'm not fooling,' Myra told him. 'The best I can see coming out of your coup is more chaos, in which case we'll need all the goddamn *assets* we can get!'

Reid took a deep breath. 'No, Myra. If you do get chaos, it'll be because we haven't won. This coup, as you call it, is the last best chance for stability. If we fail the world will go to hell in its own way. Your personal contribution to that will then be no concern of mine – I'll be dead, or in space – but you *can* help make sure it *doesn't* happen, and benefit yourself and your people in the process.' He was putting all of his undeniable charm into his voice and expression as he concluded, 'Think it over, Myra. That's all I ask.'

'I'll think about it,' she said, granting him at least this victory, for what it was worth. She looked around. 'We've arrived.'

The hotel's ornately furnished function suite was filled with people in dark clothes, standing about in small groups and conversing in low voices. Already they were beginning to relax out of their funereal solemnity, to smile and laugh a little: life goes on. Fine.

Myra and Reid walked together to the long tables on which the buffet was spread, and contrived to lose each other in the random movement of people selecting food and drinks. With a plate of savouries in one hand and a large glass of whisky in the other, Myra looked around. Over in one corner Andrei Mukhartov was deep in conversation with a lady in a black suit and a large hat; she was answering his quiet questions in a loud voice. Myra hoped this representative of the tattered Western fringe of the former United States wasn't talking about anything confidential. Possibly that was the point. She noticed that Valentina was standing alone, in an olive-green outfit whose black armband was rather shouted down by an astonishing amount of gold braid. Myra made a less than subtle bee-line for her.

'Ah, there you are,' she said, as Valentina turned. She nudged her defence minister towards the nearest of the many small tables dotted around the vast floor. They sat.

'New uniform?' Myra asked.

Valentina's rigid epaulettes moved up and down. 'Never had much occasion for it before,' she said.

'Never knew you'd accumulated so many medals, either.'

Valentina had to laugh. 'Yeah, it is a bit . . . Brezhnevian, isn't it?'

'All too appropriate, for us. The period of stagnation.'

Valentina devoured a canapé, not looking away from Myra. 'Indeed. I see you had a little chat with our main inward investor.'

'Yes. He made me an interesting offer.' Myra looked down at her plate, picked up something with legs. 'I do hope this stuff's synthetic; I'd hate to think of the radiation levels if it isn't.'

'I think we have to rely on somebody's business ethics on the radiation question,' Valentina said.

'Ah, right.' Myra peered at the shrimp's shell; it had an ICI trademark. Full of artificial goodness. She hauled the pale pink flesh out with her teeth. 'Anyway, Madame Comrade People's Commissar for Defence, my dear: our inward investor gave me to understand that he knows we've done a little less . . . outward divestment than I'd been led to believe.'

Valentina, rather to her credit, Myra thought, looked embarrassed.

'I inherited the assets from my predecessors . . . and I never mentioned them because I thought you already knew, or you didn't and you needed to have deniability.'

So it was true. The confirmation was less of a shock than Reid's original claim had been. It would take a while for the full enormity of it all to sink in.

Myra nodded, her mouth full. Swallowed, with a shot of whisky. 'The latter, actually. I didn't know. I thought they'd all been seized by the Yanks after the war.'

'Most of them were. There was one exception, though. A large portfolio of assets that made it through the crackdown, that the US/UN just couldn't get their hands on; one contract that was always renewed. Until the Fall Revolution, of course. Then it . . . lapsed, and I was left holding the babies. They were sent back to us in a large consignment of large diplomatic bags, from various locations, all controlled by . . .'

'You can tell me now, I take it?'

Valentina looked around, and shrugged.

'The original ministate, with the original mercenary defence force.'

Myra had to think for a moment before she realised just which state Valentina was talking about.

'Jesus wept!'

'Quite possibly,' said Valentina, 'quite possibly he did.'

There are times when all you can do is be cynical, put up a hard front, don't let it get to you . . . Myra joined in Valentina's dark chuckle.

'So what happened to the assets, and why is our investor concerned about them?'

'Ah,' said Valentina. 'You'll recall the Sputnik centenary a couple of years ago. We rather extravagantly launched one of our obsolete boosters to celebrate it. What I did at the time was take the opportunity to place most of our embarrassing legacy in orbit.'

'In *Earth* orbit?' Myra resisted an irrational impulse to pull her head down between her shoulders.

'Some of them,' said Valentina. 'The ones designed specifically for orbital use, you know? They're in high orbit, quite safe.' She frowned, and against some inner resistance added, 'Well, fairly safe. But the rest we sent to an even safer place: Lagrange.'

Myra had a momentary mental picture, vivid as a virtual display, of Lagrange: L5, one of the points where Earth's gravity and the Moon's combined to create a region of orbital stability, and which had, over half a century, accumulated a cluttered cluster of research stations, military satellites, official and unofficial space habitats, canned utopias, abandoned spacecraft, squatted modules, random junk . . . It was the space movement's promised land, and with the new nanofactured ultralight laser-launched spacecraft its population was rising as fast as Kapitsa's was falling.

'Oh, fucking hell,' said Myra.

'Don't worry,' Valentina assured her. 'They're almost undetectable among all the debris.'

Myra didn't have the heart to tell her how much she was missing the point.

'Why the fuck did you park them *there*?' she demanded. 'Safe, in a way, yeah, that I can understand, but didn't it occur to you that if it ever came out, we might find our intentions . . . misunderstood?'

Valentina looked even more embarrassed. 'It was – well, it was a Party thing, Myra. A request.'

'Oh, right. Jeez. Are you still *in* the fucking Party?'

Valentina chuckled. 'I am the Party. The ISTWR section, at least.'

'Now that Georgi's gone. Shit, I'd forgotten.'

They hadn't even put the fourth flag, the flag of the Fourth, on his coffin. Shit. Not that it mattered now. Not to Georgi, anyway. And not to those who'd gathered to pay their respects – the only one present who'd have understood its significance was Reid.

'Don't worry,' said Valentina.

'What does the International want with – oh, fuck. I can think of any number of things it might want with them.'

Valentina nodded. 'Some of them could be to our advantage.'

'Hah. I'll be the judge of that. You've kept the access codes to yourself?'

'Of course!'

'Well, that's something.'

'So our man's proposing in a buy-out, is he?' Valentina continued. 'Could be worth considering.'

'Yeah.' Myra stood up, taking her glass. 'I'm going to talk to him some more. Thanks for the update, Val.'

She refilled her glass, with vodka this time, and set out in a carefully casual ramble to where Reid stood chatting to an awestruck gaggle of low-level functionaries. Denis Gubanov and one of Reid's greps circled unobtrusively, keeping a wary distance from the group and from each other, each at a Lagrange point of his own. She couldn't hear the conversation. On her way, she was intercepted by Alexander Sherman. The Industry Commissar was wearing the same sharp plastic suit, its colour adjusted to black. He looked shiftier than usual; a bad sign.

'Ah, Myra. A sad day for us all.' He shook his head slowly. 'A sad day.'

'Yes,' said Myra. The phrase *get on with it* once more came to mind.

Alex took a deep breath and, as if telepathic, announced, 'I have something to tell you. It's not a good time, but . . . Well, I've had an offer from Mr Reid.'

'To buy out our assets?'

'No, no!' Alex looked surprised at the suggestion. 'An *employment* offer.'

'Oh, right,' said Myra dismissively. She waved a hand as she walked past him. 'Take it.'

She could see herself in the big gilt-framed mirrors as she walked up; they faced similar mirrors at the far side of the room, and for a moment she saw herself multiplied, a potential infinity of different versions of herself: a visual, virtual image of the many worlds interpretation. She had entertained a childish notion, once, that mirror images might be windows into those other worlds. Did the photon ever decide, she'd wondered, did it ever turn aside in its reflection?

What she saw was the endlessly repeated image of a tall, thin woman in a long black dress, moving towards the still oblivious Reid like some MIRVed nemesis. She saw the flickered glances exchange their messages, between her Security Commissar, Reid's security man, Reid, and herself, until Reid's reflected eyes met her actual eyes, and widened.

She encountered a sort of deadness in the air, and realised that the security men were, between them, setting up audio countermeasures, casting a cloak of silence around the group. Then she was through the region of dead air, where the voices were garbled and strange, and suddenly the conversation was audible – for the moment before it died on the lips of those who noticed her arrival.

'Well, hello again,' she said. Her gaze swept the half-dozen of her employees gathered around Reid; they were all making comical efforts to flee, walking backwards as discreetly as possible. 'Head-hunting my lower-middle cadres as well as my commissars?'

'Yup,' said Reid, quite unabashed. He made a fractional movement of his fingertips and eyebrows, and his supplicants – or applicants – dispersed like smoke in a draught. The grep and Gubanov continued their watchful mutual circling. A waiter went past with a salver of glasses and a tray of Beluga on rye; Myra and Reid helped themselves from both, then stood facing each other with a slight awkwardness, like tongue-tied teenagers after a dance.

'I could do some head-hunting the other way, you know,' Myra said. 'Perhaps I should buy a spy or two from you. It turns out you're better informed about our investment portfolio than I've been. Particularly its, ah, spread.'

Reid acknowledged this with a small nod.

'Puts us in a difficult position,' he said. 'You have the drop on us, frankly. Earth orbit is the high ground, after all.'

Oh? she thought to herself. So he didn't know about Lagrange? Or didn't want her to know he knew.

'However,' Reid went on, 'I'm pretty confident that you won't, um, liquidate. For obvious reasons.'

'So why the offer?'

'Peace of mind . . . nah, seriously. Between us, you and I know everyone who knows of the current level of exposure. But neither of us can guarantee that that'll last. A word in the wrong place and there could be severe market jitters on my side. Which, I hasten to add, would not be to your benefit, either, so we have a mutual—'

'Assured deterrence?'

Reid gave her a *shut the fuck up* look. 'You could say that . . . but I'd rather you didn't.'

Myra grinned evilly. 'OK,' she said. 'It's still no deal, Dave.'

He gazed back at her, expressionless, but he couldn't hide the plea in his voice. 'Will you at least agree not to dump your assets during the takeover bid? Not to make any offers to the competition?'

Oh, Jeez. This was a tricky one. She had no intention of doing any of the things he feared. On the other hand – if he were to fear them (even if only theoretically, and only at the margin, but still . . .) it might restrain him. It might keep him, and his allies, from crossing that invisible border, that terminator between the daylight and the dark. Let them hate, as long as they fear.

She shook her head, and saw her multiple reflections do the same, in solemn repetition. The act of observation collapses the wave-function, yes: the die cast, the cat dies.

'Sorry, Dave,' she told him. 'I can't make any promises.'

His gaze measured hers for a moment, and then he shrugged.

'You win some, you lose some,' he said lightly. 'See you around, Myra.'

She watched him walk away, as she so often had. His grep followed at a safe distance. Denis raised his eyebrows, rolled his eyes, came over.

'What was all that about?'

'Oh, just some old stuff between us,' Myra said. 'We don't see eye to eye, is all.' She took his arm. 'Let's see how Andrei is getting on with that lady from the Western United States, shall we?'

Not well, as it turned out. This was not the place for secret diplomacy, even if they'd been using the privacy shields, which they weren't. Juniper Bear, the West American unofficial consul, was making her diplomatic position no secret at all. Her broad-brimmed black hat with black wax fruit around its crown seemed chosen to amplify her voice, even though her pose indicated urgent, confidential communication.

'. . . Just in the last month we hit a Green guerilla incursion from SoCal, and at the same time a White Aryan Nations push across the Rockies, and would you believe the First Nations Federation, the goddamn *Indians*, lobbing significant conventional hardware on our northern settlements on the Cannuck side of the old border? Let me tell you, Comrade Mukhartov, we could do with some orbital back-up, this time on our side for a change.' She laughed, grinning at Myra and Valentina as they joined the conversation. 'Would you *believe*,' she repeated, 'the goddamn Greens are actually lobbying the old guard to keep the battlesats as asteroid defence? Like we ever really needed that, and now we got everything bigger'n a pea out there mapped and tracked, we might as well worry about a new ice age!'

'Well, that's coming,' said Valentina.

Juniper Bear's hatbrim tilted. 'Sure, the Milankovitch cycle, yeah, but it isn't a worry, now is it?' She laughed. 'Hey, I remember global warming!'

'And *that*'s happening,' Myra said. 'But, like you say, it isn't a *worry*, not any more. And the ozone holes, and the background radiation levels, and the synthetic polymers in every organic, and the jumping genes and all that, yeah, we're not *worrying*.' She felt surprised at the sound of her own voice, at how angry she felt about all that, now she was articulating it; it was as though she had a deep Green deep inside her, just waiting to get out. 'But to be honest, Ms Bear, we are worried about something else. About the plan to revitalise the ReUnited Nations. Even if they *will* be the enemies of our enemies, in the first instance. We don't want that kind of power turned against anyone on Earth, ever again.' She took off her hat, fingering the smooth hairs and running her thumb over the red star and gold sigil; realised she was standing there, literally cap in hand, begging for help.

Juniper Bear shook her head. She was an old woman, not as old as Myra; she looked about thirty, by pre-rejuvenation reckoning, when her face was in repose, but the weight of her years showed in her every facial expression, if you were old enough to notice these things. You learned to transmit and to receive those non-verbal tics, in parallel processes of increasing wisdom.

'That's what our opposition are saying,' the woman said. '"No more New World Orders!" Well, I'm sorry, but we need a real new world order, one on our side this time. It'll be only temporary – once we get enough forces out there, there's no way anyone can keep central control. Once the emergency is over, it'll just . . .' She made a downward-planing gesture.

'Wither away?'

Juniper's creased eyes registered the irony, her compressed lips her refusal to let it deflect her. 'Speaking of states that wither away,' she said, changing the subject adroitly, 'if any of you find yourselves looking for new opportunities, when all this is over one way or another . . .'

Valentina and Andrei said nothing, at least not in Myra's presence; but Myra herself smiled, and nodded, and said she'd bear it in mind.

'Well!' said Andrei Mukhartov, when the function was over and the guests had departed, the diplomats, the apparatchiks and captains of industry. Andrei, Valentina, Denis and Myra had retired to one of the hotel's smaller and quieter bars. Hardwood and mirrors, leather and glass, plush carpets and quiet music. There were plenty of people in the bar who'd had nothing directly to do with the funeral. This made for a degree of security for the four remaining Commissars, huddled as they were around a vodka bottle on a corner table, like dissidents. 'Thanks for your intervention earlier, comrades. I thought I was getting somewhere until you turned up.'

'You thought wrong,' said Myra. She didn't feel like arguing the point. 'I know Juniper, she'll seem to agree with you and then start talking about the war. Which is where we came in. You didn't lose anything.'

'Huh,' grunted Andrei. He knocked back a thumbnail glass. 'Tell me why you need a Foreign Secretary at all.'

'Because I can't do everything myself,' Myra told him. 'Even if I can do every particular thing better than anyone. Division of labour, don't knock it. It's all in Ricardo.'

Andrei and Valentina were looking at each other with eye-rolling, exaggerated bafflement.

'Megalomania,' said Andrei sadly. 'Comes to all the dictators of the proletariat, just before the end.'

'Think we should overthrow her before it's too late?' Valentina straightened her back and sketched a salute. 'Get Denis in on it and

67

we can form a troika. Blame all the problems on Myra and declare a clean slate.'

'That is not funny,' said Myra. She poured another round, watched the clear spirit splash into the crystal ware, four times. 'That is exactly how it will be. One day all the problems of the world will be blamed on me.' This was not funny, she thought. This was her deepest suspicion, in her darkest moments. She grinned at her confederates. 'To that glorious future!'

They slugged back the vodka shots and slammed down the empty glasses. Myra passed up an offer of a Marley or a Moscow Gold, lit up a Dunhill from her last trip out. The double foil inside the pack, the red and the gold of its exterior – there was still, to her, something wicked and opulent about the brand, which she'd first smoked when duty-free still meant something.

'So, what's the score, Andrei? Apart from today's subtle approaches.'

'Ah.' Andrei exhaled the fragrant smoke through his nostrils. 'Not good, I have to say. Kazakhstan's still keeping out of it – after all, they have Baikonur to think about, and the Sheenisov threat. If it weren't for previous bad blood between them and the space movement, I think they might be tempted to side with it. So their neutrality is something, when all's said and done. As for the rest – I have canvassed every country, I have checked with our delegates in New York, and frankly it looks as if next week's vote will go through.'

'Valentina?'

Myra didn't need to spell anything out. Kozlova had spent days and nights tracking reports from agents in the battlesats and the settlements. She replied by holding out her spread hand and waggling it.

'Nothing much we can do up there,' she said. 'The other side have all the resources to tip the balance their way, whichever way the argument is going.'

'Not *all* the resources,' Myra said.

'Oh, come,' said Valentina, with careful calm. 'We couldn't.' She might have been talking about cheating at cards.

'But they don't know we couldn't,' Myra said. 'We do have a hard reputation, after all. Most of the new countries, not to mention the settlements, probably think we're some kind of ruthless Bolsheviks.'

They shared a cynical laugh.

'I'm sure Reid is disabusing them of that notion right now,' said Andrei. He seemed to have picked up on what they were talking about; and as for Denis Gubanov, he was leaning back with a smug smile, as if he'd known it for years. Probably had.

'Oh, I don't know,' Myra said. 'He's a devious son of a bitch. He says his side don't know what we've got, and he might still hold out a hope of winning us over – or using us as a threat to keep his own side in order.'

She inhaled again.

'Besides,' she added, 'he doesn't know all we've got. Or so I gathered. He thinks it's all in Earth orbit.'

'It *isn't?*' Denis's smile faded instantly. 'So where is it?'

'Good question,' Myra said. 'See if you can find out.'

Valentina was intently studying the reflection of the chandelier in the bar mirror.

'Is this a joke, or what?' Denis demanded.

Myra shook her head, laid her palm on the back of his hand. 'Easy, man. Don't waste too much time on it – just treat it as an exercise, see what you can find out about what people know or suspect—'

'And I'm not to know myself?'

'Double-blind,' Myra said firmly. 'And double-bluff. I'll let you know after you've brought back some results, but I don't want your investigation dropping any inadvertent hints.'

Denis scowled. 'OK,' he allowed, 'I see the point of that.' He looked at his watch, sighed and stood up. 'Three-fifteen,' he said. 'Time I was back at the office.'

'The unsleeping sword of the Cheka,' Myra said. 'Time we all went back, I guess.'

'No,' said Andrei. 'You and Valentina stay here and get drunk.' He pushed back his chair and raised himself ponderously to his feet. 'We Russian *men* will take care of the rest of the day's business.'

'Sure?'

'Sure.' He put his hand on her shoulder. 'Relax, Davidova. The coup won't come today, or tomorrow.'

'I know that,' she said. 'But we just lost one more commissar today—'

'Alex, huh, son of a bitch. No loss. I cleared his desktop and locked him out the second he mentioned he was leaving us.'

'He was good at his job, and we don't have a replacement.'

'The economy can get along fine without a commissar for a while,' Andrei said. 'The free market, don't knock it. It's all in Ricardo.'

69

The two men walked to the bar. Andrei gallantly laid a wad of currency on it, indicating Myra and Valentina with a glance, nodded to them and left with Denis.

'So,' said Valentina, looking after them, 'what do you suppose they're up to?'

'Anything but going back to work, I hope,' Myra laughed. 'Hitting the spaceport bars, or plotting our demise. Whatever. What the fuck.' She downed another vodka; stared at the tip of a cigarette that had burnt down, unregarded; lit another.

'You're drunk already,' Valentina accused.

'And bitter and twisted. Yeah, I know.'

'I'll tell you why they left,' Valentina said. 'Apart from the spaceport attractions, that is.'

'Yeah?'

'They're giving us space, my dear. For a caucus.'

'Women's caucus? Bit dated, that.'

Valentina loosened her uniform jacket, removed her tie and rolled it up carefully. 'Not – what was it called? – feminism, Myra. Socialism. A Party caucus.'

'But I'm not even in the Party!'

'Are you so sure about that?' Valentina asked. '*I've* never seen a resignation letter from you. And I would have, you know. I'm sure you're at least a sympathiser, even if –' she giggled '– you've been missing branch meetings lately.'

Myra had to think about it. She supposed there *was* still a direct-debit mandate paying her dues to some anonymous Caribbean data-haven account. She still got the mailings, filed unread. She still wrote for *Analysis*, the International's online theoretical journal. (Its contributors had nicknamed it *Dialysis*, because of its insistent theme that everything was going down the tubes.)

Myra frowned at Valentina. The noise in the bar was louder than it had been. People were drifting in from other functions going on in the hotel: a business conference, an anime con, and at least two weddings.

'What does it matter?' she asked. 'We're nothing, we're probably among the last Internationalists in the whole fucking *world*.'

'Indeed we are,' said Valentina. 'But there's still a couple of things we can do. One is give our comrade a good send-off, by getting absolutely smashed in his memory.'

They knocked glasses, drank.

'And the other thing?'

'Oh, yes. We can see if there's anything the International is planning to do about the coup.'

'You must be fucking joking.'

'I am not. If you want my guess, that's what they wanted the assets for.'

'Whoever thought of that must be out of their tiny fucking minds. Talk about adventurism.'

'I'm not so sure. Remember, there may not be many of us left in the world, but –' Valentina leaned closer '– there isn't only one world.'

'Oh, don't be—' Myra gave it a second thought. 'Oh,' she said. 'Our friends in the sky.'

'Yeah,' said Valentina. 'The space fraction.'

'I don't want to discuss this right now,' Myra said. She looked around, wildly. The place was jumping. One beautiful Kazakh girl whom she'd thought was a bride yelled something in what sounded like Japanese. Her big white dress shrank like shrink-wrap to her body, changing colour and hardening to a costume of pastel-shaded plastic armour. A smart-suit – made from, rather than by, nanotech – was a heinously expensive novelty, offering a limited menu of programmed transformations. Myra wondered how long it would be before its price plummeted, its repertoire exploded; how long it would be before people could as readily transform their bodies. A world of comic-book super-heroes – it didn't bear thinking about. The girl struck a combative pose, to a scatter of applause from the other anime fans.

'Let's get drunk,' Myra said.

5

The Church of Man

Merrial was, as promised, waiting. She sat on the plinth, as I had done, under the Deliverer's equestrian statue. She wore a loose summer dress with a colourful tiered skirt. Something stirred in my memory, then vanished like a dream in the morning. She was in animated conversation with a man sitting beside her. They both looked up as I arrived.

'Hello,' I said warily.

He was a tall, thin man, about thirty, I reckoned; quite brown, with sharp features and dark eyes which had a sort of quirky, questioning look in them; black hair curly on top, short at the back and sides; dressed in leather trousers and jacket and a white cotton T-shirt with a red bandana. A fine chain hung around his throat beneath the bandana, its pendant – if any – below the T-shirt's round collar.

'Hello,' Merrial said warmly. 'Clovis, this is Fergal.'

The man stuck his right hand out and I shook it, noticing as I did so that one of his thumbs pressed the back of my hand and that he held on, as though waiting for some response, for about a second longer than I subconsciously expected, before letting go.

'Pleased to meet you, Clovis,' he said. His voice was low and deep, his accent was hard to place: correct, but by that very correctness of intonation in each syllable, somehow foreign; it reminded me of a Zanu prince I'd once heard speak at the University.

'Let's get some drinks,' he said, rising to his feet. We strolled to the nearest vacant table outside The Carronade. Fergal took our requests and disappeared inside.

'Who is that guy?' I asked.

Merrial favoured me with a slow smile. 'You sound jealous,' she teased.

'Ah, come on. Just curious.'

'I've known him a long time,' she said. 'Nothing personal. Just . . . one of us.'

'Well, I had kind of figured he was a tinker.'

Merrial's eyes narrowed slightly. 'Yes, that's it,' she said.

Fergal returned in a few moments, taking his seat beside me and opposite Merrial. I offered him a cigarette, which he accepted with an oddly ironic smile.

'Well,' he said, lighting it, 'you know about the . . . concern, for the ship?'

I nodded. 'Yes, but Merrial said nothing about its being shared.'

He grinned. 'Oh, it's quite widely shared, I can tell you that. It's a brave offer you've made, and –' he spread his hands '– all I can say is, thanks.'

I was more puzzled than modest about this reference to the bravery of my offer, so I just shrugged at that.

'Are you on the project too?'

He seemed amused. 'I'm not on site, but I am on the payroll, if that's what you mean,' he said. 'All of –' he glanced at Merrial '– our profession are very much involved in the project as a whole.' He took a long swallow of beer, and a draw on his cigarette, becoming visibly more relaxed and expansive as he did so. 'Its success matters a lot to us. We're very keen to see the sky road taken again.'

'I like that,' I said. '"The sky road".'

'Yes,' he said. 'Well, it took you people long enough to get back on it.'

'Back?'

'You walked it once.' Another glance at Merrial, then a smile at me. 'Or we did.'

'Our ancestors did,' I said.

'That's what I meant to say,' he said idly. 'But to business. I'll have to get a piece of equipment that you – or rather, Merrial – is going to need. That's going to take some time, but I'll manage it this weekend. You'll have to book some time off and seats on the Monday train.' He smiled wryly. 'Not much point trying to travel on the Saturday or the Sunday, anyway. No trains and damn slow traffic, even if you wanted to drive.'

I nodded. 'And the University would have all its hatches battened anyway.'

73

'Yeah, that's a point. Still, can't complain – the free weekend is one of the gains of the working class, eh?'

'You could call it that,' I said. 'Mind you, whether what goes on at the University should count as work—'

We went on talking for a bit. Fergal was cagey about himself, and I didn't press him, and after another couple of beers he got up and left. We had the evening, and the weekend, to ourselves.

Merrial slept, leaning against my shoulder, all the way from Carron Town to Inverness. It seemed a shame for her to miss the journey, but I reckoned she must have seen its famously spectacular and varied scenery before, many more times than I had. Besides, I liked watching her sleep, an experience which, in the nature of our past three nights, I had hitherto not had much time to savour.

We had caught the early train, at 5.15 on the Monday morning. Each of us had separately arranged to have the first two days of the week off, by seeking out our different supervisors in the Carron bars on the Friday evening. It was to be hoped that Angus Grizzlyback would remember that I was not coming in this morning; but if he didn't, I was sure my loyal friends would remind him, with predictable and – as it happened – inaccurate speculation as to how I intended to spend the day.

We had, in fact, spent the Saturday and the Sunday in just that way, very enjoyably, in bed or out on the hills. On the Saturday afternoon Merrial had guddled a trout from a dark, deep pool in the Alt na Chuirn glen; leapt up with the thrashing fish clutched in her hands and danced around, sure-footed on the slippery stones. Again, something had moved in my mind, like a glimpsed flick of a tail in the water, which had – as soon as the shadow of my thought fell on it – flashed away.

The sun rose higher, the shadows shortening, apparently in the face of the train's advance. We stopped at all the small, busy towns built around forestry and light industry and – increasingly as we moved east – farming: Achnasheen, Achnashellach, Achanalt, Garve . . . The electric engine's almost silent glide surprised the short-memoried sheep, rabbits and deer beside the track, and set up a continuous standing wave of animals, sauntering or lolloping or springing away. I saw a wolf's grey-shadowed shape at Achanalt; as we rounded the cliff-face at Garve I saw a wild goat on a shelf; and spotted an eagle patrolling the updrafts above the slope of Moruisg.

74

I didn't wake Merrial for any of them.

I smoked, once, with a coffee brought around on a rattling trolley by a lass in tartan trews. Neither the sound nor the smell nor the smoke stirred Merrial at all, except to a few deeper breaths, long ripples in the spate of her hair across her breast and over my chest. I let her head nestle in the now awkward crook of my left arm, and alternated the cup and the cigarette in my right hand. It was a quiet train, for all that it was busy, with clerks and traders on their weekly commute from their coastal homes to their work in Inverfefforan or Inverness.

On Merrial's lap, with her left arm – crooked like mine – protectively over it, lay a bulky poke of polished leather, fastened with a drawstring thong. It may have bulged a little larger, and weighed a little heavier, than the kind of bags that lasses tend to lug around, but it would have taken a close and sharp observer to notice. Inside it, concealed by a layer of the sort of oddments one would expect to find in such a poke – a cambric kerchief, cosmetics, small-bore ammunition and the like – was the complicated apparatus that Fergal had delivered to her house early on the Sunday evening. It was built around a seer-stone about fifteen centimetres in diameter, nested in neat coils of insulated copper wire. The strangest aspect, to me, of this device was an arrangement of delicate levers, each marked with a letter of the alphabet, queerly ordered:

QWERTYUIOP...

Probably, I thought, a spell.

'Grotty old place,' said Merrial, rubbing her face with her hands and looking around the damp, flagstoned concourse of Inverness station. Her cheeks reddened, her eyes widened under the smooth friction of her palms. Her dress, this time of blue velvet, looked a bit rumpled. We were standing at the coffee-bar, having twenty minutes to wait for the 8.30 to Glasgow.

I looked up at the creosoted roof with its wide skylight panels and suspended electric lamps. 'At least it doesn't have pigeons.'

'Can't say herring-gulls are much of an improvement.' She kicked out with one booted foot, sending a hungry, red-eyed bird squawking away. One end of the station opened to the platforms, the other to the main street. The arrangement seemed peculiarly adapted to set up cold but unrefreshing draughts. Despite its mossy walls and paving, the station was more recent than the buildings outside, most of which pre-dated the Deliverance, if not all three of the world wars.

I finished my bacon roll, smiled at Merrial – who was mumbling, half to herself and around mouthfuls of her own breakfast, some irritated speculation about the degenerative evolution of scavenging sea-birds – and wandered over to the news-stand. There I stocked up on cigarettes and bought a copy of the *Press and Journal*, a newspaper which outdoes even the *West Highland Free Press* in its incorrigible parochialism and venerable antiquity. Most of its pages consisted of small advertisements, to do with fishing, farming, uranium and petroleum mining and, of course, Births, Marriages and Deaths. The last of these could take up half a tall column of small print: 'Dolleen Starholm, peacefully in her sleep, aged 251 years, beloved great-great-grandmother of . . .' followed by scores of names; and sometimes (as in this case) the discreet indication of cult affiliation: 'RIP' or 'IHS'. More frequent, and more prominent, were proud affirmations of the orthodox hope: 'Returned by the Flame' (or the Sky or the Sun or the Sea) 'to the One'.

I went back to the counter and, while Merrial finished off her breakfast, scanned the sparse snippets of national and international news that had managed to wedge their way in among the earth-shakingly important football and shinty reports, fishing disputes and Council debates.

The Congress of Paris had ceremonially opened its ninety-seventh year of deliberations, and had immediately plunged into bitter controversy about a proposal to empower the Continental Court to adjudicate border problems between cantons and communes; the apparently more difficult matter of disagreements between countries having been resolved by the Congress long ago, its success had apparently gone to its collective head.

I sighed and turned the page. Another American republic had voted a contribution from tariff revenue to the spaceship project, which was gratifying but mysterious – there was even an editorial comment about it, full of sage mutterings about how their ways were not ours, and that we should not disdain such assistance, immoral though it might seem to us. I wasn't too sure; to me, it smelt of stealing money, but the Americans have a much greater reverence for their

76

governments than people have in more civilised lands. If offered some loot by an African king or Asian magnate or South American cacique, I should hope the International Scientific Society would politely decline, and this case seemed little different. But all of this was, at this moment, quite theoretical, as no such offer, and indeed no news at all, from Asia or Africa appeared in today's edition. I rolled it up and decided to leave the national news until later.

Merrial brushed crumbs from her lips and looked at me with amusement. 'You really look as though you're paying attention to all that,' she said, picking up her leather poke. I hitched my canvas satchel on my shoulder and we strolled to the Glasgow train.

'Well, I do follow the news,' I said, somewhat defensively, as we took our seats, this time facing each other across a table. 'What's wrong with that?'

Merrial shrugged. 'It's so . . . ephemeral,' she said. 'And unreliable.'

'Compared with what?'

'Don't misunderstand me,' she said. 'I'm sure this, what is it –' she reached for the paper, and spread it out '– Congress here is real, and really did do what the article says it did. But it is only a tiny part of the truth, and perhaps not the most important part of what is going on there in Paris. Let alone what is going on elsewhere in Paris. So that, and all the other such pieces give you, really, a false picture of the world.'

I could have been offended, but was not. 'I'm a scholar of history, remember?' I said. 'I understand how newspaper reports, even documents aren't everything—'

'Oh, you don't want to hear what I think about *historical documents*!'

'So what else can you do?'

She frowned at me, puzzled. 'You travel around and find things out for yourself.'

'Aye, if only we all had the time.'

She touched the tip of my nose with the tip of her finger. 'It's what tinkers do, and they have all the time in their lives for it.'

The train pulled out, the Moray Firth in sight at first, with its kelp fields and fish-farms, and then nothing to see for a while but the close-packed pines of Drumossie Wood as the train turned and the engines took the strain of the long, slow ascent to Slochd.

A couple of hours later, maybe, after Speyside of the malts and bleak Drumochter, we were in the long and beautiful glens between Blair Atholl and Dunkeld. On one side of the line were streams full of trout and turbines, on the other hillsides buzzing with the saws and drills of workshops. The train stopped for five minutes at Dunkeld. A small, old town of stone, still with its Christian cathedral.

Merrial looked out of the windows, around at the scene, and sat back with a slight shudder.

'A strange place,' she said, 'with the hills around it like an ambush.'

'But that's why it's a great place,' I said, and told her the story of how the Cameronians had held off the Highland host and saved the Revolution to which they owed their freedom. She listened with more interest, even, than my telling of the tale deserved, and leaned back at the end and said, 'Aye well, maybe there's some use to history, after all. I'll never be afraid of these hills again.'

It was two in the afternoon by the time the train reached Glasgow's Queen Street Station, and glad enough we were to get off it. Sometimes two people who can fascinate each other endlessly when alone together, and who can spark off each other in convivial company, find themselves inhibited among strangers who are unignorably in earshot, and find themselves growing shy and silent and stale. So it was with us, towards the end of that journey. I couldn't even find it in my heart to talk about the Battle of Stirling when we passed through the town.

We both brightened, though, on jumping down on the platform. The familiar Glasgow railway-station smell – of currying fish, and curing leaf, and spark-gapped air, and old iron and wood-alcohol and hot oil and burnt vanilla – hit my sinuses like a shot of poteen. Merrial, too, seemed invigorated by it, taking a deep breath of the polluted stench with a look of satisfaction and nostalgia.

'Ah, it's good to be back,' she said.

I glanced sidelong at her as we walked down the platform. 'When were you in Glasgow? And how could I have missed you?'

She smiled and squeezed my hand. 'Oh, I forget. Ages ago. But the smell brings it back.'

'That and the noise.'

'The what?'

'THE—'

But she was laughing at me.

78

We crossed the station concourse, agreeing that, on balance, pigeons were a worse nuisance than sea-birds (though, as Merrial gravely pointed out, better eating). This comment, and some of the more appetising components of the smell, reminded us that we were ravenous, so we bought sandwiches and bottles of beer from a stall in the station and carried them out to George Square.

We sat down on a bench by a grassy knoll under the statue of the Deliverer.

'Shee that,' Merrial said, pointing upwards as she munched. 'It'sh mean.'

'What?'

She swallowed. 'The statue. The old city fathers must have been a bit stingy.'

I looked up. 'No argument about the city fathers,' I said. 'They're still tight-fisted. But that statue looks fine to me.'

'The horse is black,' Merrial pointed out. She tapped the handle of her knife on a fetlock. 'And cast in bronze. The lady herself is green – just copper. They got out the oxy-acetylene torches and hacked off the original rider, a king or general or whatever, and stuck the Deliverer in his place!'

I stood up and paced around it, peering.

'You're right,' I said. 'You can see the joins. I must have looked at that statue a hundred times, and not noticed anything wrong with it.' I looked up at the lady's head. 'And she has a different face from the one in Carron Town, and they're both different from any pictures I've seen of the Deliverer.'

'Well, there you go, colha Gree,' she said. 'Some things a tinker can teach a scholar, eh?'

'Oh aye,' I said. I sat down again. 'Mind you, it could hardly be just parsimony – it's a fine piece of work after all, and they've done her hair in gold.'

'Yon's gold *paint*,' she said scornfully. 'And as for artistry, the breed and the trappings of the horse are all wrong for the time and the circumstances.'

She was right there, too, when I looked. This was no steppe horse, bare-back broken, roughly saddled, such as was shown quite authentically in Carron Square. Instead, it was a hussar's mount, in elaborate caparison. But I thought then, and still think, that the representation of the Deliverer herself was well done. A fine example of the Glasgow style; which, perhaps, makes the equine bodge appropriate, and part of the artist's point.

We binned our litter and headed for the nearest tramway stop, in Buchanan Street. The transport system is one of Glasgow City Council's proudest public works, a more than adequate replacement for the great Underground circle, which was – it's said – one of the wonders of the ancient world. Judging by the remnants of it that here and there have outlasted centuries of flooding and subsidence, it is quite possible to agree that such it must have been.

The tram came along, bell clanging, and we jumped on and paid our groats and clattered like children up the spiral steps to the upper deck. The bell rang again and the tram lurched forward, creaking up Buchanan Street and swaying as it turned the corner into Sauchiehall.

Glasgow's main drag looked clogged with traffic, but everything – steam-engine and motor-car and horse-cart and bicycle alike – made way for the tram's implacable progress. The pedestrians, at this time of the day, were mostly women shopping. But all of them, whether young lasses just out of school or mothers with young children or retired ladies at their leisure, had to pick up their skirts, their pokes or their weans and run for their lives when the tram bore down on a crossing. The shops and offices from recent centuries are built of logs and planks, and rarely go higher than two storeys. The older, pre-Deliverance buildings are of stone; some have as many as five floors. In ancient times there were much higher buildings, but most of them were made of concrete, which doesn't last well, and – agonising though it may be for archaeology – almost all of their structures have long since been plundered for steel and glass. Their foundations give rectangular patterns to the growth of trees in the forests around Glasgow: Pollock Fields, Possil Wood, Partick Thorn.

Farther away, to the west, we could just make out the haze and smoke from the Clydeside shipyards, on which most of Glasgow's prosperity depended. The shipyards were the seedbed of the skills which – along with Kishorn's deep-water dock, almost unique on this side of the Atlantic – had made Scotland the logical site for the launch-platform's construction.

At the top of Sauchiehall there's a new stone bridge, to replace the original concrete one that has crumbled away. It carried us over the Eighth Motor Way and into Woodlands Road, which runs along beside the Kelvin Woods. (They, and the river that runs through them, are named after Lord Kelvin, who invented the thermometer.)

We stepped off the tram at the crest of University Avenue, and stood for a moment looking at the main building, a huge and ancient pile called Gilmorehill. It looks like a piece of religious architecture that has run wild, but it is solely devoted to secular knowledge, a church of Man.

'It's not as old as it looks,' Merrial said, as though determined not to be impressed. 'That's Victorian Gothic.'

I didn't believe her, but I didn't argue. I had felt in its chill stone and warm wood the shades of Scotus and Knox and Kelvin, of Watt and Millar and Ferguson, and no disputed date could shake my conviction that the place was almost as old as the nation whose mind it had done so much to shape.

'Whatever,' I said. 'Anyway, the department we're going to isn't there.'

'Just as well,' Merrial said.

It was actually in one of the small side streets off University Avenue, all of whose buildings date back at least to the twentieth century. The trees that line it are probably as old, gigantic towers of branch and leaf, taller than the buildings. Their bulk darkened the street, the leaves of their first fall formed a slippery litter underfoot.

'So we just walk up and knock on the door?' Merrial asked.

'No,' I said. 'I've got a key.'

She glanced down at her leather bag. 'And you're sure we won't be challenged?'

'Aye, I'm sure,' I said. We'd been over this before. As a prospective student, with my project already accepted even if as yet unfunded, I had every right to be here – in fact, I should have been here more often, through the summer. So no one should question us, or our presence in the old archive. We'd planned how we'd do the job, but its proximity seemed to be making Merrial more nervous than I was.

'All right,' she said.

The key turned smoothly in the oiled lock, and the tongue clicked back. I pushed the heavy door aside and we stepped in. I locked it behind us. The place was silent, and as far as I could tell it was empty. The hallway was dim and cool, its pale yellow paint darkened by generations of nicotine, and it divided after a few metres into a narrower corridor leading deeper into the Institute and a stairway leading to the upper floors. The place had a curious musty odour of old paper and dusty electric light-bulbs, and a faint whiff of pipe-smoke. I checked the piles of unopened mail on the long wooden table at the side. A few notes for me, which a quick check revealed were refusals of various applications for patronage. I stuffed them in my jacket pocket and led the way up two flights of stairs to the library, switching on the fizzing electric lamps as we went.

Merrial wrinkled her nose as I opened the library door and switched on the lights.

'Old paper,' I said.

She smiled. 'Dead flies.'

I made to close the door after we entered the room, but Merrial touched my arm and shook her head.

'I couldn't stand it,' she said.

'You're right, me neither.' The still, dead air made me feel short of breath.

I held her hand, as much for my reassurance as for hers, as we threaded our way through the maze of ceiling-high book-cases. Merrial, to my surprise, once or twice tugged to make me pause, while she scanned the titles and names on cracked and faded spines with a look of recognition and pleasure.

'*The Trial of the Anti-Soviet Bloc of Rights and Trotskyites*!' she breathed. 'Amazing! Do you know anything about that?'

'It was some kind of public exorcism,' I said, hurrying her along. I'd once glanced into that grim *grimoire* myself, and the memory made me slightly nauseous. 'People claimed they had turned into rabid dogs who would go out and wreck machinery. Horrible. What superstitious minds the communists had.'

Merrial chuckled, but shot me an oddly pleased look.

At the far end of the library the ranks of book-cases stopped. Several tables and chairs were lined up there, apparently for study – but no one, to my knowledge, ever studied at them. The most anyone could do was to put down a pile of books or documents there for a quick inspection of their contents under the reading-lights, before rushing out of the library. I recalled Merrial's comment that people today are more claustrophobic than their ancestors.

Beside these tables was another door, of iron, with a handle but no lock. The mere thought of the possibility of that door's having a lock was enough to give me a cold sweat.

'Here we are,' I said, and added, to make light of it, 'the dark archive.'

'What's inside it?'

'I don't know,' I said. 'I've never been in it.'

She frowned. 'Is it off limits, or what?'

'No, no.' I shook my head. 'It's not forbidden or anything. Hardly anybody wants to go in.'

'No point in hesitating,' said Merrial. 'Let's get it over with.'

I turned the handle and pulled the door back. To fit with my feelings, it should have given off an eldritch squeak, but its heavy hinges were well-lubricated. A couple of times I worked the handle from the inside. It appeared to be in good order, but I dragged one of the chairs over and used it to prop the door open, just in case it closed accidentally.

I switched on the overhead light and stepped with an assumed air of boldness across the threshold. The small back room appeared innocent enough. It had a desk, with a couple of chairs in front of it and on its top a cluster of boxy, bulky structures like models of ancient architecture. Aluminium shelves lined the walls on either side. The air held a different, subtler smell, almost like the smell of washed hair or polished horn, with a sharp note of acetones.

Merrial sniffed. 'Like a rotting honeycomb,' she remarked cheerfully. I fought down a heave.

'Would smoking get rid of the miasma?' I suggested.

'Yes, but it might damage the disks.'

While I was still looking around for anything that remotely resembled a disc, Merrial began rummaging along the shelves. The boxes arrayed there were translucent, the colour of sheepskin, with dusty, close-fitting lids. They contained flat black plates about nine centimetres square and two millimetres thick. She picked out a few at random, held them up and shook them slightly. From every one, a sooty black dust drifted down. Oxidation crystals crusted the small metal plates at their edges. She shook her head. 'Hopeless,' she said.

In other, smaller boxes there were smaller, shiny wafers. These, when she picked them out, simply crumbled to the touch.

'So much for them,' she said. 'We'll just have to see if there's anything on the hard drive.' She pulled up a seat in front of the machines. The largest, before which she sat, had a sort of window-pane on the front of it. She opened her poke, rummaged out the clutter on top and carefully extracted her strange devices. She laid them on the table: the seer-stone glowing with random rainbow ripples, a small black box and the frame of lettered levers, all connected by the coils of insulated copper wire.

'Oh, look, that thing there has the same—'

'Don't touch it!'

'All right.'

She glanced up at me. 'Sorry to snap. I'm a bit jumpy.'

'Aye, well, me too.'

'Also I'm in tinker mode.' She smiled. 'Courtesy doesn't come into it. If you want to help, see if you can find a power source for this thing while I set up my system.' She waved a hand vaguely in the darkness under the table.

Suppressing a qualm, I stooped down into that darkness, and after a moment while my eyes adjusted I saw a dusty power-socket, with three holes. A centimetre-thick cable hung from the back of the table and ended in a three-pronged plug. Deducing how plug and socket fitted together was the work of a moment, as was inserting the one into the other.

The light around me brightened suddenly. Merrial's boot hit my ribs, and she simultaneously uttered an odd imprecation.

'What?'

'Christ, don't *do* that!'

Another strange prayer. I crawled backwards from under the table. Merrial gave me a glare.

'I thought that was what you wanted me to do,' I protested.

'Oh.' She thought about it. 'I suppose you could have taken it that way, yes. I forgive you. Now come here and sit down.' She patted the seat beside her.

As I got to my feet I noticed what had happened to the machine, and where the extra light was coming from. The window on the front of the box was glowing a pearly grey with darker and lighter flecks swirling through it, like the sky above a port on a snowy day. I took a step backwards. The temperature in the room seemed to have dropped a few kelvins. Now I understood why she'd been making these invocations. At moments like that even the most rational person will utter whatever name of the deity springs to mind.

'It won't bite,' she said.

I sidled forward, keeping a wary eye on the thing, as one might do towards a dog about whom one had received just such an assurance. With the hand that Merrial couldn't see, I made the sign of the Horns, then realised that this was shamefully superstitious and began instead mentally to recite a few Names of the One, and of the Prophets: Allah, Buddha, Christ, Deity, Jordan, Justice . . .

'Did I do that?' I asked.

Khomeini, Krishna, Mercy, Mary, Odin, Necessity, Nature . . .

'When you switched the power on, yes.'

Paine, Providence, Quine, Reason, Yaweh, Zoroaster. That should do.

She gazed into my eyes with impish amusement, and reached forward and stroked my face. The rasp of my stubble sounded uncannily loud.

'It's all right, *mo gràidh,*' she said. 'I'm a tinker. I know what I'm doing. This thing here –' she patted the top of it '– is just a machine that does the same thing as the seer-stanes, only not so well. It's no a deil, ye ken. It's a computer.'

'Aye, I know that . . .'

'Well, start acting as if you believed it,' she said.

'But is it a *television*?' I shuddered inwardly at naming that dark instrument of the Possession.

She shook her head. 'No. This here is a keyboard, and this here is a screen. The screen, or monitor, works on a similar principle to a television, but it is not a television. And even if it was, it couldn't do you any harm.'

Easy enough for her to say that, I thought, but wisely didn't say.

'Assuming it still works at all,' she added cheerfully. 'The chips got fried in the Deliverance, for the most part.'

(Me neither, but that's what she said.)

She rattled a few keys. The screen's snowstorm responded not at all.

'Control alt delete,' she said to herself, and hit three keys simultaneously.

Nothing happened, again.

'Hmm,' she said. She reached forward and prodded a stud on the machine. The screen turned black.

'So much for that one,' she said. She stood up and leaned over the table and started looking more closely at the various boxes.

'Hey!' she said. 'Got it! One of these looks like it's radiation-hardened!' She reached in among the boxes and started fiddling dangerously with live cables, removing a lead from the back of the box we'd used and sticking it in the back of another one. What had seemed to be merely the blank front of that box suddenly lit up, a smoothly shining grey, revealing itself to be a screen.

'Yess!' said Merrial, punching the air.

By this point I was beginning to get a grip on myself, though I must admit I almost lost it completely when Merrial turned around and prodded a letter on the keyboard and the words 'Demon Internet Software' flashed up on the screen.

Allah, Buddha, Christ . . .

'All right,' Merrial said briskly, as the screen with the three sinister names disappeared and was replaced by a picture with lots of tiny pictures spread out on it. 'We've got this bugger up and running, but Christ knows how long it'll stay up.' (She talked this way, I'd come to notice, with its curious combination of obscure sexual and religious references, when she was in what she'd called her 'tinker mode'.) 'So what we better do is whip the stuff out of it ay ess ay pee.'

'Out of it what?'

'As. Soon. As. Possible.'

'Oh, right. Toot sweet.'

'What?'

I waved a hand. 'Let's get on with it, as you say.'

'Yip.'

She carefully uncoiled one of the strands of copper wire, and attached a little peg with a copper pin to the end. This she inserted in a round hole (which, she explained, did not fucking have to be round the fucking back, but fucking was) in the pediment of the computer.

'Right,' she said. The tip of her tongue between her lips, she tapped out the words 'Myra Godwin', the name of the Deliverer, on the keyboard. They simultaneously appeared on the screen and on the now black seer-stone.

'Go,' she said, hitting another key.

A few seconds passed (tongue between the teeth again) and the screen and the stone filled with a list of titles which crept slowly upwards, its top moving out of sight, and which kept on going for several minutes.

When the list had stopped its crawl she said, 'OK, copy,' and rat-tled at the keyboard again. A picture of an hourglass appeared on the screen, and the sand began to run. The seer-stone, meanwhile, showed a tree, branching and budding and growing leaves.

After about a minute and a half the sand had all flowed from the top half of the glass, and the stone was filled with green. Both displays vanished.

'That's it,' Merrial said.

'That's all?'

'Yes,' she grinned. 'That's all the files that mention Myra Godwin transferred, from the dark storage to the stane. No bad going, eh?'

'Brilliant,' I said. She stood up, leaned around behind the com-puter again, disconnected her wire and wound it quickly around her hand. Then she poked a few more keys on both keyboards. The screen went that shining grey again, and the stone went back to black.

She smiled at me. 'You have my permission to turn the power off.'

We left the small room, and the larger library, exactly as we had found them, and walked quietly down the stairs and out of the Institute. When we were a few metres down the street and away we hugged each other and yelped.

'We did it!' Merrial gloated. 'We actually fucking did it!'

'Yes, I still can hardly believe it,' I said. I caught her hand. 'Now what do we do?'

'We look at what we've got,' she said. 'Somewhere no one will see us, or bother us.'

I knew just the place.

Because it was vacation time there were few students around, so my landlady was happy to rent me my usual small room above the book-shop on Southpark Avenue for one night. She didn't raise an eyebrow as she took my five marks and handed over a bedroom key, even though it was only about half past four in the afternoon. I suppose she assumed we wanted to use the room for sex.

She gave us a quick cup of coffee and shared a smoke, and a couple of months' worth of local gossip, in the back of her kitchen, then waved us upstairs with a wink at me. The room had a fairly generous, though notionally single, bed and a chair and table and power socket. The window had been left open, but its only view was of the back yard. Still, one could look out and see the sky any time one wanted.

'Perfect,' Merrial said.

She unloaded the seer-stone and its peripheral pieces again and set them up on the table, running a small cable from the black box to the wall socket. The little box began to hum faintly, and at the same moment a human face loomed out of the dark of the seer-stone, mouthing distress.

'Ah, fuck that,' Merrial said. She rubbed the stone with a cuff, and the face fell apart into flecks of colour. 'Now,' she said, 'let's get on with sorting and searching. We're looking for stuff from before the Deliverance, but finding it in this lot won't necessarily be easy. Let's hope the files are date-stamped.'

She sat in the chair, motioning to me to perch on the table, and started tapping away at her version of a keyboard. 'Ah, good, we can sort by date.'

The list reappeared in the depths of the glassy stone, this time with a stack of articles at the top with a single date of 28 May 2059. Merrial stroked with her finger gently and slowly along a tiny bar on the keyboard, then tapped another key. 'Let's see what this is.'

We peered together into the glass and began to read.

> *Bankrupt of any perspective for overcoming the crisis, the ruling elite can only sit and watch as society disintegrates beneath it. Factories fail to fulfil their obligations, corruption is rife, and the real value produced in the economy continues to plummet. Many industrial sectors actually produce negative value: their output is worth less – in market or any other terms – than the raw materials they take in; in essence, they are vast organisations for spoiling resources.*
>
> *In the absence of any genuine move towards a market, or – from the other side – any initiative from the workers, the system can only continue to disintegrate.*

'Sounds like 2059 all right,' Merrial said. 'That was what the Deliverance delivered us *from*.'

I nodded, cautiously. 'Let's just look further down . . .'

> *What cannot be ruled out is that the Moscow oligarchy could launch some diversionary military adventure, but this too would*

rapidly develop its own problems, and intensify those of the centre.

'Damn!' I said.
'What?'
'This isn't 2059, it's more like 1999!'

The invasion of Afghanistan must be seen in this context.

'No, it's 1979! Well –' I frowned at the date at the foot of the article '– actually 1980, but it was written about the situation in '79. In the Soviet Union.' I laughed bitterly. 'The reason it's a bit difficult to tell at first what period she's talking about is that it was in the Soviet Union that the collapse started, right there in the 1970s. After the Soviet Union disintegrated it just got worse, and spread.'

This much was a fairly well-accepted historical account, which I'd covered in my undergraduate studies in Ancient History.

'So why's it dated 2059?' Merrial asked. She stroked the bar and rolled the list down again. 'Hah!' she said. 'This file, and a whole lot of others by the look of it, were put *on to* the computer at that date. Which doesn't mean they were created then. I don't know if I can extract the original creation date, either.'

'Wait a minute,' I said. 'Maybe this is where I can help. I should be able to tell the rough date from the titles of the files, or maybe a quick look at their contents.'

'There are thousands of files in there,' she pointed out. 'If dating each of them takes as long as it did to date that one, we'll be here all night.'

I smiled. 'Why should that be a problem?'

It turned out not to be a problem. Although the bulk of the files had the same date in the 'date' column of Merrial's machine, and she gave up looking for a way to find what she called the 'create-date', quite a large number of the files had a date reference of some kind in their titles. These were apparently articles from magazines or newspapers, by Myra Godwin or about her. We quite quickly got into a way of working that let me identify such files, and Merrial deal with them, copying the date from the title to another 'date' column. After ten minutes of this she hit her forehead with the heel of her hand and cried, 'Stop!'

'What is it?'

'We're wasting our time. *I'm* wasting our time, I mean.' She rubbed her hands. 'What we need here is a wee program, to scan the titles for dates, extract them, reformat them and then sort by date . . .'

'I'll take your word for it,' I said, not having understood all of her words. She waved me away, with a look of abstracted concentration on her face.

'This'll be easy,' she said. 'It'll save us hours.'

I sat on the windowsill, smoking a cigarette, while her fingers flickered over the small keyboard, making a pattering noise like rain on a roof. It struck me that there seemed to be no discernible difference between the white logic and the black, but no doubt this only showed my ignorance.

'Yess!' she said. 'No bother.'

She hit a key and sat back. Then she leaned forward again, peering at the stone.

'Oh fffuck!'

I eyed her warily.

'I used fucking two-digit year-dates. Force of habit. Fucking thing falls over on the year 2000.'

The pattering started again.

About half an hour later Merrial had the files partially ordered by date, and we could dig about in them with a little more confidence in their relevance to our concerns.

'"Defence Policy Contract (Expiry), Vatican City, 11 December 2046",' Merrial read out. 'That looks interesting.'

She pressed one of her keys and the file, as she put it, opened: instead of the title glowing a little brighter among the others, we could see the whole document. Parts of it were in impenetrable legal language (parts of it, in fact, were in Latin) but there was enough there for us to form a good idea of what it was about.

Merrial paused before opening another file, one labelled 'Mutual Protection/Space Merchants/2058'.

We looked at each other, both a little pale, each waiting for the other to speak first.

Merrial swallowed hard, and reached for one of my cigarettes.

'You do know,' she said slowly, 'just what the Deliverer had to do to make a living, under the Possession?'

'Well . . .' I could feel my lower lip moving back and forth over the edge of my teeth, and stopped it. 'Yes. It's one of the aspects of history that historians tend not to talk about. In popular works, that is.'

'Ohh!' Merrial let out a held breath in relief. 'You know about the slave camps, then.'

'What?' For a fleeting instant, I literally saw a black shadow before my eyes. I pointed at the seer-stone's script. 'I thought you were talking about the nuclear blackmail!'

Merrial looked puzzled. 'Nuclear blackmail? I know she got some nuclear weapons from the *Papanich*, that's right here. What has that to do with how she made her living?'

'Oh, Reason above!' I clutched my head. 'Let's get this straight. *You* think the dirty secret is that she ran *slave camps*. I think it's that she trafficked in nuclear threats.'

Merrial sighed. 'Yes, that's it.' She unfurled her hand and forearm with parodied politeness. 'You first.'

'All right.' I noticed that my left knee was juddering up and down; I stood up, and paced the floor as I spoke. 'You know about nuclear deterrence?'

'Oh, aye,' she said, with a grimace.

'Well, yes, to us the policy of threatening to burn to death many great cities and their inhabitants seems wicked, but the ancients didn't see it that way. In fact, some of them began to see nuclear deterrence as a good, which like all goods would be better bought and sold by businesses than provided by governments. The trouble was, all nuclear weapons were owned by governments, and were impossible to buy and hard to steal.

'So Myra Godwin and her husband, Georgi Davidov, stole a government. Davidov was a military man, and he carried out a military coup in a part of Kazakhstan, in a region which was very unpleasant and barren but which did happen to have a large stockpile of nuclear weapons. In a way, what happened was that the soldiers who manned the nuclear weapons decided to claim some territory, and nobody dared gainsay them.

'The local people had suffered grievously under the rule of the Communists. Stalin had starved at least a million of them in the 1930s. But things had improved a lot, and after the fall of the Communists they found themselves worse off under the lairds and barons and usurers. The real answer to their problems was not known at the time, or not known widely enough, and they began to hanker for the secure if limited life they had known before.

'This was where Myra and Georgi had their stroke of genius. While Myra was studying here she was a follower of a man called Trotsky, who had been killed by Stalin and who became a banner for a different kind of communism, purged of Stalin's crimes. As if there could be such a thing!'

'What do you mean?' Merrial asked, narrow-eyed.

'Oh, come on, you know, *communism*—' The word made me physically nauseous, as though dirty hands were pawing me. 'Everybody minding each other's business, everybody *owned* by everybody else, and that's just the ideal! What could that be but evil? Let alone the reality, of a small ruling group doing the minding and the owning!'

'How did that help the Deliverer?'

I shrugged. 'She may have believed it when she was young. Nobody's perfect. But when the Davidovs set up their state, they did so in the name of Trotsky, even though they did not really believe in him any more. They kept enough communism to keep people secure, and enough freedom to let them be happy and rich.'

Merrial's face was set in an interested but carefully neutral expression.

'And the way they got rich,' I went on, 'was this. They started selling options to use the nuclear weapons they held. That way, states that had no nuclear weapons of their own could have nuclear deterrence. They were quite open about it, but they had to stop after the Third World War, when the last empire consolidated its grip.'

I sighed and shrugged. 'It's a blot on her record, I'll give you that. But they never actually used them.'

Merrial looked a bit shaken. 'So the scholars have known that all along? Well, I know what Godwin's people did after they lost their little nuclear threat business.' She smiled, thin-lipped. 'It seems you don't.'

She opened the other file. This one, which I read with growing horror, was about a very different contract. It was a monthly report on work done by prisoners, guarded by a company called Mutual Protection, for another company called Space Merchants.

'Prison labour was another *good*,' Merrial said, 'that our Deliverer thought best to supply on the free market.'

'But that's slavery!'

'Indeed it is,' said Merrial. 'That's why we don't talk about it. I wouldn't be surprised if some of your scholars have covered it up too.' Her eyes narrowed. 'Maybe some of the senior tinkers know about this nuclear business, and all. But they don't talk about it.'

We sat looking at each other, with the sudden passion of people who have lost something that they believed in, and have only each other left. It was all the more bitter because we each had separately thought we had been told the worst about the great woman, had smugly thought we were mature enough to know it and keep it quiet from the gullible populace, and we each had found that we had ourselves been gulled by our own guild; that there was an even darker tale to tell. My mind was racing, and I could feel a headache coming on. At the same time I felt a sense of release, a small deliverance, as the image of the Deliverer toppled in my mind.

With a short break when we wandered out into the warm evening for dinner in a fish restaurant by the Kelvin, we worked through the files. We found plenty about Myra Godwin's strange career – more than enough to write a pretty sensational biography – but nothing about what had happened around the time of the Deliverance itself. It was after nine when Merrial jumped up and hissed, 'Shit! Shit!'

'What's the matter?'

'I've found a catalogue file. No meaningful title, wouldn't you just fucking believe it. And it's got far, far more entries than we've got files here. We just got the low-security stuff! The rest is still in the University's dark storage.'

I rubbed my sore eyes, and reached out for Merrial's hand. 'So what's still there might be *worse?*'

'You said it. It might even contain the stuff we're looking for. We have to go back.'

6

Light Weapons

Long ago there had been another country, called the International. It was a country of the mind, a country of hope, and it encompassed the world. Until one day, in August 1914, its citizens went to war with each other, and the world ended. Everything died in that war, God and Country and International and Civilisation; died, and went to hell. Everybody died. The survivors thought they were alive, but they were not. After August 1914 there had been no living people in the world – only dead people on leave, the damned and the demons.

The last morally responsible people in the world had been the Reichstag fraction of the German Social-Democratic Party. They had voted the credits for the Kaiser's war, against every resolution of their past. They had known the right thing to do, and they had chosen the wrong. All subsequent history had been that of the damned, of poor devils struggling in the hell these men had pitched them into; and nobody could be judged for how they behaved in hell.

This thought, with its bleak blend of Christian and Marxist heresies, had originally been expounded to her by David Reid, one night many decades ago, when he was very drunk. It had sustained Myra through many a bad night. At other times – in the days, and the good nights – it seemed a callow undergraduate nihilism, shallow and wicked and absurd. But in the bad nights it struck her as profound and true, and, in its way, life-affirming. If you thought of people as *alive* and *each having a life to live*, you'd get so depressed at what so many had got instead, this past century and a half, that on a bad night you'd be tempted to add your own death to theirs, and thus make an undetectable increment to that already unimaginable, unthinkable number.

A number which Myra, on her bad nights, suspected she had already increased quite considerably. Not directly – if she had sinned at all, it had been a sin of omission – and nobody had ever blamed her for it, but she blamed herself. If she had sold the deterrence policy to the German imperialists when they'd needed it, torn up all her existing contracts and sorted them out later, how many people would now be alive who now were dead? On the bad nights the answer seemed to run into millions. At other times, on more sober reflection, she realised she wasn't in that league; she wasn't up there with the Big Three; there was almost a sort of adolescent self-dramatisation in the pretension; if she belonged in that company at all it was in the second or third rank, below the great revolutionaries but up there with the more destructive of the great imperialists, Churchill and Mountbatten and Johnson and people of that ilk.

Her shoes were kicked off under a chair, the black crêpe and dévoré dress was across the back of the chair, the sable hat was flung in a corner, the black fur coat was on the floor, the whisky bottle was open on the table and Leonard Cohen's black lyrics disturbed the smoky air: Manhattan, then Berlin, indeed.

Myra was having one of her bad nights.

The late-spring night outside the thin, old curtains was cold, and the central-heating radiator didn't do much to hold back the chill. The main room of the flat felt small, almost cramped, like a student bedsit. She had a kitchen, a bathroom, a bedroom; but most of what defined her life was crammed into this living-room. The shelves were lined with books, two or three rows deep, though she had the entire 2045 edition (the last) of the Library of Congress, sharing space with its Sterling search engine on a freebie disk somewhere in the clutter. Her music, her computer software and hardware, her pictures, all were piled up in similarly silted layers of technological generations, with the most recent stuff at the top or on the outside, and everything back to CDs and PCs and even, at some pre-Cambrian level, vinyl, in the strata below. She had, in her eyeband, ready access to any scene on Earth or off it, but she still had posters on the walls.

Once, these posters had consisted mainly of old advertisements for the ISTWR's exports. But in recent years, one by one, the tacked-up shots of lift-offs and payloads, missiles and explosions had been tugged down in moments of shame and fury, to be crumpled and binned, and replaced by scenes of Kazakh nature and tradition.

Mountains and meadows, horsemen and peasants, dancers in embroidered costumes – a whole oriental Switzerland of tourist attractions. Kazakhstan was not doing too badly, even today. It had moved away from its disastrous, Soviet-era polluting industries and extractive monocultures, and put its prairies to a more productive and natural use in cattle-raising. The Kazakh horsemen were back in the saddle.

Myra leaned back and stretched. It was nearly midnight. She'd had far too much to drink. Her few hours in the bar with Valentina had been followed by an hour or two of drinking on her own. She was so drunk she was lucid, 'fleeing' as Dave used to call it. Or possibly she was sobering up, smoothly and gradually, and was in the state where repeated applications of the hair of the dog were postponing the inevitable hammer-blow of the hangover. But drunk or sober, with or without Reid's antinomian justification, she had to act. She had to reach the International.

There were two Internationals ('for large values of two' as Reid had once put it, alluding to the numerous splits): the Second and the Fourth. When most people talked about *the International*, they meant the Second – the successor of the one that had torn itself apart in 1914, and had painfully reassembled its severed limbs in the course of three world wars, five world slumps and one successful world revolution. Even today it was massive: the Socialist International's affiliated parties and trade unions and co-operatives and militias had an aggregate membership in the tens of millions, still.

What Myra meant, and Valentina meant, and Georgi had meant by *the International* was a less imposing institution, a remnant of a fragment, most of it embedded in the greater body of the Second, a splinter travelling slowly through its veins. The Fourth International's membership was in the low thousands, scattered around the world – and, as Valentina had reminded her, off the world, thanks to its pioneering efforts at unionising the space rigs back in the 2020s. It was now almost dormant, a tenuous network of old comrades who couldn't quite say goodbye to each other, or to the dreams of their fervent younger days.

The radical sects of the English Revolution, the Muggletonians and Cameronians and Fifth Monarchy Men, had persisted as dwindling, marginal congregations for centuries after their Kingdom had failed to come; so it would be, Myra thought, for the erstwhile partisans of the Fourth. She knew that, but still she had paid her dues.

Now it was time to get something back for her money. For a start, she could find out what her comrades had done with her country's nukes.

Myra flew through virtual space, drunk in charge of a data-drive. New View floated before her, its image filling her eyeband's field. The habitat was a sort of orbital commune – world socialism, in a very small world – which had been put together by the left wing of the space movement, back when such ideas seemed to matter. The graticule showed it was hundreds of metres across, a circular accretion of habitats, salvaged fuel-tanks, cannibalised spacecraft. She reached out and turned it about in her datagloved hands, mildly amused at the chill, prickly tactile feedback, and peered at the small print of addresses on the hull until she found the name she sought.

Logan; whether forename or surname, real name or party name she didn't know; she'd never heard the man called anything else. There it was, scribed on a hull panel from an old McDonnell Douglas SSTO heavy-lifter. She tapped it and the view zoomed in, to show a window with the man's face peering out. It was an engagingly apt interface. Myra zapped a hailing code, and the face at the window responded.

'Oh, hi? Myra Godwin? Just a moment, please.' The fetch wavered and Logan's real face, subtly different, seamlessly replaced it, pulling back as the window icon widened to an interior view of an actually windowless room.

The compartment was full-spectrum strip-lit, the glowing tubes like shafts of sunlight among intertwined vines and branches, cables and tubes. Logan floated in the centre of the room. His cropped white hair matched his white stubble. He wore a faded blue singlet and baggy pants. Around his brow was a toolkit headband on which a loupe and a light were mounted; a standard eyeband was shoved higher up on his forehead. He was bent around the open back of a control-panel which he had gripped between his feet and was working on with a hand laser and a set of jeweller's screwdrivers.

He flipped the loupe up from his eye and grinned at her.

'Well, Myra, long time no see.' He still had the London accent, overlaid with a space-settler drawl. His space fraction had picked up a lot of people she and Georgi had known in Kazakhstan, tough trade-union militants blooded in the Nazbarayev years.

'Yeah, I've missed you too, Logan. How's life on New View?'

97

Logan gestured with one hand, automatically making a compensating movement with the other. 'OK. We've got pretty much up to complement population-wise, near a thousand last time I checked. We're making a good living, though – got a lot of products and skills the white settlers need. And the old Mars project is chugging along.'

'You're still doing *that*?'

Logan turned up his thumb. 'Kitting out the expedition, bit by bit. No intention of hanging around here forever – not with the white settlers staking out the Moon, anyhow. Nobody's even got much scientific interest in Mars any more, 'specially after that contamination thing came out.'

Myra nodded glumly. It had indeed come as a bit of a disappointment that Mars had an entire biosphere of busily evolving micro-organisms, of recent origin; in the 1970s the Soviets had proudly deposited a piece of paper autographed by Leonid Brezhnev on the Red Planet, which was now being very slowly terraformed by the descendants of bacteria from the General Secretary's sweat.

'So we're gonna go for it,' Logan went on. 'Some time in the next couple of years, we're moving it out.'

'You're going to move *New View*?' Myra smiled at Logan, and at herself – each question so far had ended on a high note of astonishment.

'Minus a few hundred tons of stuff we won't need, but basically, yes. Fill her up – well, fill up a few tanks, I mean – with Lunar polar water, buy a fusion engine from the white settlers and push off on a Hohmann orbit. We got enough old spacecraft lashed into this junk-heap to build landers, then habitats on the ground.'

'You've got it all worked out, I see,' said Myra. 'Well, good luck to you with that.' The Mars colony scheme had been pending, Real Soon Now, on Logan's agenda for as long as she'd known him. 'However, I've got something a bit more urgent to ask you. These white settlers of whom you speak, they aren't by any chance the people I once made a lot of money out of sticking on top of Protons and Energias and sending out there?'

'That's the ones,' Logan said. 'And the new lot coming out on the diamond ships, of course.' He laughed. 'The colonial bourgeoisie!'

'Well, whatever you want to call them,' said Myra, 'you know they're planning to take charge, through the ReUN and the battle-sats?'

'Oh, sure,' Logan said. 'Everybody knows that.' He shrugged. 'What can you do? And anyways, what difference is it gonna make to us?' He flourished his tiny laser. 'We're safe.'

'No, you're not,' said Myra. She flicked her gaze upwards, checking the firewall 'ware. It was sound. 'I've just learned – from my Defence Minister, no less – that *I* have a clump of city-buster nukes stashed somewhere in the clutter around you.'

'Is that a problem?' Logan asked. 'Best place for them, surely.'

She had to admire his cool.

'Somehow I don't think that was why the International asked for them to be put there.'

'Ah,' said Logan. 'So you know about that.'

'Yeah,' said Myra. 'Thanks a bunch for not telling me.'

Logan mumbled something entirely predictable about need-to-know. Myra cut off his ramble with an angry chop of her hand.

'Give me a fucking break,' she said, exasperated. 'I can figure that out for myself. The nukes are an element of the situation, but they're not my main concern right now. I just thought I should let you know that I know about them, for the same reason that you should've told me: for the sake of politeness, if nothing else. OK?'

'Well, yeah, OK,' Logan allowed, grudgingly. 'So what is your main problem?'

'I was wondering,' said Myra, 'if you'd grabbed them because you intended to do something about the coup. Like, you know, stop it.'

Logan laughed. 'Me personally?'

'No. The International. And don't tell me you *personally* are the only member it's got up there.'

'Oh, no, not at all.' Logan stared at her, obviously puzzled. 'We got plenty of comrades, I mean New View is basically ours, but it's been a long time since the Party had an army, Myra, you know that as well as I do. We do have a military org, like, but it's just a . . . a small cadre.'

'Of course I know that. But I also know what a small military cadre is *for*. It's so that when you do need an army you can recruit your soldiers from *other* armies. You telling me the space fraction's done no Party work on the battlesats? In all those years?'

Logan looked uncomfortable. 'Not exactly, no, I'm not saying that. We have – well, naturally we have sympathisers, we get reports—'

99

'And so do we,' she said. 'Some of them from the same comrades as you do.' She wasn't entirely certain of this – need-to-know, again – but it would give him something to think about. 'Who actually knows about the nukes?'

'Valentina Kozlova,' said Logan. 'And your ex-husband, Georgi Davidov.' If Logan noticed Myra's involuntary start at this news, he gave no sign. 'And me, obviously. That's it. The only people who know. Unless there's been a leak.'

'Hmm,' said Myra. 'Reid doesn't seem to know about them – he knows we have nukes in space, but he thinks they're all in Earth orbit.' She paused. 'Wait a fucking minute. If you're the only person up here who knows about them, then the request from the Party a couple of years ago was in fact a request from you. You, personally.'

'Well, yeah,' Logan said. He didn't seem bothered at all. 'In my capacity as Party Secretary for the space fraction, that is.'

'You took it upon yourself to do *that*? What the fuck was on your *mind*?' God, she thought, there I go again with the incredulous screech. She added, in a flat, steady voice, 'Besides, what gave you the right to interfere in my section, and in my section's state?'

Logan squirmed, like someone shifting uncomfortably in an invisible chair. 'I had a valid instruction to do it. From the military org.'

'Ah! So there *is* someone else who knows about it!'

'Not as such,' said Logan. 'The military org is . . .' He hesitated.

'Like you said, a small cadre?' Myra prompted.

'In a manner of speaking,' said Logan. He looked as though he was steeling himself for an admission. 'It's an AI.'

Myra felt her back thump against the back of her chair – she was literally thrown by this statement. She took a deep breath.

'Let's scroll this past us again, shall we? Tell me if I've got this right. Two years ago, at the Sputnik centenary, Val gets a message from you, asking for part of our stash of nukes. It's a valid Party request, she decides I don't need to know, and she blithely complies. And the reason this happened is because *you* got a request from a fucking *computer*?'

'An AI military expert system,' Logan said pedantically. 'But yeah, that's about the size of it.'

Myra groped blindly for a cigarette, lit it shakily.

'And just how long has the Fourth International been taking military advice from an AI?'

Logan did some mental arithmetic.

'About forty years,' he said.

It was no big secret, Myra learned. Just one of those things she'd never needed to know. The AI had originated as an economic and logistic planning system devised by a Trotskyist software expert in the British Labour Party. This planning mechanism had been used by the United Republic of Great Britain, and inherited by its self-proclaimed successor, the underground Army of the New Republic, after Britain had been occupied, and its monarchy restored, by the Yanks in the Third World War. It had acquired significant upgrades, not all of them intended, during the twenty-year guerilla war that followed, and had played some disputed role in the British national insurrection during the Fall Revolution in 2045. Its central software routines had been smuggled into space by a refugee from the New Republic's post-victory consolidation. It had been expanding its capacities, and its activities, ever since.

'Most people call it the General,' Logan told her. 'Aces the Turing, no sweat.'

'But what's it doing?' Myra asked. 'If it's such a shit-hot adviser, why aren't we winning?'

'Depends what you mean by "we",' Logan said. 'And what you mean by "winning".'

Myra had, she realised, no answer to that. Perhaps the AI adviser had picked up on the *Analysis* analysis, and agreed that the situation was hopeless.

Logan was looking at her with sympathetic curiosity, a sort of reversed mirror-image of the hostile bafflement she was directing at him. He must have gone native up there; he'd got used to this situation, and to this style of work, over the decades, and had forgotten the common courtesies of even their notional comradeship.

'Anyways,' he was saying, 'you can ask it all that yourself.' He poked, absently, at the control-panel between his feet; looked up; said, 'Putting you through.'

Before Myra could so much as open her mouth, Logan had vanished, and had been replaced by the military AI. She'd had a mental picture of it, ever since Logan had first mentioned it: something like the *Jane's* software, a VR gizmo of lines and lights. At best a piece of simulant automation, like Parvus.

He was a young man in sweat-stained camos, sitting casually on a rock in a clearing in temperate woodland: lichen and birch-bark, sound of water, birdsong, leaf-shadow, a wisp of woodsmoke. It looked like he'd paused here, perhaps was considering setting up a camp. The man looked every inch the commandante – his long, wavy black hair and his black stubble and dark eyes projected something of the glamour of Guevara, the arrogance of Trotsky. He also reminded Myra, disturbingly, of Georgi – enough to make her suspect that the image she saw was keyed to her personality; that it had been precisely tuned to give her this overwhelming impression of presence, of charisma.

'Hello,' he said. 'I've wanted to meet you for a long time, Myra.'

She opened her hands. 'You could have called.'

'No doubt I would have done, quite soon.' The entity smiled. 'I prefer that people come to me. It avoids subsequent misunderstandings. Anyway – I understand you have two concerns: the nukes at Lagrange, and the space-movement coup. Regarding the first – the nukes are still under your control. Your Defence Minister still has the access codes. I requested that the weapons themselves be moved here for security.' He shrugged, and smiled again. 'They're all yours. So are the weapons in Earth orbit – which are, of course, more immediately accessible, and usable. This brings me to your other concern – the coup. It is imminent.'

'How imminent?'

'In the next few days. They'll ram through the vote on reorganisation of the ReUN, and the new Security Council will issue orders to seize the battlesats. They have the forces to do it.'

He paused, looking at her, or through her. 'But we have the forces to stop it. I can assure you, Myra, it's all in hand.'

She shook her head. 'That isn't what our intelligence indicates. I've checked, my Defence and Foreign ministries have checked. We have agents in the battlesats, as you must know – hell, some of them must be in your own military org! *If* such a thing exists.' She wished she had read some of those mailings.

'It most certainly does exist,' the General said firmly. 'And it's been feeding you disinformation.'

'*What?*'

The entity stood up and stepped towards her in its virtual space. It spread its hands and assumed an apologetic expression, but with a sly conspiratorial gleam in its eyes.

'Forgive me, Comrade Davidova. This was not done against you. It was done against our common enemy: Reid's faction of the space movement.'

'How—' she began, but she saw, she saw.

'I'm telling you this now,' the General said, 'because today you lost your last disloyal Commissar. Alexander Sherman has been passing on information to Reid for months. He wasn't the first, but he was the last.'

'Who were the others?'

The General moved his hand in a smoothing gesture. 'I can't tell you that without compromising current operations. That particular information is of no further use to you anyway.'

'I suppose not,' Myra concurred reluctantly. She wished she knew who the traitors were, all the same; hoped Tatanya and Michael hadn't been among them. She'd quite liked those two . . .

'So you used them – and *us* – as a conduit for disinformation?'

The General nodded. 'And for information going the other way – your updates to *Jane's* have been most helpful.'

'Jeez.' Her reactions to this were interestingly complicated, she thought distantly. On the one hand she felt sore at having been used, having been lied to; on the other, she could admire the stagecraft of the deception. Above all she felt relieved that the gloomily negative assessments she'd worried over were all wrong.

Unless the situation was even *worse* than she'd thought—

'The situation is better than you think, by far,' said the General. 'We have our people in place – the battlesats won't be taken without a struggle, which in most cases we expect to win.'

'*Most cases* won't be enough. Even one battlesat—'

'Indeed. Which is where your orbital weaponry comes in. The lasers, the EMP bursters, the smart pebbles, the hunter-killers, the kinetic-energy weapons . . .'

Myra hadn't known her arsenal was so extensive. (God, to think that stockpile had once belonged to the Pope! Well, to the Swiss Guards, anyway – quite possibly His Holiness had been discreetly left out of the loop on that one.) She shivered in her wrap, tugged it around her shoulders, lit another cigarette. She didn't know what to say; she felt her cheeks burning under the General's increasingly quizzical regard.

'What do you want us to do with them?' she asked at last.

'I'm sure you can work that out,' he said. 'I'll be in touch.'

'But—'

He gave her a smile; heartbreaking, satanic.

'I hope I see you again,' he said. He reached out a hand and made some fine adjustment to the air. The link went down.

Myra took off her eyeband and rubbed her eyes. Then she walked unsteadily to the kitchen and made some tea, and sat drinking it and smoking for about ten minutes, staring blankly into the virtual spaces of her mind. She supposed she should do something, or tell someone, but she couldn't think what to do, or whom to tell.

Time enough in the morning, she decided.

Her bedroom was small, a couple of metres' clearance on three sides of the double bed giving barely enough space for a wardrobe and dressing-table. Over the years the room had accumulated a smothering snowfall of soft furnishings, needlework and ornaments; pretty things she'd bought on impulse and never had the heart to throw out. The process was a natural selection for an embarrassingly large collection of grannyish clutter. Now and again – as now – it infuriated her in its discrepancy with the rest of her life, her style, her look. And then, on reflection, she'd figure that the incongruity of the room's appearance was what made it a place where she could forget all care, and sleep.

In the morning it seemed like a dream.

All the more so, Myra realised as she struggled up to consciousness through the layers of sleep and hangover and tangled, sweat-clammy bedding, because she *had* dreamed about the General. She felt vaguely ashamed about that, embarrassed in front of her waking self; not because the dream had been erotic – though it had been – but because it had been besotted, devoted, *servile*; like those dreams the Brits used to have about Royalty. She sat up in the bed and pushed back the pillow, leaned back and tried to think about it rationally.

The entity, the military AI, would have had God only knew how many software generations to evolve an intimate knowledge of humanity. It had had time to become what the Japanese called an *idoru*, a software representation that was better than the real thing, smarter and sexier than any possible human mind or form, like those wide-eyed, faux-innocent anime brats or the simulated stars of pornography and romance. Sex wasn't the half of it – there were other codes, other keys, in the semiotics of charm: the subtle suggestions of wisdom, the casual hints at a capacity for violence, the assumed readiness to command, the mirroring glance of empathy; all the elements that went to make up an image of a man that men would die for and women would fall for.

So, she told herself, she wasn't such a pathetic case, after all. Happens to the best of us. As she reached for her medical kit and clicked out the tablets to fix the hangover, she caught herself smiling at the memory of the General's smile. Annoyed with herself again, she got out of bed and padded to the kitchen in her fluffy slippers and fuzzy nightgown, and gulped cold water while the coffee percolated. She added a MoodLift tab to her ReSolve dose and her daily intake of anti-ageing supplements and knocked them back all at once. She felt better.

The time was 8 o'clock. She put her contacts in and flicked on a television tile and watched it while spooning muesli and yoghurt and listening to the murmured morning briefing from Parvus. The news, as usual, was bad, but no worse than usual. No martial music or ballet on all channels – that was enough to count as good news. After a coffee and a cigarette she felt almost human. She supposed she might as well get up and go to work.

The walk to the government building woke her up even more, boosted her mood better than any tab. The air was crisp, the morning sky unexpectedly colourful, reds and oranges and yellows shading to green at the horizon. She noticed people staring up at the sky.

Its colours were changing visibly, flowing – suddenly she realised she was looking at an aurora, thousands of miles south of where aurorae should be seen. As she stopped and looked up, open-mouthed, the sky brightened for a few seconds from some great illumination below the horizon.

She ran. She sprinted through the streets, barged through the doors, yelled at Security and bounded up the stairs. As she strode into her office her earpiece pinged, and a babble of tinny voices contended for her attention. She sat heavily on the edge of her desk and flipped down her eyeband, keyed up the news.

The tanks were rolling, all around the world.

Without taking her eyes off the newsfeeds, Myra slid across her desk and lowered herself into her chair. She rattled out commands on

105

the armrest keypads, transforming the office's walls into screens for an emergency command-centre. The first thing she did was secure the building; then she hit the emergency call for Sovnarkom. The thrown fetches of Andrei, Denis and Valentina sprang to attention on the screens – whether their physical bodies were in their offices, on their way in or still in bed didn't matter, as long as their eyebands were online.

Myra glanced around their virtual presences.

'OK, comrades, this is the big one,' she said. 'First, is everything clear with us?'

It was unlikely that the ISTWR's tiny Workers' Militia and tinier People's Army would have joined the coup, but more unlikely things were happening before her eyes every few seconds. (A night-time amphibious landing at South Street Seaport! Tanks in Pennsylvania Avenue! Attack helicopters shelling Westminster Bridge!)

'We're sound,' said Denis. Even his fetch looked drawn and hung-over. 'So's Kazakhstan, they're staying out of this. Army's on alert, of course. Baikonur cosmodrome's well under government control. So's the airstrip at Yubileine. Almaty's mobilised, militia on the streets, but they're loyal.'

You hope, Myra thought. The neat thing about a military coup was that mobilisation against it could quite easily become *part* of it, as the lines of command writhed and broke and reconnected.

'Good, great. North-eastern front? Val, you awake?'

'Yeah, I'm with you. No moves from the Sheenisov so far.' Valentina patched in a satellite feed, updated by the second: the steppe was still.

'What about Mutual Protection here?'

'Haven't moved from the camp – and the camp's quiet.'

Myra relaxed a little. 'Looks like our immediate surroundings are secure, then. Any word from orbit, Val?'

Valentina shook her head. 'All comms are very flaky, can't get anything coherent from the settlements, the factories, the battlesats—'

'That's impossible!' She thought about how it might be possible. 'Oh my God, the sky—'

'About ten minutes ago,' Andrei announced, from some glassy trance, 'somebody nuked the Heaviside Layer. Half a dozen bursts – not much EMP, but quite enough of that and of charged particles to scramble radio signals for a good few hours.'

'So how are we getting even the news?' Myra demanded.

'Cable,' said Andrei. 'Fibre-optics aren't affected. And some stuff's getting through by laser, obviously, like Val's spysat downlink. Should increase as people switch, or improvise. But for the moment it's dust in everybody's eyes.'

'Didn't know the space movement had orbital nukes,' Denis said. 'In fact, didn't know anybody but us had *any* serious nukes.'

That was a point. Nuclear disarmament had been the only universally popular, and (almost) universally successful, policy of the US/UN after the Third World War. Even Myra, at the time, had not resented or regretted the confiscation of the ISTWR's complement, along with all the rest. Only by sheer accident had an independent stockpile survived, in the hands of a politically untouchable institution that counted its supporters in billions, its age in millennia and its policy in centuries. All other strategic nuclear weapons had been dismantled. There were thousands of battlefield tactical nukes still around, of course, but nobody'd ever worried much about *them*: the consequences of their use had never been shown live on television.

(The images went through her mind, again, and the names of cities: Kiev, Frankfurt, Berlin. She shook her head with a shudder, shutting them out.)

Valentina was giving her a hard stare. 'They weren't *ours*, were they?'

'Not as far as I know,' Myra said. 'Unless you happened to turn over the access codes to somebody else, eh?'

Valentina shook her head, thin-lipped. 'No. Never.'

'Right, so much for that theory,' Myra said briskly, to assure Val that she wasn't under any suspicion. 'Andrei, any ideas?'

'Excuse me,' said Andrei. 'I'm still trying to get through the front door.'

'Oh, fuck!' Myra tabbed a code to let him in.

'Thanks . . . OK, I think the nukes were from the UN side, against the coup.'

'And where did they get them?'

'What I think is that the UN hung on to some nukes for itself, the secret stayed with some inner cadre of bureaucrats who made it through the Revolution and the purges, and they put it at the disposal of the current Secretary General.'

'Makes sense, I suppose,' said Denis. 'What I'd do.'

107

'What's the politics of this, Andrei?' Myra asked. 'We were so sure they'd wait for the ReUN vote—' she stopped and laughed. Trotsky himself had used just such a stratagem. 'Have the coup before the vote – I wonder where they got that idea. Still, it kind of undermines the appeal to legitimacy.'

She still had one eye on the virtual screens of the cable news. 'Ah, wait, something coming in—'

They sat in silence as the presenter read out a communiqué from a large group of small governments calling themselves the Assembly Majority Alliance. The gist of it was that the present Security Council had violated the Revised Charter of 2046 by planning to use nuclear weapons in space; and a call for immediate action to depose the conspirators and usurpers. The forces of the Alliance governments and of Mutual Protection were offered for immediate, co-ordinated action to that end. A swift resolution of the emergency was anticipated. The population was urged to remain calm and stay away from work for the day.

'God, that is so cynical,' Val said. 'They must have had dozens of back-dated statements, prepared for every contingency, so they could claim to be acting to prevent whatever the Security Council decided to do.'

'Yes, yes,' Myra said. 'All SOP for a coup. And a diversion, anyway. It's in space that the real battles are being fought. Maybe right at this moment! The whole thing will be decided at the speed of light. Come on, let's get into command mode.'

The others nodded, fell silent, turned to the screens and started pulling in all available data and throwing analysis software at it. After a minute or two they'd begun to mesh as a team in their common virtual workspace. Information flashed back and forth between their personal networks, the government network, the *Jane's* system, the newsfeeds, and field reports from their own troops and agents.

The big picture became as clear as the situation it revealed was chaotic. Myra clocked through most of the world's significant capitals: Beijing, Pyongyang, Tokyo, Vladivostok, Seattle, LA, Washington DC, New York, London, Paris, New Berlin, Danzig, Moscow. All of them reported military strikes of one kind or another, but they all had the aspect of *putsches* – short-term grabs of public buildings or urban strongholds, which could be held more by the reluctance of the government forces to reduce them than by the strength of their occupiers. It all had a suspiciously diversionary look about it.

All of the committed technophobe governments, from the Khmer Vertes rulers of Bangkok, through the Islamic Republicans of Arabia to the White Nationalists of Dallas, had their forces on full alert and their media screaming imprecations against the enemies of God, Man or Gaia (depending on local ideological taste); but Myra judged them well aware that they were not, themselves, immediate targets – it was the more liberal governments, those who compromised between the pro-tech and anti-tech forces, which were taking the fire.

The more serious action was taking place in the imbricated global hinterland of enclaves and ministates and company countries; along their fractal borderlines the local defence forces were massed and mobilised, in a posture that was aggressive in the Assembly Majority Alliance statelets, generally defensive in the rest. Meanwhile, in the shadowy lands beyond and behind even these anarchic polities, the forests and plains and badlands and shanty towns bristled as the Green neo-barbarians, the marginals and tribals awoke to the unlooked-for opportunities of this new day.

Jane's Market Forces registered unexpected shifts in the balance of power; minor skirmishes could have major effects, putting troops and tactics and weapons to the test in new conditions, or in real rather than simulated combat. Not much blood was being shed, but fortunes were being made and lost, alliances and antagonisms updated; the process had its own gory fascination. Myra felt she could sit and look at it for hours.

But this was Earth, this was not where it was at. The battles here, real or virtual, were fundamentally a diversion, and she was duly being diverted. She turned her attention determinedly skyward.

With Val's well-practised help she spun a neon orrery of near-Earth space, separating out the relevant threads from the skeins of commercial and military orbits. The planet itself appeared as a transparent globe, etched with political and geographical outlines, clouded with weather patterns, cross-hatched with confrontations, pin-pricked with flashpoints. Again its intricate patterns compelled her attention; again, she turned away.

Their own space-borne *matériel* – nuclear and kinetic-energy weapons – were depicted as black rods and cones, deep in the ever-growing ring of space-junk that tracked the main orbital thoroughfares.

109

'Anything coming through yet from the battlesats?'

'Some,' said Val, sounding distracted. 'I'm pulling in laser comms via various ground stations. Shit, this is tricky – hold it, hold it . . . ah!'

The battlesat locations lit up, one by one; those with which communication had been established blinked invitingly. Myra zoomed in on one of them. A classic von Braun space station, with a rotating tubular ring joined by thinner tubular spokes to an inner ring surrounding the contra-rotating spin-compensated axial tower. The living-quarters and hydroponics were around the ring, in the fake gravity of the spin; the laser-cannon and rocket-racks and particle-beam weapons and military command-centre were in the free-fall hub. The whole enormous mandala had a camp Nazi grandeur, spoiled only by the ungainly arrays of solar panels it had sprouted while its nuclear reactor had run down.

It was one of dozens in various orbits. Space Defense had enforced the Pax Americana of the US/UN Imperium, a twenty-year Reich between the Third World War and the Fall Revolution. In that revolution the battlesats had passed into the hands of their personnel – soldiers' soviets in space – and, ever since, they'd sought a role to replace their lost empire. Everything from power-beam transmission to asteroid defence had been tried, to little profit. The stations survived on a trickle of subsidy – or 'user fees' – from the similarly diminished UN, paid mainly to prevent the battlesats' going rogue out of sheer desperation.

Now the forces of the coup were offering them a new empire, one a lot more justifiable and enforceable than the old.

'So what's the score with this one?' Myra asked.

'Still loyal,' replied Val. 'They just reported in to say they weren't going with the Alliance.'

'Any way of checking that?'

'Don't know, I'm hailing them – ah! they're letting us in.'

'I'll go,' said Myra, 'you stay with the big picture.'

With a clunky, disorienting transition, she found herself standing in a real-time representation of the battlesat's bridge. It was about fifteen metres across, and crowded. The interior matched the exterior's style: banks of flashing lights among chrome and black surfaces; a cluttered overgrowth of retrofitted modern kit among a profusion of plants, like in a civilian space settlement. The layout was optimised for free-fall, with the crew-members strapped into seats and couches at unexpected angles to each other. In this section of the shaft there were actual windows, through which she could see the great wheel turn in the sunlight, and the Earth's swirling clouds below. She blinked, and overprinted the real view with its software image.

The crew were wearing eyebands, and some of them could see Myra's fetch in their own virtual palimpsests of the scene – but they spared her no more than a glance. Another spectral presence had all their attention.

The General sat on a window sill, surveying the bridge with narrowed eyes. He'd been saying something; his words seemed to hang in the air, resonating in the circuits of the display. He interrupted himself and turned to face her.

'Ah, Comrade Davidova – thanks for coming.'

'I wasn't aware I'd been asked,' she said.

'Oh, you were,' the construct said. 'This is, as they say, no accident.'

Myra nodded. No doubt it was indeed no accident that the first battlesat to allow her into its internal systems was the one in which the General was addressing his troops.

He waved a hand. 'Welcome to a quick emergency session of the military org's local cell.' He grinned. 'Which is pretty much the command of this station.' The watching crew-members gave her longer looks now; some of them even smiled.

'We need your help,' the General told her flatly. 'Nice display,' he added. 'May I?'

He reached over, thumb and forefinger pinching into her translucent globe, and with frightening insouciance overrode all her protocols and relocated her virtual view of the Earth and near-Earth space into the centre of the bridge.

She stared at the spinning shapes, fuming. He shouldn't have been able to *do* that—

'We still hold most of the battlesats.' A quick sharp look. 'That is to say, the anti-coup forces do, whatever their other alignments. But the struggle is still in the balance. We have about a sixth of the battle-sats securely on our side, the enemy likewise, and the others undecided.'

Myra was momentarily stunned. Despite what the General had said to her earlier, she'd had no idea, no expectation that the military org's penetration of Space Defense was so thorough – it must have

111

taken years of work. But the General gave her no time to question or congratulate.

'Here, here and here.' He stabbed a forefinger at three battlesats, whose footprints between them covered most of the planet. 'These are in enemy hands. We can't hit them from the battlesats we hold, because that would risk a spasm of retaliation. But we need to hit them fast, to warn any others who are about to go over to the enemy. Take them out.'

He ran a finger lightly around the republic's orbital caches of smart pebbles, lasers, KE weapons.

'I can't,' Myra said. 'I don't have the skills, I don't have the automation. None of us do.'

The General snapped his fingers. 'The keys, Comrade, the keys. That's all I need. The access codes.'

'Let me consult my Defence Minister,' said Myra, and backed out hastily. It was a relief – even with the sudden, swallowed surge of cyberspace sickness that it brought on – to find herself back in her office, looking at screens.

'Val—' she began.

'I got that,' said Valentina. 'Kept half an eye on you with a partial piggyback. Who *is* that guy?'

Myra looked sidelong at her. 'Good for you,' she said. 'That was the head of the FI military org. An AI. Our very own electric Trotsky.'

'Fuck your mother,' said Val, in Russian.

'Right. We gonna give it the codes?'

'Up to you,' said Val. 'You're the PM.'

'What,' said Myra through clenched teeth, 'would you *advise*?'

Val licked her lips. The others were either pointedly ignoring them or concentrating on their own areas.

'Well, hell. Go with the military adviser, I'd say. Give it the codes.'

'Will that work? Do we really have munitions up there that can down battlesats?'

'Hard to say,' said Valentina. 'Ancient, never combat-tested, poorly maintained – but so are the battlesats! In theory, yes, they can overwhelm a battlesat's defences.'

Myra was trying to think fast. It struck her that the battlesats themselves might be a diversion – old and powerful, but inflexible and vulnerable: an orbiting Maginot Line. Perhaps the General was fighting the last war, and *winning* it, while the real battles raged elsewhere.

She hesitated, then decided.

'Give me the codes for the smart-pebble bombs,' she said. Val zapped them across; Myra tabbed back to the battlesat and passed them to the General. He was waiting for her, with puzzled impatience.

'Thank you,' he said heavily, then disappeared. Myra looked around at the now frantically active crew, gave them an awkward, cheery wave, and dropped back to her own command-centre.

'That was quick.' Valentina pointed at the display. Already, some of their orbital weapons had been activated. Myra devoutly hoped that what she was seeing as a representation wasn't appearing on the enemy's real-time monitors. In three places a cloud of sharp objects had burst out of cover and were moving in the same orbital paths as the three enemy battlesats, but in the opposite direction. They were due to collide with the battlesats in ten, eighteen and twenty-seven minutes.

What happened next was over in less than a second – a twinkle of laser paths in the void. The action replay followed automatically, patiently repeating the results for the slow rods and cones and nerves of the human eye.

Myra watched the battlesats' deep-space radar beams brush the oncoming KE volleys; saw their targeting-radar lock on. Her laser-platform drones responded to that detection with needles of light, stabbing to blind the battlesats – which had, in the momentary meantime, released a cloud of chaff to block that very manoeuvre. Then the battlesats struck back, with a speed still bewildering even in slow motion. Each one projected a thousand laser pulses, flashing like a fencer's swift sword, slicing up the KE weapons and their laser-platform escorts.

'Wow!' she said, admiring despite herself.

'Yeah, that's some defence system,' said Valentina. 'Not standard issue for a battlesat, I'll tell you that.'

Myra zoomed the view. Each attack cloud was still there, as a much larger cloud of much smaller objects. They would bombard the battlesats, sure enough, they'd even do some damage, but it would be more like a sand-blasting than a shelling.

The time was 09.25. Forty minutes had passed since the Heaviside nukes. The disruption they'd caused was easing off; radio comms were still haywire, but more and more centres were coming back on-line via patches and work-arounds. The outcome of this first serious exchange was already being analysed. Myra cast a quick glance at *Jane's*. The coup's stock was fluctuating wildly.

'Shit—'

She was about to transfer her workspace to the battlesat again but the General beat her to it. He – or it – suddenly appeared in the command-centre, as a recognisable if not very solid figure. Andrei and Denis, by this time evidently having been brought up to speed by Val, didn't react to the apparition with more than open-mouthed astonishment.

'Too bad,' the General said, staring sadly at the display. 'These defences are portable, not fitted to the station but brought in by the conspirators.'

'Any other battlesats have them?'

A sketch of a shrug. 'We don't. Maybe they're already being deployed among the waverers. Mutual Protection nanofactures, is my guess.'

Better than a guess, Myra reckoned.

'You want another strike?'

'No. Only one thing for it now. Nuke 'em.'

Myra glanced at Valentina. 'Wait. Give us a first-cut sim, Val.'

Valentina ran down the locations of their orbital nuclear weapons and launched a simulation of an immediate strike, in the light of the new information about the battlesats' capabilities. Stopped. Ran it again; and again; all in a few seconds, but a waste of time nonetheless. The answer was obvious. The nukes could get close enough to the battlesats to take them out – but near-Earth space was a lot more crowded than it had been when the doctrine of that deployment had first been developed. There was no way to avoid thousands of innocent casualties and quadrillions of dollars' worth of damage to space habitats and industries.

'It's worse than that,' Valentina pointed out. 'The direct effect of the explosions and the EMP would be just the beginning – there's every possibility that the debris would set off an ablation cascade – each collision producing more debris, until in a matter of days you'd have stripped the sky.'

The ablation cascade was a known nightmare, one of the deadliest threats to space habitation, or even exploration. Myra had seen discussions and calculations to suggest that a full-scale cascade would surround the Earth with rings of debris which could make space travel unfeasibly dangerous for *centuries* . . .

114

The General had a look which indicated that he was weighing this in the balance. She could just see it now, that calculation – even with a cascade, it was possible that the new diamond ships could dodge and dogfight through the debris – the barrier might not be impenetrable after all, and meanwhile . . .

'Forget it,' Myra said. 'We aren't going to use the nukes.' Her fingers were working away, codes were flashing past her eyes – she was trying to find the channel the General's fetch had ridden in on.

Something in her tone told the General there would be no argument. Instead, he turned to the others and said, quite pleasantly, 'The comrade is not thinking objectively. Are you willing to relieve her of her responsibilities?'

'No,' they told him, in gratifying unison.

'Very well.' He smiled at them, as if to say he was sorry, but it had been worth a try.

'And you can fuck *right* off,' said Myra. She tapped her forefinger, triumphantly, on an input-channel key, and tuned him right out.

7

The Claimant Bar

Out we went into the summer dusk. Moths sought the sun in street-lamps, baffled. The few quiet roads between the house and the Institute were crowded now, with local residents taking advantage of the slack season in bars normally jammed with students. Lads strutting their tight dark trousers, lasses swaying their big bright skirts. We must have looked a less happy couple, harried and hurrying.

A few lights burnt in the Institute, one of them the light in the corridor. As we stepped in and closed the door, the smell of pipe-smoke was stronger than before, and familiar.

'Someone's around,' Merrial whispered.

'Yes,' I replied, 'it's—'

Right on cue, an office door down the corridor opened and Anders Gantry stepped out. A small man with strong arms and a beer-barrel of a belly, hair curling grey like the smoke from his inseparable pipe. His shirt was merely grubby – his wife managed to impose fresh linen on him every week or so – but his jacket had not been cleaned in years. It smelled like it had been used to beat down fires, which it had.

He was the best historical scholar in the University, and quite possibly in the whole British Isles; and the kindest and most modest man I'd ever met.

'Ah, hello, Clovis,' he boomed. 'How good to see you!' He strode up and shook hands. 'And who's your friend?'

'Merrial – Dr Anders Gantry,' I said.

He held her hand and inclined his head over her knuckles. 'Charmed.' He looked at her in a vaguely puzzled way for a moment, then turned to me. 'Now, colha Gree, what can I do for you?'

Gantry had agreed to supervise my project; it was a persistent irritant to my conscience that I hadn't seen or written to him all summer.

116

'Oh, nothing at the moment, Dr Gantry. I've been doing a fair bit of preliminary research up North, and I've about finished the standard references.' I rubbed my ear, uneasily remembering the dust on the books. 'And I thought I'd take the opportunity of a wee visit to Glasgow to drop by the library.'

'That's very commendable,' he said. I was unsure of the exact level of irony in his voice, but it was there. 'We've rather missed you around here.'

'He works very hard,' Merrial put in. 'The space-launch platform project is on a tight schedule.'

'Oh, so that's where you are. Kishorn. Hmm. Good money to be made up there, I hear. And you, miss?'

'I have an office job there,' Merrial said blandly. She shot me a smile. 'That's how I know he works hard. He's saving up money to live on next year.'

'Well, I suppose there are ways and ways of preparing for a project,' said Gantry, in a more indulgent tone. 'No luck with patronage yet, I take it?'

'None so far, no.'

He clapped me around the shoulders. 'Perhaps you should try to extract some research money from the space scientists,' he said. 'Our great Deliverer had much to do with spaceflight herself. There might still be lessons in her life story, eh?'

Merrial's face froze and I felt my knees turning to rubber.

'Now that's a thought,' I said, as calmly as possible.

Gantry guffawed. 'Aye, you might even fool them into thinking that!' he said. 'Good luck if you do. Now that you're getting stuck in, Clovis, I have something to show you.' He grinned, revealing his teeth, yellow as a dog's. 'It's in the library.'

With that he turned away and bounded up the stairs. I followed, mouthing and gesturing helplessness to Merrial. To my relief, she seemed more amused than alarmed.

By the time we arrived at the open door of the library he'd vanished into the shadows.

'What are we going to do?' I whispered to Merrial.

'If he stays around, you keep him busy,' she said. 'I'll get the goods.'

I was about to tell her how unlikely she was to get away with that when Gantry came puffing up, carrying a load of cardboard folders that reached from his clasped hands at his belt to his uppermost chin.

117

'Here we are,' he said, lowering the tottering stack on to a table. He sneezed. 'Filthy with dust, I'm afraid.' He wiped his nose and hands on an even dirtier handkerchief. 'But it's time you had a look at it: Myra Godwin's personal archive.'

'That really is amazing,' I said. My voice sounded like a twelve-year-old boy seeing a girl naked for the first time. I picked them up and put them down, one by one. Eight altogether: bulging cardboard wallets ordered by decade, from the 1970s to the 2050s.

I hardly dared to breathe on them as I opened the first one and looked at the document on the top of the pile, a shoddily cyclostyled, rusty-stapled bundle of pages with the odd title *Building a revolutionary party in capitalist America. Published as a fraternal courtesy to the cosmic current.*

'Why haven't I seen these before?' I asked.

Gantry shuffled uncomfortably. He glanced at Merrial, rubbed his chin and said, 'Am I right in thinking you're a tinker?'

'You're right, I am that,' Merrial said, without hesitation.

Gantry smiled, looking relieved. 'Um, well. Between ourselves and all that. Scholars and tinkers both know, I'm sure, that we have to be . . . discreet, about the Deliverer's . . . more discreditable deeds and, ah, youthful follies. So, although previous biographers have seen these documents, we don't tend to show them to undergraduates. What I hope, Clovis, is that you'll see a way to go beyond the, um, shall we say hagiographic treatments of the past, without . . .' He paused, sucking at his lower lip. 'Ah, well, no need to spell it out.'

'Of course not,' I said.

I looked at the master scholar with what I'm sure must have been an expression of gratifying respect. 'Shall we have a look through them now?'

Gantry stepped back and threw up his hands in mock horror. 'No, no! Can't have me looking over your shoulder at the raw material, Clovis. Unaided original work, and all that. This is yours, and there's a thesis in there if ever I saw one. No, it's time I was off and left you to it.' He hesitated. 'Ah, I shouldn't need to tell you, colha Gree, but not a word about this, or a single page of it, outside, all right?'

I had a brief, intense tussle with my conscience, which neatly tripped me up and jumped on me. 'Nothing for the vulgar, of course,' I said carefully. 'But in principle I could, well, show it to or discuss it with other scholars?'

'Goes without saying,' Gantry confirmed jovially. He tapped the side of his nose. 'If you can find anyone you'd trust not to claim it as their own.' He winked at Merrial. 'Untrustworthy bunch, these scholars, I think you'll find.' He punched me, playfully as he thought, in the ribs. 'Confidence, man, confidence! I'm sure you have the wit to understand and explicate this lot yourself, and it'll make your name, you mark my words!'

'Thank you,' I said, after a painful intake of breath. 'Well . . . I think I'll make a start right now.'

'Yes, indeed. Splendid idea. Don't stay up too late.' His complicitous grin made it obvious that he thought it unlikely that we'd stay up too late. 'Best be off then,' he said, as though to himself, then backed to the door and turned away.

'Good night to you, sir!' Merrial called out after him.

'Good night,' came faintly back from the stairwell.

Merrial let out a long breath.

'What a strange little man,' she said, in the manner of someone who has just encountered one of the Wee Folk.

'He's not entirely typical of scholars,' I said.

'I should hope not,' Merrial said. 'Wouldn't want you turning into something like that.'

'Heaven forbid,' I said, adding loyally, 'but he's a fine man for all his funny ways.' I looked down at the stack of folders. 'Maybe it would be a good idea,' I said slowly, 'if you were to do your thing with the computer, and I could stay here, just in case he comes back.'

'Oh, and leave me to face the deils all on my own?' Merrial mocked, then laughed, relenting. 'Aye, that is not a bad idea. If he or anyone else comes in, keep them busy. I'll not be long, and I'll be fine.'

'What about this security barrier?'

She waved a hand and made a rude noise. 'Faugh! This wee gadget here has routines that can roast security barriers over a firewall and eat them for breakfast.'

Considering how she'd had to program something a lot simpler than that to sort out the dates, I doubted her, but supposed that was the black logic for you.

She smiled and slipped away; after an anxious minute of listening, I heard the sound of the inner door being opened and the scrape of a chair being dragged across the floor and propped against it. I relaxed a little and turned again to the files – to the paper files, I

119

mentally corrected myself, for the first time making the connection between 'files' in Merrial's and, I presumed, tinkers' usage, and my own.

I was eager to get into the early decades, but I knew that would be somewhat self-indulgent, and that I would have plenty of time for that. It was the later years, closer to the time of the Deliverance, that were hidden from history. I picked up the folder for the final decade, the 2050s, and was about to open it when I heard Merrial scream.

I don't remember getting to the door of the dark archive. I only remember standing there, my forward momentum arrested by a shock of dread that stopped me like a sparrow hitting a window. The file folder, absurdly enough, was still in my hands, and I held up that heavy mass of flimsy paper and fragile cardboard like a weapon – or a shield.

Merrial too was holding a weapon – the chair she'd been sitting on, and had evidently just sprung out of. In front of her, and above the computer, in a lattice of ruby light, stood the figure of a man. He was a tall man, and stout with it, his antique garb of cream-coloured jacket and trousers flapping and his shock of white hair streaming in the same invisible gale that had blown his hat away down some long corridor whose diminishing perspective carried it far beyond the walls of the room. His face was red and wrathful, his fist shaking, his mouth shouting something we couldn't hear.

Holding the chair above her head, her forearm in front of her eyes, chanting some arcane abracadabra, Merrial advanced like one facing into a fire, and seized her seer-stone and machinery from the table. Its wire, yanked from its inconveniently placed socket, lashed back like a snapped fishing-line. The little peg at the end, now bent like a fish-hook, flew towards me and rapped against the file-folder. Merrial whirled around at the same moment, and saw me. She gave me a look worth dying for, and then a calm smile.

'Time to go,' she said. She let the chair clatter down, and turned again to face the silently screaming entity she'd aroused. As she backed away from the thing, it vanished. A mechanism somewhere in the computer whirred, then stopped. A light on its face flickered, briefly, then went out.

All the lights went out. From downstairs we faintly heard an indignant yell. I could hear Merrial stuffing her apparatus back in its sack. She bumped into me, still walking backwards.

120

Holding hands as though on a precipice, we made our way through the library's suffocating dark. I could smell the dry ancient papers, the friable glue and frayed thread and leather of the bindings. From those fibres the ancients could have resurrected lost species of trees and breeds of cattle, I thought madly. Pity they hadn't.

After a long minute our eyes began to adjust to the faint light that filtered in past window-blinds, and from other parts of the building. We walked with more confidence through the maze towards the door. On the ground floor of the building we could hear Gantry blundering and banging about.

Then, behind us, I heard a stealthy step. Merrial heard it too and froze, her hand in mine suddenly damp. Another step, and the sound of something *dragging*. I almost broke into a screeching run.

'It's all right,' Merrial said, her voice startlingly loud. 'It's a sound-projection – just another thing to scare us off.'

Behind us, a low, deep laugh.

'Steady,' said Merrial.

My thigh hit the edge of the table by the door. 'Just a second,' I said. I let go of her hand, grabbed one more file-folder, put it in my other hand and then caught Merrial's hand again.

We reached the library door, slammed it behind us and descended the stairs as fast as we safely could, or faster. Then we lost all caution and simply fled, rushing headlong past Gantry's angry and puzzled face, lurid in the small flame of the pipe-lighter he held above his head, and out into the night.

Night it was – for hundreds of metres around, all the power was off. We stopped running when we reached the first functioning street-lamps, on Great Western Road.

I looked at Merrial's face, shiny with sweat, yellow in the sodium puddle.

'What in the name of Reason was that?'

Merrial shook her head. 'My mouth's dry,' she croaked. 'I need a drink.'

My feet led me unerringly to the nearest bar, the Claimant. It was quiet that evening, and Merrial was able to grab a corner seat while I bought a couple of pints and a brace of whiskies. By the empty fireplace a fiddler played and a woman sang, an aching Gaelic threnody of loss.

Merrial knocked back her whisky in one deft swallow, and summer returned to her face.

'Jesus!' she swore. 'I needed that. Give me a cigarette.'

I complied, gazing at her while lighting it, glancing covertly around while I lit my own. The pub, which I'd patronised throughout my student years, was a friendly and comfortable place, though its wall decorations could chill you a bit if you pondered on them: framed reproductions of ancient posters and notices and regulations about 'actively seeking employment' and 'receiving benefit'. It was something to do with living on public assistance, which is what many quite hale and able folk, known as claimants, had had to resort to in the days of the Possession, when land was owned by lairds and capital by usurers.

The usual two old geezers were recalling their first couple of centuries in voices raised to cope with the slight hearing impairment that comes with age; a gang of lads around a big table were gambling for pennies, and several pairs of other lovers were intent only on each other; and the singer's song floated high notes over them all.

'You were about to say?' I said. My own voice was shakier than Merrial's had been at any point in the whole incident. At the same time I felt giddy with relief at our escape, and a strange exciting mixture of dread and exaltation at the sure knowledge that my life was henceforth unpredictable.

'I wasn't,' Merrial said, 'but I'll tell you anyway. That thing we saw was the deil that guards the files. But,' she added brightly, 'blowing fuses for several blocks around was the worst it could do.'

'Hey, that's comforting.'

'Yes, it is,' she said, in a very definite tone. 'Better that than an electric shock that burns your hands or a fire that brings down the whole building. Or—'

'What?'

'I've heard of worse. Ones that attack your mind through your eyes.'

'And there you were laughing at the very idea, back at the yard.'

'Aye, well,' she said. 'It was just me that had to face them. No sense in getting you worried.'

'Oh, thanks.'

She took my hand. 'No, you were brave in there.'

'Ach, not a bit of it,' I agreed.

'So, after all, we didn't get much,' I said, returning to our table with refilled glasses about two minutes later. Outside, I could hear a growing commotion of militia rattles and whistles and fire-brigade bells. Somewhere across the street, a vehicle with a flashing light trundled slowly past.

Merrial looked up from riffling through the folders.

'Well, you got the 2050s and the 1990s,' she said. 'That's something. What *I* got –' she patted her bag, grinning '– was a whole lot more. Maybe everything, I don't know yet.'

I put the glasses down very carefully.

'The . . . um, barrier . . . didn't work, then?'

'Up to a point. Like I said, my machine, and the logic on it, are stronger than the other one. It just couldn't stop that thing from doing what it kept warning it *would* do. You can steal a bone from a dog if you ignore the barks and don't mind the bites.' In a less smug tone, she added, 'But it all depends on how much I pulled out before I had to . . .'

'Pull out!'

'Yes.'

'So what do we do now?' I looked down at the folders. 'I suppose I'll have to try and square things with Dr Gantry.' Confused thoughts fought in my mind, like those programs Merrial talked about. One sequence of impulses made me think through a scheme of grovelling apology and covering up and smoothing over. Another made me realise that I was almost certainly in very deep trouble with the University authorities, and had quite possibly affronted Gantry in ways that he might find hard to forgive.

'Oh, and how are you going to do that?' Merrial asked. 'I reckon he won't be too pleased about your running off with this lot.'

'That he won't,' I said gloomily. 'But I could always say I grabbed them to save them, or something, and that I'll return them in a few days. After photocopying them, of course. No, it's the other thing that'll have him pissed off. Heaven knows what damage that thing did – I doubt it was just a power cut. More like blown fuses all over the place, maybe worse. That'll be looked into, and not just by the University. And he's going to want to know who you are and what we were up to.'

'Hmm.' Merrial blew out a thin stream of smoke, observing it as though it were a divination. 'Well, seeing as he knows my name, and where I work . . . tell you what, colha Gree. Assume he does make a fuss, or somebody else asks questions. What I do not want getting out is that this has anything to do with the ship, or with . . . my folk. What we can say, and with some truth, is that you were led by excess of zeal to poke around in . . . the dark place. That you inveigled me into helping you. That you're very sorry, you got your fingers burned, and you won't do it again. And that of course the files you took will not be seen by anyone outside the community of scholars. Their *photocopies*, now, they might be seen, but you need say nothing of that.'

I had been thinking of counting Merrial as an honorary scholar in my own version of that bit of casuistry, but hers would do at a pinch. My two conflicting programs meshed: I was in trouble, yes, but I could get out of it, by the aforementioned grovelling and covering up.

The clock above the bar showed the time was a quarter past ten.

'I doubt Gantry's still around,' I said. 'And I don't know where he lives, or his phone number, if he has one. I suppose the best thing to do is see him in the morning, before we leave.' I took my return ticket from my pocket. 'Train leaves at forty minutes before noon. I'll be round to see him at nine, and try and straighten things out.'

Merrial nodded. 'Sound plan,' she said. She cocked an ear. 'Things seem to be quietening down, but I don't think wandering around back there would be a good idea right now.'

'D'you want to go back and check over what we've got?'

'*Dhia*, no! I've looked at enough of that for one day. I want to stay here and drink with you, and maybe dance with you – if a wee bit of siller can make that fiddler change his tune – and then go back to the lodging and test the strength of that bed with you.'

That is not what we should have done, I grant you; but are you surprised at all that it is what we did?

I sat on the steps outside the Institute, in the still, chill morning under the shadows of the great trees, and looked at my watch. Ten to nine. I sighed and lit another cigarette. A couple of hundred metres away a pneumatic drill started hammering. Brightly painted trestles and crossbeams and piles of broken tarmac indicated that some similar work had been done already during the night.

The path of power, indeed. One reason why it's called that is that electronic computation is inextricably and unpredictably linked to electrical power generation, and can disrupt it in expensive and dangerous ways. I had an unpleasant suspicion that the cost of all this was, one way or another, going to meander through some long system of City Council and University Senate accountancy, and arrive at my feet.

'Good morning, Clovis.' I looked up at Gantry. He had his pipe in one hand and a key in the other. 'Come on in.'

His office had a window that occupied most of one wall, giving a soothing view of a weed-choked back yard, and bookcases on the others. Every vertical surface in the room was stained slightly yellow, and every horizontal surface was under a fine layer of tobacco ash. I wiped ineffectually at the wooden chair in front of his desk while he sat down on the leather one behind it.

He regarded me for a moment, blinking; ran his fingers through his short hair; sighed and began refilling his pipe.

'Well, colha Gree,' he said, after a minute of intimidating silence, 'you have no idea how much my respect for you has increased by your coming here. When I saw you a moment ago, stubbing out your cigarette on the pavement, I thought, "Now, there's a man who knows to do the decent thing." Considerable improvement on your blue funk last night; considerable.'

I cleared my throat, vaguely thinking that whatever the doctors may say, there *must* be something harmful in a habit which makes your lungs feel so rough in the morning. 'Aye, well, Dr Gantry, it wasn't yourself I was afraid of.'

'Oh,' he said dryly, 'and what was it then, hmm?'

Without meaning to, I found my gaze drifting upward. 'It was, uh, the demon internet software that I'm afraid I and my friend, um, accidentally invoked.'

Gantry lit his pipe and sent out a cloud of smoke.

'Yes, I had gathered that. And what on earth possessed you – so to speak – to poke around in the dark storage when I'd just given you more than enough material for years of study?'

I met his gaze again. 'It was my idea,' I said. 'Call it – excess of zeal. I got the idea before you gave me the papers, of course, but even after that I thought we might as well go through with it. I'm afraid I was – rather blinded by the lust for knowledge.'

'And by another kind of lust, I shouldn't wonder,' Gantry said. 'This *friend* of yours, she's more than that, am I right?'

There seemed no point in denying it, so I didn't.

125

'All right,' he said. He jabbed his pipe-stem at me, thumbed the stubble on his chin, and gnawed at his lower lip for a moment. 'All right. First of all, let me say that the University administration has a job to do which is different from the self-administration of the academic community. It has to maintain the physical fabric of the place, and its supplies and services and so forth, and with the best will in the world I can't interfere with any measures of investigation *and discipline* which it may see fit to take in this unfortunate matter. You appreciate that, don't you?'

'Yes, of course.'

'Fine. Well . . . as to any academic repercussions, there I can speak up for you, I can . . . refrain from volunteering information about how the demonic outbreak took place. But I can't lie on your behalf, old chap. I'll do my best for you, because I think it would be a shame to throw away someone with so much promise over what, as you say, was excess of scholarly zeal. Very understandable temptation, and all that. Some of the Senatus might well think to themselves, "Been there, done that – young once myself – fingers burnt – learned his lesson – say no more about it," and all that sort of thing.'

I relaxed a little on the hard chair. I'd been fiddling with a cigarette for a while, unsure if I had permission to smoke; Gantry leaned over with his lighter, absently almost taking my eyebrows off with its kerosene flare.

'Thank you.'

'However,' he went on, leaning back in his own chair, 'there are some wider issues.' He waved his pipe about, vaguely indicating the surrounding shelves of hard-won knowledge. 'We British are beginning to get the hang of this civilisation game. When the Romans left, there wasn't a public library or a flush toilet or a decent road or a postman to be seen for a thousand years. When the American empire fell, I think we can honestly say we did a damn sight better, and indeed better than most. We lost the electronic libraries, of course, and a great deal of knowledge, but the infrastructure of civilisation pulled through the troubled times reasonably intact. In some respects, even improved. A great deal of that we owe to the very fact that the electronic records were lost – and along with them the chains of usury and rent, and the other . . . dark powers which held the world in what they even then had the gall to call "The Net".'

126

He stood up and ambled along to a corner and leaned his elbow on a shelf. 'What we have instead of the net is the tinkers.' He waved his hands again. 'And telephony and telegraphy and libraries and so forth, of course, but that's beside the point. The tinkers look after our computation, which even with the path of light most of us are . . . unwilling to do, because of what happened in the past, but are grateful there's somebody to do it. This makes them . . . not quite a pariah people, but definitely a slightly stigmatised occupation. And that very stigma, you see, paradoxically ensures – or gives some assurance of – the purity of their product. It keeps the two paths, the light and the dark, separate. You see what I'm driving at?'

'No,' I said. 'I'm afraid I don't.'

'Oh.' He looked a little disappointed at my slowness on the uptake. 'Well, not to put too fine a point on it, it's one thing for scholars to risk their own bodies or souls with the dark storage. Not done, so to speak, but between you and me and the gatepost, it *is* done. It's quite another for a tinker to do it. Could contaminate the seer-stones, y'see. Bad business.'

He stalked over and stared at me. 'The upshot, my friend, is that you had better get your tinker girlfriend back here with whatever she took, and get those file-folders you *borrowed* back here with it, if you want to have this episode overlooked. Clear?'

'Yes, but—'

'No "buts", Clovis. You don't have much time. Get out and get back before anyone else notices, that's the ticket.'

'I'll do what I can,' I said, truthfully enough, and left.

As I hurried back to the lodging I kept trying to think what the hell we could do. I'd been hoping to hang on to the paper files for at least a week, which should give me enough time to see if there was anything of urgent significance in them. There was no way, however, that Merrial could 'return' whatever computer files she had managed to retrieve. She could pretend to delete them from her seer-stone's memory, but I doubted if that would fool Gantry. He would want the stone itself, and she was most unlikely to give it to him.

The landlady let me in, because I'd left the outside door key with Merrial. I gave her a forced smile and ran up the stairs, and knocked on the door of the room where I'd left Merrial drowsing. No reply came, so I quietly opened the door.

Merrial wasn't there. Nor was anything that belonged to her. Nor were the two file-folders. I looked around, bewildered for a moment, and then remembered what Merrial had said about photocopying the documents. I felt weak with relief. I gathered up my own gear, checked again that there was nothing of ours left in the room, and went downstairs.

'Aye,' said the landlady, 'the lassie went out a wee while after you did. She left the key wi' me.'

'Did she ask about photocopying shops around here?'

'No. But there's only one, just around the corner. You cannae miss it.'

'Aw, thanks!'

I rushed out again and along the street and around the corner. The shop was there, sure enough, but Merrial wasn't. Nobody answering to her – fairly unmistakable – description had called.

I wandered down Great Western Road in a sort of daze, and stopped at the parapet of the bridge over the Kelvin. The other bridge, which we'd crossed on the tram, was a few hundred metres upstream; the ruins of an Underground station, boarded-off and covered with grim warnings, was on the far bank. The riverside fish restaurant, where we'd eaten last night, sent forth smells of deep-fried batter. The river swirled along, the ash of my anxious cigarette not disturbing the smallest of its ripples.

She could not have just gone off with the goods; I was loyal enough to her to be confident in her loyalty to me, and did not even consider – except momentarily, hypothetically – that she'd simply used me to get at the information she sought. The most drastic remaining possibility was that she had somehow been got at herself, and had left under some urgent summons, or duress. But the landlady would surely have noticed any such thing, so it couldn't have happened in the lodging.

Between there and the copy-shop, then. I formed a wild scheme of pacing the pavement, searching for a clue; of questioning passers-by. It seemed melodramatic.

More likely by far, I told myself, was that she'd simply gone somewhere for some reason of her own. She had her own return ticket. She'd expect me to have the sense to meet her at the station. I could picture us laughing over the misunderstanding, even if some frantic calls would have to be made to Gantry.

Or even, she could have gone to another copy-shop!

A militiaman strolled past, his glance registering me casually. I stayed where I was until he was out of sight, well aware that heading off at once would only look odd; and also aware that staring with a worried expression over a parapet at a twenty-metre drop into a river might make the least suspicious militiaman interested.

By then, naturally, I was wondering if she'd been arrested, for unauthorised access to the University, necromancy, or just on general principles; but then again, if she had been, it was not my worry on anything but a personal level: as a tinker, she'd have access to a good lawyer, just as much as I would, as a scholar.

So the end of my agitated thinking, and a look at my watch, which showed that the time was a quarter past ten, was to decide to go to the station and wait for her.

The train was due to leave at eleven-twenty. At five past eleven I put down my empty coffee-cup, stubbed out my cigarette and strode over to the public telegraph. There I tapped out a message: GANTRY UNIV HIST INST REGRET DELAY IN FILE RETURN STOP WILL CALL FROM CARRON STOP RESPECTS CLOVIS.

I was on the point of hitting the transmit key when I smelled the scent and sweat of Merrial behind me. Then she leaned past my cheek and said, in a warm, amused voice, 'Very loyal of you, to him and to me.'

I turned and grabbed her in my arms. 'Where the hell have you been?'

'Just fire off that message,' she said. 'I'll tell you on the train.' She was grinning at me, and I felt all worries fade as I hugged her properly, then stepped back to hold her shoulder at arm's length as though to make doubly sure she was there. Her poke looked even larger and heavier than before.

'You've got the paper files?'

'Yes,' she said, hefting the bag. 'Come on.'

I transmitted the message, and we dashed hand in hand down the platform. The train wasn't heavily used, and we found a compartment – half a carriage – to ourselves and swung down on to the seats and faced each other across the table, laughing.

'Well,' I said. 'Tell me about it. You had me a wee bit worried, I have to admit.'

She curled her fingers across the back of my hand. 'I'm sorry,' she said. 'But I thought it seemed like a good idea to disappear. That way, if Gantry or anyone else leaned on you to give the files or the, you know, other files back, you could honestly say you couldn't, you really wouldn't know where I was and would look genuinely flummoxed, say if they went so far as to come back to our room with you.'

'Oh, right. I was genuinely flummoxed, I'll give you that. But if anyone was with me they could have made the same guess as I did, and come to the station.'

She shrugged. 'I'd have kept out of sight.' She combed her fingers through a hanging fall of hair, smiling coyly. 'I'm no bad at that.'

'And caught the train at the last second?'

'Or something.' She didn't seem interested in raking over speculative contingencies. 'Anyway, we're here, and we've got the goods. Nothing Gantry can do to get them off us now.'

'Aye. Still, I'll have to wire him from Carron, reassure him they're in safe keeping.'

'Like you said. So it's all square.'

The train began to move. I looked out at the apparently shifting station and platform, gliding into the past in relative motion, then looked back at her.

'No,' I said. 'It isn't as straightforward as that.'

She listened to my account of what Gantry had said about the tinkers and the dark storage. When I'd finished she shook her head slowly.

'You should have just covered up about my being a tinker,' she said.

That was a shock. 'How could I?' I protested. 'He'd figured it already, and it would be easy enough to check. I didn't want to lie to him. Especially not lie and get found out as soon as he picked up a phone.'

Her mouth thinned. 'I suppose not. Fair enough. Your man's trust matters in the long run. And maybe even being evasive would've confirmed his suspicion.' She looked as if a weight had settled on her shoulders at that moment.

'I would have been evasive – Truth help me, I would have *lied* if you'd asked me!'

'I couldn't do that,' she said. 'Ach, this is so complicated!'

'Hey, it's all right,' I said. 'We'll think of something. I'll string

Gantry some kind of line, give us time to check out the files, and we'll have them back in a week. Take next Monday off too if I have to.'

Merrial's eyes suddenly brimmed. She blinked hard.

'*Dhia*, I hope it's that easy!' She sighed. 'I wish I could tell you more right now.' She shook her head. 'But I can't.'

'Why not?'

'Oh, *mo chridhe*! I'm a tinker, and tinkers have to mind their tongues. Even if – especially if – their tongues are spending time in other mouths!'

'So you have secrets of your craft,' I said dryly, 'which you have to keep. That's all right with me.'

She looked as if she were about to say something urgent, and then all she said was, 'I shouldn't worry so much. It'll probably all turn out all right.'

'Yes, sure,' I said, pretending to agree with her. 'Oh, well. Shall we have a look at the files, then?'

'OK,' she said, pulling them out. 'Tell you what. You can look through the early one, and I'll look through the late. That'll increase the chances that either of us will find something we can *understand*.'

'Fair enough,' I said.

I opened the folder from the 1990s and flipped impatiently through thoroughly dull and worthy stuff about medical charity, and some fascinatingly improbable economic statistics from Kazakhstan. Towards the end I found something more personal: pages ripped from a spiral-bound notebook, apparently a diary. I pored over the Deliverer's scrawl:

Thurs Jul 16 98. Trawl of NYC's remaining left bookshops – nostalgia, I guess. Picked up *Against the Current* in St Mark's – trendy place, left pubns marginalised, seems apt. The old Critique clique still banging on – Suzi W in AtC, etc. At least they're loyal – unlike moi, huh. Then trekked over to Revo Bks – Avakian's lot, madder than ever. They have a dummy electric chair in the shop for their Mumia campaign. Flipped through old debates on SU etc. Depressing thought 'Marxism is a load of crap' kept coming to mind. Then Unity Books on W 23d. Couldn't bear going to Pathfinder. After my little adventure, not sure I want to face the Fourth International cdes either. Or they me. Agh.

Fri Jul 17 98. Hot humid afternoon, rainstorm later. Met M on Staten Isl ferry. Leaned on the rail and looked at old Liberty thro near fog. M seems to know I'm telling the old gang about his approaches. Thing is he doesn't seem to mind. (Girl with pink hair on the ferry. *Swear* same girl was in Boston. Am I being followed or getting paranoid?)

I couldn't make head nor tail of this, and turned over to the last of the entries.

Thurs Dec 17 98. Almaty again. Hotel lounge TV tuned permanently to CNN. Green light of city falling in the night. Hospital filling up. Fucking Yanks. Here I am trying to help development, there they are trying to roll it back.

After that, nothing but a stain and an angry scribble, where the pen had dug into and torn the page. Perhaps she'd reached the end of that notebook, or stopped keeping a diary. I leafed through the rest of the papers, with an oppressive feeling that seeing through their present opacity would take even longer than I'd thought. Then an idly turned page brought me to a stop.

It was a photocopy of an old article she'd written, but it was a small advertisement accidentally included at its margin that caught my eye. It was for a public meeting on 'Fifty Years of the Fourth International' and it had in one corner a symbol which was identical to the monogram on Merrial's pendant. It was all I could do not to knock my forehead or cry out at my own stupidity. What I'd thought were the letters 'G' and 'T' were in fact the hammer and sickle of the communist symbol, and the meaning of the '4' was self-evident. I'd missed the connection just because the symbol faced in the opposite direction to the one on the Soviet flag.

The sinister significance of the hammer and sickle made me feel slightly nauseous; the implication of that same symbol appearing across such a gulf of time induced a certain giddiness.

I closed the file and looked up, and found myself meeting Merrial's equally baffled eyes.

'It's all either not very interesting, or completely fucking incomprehensible,' she said.

'Same here,' I said. 'Let's leave it.'

All that long afternoon, we talked about other things.

Battles, mostly, as I recall.

*

132

The train pulled into the station at Carron Town on the dot of six. The sun was still high, the late afternoon still warm. Once again tired and jaded by our journey, Merrial and I left the train with an access of energy and a surge of hunger. Merrial led the way straight to The Carronade, and we settled into a dark corner of the strangely polished-smelling bar with plates of farmed trout and fresh-picked peas and new potatoes, accompanied with a shared jug of beer.

'I can't wait to get back to your place,' I said, 'get a bit of privacy, and get my face right down into . . . the files.'

She laughed. 'Aye, it'll be great to get a good look at them at last, without having to look over our shoulders.'

But as she said it she was looking over my shoulder, as she had done every minute or so all through the meal. She had her back to the wall, I had my back to the bar. The pub was beginning to fill up with people from the project, in for a quick drink on their way home or to their lodgings. As yet I'd heard no voices I recognised.

'You seem a wee bit on edge,' I said.

'Aye, well, like I said on the train . . .'

'Fergal?'

'Yes.'

'You're expecting to meet him here?' I asked, remembering that we were in this bar on her – albeit welcome – suggestion.

She opened her hands. 'Maybe. Depends.'

'On what?' I piled up our empty plates and lit a cigarette.

'Och, on how they want to play it,' she said, sounding unaccustomedly bitter.

'Secrets or no secrets,' I said, trying to keep my tone light, 'you're going to have to let me in on this, sooner or later. I'm getting thoroughly tired of seeing you looking worried.'

'I don't *have* to do anything!' she flared. 'And you don't *have* to see me looking like anything!'

I said nothing, staring at her, shocked and annoyed but already forgiving her; she'd been under a lot of tension, for reasons I knew about and reasons I knew I didn't.

'Ach,' she said, gentle again, 'I didn't mean that, colha Gree. You've not been taught as I have, to be hard.'

At that I had to smile; she seemed more vulnerable than hard, at that moment. Her eyes widened. I heard a footstep behind us, and then Fergal swung uninvited on to the bench beside me.

133

'Hello,' Merrial said, not warmly. Her glance returned to me.

'Oh, hi,' I said. He looked at our drinks. 'My round, I think.' He reached back over his shoulder and snapped his fingers; most people wouldn't have gotten away with that, but he did. In half a minute the barmaid was laying another full jug on the table.

'So, Merrial,' he said quietly, 'you got it?'

'We did,' said Merrial. 'As far as I can tell. I checked through it all this morning, and it's the whole archive.'

'And where did you do that?' I butted in, a little indignantly.

'Kelvin Wood,' Merrial said, giving me a disarmingly unabashed grin. 'In the bushes.'

'So that's what you were up to.'

Merrial nodded, with a flash of her eyebrows. Fergal looked at her, then at me, as though to remind us that he had more important things on his mind.

'Fine,' I said.

'That's good news,' Fergal said, to Merrial. He laughed briefly. 'To put it mildly, eh?'

'Aye,' she said. 'It is that.'

'Anyway, Clovis,' Fergal said, 'you'll appreciate that the information you've helped to retrieve needs to be looked at with an expert eye. Rather urgently, in fact, considering how long it may take.'

'Of course,' I said. 'Any chance that I could take a look at it first, just glance through it?'

He shook his head. 'Sorry, Clovis. You have no idea – no offence – of how much is there. It's an incredible quantity of not very well organised information. In the time it would take for you to make sense of any of it, we could be searching for information we *know* how to interpret. Every hour might count.'

'Just a minute!' I said, dismayed and indignant. 'Nobody mentioned anything about this. I want to get a look at them too, and not have them disappear into—'

'Some tinker hideaway?' Fergal raised his eyebrows. 'It won't be like that, I assure you. You have my word that we won't keep them long – weeks at the most – and that you'll get to see them and search them at your leisure as soon as we've finished.'

'But,' I said, 'how will I know they haven't been changed – even accidentally? Because I have to be able to rely on it.'

Merrial was looking desperately uncomfortable. She gave Fergal a quick, hot glare and leaned closer to me across the table.

'Think about it, man,' she said quietly. 'This stuff is all illicit anyway – you could not exactly cite it in footnotes, could you? You can only use it to find leads to material you *can* refer to. So you'll just have to trust us – trust me – that the information won't be tampered with.'

'All right,' I said reluctantly.

'Good man!' He drained his glass and stood up. 'Thanks for your help.' Fergal reached out a hand across the table. Merrial was already emptying her personal clutter out of the leather bag. She tightened its thong and passed it over; Fergal had caught it while I was still gazing, puzzled, at Merrial's actions.

'Wait!' I said. 'The paper files are still in there. You can't take them!'

Fergal raised his eyebrows. 'Why not?'

'These papers belong to the University.'

'I'm afraid they don't,' said Fergal, sounding regretful. 'They belong to us.'

I looked frantically at Merrial, who only gave a small, sad nod.

'Who the fuck is this "us"?' I demanded, though I already suspected the answer. 'Come on, I can give you photocopies if you must.'

'Not good enough, old chap.'

'Then give me them back.'

'Sorry,' said Fergal. 'I can't.'

I shifted on my feet, moved my elbow; all by reflex. Fergal's eyes narrowed.

'Don't,' he said very quietly, 'even *think* of messing with me.'

I was actually thinking of yelling out and calling on the others in the bar, some of whom had their eye on this confrontation. But something in Fergal's stance and glance suggested that the only outcome of such a brawl would be his escape after inflicting some severe damage on our side, starting with me. And whichever side Merrial came in on, or even if she tried to stay out of it, she was likely to get hurt.

My honour wasn't at stake in preventing Fergal's departure with the papers – it would be at stake in getting them back – and for now I had no right to risk life and limb of myself or others over it.

'Take it, tinker,' I said. 'I can bide.'

He smiled, without condescension.

'I hope I see you again,' he said, and was out the door.

I looked over at a few curious, tense faces at the bar, shrugged and returned to the table, where Merrial was shakily lighting one of my cigarettes.

'Some explanation might be in order,' I said, as casually as I could manage. One of my knees was vibrating.

Merrial took a long breath and a long draw with it.

'Sorry,' she said. 'I can't, really.'

'But look,' I said. 'Why didn't you just tell me to hide the files, or say we'd put them back—'

I was getting exasperated and confused, and then the penny, finally, dropped.

'You agree with him!' I said. 'You actually *agree* that he has some kind of a *right* to those papers, and to see the files first, and that nobody else can so much as look at them without his sufferance. Including me.'

She looked levelly back at me.

'And you're not going to tell me why.'

A small shake of her head.

'And you knew all along this could happen.'

A smaller nod.

'All right,' I said. There were still two half-litres in the jug; I poured for both of us, and lit a cigarette myself, leaning forward into Merrial's smoke, almost into the tent of her hair. 'All right.' The heel of my hand was rubbing beneath my eye; irritated with myself, I stopped doing that and fiddled with the cigarette instead. The sound of the laughter and conversation at the bar was like the noise of a burn over a rock, washing over and hiding our talk. We could say anything.

'I'm really at a loss,' I said. 'I can't believe you just set me up, but unless you tell me what's really going on—'

'I told you,' she said. 'I can't. Can't you trust me on that?'

'Oh, I can trust you on that all right,' I said. 'But if I don't get those files back like I promised, nobody at the University will ever trust me again.'

She looked as tense, as torn, as I felt.

'I'm very sorry about that,' she said. 'But there's nothing I can do about it.'

'Come on,' I said. 'There must be. Hell, if I get the files back, I can give your lot copies of all the files. Isn't that worth more to them than just what they've got?'

'You don't understand,' Merrial said. 'Now that we know about the other files, we're going to have to get them all. Like Fergal said, they're ours.'

'Ours', indeed! I was unwilling, or unready, to challenge her about the society to which that might refer. I spread my hands. 'You can't expect me to accept that without a damn good reason, which you're not giving me.'

'I've told you. I can't. So why don't we just forget about all this?'

'Merrial,' I pleaded, dismayed at the depths of her lack of understanding, 'these files are part of my work, my whole career depends on them. So, please—'

I reached out, touching her hair.

Her eyes glinted.

'Oh, *fuck off*!' she told me, not quite a yell but loud and emphatic enough to turn heads.

'I'll do that,' I replied, and rose and stalked out. I glanced back from the door, and saw only the top of her head, and the forward fall of her hair, and her hands over her face. The door swung shut behind me.

8

Western Approaches

'It's over,' Valentina was saying.

'What's over?' Myra asked. She shook her head, looking around her office. Val and Andrei and Denis were all there, perched on desks or window sills. The command-centre screens had vanished like a dream. Parvus hovered on the edge of her vision, looking as though about to speak.

'The *putsch*,' Valentina explained.

'Just like that?'

Myra stared, blinking through options presented by Parvus. The personal had its own analysis, and it was busy agreeing with Valentina. The battlesats seized by the space movement were enough to guard their beleaguered enclaves and launch sites, but not to tilt the balance of world power in their favour. The Security Council nations retained their control over the ReUN, but the battlesats that had resisted the coup had done so in their own name, not that of the ReUN. They remained dangerously autonomous.

At ground level all sorts of local balances had been tilted, almost entirely by the rapid re-evaluations of the real weight on the various sides that the bloody flurries of actual combat had induced. Disputes had been resolved or reopened, entire armies had mobilised or disbanded on the strength of the gigantic shadows thrown on the screens of analysis by the small engagements in the field.

'God,' said Myra disgustedly. 'This is *so* decadent.' It reminded her of the Renaissance mercenaries that Machiavelli had moaned about in the *Discourses*, working out who would have won if they'd fought and abiding by that decision like gentlemen, while omitting the bloody business of actual battle. 'Nobody wants a real fight, they'd rather follow the sims. Talk about the pornography of violence. Wankers.'

'It's worse than that,' Denis said coarsely. 'We're fucked.' He threw a projection of a time-slice from *Jane's* and laser-pointed the relevant areas. 'Look.'

The ISTWR's military profile and general credibility was no longer something that cautious strategists, estimating from past actions and present rumour, rated highly. It was negligible.

'We've been found out,' said Denis Gubanov. 'In exactly the wrong way. They must have always reckoned with at least the possibility that we had nukes. Mutual Protection – or Reid, anyway – knew we had them. Point is, we didn't use them, so it's assumed we either don't have them or don't have the stomach to use them. We've gone from being Upper Volta with nukes to being Upper Volta without. And the weapons we did use didn't work.'

'They worked—' Valentina began, rather defensively.

'Huh!' Myra snorted. 'They worked just fine, only they didn't destroy the targets. Yeah, I can see that doing our deterrence posture a power of good.'

The hotline phone – a solid, old-fashioned, unambiguous red phone on Myra's desk – began to ring. She looked at it doubtfully for a moment, then shrugged and picked it up.

'Myra Godwin-Davidova.'

Pause.

'Hello, Myra. Dave here.'

She gave him a moment of nonplussed silence.

'Myra? It's *David Reid*.'

'Yes. Hello,' she said. 'What do you want now?'

There was a second's delay in his reply.

'What do you want, is more like it.' Even over the crackly laser-to-landline link, she could hear his fury. 'You had the whole situation in the balance, you know that? You had the fucking *casting vote*, Chairman Davidova! You had the nuclear option, and you threw it away! I'd almost rather you had used your goddamn nukes against us – at least that way the Security Council would have had control, and would've had to take responsibility. There'd be some chance of an end to the chaos, which is all we really wanted. As it is you've turned what should've been the endgame into another fucking stalemate.'

'I don't see how that makes you any worse off.'

She heard a knocking noise and realised after a moment that he was banging something on his head.

'It's made us *all* worse off! It's like entropy, Myra, can't you see that? Everybody's climbed up a few flights, *escalated*, that's the fucking word for it. We're all higher up but relatively we're no better placed, and we've lost energy, wasted work in the process. And you know the only people who'll gain from that? The marginals, the fucking barb, that's who. Including your local godless communists.'

'It's you who should have thought of that. Before you launched your bloody coup.'

Reid took a deep breath, a long sigh down the wire.

'Yeah, you're right. It is my fault. Didn't expect a counter-coup, that's all.'

'What counter-coup?'

Again the odd delay.

'Don't play the innocent. Somebody's taken over most of the battle-sats, and it sure wasn't my lot. Nor the UN's, come to that.'

'You don't know who it was?'

'No. So who was it? You must know.'

Myra thought about this. Ah, hell, he'd find out anyway.

'The Fourth International,' she told him. 'Space fraction, mil org.'

A second ticked past, then she heard Reid's loud laugh. 'Ha-ha-ha! OK, Myra, be like that. I'll find out anyway. Meanwhile, take a look at the north-eastern border, and see if it all still seems so funny. I'm well out of it – I'm on a shuttle for Lagrange. Bye.'

He closed the connection in some manner that sounded like slamming down the receiver on an old-fashioned phone, with an impact that made her wince.

Before she could look at the north-eastern border, Parvus stepped into frame and raised a hand. Myra gestured to the others to wait.

'Yes?'

The stout phantom waved his hands expansively. 'Ah, Myra, I have had to move fast on your investments. I received the hot inside tip –' he laid a yellowed finger to his ruddy nose '– that Mutual Protection are liquidating their assets.'

'What!' Myra had by this time got so used to 'assets' being a euphemism for 'nukes' that she almost ducked under the desk. Her startled gaze raced down the latest news bulletin – nothing.

'Oh, you mean *financially*.'

'Of course financially. When the last war starts I will tell you straight. No, Mutual Protection are selling up, pulling out.'

'Pulling out from where?'

'From here. From Kazakhstan.' He looked at her sadly, almost sympathetically. 'From Earth.'

Over the next few days it became clear that the main gainers from the brief lurch into actual violence were the marginals, who took their own advantage of the distraction – and Mutual Protection's hasty liquidation – to expand their domains in country after country; and the Sheenisov.

They made a push along the pass at Zaysan, to the south-east. Kazakhstani long-range bombers pounded the Sino-Soviet combat drones – devices of unsettling and diverse appearance, combinations of almost Soviet mechanical clunkiness with quasi-organic nanotech sheen. Their wrecks, or corpses, littered the roads and hillsides outside Buran. Any functioning components had a disturbing tendency to reassemble. The Kazakhstani bombing-runs stopped as supplies of bombs began to run out. Sheenisov *spetsnatz* teams – casting hologram feints, radar ghosts, sonic body-doubles – skirmished among the wreckage and dug in at the furthest limit of their advance. Meanwhile, a tank-borne human army, or horde, was outflanking the Altay Mountains at the northern end of the range: rolling south and west from the Katun basin, and down the road and railway from Barnaul, unopposed. By the end of the fourth day after the coup attempt they'd crossed Kazakhstan's northern border, and paused.

The *oblys* council in Semipalatinsk – evidently softened by intimidation or subversion – invited them in, and they cheerfully accepted the invitation. They rode in like liberators, welcomed by cheering crowds, and settled down with every appearance of being there to stay.

The red phone rang again.

'Chingiz Suleimanyov,' the caller identified himself. The current President of Kazakhstan; his nickname of 'Genghis President' was not quite fair. 'I have a proposal for your government, Madame Davidova, and for you personally . . .'

The following morning Myra got up and dressed, and packed. She had most of her luggage sent on to the airport. She loaded stacks of old files, in formats going back all the way through floppy disks to actual paper, into a couple of crates, sealed and diplomatic-bagged and sent off to another destination. Then she began stripping her flat, with a kind of rage at herself. She commandeered some kids from the militia to take the stuff down the stairs – physically, she wasn't up to that, and she knew it.

The bedroom's contents went first, all the cushions and throws, the tatting and trim, the lacework and lacquer and lapis lazuli – out, all of it, into big black plastic sacks that went straight to the nearest craft-market stall for a derisory sum. Let them make their own way again, let them travel the circuits like trade-goods, like cowrie shells and crated Marlboros, back to the Camden Locks and Greenwich Villages of the world. The posters on the walls went next, to another stall, for other collectors. The vinyl records and the compact discs – that was what they were called, she thought with a smile, as she hefted their stacked bulk – to a third.

And then the books. That did hurt, but she went on with it; grimly, grimily hauling them down from their shelves, sorting and stacking. Again and again tempted to sift, to stray; now and again lost in a book, or in the reminiscences it provoked. Blink, knuckle the eye, slam the covers shut, sneeze out the dust, move on. Her eyes reddened, her fingers blackened and her shoulders ached.

Most of the books, too, went to the bazaar. The remainder she had loaded in the back of a small truck. She washed herself and looked around the echoing emptiness of her flat. It was still habitable; it was a place to which she could return; but in it nothing of herself remained.

She shoved her 2045 Library of Congress and her other libraries and concert halls, art galleries and archives into the top of her overnight bag, and distributed her knives and pistols about her belts and pockets. The lads who'd lugged her stuff to the market came back one by one, with sheaves of money. She peeled off more than enough to pay them, one by one.

The truck with the books went ahead of her, well ahead, as she hefted her overnight bag and herself on to the horse, and rode out for the last time to the camp.

'Open up!'

Myra yelled, rattling the iron gate. The truck had parked itself in front, waiting with robotic patience for the obstacle to clear. Any electronic pleas it had made had evidently been ignored.

Myra could see why. There wasn't much left of the camp but the fence, and away to one side – too far away to be useful for her – she could see men taking it apart with wire-cutters and rolling it up in great bales and wheels. Nothing but grass and roadway stretched ahead of her for a few hundred metres. Where the huts had been she could see only clumps of dark material on the steppe, with men and women wandering around and children racing about. The factories were not gone, but they were visibly shrivelling, as though their construction were being run in reverse.

She flipped down her eyeband, upped the gain, gazed at the scene. Nobody'd heard her shouts. Damn. She eased her old New Vietcong knock-off Glock from its holster, steadied and soothed the horse, and fired not into the air but carefully at a tussock a few tens of metres distant. The mare shied and the bullet ricocheted anyway, but the shot got the result she wanted. A figure detached itself from the milling crowd and marched towards her. Kim Nok-Yung, carrying a rifle.

'Hi, Myra.' He couldn't stop smiling. He tapped a code into the lock's plate. The gate creaked open, and he left it open. Myra led the horse through, and the truck followed, then kept pace beside her. Nok-Yung hopped on the running-board and hung on with one hand, flourishing the rifle triumphantly with the other, as if he was riding a tank into a liberated capital.

'Isn't this great!'

She got caught up in his enthusiasm.

'Yes, it's wonderful. I'm so glad it's over, Nok-Yung.'

They passed one of the factories, vanishing before their eyes, crumbling back from its edges into curiously ordered dust, dust that trickled like columns of ants along paths on the remaining machinery, or on the grass. Some of the dust heaped itself up into blocky stacks that hardened into colour-coded cubes, inert, from which the wind blew not a speck. Other lines of dust coalesced into glassy spheroids, obsidian-black or crystal-clear, that lay in the tall grass like gleaming pebbles and stones and boulders.

'Control components, computers and so on,' Nok-Yung indicated. 'The cubes are construction material.'

'Will anyone collect them, I wonder?'

The Korean laughed. 'We'll take some of the control parts with us – they might be valuable, where we're going.'

'Oh?'

He glanced sidelong at her, almost apologetic. 'Semipalatinsk,' he said. 'To the Sheenisov.'

Myra restrained herself from reining in the horse. 'What? Why, for God's sake?' She waved an arm, wildly, around and behind. 'You can stay with us – you're welcome here, in our republic or anywhere in Kazakhstan. Hey, man, Baikonur will take you on, think of that!'

He shook his head. 'Some of the prisoners will settle here, of course. But I and Se-Ha and the others, we are going to the Sheenisov. Some of us have friends and family with them already. There is no other place for us. Even with Mutual Protection –' he turned aside and spat on the grass '– gone, we still have the debts, and the black-lists. No work to be had back home but debt-bondage. Among the Sheenisov we will be free.' He grinned, no longer apologetic but feral. 'And there is work to be done there – work for us. They are the future.'

'But you don't know anything about what they're really like. Just because they call themselves communists doesn't mean they're *nice* – you should know that!'

Nok-Yung laughed harshly. 'They have no Great Leader or Dear Leader, you can love it or leave it, and we're going to try it.'

By this time they had reached the edge of the crowd. Myra reined in the horse and signalled the truck to stop. Nok-Yung jumped off the running-board. What had seemed from a distance like aimless wandering resolved itself into people moving about purposefully, retrieving and stacking their possessions from the self-disassembling huts. Most of them ignored her arrival. Myra was not surprised or put out. The benefits of her oversight were easy enough to overlook, and the camp committee itself was not a popular body among the prisoners, elected though it was. Like a company union, it had partially represented the interests of the labourers, while often enough relaying the will of the owners.

She noticed Shin Se-Ha, dapper in a sadly dated *sarariman* suit which he'd probably worn for the first and last time at his trial, but which for now signified his new freedom. He carried a small case through the scooting children and trudging adults. By now other vehicles and beasts were trundling or plodding into view, summoned by phones restored to their proper owners.

Myra stood, fondling the mare's neck, quieting it, as the Japanese mathematician picked his way towards her. She tried to search her

144

memory of what he'd been sent down for: misuse of company resources or some such pretext – he'd run refinements of Otoh's neo-Marxian capital-reproduction schemata, primed with empirical data, on the university's computers. The real reason was his results, which he'd indiscreetly spread-sheeted around: the sinister algebra of the Otoh equations added up to complete breakdown in two more business-cycles.

That had been one boom and one slump ago.

'Hello, Myra,' he said. He put the case down. Probably contained all he owned, he was that sort of guy. Frightening, in his way.

'Hi, Se-Ha. Nok-Yung tells me you're going –' she nodded forward '– East.'

'I am. Sorry if you do not approve.'

Very direct! The sun shone in her face like an interrogation-lamp and the wind made a constant white noise. It was a time for telling the truth or facing worse ordeals.

'Whether I approve or not is not the point,' she said. 'You're free, and I have no say in what you do. But I should warn you that the Kazakhstani Republic will resist the Sheenisov, and so will I. We will not be rolled over. I would be sorry to be on the opposite side to you in a battle, but—'

She shrugged.

'I would be sorry too,' said Shin. 'But "so it goes", *ah-so?*'

'*Ah-so* indeed,' she smiled, and suddenly realised how Reid had been able to keep up his no-hard-feelings enmities for so long. 'Meanwhile, I have something for you.' She waved a hand at the truck. 'This, and everything in it.' She tossed him the truck's control-panel, which he deftly caught. 'Go on, have a look.'

Doors clicked open, banged shut. He came back. He caught her hand; he bowed over it, as though about to kiss her knuckles, and stepped back.

'I am in your debt,' he said, stiffly. Then he spread his hands, looking Western and abashed rather than Eastern and indebted. 'What can I say, Myra? You're very kind.'

'Ah, don't be silly, my friend,' she said. 'You and Nok-Yung and the others made my work here a lot more rewarding than it would otherwise have been. I owe you it, if anything.' She shared with him a conspiratorial chuckle. 'And a library of revolutionary theory might just come in handy where you're going, eh?'

145

'Yes. I don't know if I can take the responsibility.' He shook his head, thinking about it. 'There are books and documents in that van which have *never been scanned in.*'

Myra patted a pocket. 'Not even in the 2045 Library of Congress?'

'Not even that!' He seemed to find the thought awesome, a violation of the order of nature. It gave pause even to Myra's resolution, as half a lifetime's easy assumption that everything was archived, that every jot and tittle lived unchanged in silicon heaven, was suddenly confronted with the reality that some thoughts might only face eternity in the frail ark of woodpulp, and that she was responsible for them. Her commitment rallied.

'Oh, well. I should have read them by now, and if not, it's too late for me.'

The bustle around them was increasing. Vehicles were whining, horses and camels were whinnying and spitting. Some children, even some adults, were in tears at leaving this place, which for all its duress had not imposed any too severe privation, and which was familiar. Some folk were assiduously picking up the glassy stones, whether as talismans or as trade-trinkets Myra couldn't tell. The thousands of former prisoners were dispersing to all the round horizon.

Half a dozen other men were converging on where she stood, gathering around, talking in Korean or Japanese, smiling at her and climbing into the back of the truck. Nok-Yung came up and shook hands.

'We'll keep in touch.'

There was so much to say, so much that could not be said.

'We'll meet again,' Myra said. 'All the best, guys. Good luck with the commies.'

'Hah!' Nok-Yung raised a clenched fist and grinned at her. 'You'll be with us some day, Myra, you'll see. Goodbye, and thanks!'

He threw his bag in the truck and sprang into the driving-seat, then laughed as Shin Se-Ha climbed through the opposite door and flourished the control-panel under his nose. Still shouting and waving, the men drove off, bumping across the steppe, resolutely north-east.

Myra watched them out of sight and then mounted her horse and rode back to the town. Only once did she look behind, and saw that there was nothing left to see.

The airport of the capital of the International Scientific and Technical Workers' Republic had only one terminal building. It was a big,

146

open-plan space, dotted with franchises. They'd never bothered with Customs, or Immigration Control. Between the floor-to-ceiling windows – with their charming views of steppe, runway, apartment-blocks, gantries and more steppe – hung equally gigantic posters of Trotsky, Korolev, Kapitsa, Gagarin and Guevara. The idea, many years ago, had been to make the concourse look Communist: a bit of macho swagger. Right now it had the look of a place about to *fall* to the com-mies, rather to Myra's disgust. Crowded with people sitting on too much luggage, their expressions flickering between impatience and resignation with every change on the departure screens. For heaven's sake, thought Myra – Semipalatinsk was a hundred miles away, they were over-reacting.

Her own flight's departure-time was not for another hour. She con-firmed her booking at the check-in, made sure her luggage was on board, and declined the offer of waiting in the first-class lounge. Instead she made her way to the old Nicafe franchise, and sat down with a coffee and a cigarette, to rest her feet and indulge in a little nostalgia.

In the good old days before the Third World War she'd sipped many a coffee here, with many a man on the other side of the table. Always a different man, and almost never one that she'd liked: ugly, jowly military men for the most part, jet-lagged and stubbled, in creased dress uniforms heavily medallioned; or diplomats or *biznesmen*, sleek and shaven and cologned in silk suits. And always, hanging around a few metres away, outside the glowering ring of bodyguards, would be the photographers and reporters, there to record the closing of the deal. The ISTWR had never gone for secret diplomacy – openness was the whole point of tradable nuclear deter-rence.

It had worked fine, until the nuclear war.

The Germans had launched the War of European Integration with-out a nuke to call their own. This hadn't been an oversight – it had been essential to the element of surprise. Once their first wave of tanks was safely over the Polish border they'd made Myra a very gen-erous offer for some of her tradable nuclear deterrence. Myra's frantic ringing around her clients had found no one willing to deal: not for any amount of money, on the entirely rational basis that the Third World War was not a good time to sell. Myra had considered cutting them out and selling the Germans the option anyway, but her business

147

loyalty had got the better of her. It had also got the better of the German occupiers of Kiev, and the German civilians of Frankfurt and Berlin. She still felt guilty about that.

For want of company, she flipped down her eyeband and summoned Parvus. For a laugh, she sat his virtual image in the seat across the table from her. The construct triangulated his apparent position, saw the joke and smiled.

'What can I do for you, Myra?'

'Tell me what you think of the General.' She wasn't bothered by appearing to talk to empty air; she wasn't the only person in that café area consulting a familiar or a fetch.

'That is a tricky one,' said Parvus. He ran his fingers through his thatch, rummaged in his crumpled jacket for cigarettes. Lit up and relaxed; the addictive personality was part of the package, an aspect of how the thing hung together. 'There are of course rumours –' dismissive smoketrail '– that the FI has long had access to a rogue AI. Or the other way round, according to its opponents.' Parvus showed his teeth. 'It goes back to when AIs of that sophistication were rare – before the Revolution, or the Singularity.'

'This is the Singularity?' It was Myra's turn to wave a cigarette. 'Not like you'd notice.'

'It's one of these things you don't notice, when you're in the middle of it,' agreed Parvus. 'Like the mass extinction event that's going on around us right now.'

'But that's slow, that's the point. The Singularity's supposed to be fast on something more than a geological scale.'

'It was.'

'Oh.' She wasn't sure she wanted to take this discussion any further. 'Anyway, back to the General, and what you make of him.'

'Ah, yes. Well. Very dangerous, in my opinion. His use of face and voice is remarkably effective at getting under the skin of . . . people with skin. Count yourself lucky he can't use pheromones, at least not over the net.'

'You're impervious to his charm yourself, I take it.'

'Yes,' Parvus sighed. 'Fortunately for me, I lack self-awareness.'

Myra was still gaping at her familiar's unexpected remark – surely ironic, though she wasn't sure on what level – when Parvus's place was occupied by a Kazakh man with smooth clothes and a lined face. He had a distracting small child in tow, and a silently accusing puffy-eyed woman behind him. The woman took another chair, held the squirming toddler in her lap.

Myra blinked Parvus out of her sight, vaguely hoping that the AI wasn't offended, raised her eyeband and smiled at the man and his family. His returning smile was forced.

'Good morning, Madame President. Why are you leaving us?'

Myra looked around. Nobody else seemed to have noticed her. The cult of personality was another strategic omission from their socialist democracy. Just as well – she didn't want to be mobbed on her departure. 'I'm not leaving you,' she said earnestly, leaning forward and speaking as though confidentially. Her mission had not yet been publicly announced, but she had no objection to starting a truthful rumour in advance. Only the details were sensitive, and at that level secrecy was pointless – she was confident that her full itinerary was already circulating the nets, buried among hundreds of spurious versions, all of equally authoritative provenance. 'I'm going to the West, to get help. Economic and military assistance.'

The man looked sceptical. 'Against the Sheenisov? But we haven't a chance, against them. We have no defensible borders.'

'No, but Kazakhstan has – and it's on behalf of Kazakhstan that I'm going.'

'For Chingiz?' The man's face brightened; he glanced at his wife, as though to cheer her up. 'So we are going to drive the Reds out of Semey?'

'We can't bomb Semey,' Myra said, repeating exactly President Suleimanyov's words to her. 'But we can hold the pass east of Lake Zaysan, and we can stop any further advance in the north-east. If we get help soon. The SSU forces are unlikely to try anything for some weeks, because they're stretched. And they don't like frontal fighting. As long as the Kazakhstani Republic stays hostile to them, they won't come in.' She grinned encouragingly. 'And I can be sure our own republic will stay hostile.'

She was not sure at all. There was enough social discontent, understandable enough, in her redundant workers' state for the Sino-Soviets to work on. No doubt the first agitators were already drifting in, among the first refugees from Semipalatinsk. But the man took her words to heart.

'Yes,' he said, adding, 'if Allah wills. But we are leaving, with all we have.'

'I can't blame you,' Myra said. 'I wish you well. I hope you see your way clear to come back, when things are more . . . settled.'

'Perhaps.' The man shrugged, the woman smiled thinly, the child suddenly bawled. They departed, looking up disconsolately at the screens, leaving Myra depressed.

The man had looked like a small trader, one of the large middle class raised by the republic's mixed economy. Despite all the devils it painted on its walls, the ISTWR had always stood more for a permanent NEP than a permanent revolution: only its defence and space industries were state-owned, and apart from the welfare system everything else (which in GNP terms didn't add up to much, she had to admit) was more or less *laissez-faire*. She wondered what the family had to fear from the Sheenisov, who by all accounts would have left their property and piety alone. In a way it was not surprising: the Sheenisov had made their advances by bluff and intimidation, by looking and sounding more radical and communistic than they actually were, and their absence from the comms net left a great blank screen for the most sinister speculations to play on. So perhaps this kind of unwarranted fear was the price of their progress.

Well, she would make them pay a higher price, in a harder currency. She drained her coffee and headed for the departure lounge.

At Almaty she picked up her documents, diplomatic passport and line-of-credit card in a snazzy Samsonite Diplock handed over by a courier, and on the flight to Izmir she sifted through them. The papers were literally for her eyes only, being coated with a polarising film tuned to her eyeband which in turn was tuned to her. Even so, and even sitting in the company class section at the front of the jet, alone apart from the flight-attendant, Myra felt the impulse to hunch over the papers, and wrap her wrist and elbow around their corners like a kid in class trying not to be copycatted.

Suleimanyov had struck a bold deal with the ISTWR, and with her. It was a deal which had been proposed by Georgi Davidov, who'd died before he'd been ready to return with it. Myra's lips tightened whenever she thought of that; her suspicions stirred and were not soothed back to sleep. He'd had the contracts drawn up in the briefcase that was found with his body in the hotel room. The terms were simple, a straightforward offer of economic union and military alliance. Kazakhstan would take over the ISTWR's residual social responsibilities, assimilating all of its inhabitants who wished to become Kazakhstani citizens, subsidising the rest. It would provide for the smaller state's conventional defence, leaving to its People's Army and Workers' Militia the only functions for which they were actually fitted – internal security and border patrols, principally the guarding of the spaceport and airport. In return, Myra's government would integrate its space-borne weapons, including the nukes, into the greater republic's defence forces. They would retain ultimate operational control – there was no way Suleimanyov could expect them to surrender that – but for all public and diplomatic and military purposes, they'd work together under one command. At a stroke Kazakhstan would have a military force commensurate with its land area rather than its population.

This new Great Power could then negotiate assistance from the West. It could stand as a solid bulwark – possibly even an entering wedge – against the Sheenisov, which the inchoate regimes of the Former Union and warlorded China could not. The nuclear weapons would be their bargaining counter. Useless themselves – in any but the shortest term – against the Sheenisov, they could be made available to the US or UN in exchange for the hardware and orbital back-up and even, at the outside, troop deployments that *could* hold back this new Red tide.

Myra, as the oldest available politician, with the longest experience and the widest range of Western knowledge and contacts, would make the initial approaches. In a way she would be going back to her old business of selling nuclear deterrence policies; the only difference being that there was, now, only one logical customer. And because it would be an arduous job, on a tight schedule, they were going to give her a week's break before she started, and a lot of money. She was to use that time and money to get young again.

Rejuvenation was something she should have done long ago. Now, thinking it over, she found it difficult to disentangle her reasons for procrastinating. It wasn't that the process was unaffordable, or even obscenely privileged – many of her own citizens and employees had made a trip to some Western clinic. Dodgy black-market strains of the relevant nanoware circulated wherever health services existed at all, and patches for their shortcomings were a widespread and legitimate trade. But Myra'd never gotten around to it, partly because she had been satisfied with her present condition – attractive enough to pull interesting and interested men, fit enough for her work and her unde-manding exercise routines, but in no way good enough to fool anyone that she was actually young, once they saw more of her than her face, or saw her face close up.

Another aspect, she realised, was a certain patriotic stubbornness, of the kind that kept her driving her ancient Skoda Traverser. She didn't want to buy youth from . . . not so much the West as . . . the new breed, the post-nanotech generation. She wanted to muddle along with the fixes that had worked for her so far: the Swiss collagen jabs, the British circulatory-system microbots, the Georgian bacterio-phage immune-system back-ups, the Vietnamese phytochemical neural regenerators, the American telomere hack . . . all assembled in a post-Soviet package deal that the health services of the Former Union and the communistans had been doling out for decades.

The Kazakhstani President had taken about thirty seconds to per-suade her that it was her personal right and patriotic duty to go for the full works, the one-shot nanotech silver bullet for death. Freed from the burden of responsibility for the ISTWR, given a mission on which even history might some day smile, that legitimacy somehow legitimised her selfish stab at immortality.

But still, *memento mori*, when her mind drifted the words came back.

Death follows me.

She thought that death had caught her several times over the next few hours. The journey from Izmir's airport, Adnan Menderes, to Olu Deniz on the Aegean coast was terrifying, even in the armoured limo. It wasn't just the hairpin bends, the appalling driving, the precipitous drops and – after nightfall – the way the headlamp beams swung out into empty black space. It was all that, and the dead men.

The car had just laboured up an incline, overtaking a couple of coaches with centimetres to spare between the booming metal of the coaches on one side, and a tyre-width away from the drop on the other, and two seconds to get out of the way of an oncoming truck. In the crook of the bend, a stand of pine a little away from the main forest; three bloodied men hanging from the branches, by the neck, dead. The mind retained from the sight a shocking impression of absences: at the faces, at the ends of limbs, at the crotch. Blink and you'd miss it.

152

Myra yelped. The driver's gaze met hers in the mirror. The crinkles around his eyes deepened to a smile.

'Greek partisans.'

He started telling her the story, of how Izmir had once been Smyrna before Kemal liberated the nation, and had – only thirty-five years ago –̇ been Smyrna again, and the airport had been named after the Greek fascist Grivas rather than the Turkish democrat Menderes, and how the Greeks had begun to re-colonise, and how the New Turks had risen to again drive out the Hellenic chauvinist pawns of imperialism, and . . . and so on. Myra listened intently to the long, winding tale of nationalist grievance; it distracted her, it kept her mind off all but the worst of the roadside attractions and the most heart-stopping turns in the road. This was a place where the small wars were real, with no simulations played and no quarter given.

Why had Suleimanyov booked her into a clinic here, of all places? She knew the answer had something to do with the complex diplomacy of the rest of her journey – the Turkish Federation was as usual in dispute with the Russians, who were backing the Bulgars and Serbs and Greeks, and most of the US successor regimes were backing Turkey, and Kazakhstan's on-again-off-again relations with the rest of the Former Union were currently in 'off' mode, so . . .

But still.

At last, in the darkness, she saw that they were heading down a long incline, towards the bottom of a valley that opened to the sea. Lights dotted along the roadside and along the sides of the valley increased in frequency to a cluster behind the beach, beyond which were the lights of ships. As the road levelled out the driver turned left, then right through a big iron gate which opened for them. Concrete walls topped with coils of razor wire, a short gravelled drive. She stepped out and looked around. She could see a swimming-pool with a bar, and multi-level apartments. The driver handed her luggage to a couple of lads in jeans and polo-shirts. She tipped the driver, checked in, followed the guys to her room, dumped her gear, tipped the lads and made her way down the stairs and over slippery tiles to the bar, where she ordered a Pils. She sank it in seconds. After the air-conditioned interior of the car the heat was horrendous.

She was on to her third lager and fourth cigarette when a small, dark woman in a white lab-coat strolled over to her.

'Madame Davidova?' She stuck out a hand. 'Dr Selina Masoud.'

'Hi. Pleased to meet you. You're looking after me?'

'Yes.' Dr Masoud clicked a tablet out of a dispensary. 'Swallow this. Wash it down with—'

Myra swallowed. Dr Masoud smiled. She had curly hair and pretty white teeth. 'Something non-alcoholic, I was going to say. But it's all right – it'll just make you sleepy, now, that's all.'

'Fine,' said Myra, covering a yawn. 'I'm tired already. Smoke?'

'Thank you.' The doctor took her cigarette and flipped a gold lighter, slipped it back into her pocket, inhaled gratefully. 'Ah . . . I needed that.' She sat up on the stool beside Myra, ordered a Coke.

'So when do I go for treatment?' Myra asked.

Dr Masoud flashed her brows. 'That *was* your treatment,' she said. 'You stay a week in case there are any complications, any bad reactions. There won't be. Slightly feverish is normal.'

'Oh,' said Myra. It seemed something of an anti-climax. 'So what should I do?'

'Relax. Drink a lot – mainly non-alcoholic, to avoid dehydration. If you want to help the process along, smoke and sunbathe as much as you can. Both are carcinogenic, and they denature collagen too, you know—'

She said it as though relaying a recent and controversial discovery.

'Yes,' said Myra. 'And?'

'They catalyse the telomerase reactions.'

She smiled, downed the Coke, hopped off the tall seat. 'I must go. Enjoy your stay.'

The muezzin's taped cock-crow cry from the minaret's tannoy woke her before eight. She lay for a while enjoying the coolness of the room, and the fast-growing light. The room was, compared with her own, refreshingly uncluttered: painted and furnished in shades of white, the crisp straight lines of the decor and fabrics jiggled here and there with a twiddle of eyelet or a tuft of lace, as though the white ambience wavered between clinical and bridal, undecided whether it signified a hospital or a hotel. Not a bad honeymoon destination, Myra guessed – she'd noticed plenty of young, loud couples at the bar the previous evening, though she couldn't help wondering if the implications of staying together *for ever* might not strike home a little too hard, too soon, in a place like this.

By the pool she sat on a lounger and rubbed suncream on her limbs and torso. Her hands were as claw-like (but supple), her muscles as stringy (but strong), her skin as mottled (but taut) as they had all been for forty years.

On her left, behind the clinic's main buildings, the ground rose as a farmed foothill to a high, barren cliff. Across the kilometre or so of valley bottom, it faced a lower cliff, which sprouted scrub and trees. Overhead, the sky was deep blue. Paragliders, their canopies shaped like brightly coloured nail-parings, drifted by, from a higher range far behind the high cliff, to the beach a mile or so distant. Cicadas whirred like small electrical devices. The rest of the people here seemed to be either young, getting their fix, or old like her, getting their rewind.

For two days it was great. The sun rose above the cliff on the left, set behind the cliff on the right, regular as clockwork. In the evenings the barren cliffs looked red and martian, and the clinic like a Moon colony, a little artificial environment over which the gravity-defying paragliders swooped. Myra spent her days in sunshine and swimming and not dying. It was better than heaven. She rolled over and let the sun bake her back.

Big bare feet stopped in front of her face, in a spreading stain of water on the concrete tiles. Her gaze tracked up hairy brown legs, wet stretched trunks, hairy brown chest, to a face. Beaky nose, bright brown eyes, dark red-brown strandy hair swept back. The man smiled down at her, nodded unconsciously to himself.

'Myra Godwin?'

'Yeah?' Like, what's it to you?

He squatted. Big, white, irregular teeth.

'Jason Nikolaides,' he introduced himself. 'I've been asked to speak to you.'

She felt slightly befuddled.

'You're Greek?'

He laughed. 'Oh no. Not for generations. American.' He bowed slightly. Drops of water fell from his hair. 'CIA. We have a few things to talk about.'

Myra rolled over, swung her legs round, sat upright. Fumbled a cigarette. She looked at him, eyes screwed up against the sunlight and the smoke. She sighed.

'It's been a long time,' she said.

9

The Sickle's Sang

I looked back at the pub door, shook my head, and then walked along the side of the square and turned a corner to the street where I lodged. I went to my lodging, ran upstairs and dumped my bag, then downstairs and out again.

Without taking thought, I turned right, in the opposite direction from the station and the square. I crossed a pedestrian bridge over the railway and walked along the road out of the town, past the flood-plain of the Carron River and along the southern shore of the Carron Loch. The railway line was on my right, between the road and the sea. The sun was lowering ahead of me, but not yet shining into my eyes. On my left the wooded hills shouldered up. I walked past the hamlet and glen of Attadale, and on beside and beneath the slope of Carn nan Iomairean.

I'd walked about five kilometres before I stopped, walked over the railway line and sat down on a rock on the shore at Immer. The tide was high and the loch was still; I could hear clear across it the fiddler playing at some revel in the wood at Strome Carronach. The Torridonian hills, their rocks older than life, older than the light from the visible stars, loomed black behind the hills of Strome.

In all that walk I'd met no one, and encountered few vehicles. The whole landscape seemed to shut me out, and to remind me that I was a stranger here, excluded from everything but God's terrible love. A couple of hundred metres away, a man with a scythe was working the long grass of a meadow, as his ancestors had done and his descendants, no doubt, would do. Merrial had, on Saturday up in the hills, recited a bit of tinker doggerel that meant more to her than it did to me:

The hammer rang in factory
The sickle sang in field
The farmer proved refractory
The hammer made the sickle yield.

No hammer, no factory had stopped this man's scythe; its rhythmic swing slashed the grass as though the centuries had never been.

Then the man laid it carefully aside, and jumped to the seat of his tractor, and its methane-engine's fart scared the birds as he lowered the baler and set about raking up the hay.

I laughed at myself, and stood up, and walked back to the town.

She'd left, the barmaid told me, shortly after our quarrel. I thanked the girl, avoided my mates and headed for the tinker estate.

'She isna here.'

I turned from my futile chapping on Merrial's white door. A small boy in shorts and shirt, both too big for him, regarded me solemnly from the path. I stepped over.

'Do you know where she went?'

He was very clean, as far as I could see in the low sunlight, except for a red and evidently sticky stain on his chin, furred with fluff. I resisted the urge to spit on my finger and wipe it.

'I canna say,' he told me, with artless guile.

'Well, can you take me to somebody who can?'

As he shook his head I became aware of the crunching of gravel around me and realised that I need not look far. A dozen tinkers, young and old, male and female, seemed to drift in from nowhere. They gathered in a loose semi-circle around me, none closer than three metres away. Some of their faces I'd seen on my previous visits to the camp; others were altogether strangers to me. All of them were dressed in that mixture of simplicity and artifice which I was beginning to recognise as a peculiarity of tinker garb; it was as though the rest of us wore the cast-off finery of some reduced aristocracy, while the tinkers alone cut their own elegant cloth.

'I'm looking for Merrial,' I said, boldly enough; in the silence my voice sounded as startling and thin as a curlew's in a field.

'Aye, we know that,' said a young man. 'But you'll not find her here.'

'And I know that,' I retorted. 'So where can I find her?'

157

He shrugged. Somebody tittered. Finally, and as though with sympathy, an older man added, 'That's for her to say. If she disna want you to find her, it's no for us to help you do it. If she does, you'll find her soon enough.'

'So you do know where she is?' I sounded, even to myself, pathetically hopeful. The only response was more shrugs and a giggle.

'There's someone else I want to see,' I said. 'Fergal.'

'Oh,' said the older man, with a pretence at puzzlement, 'there are a lot of men by that name. You wouldn't happen to know his surname, would you?'

'You know damn well who I mean,' I said. 'Let him know I want to see him.'

Everyone took a step closer. The semi-circle became a close-packed horseshoe of people who began to move so that the open end was in the direction of the road. I had never thought of the tinkers as intimidating to one of the settled folk – more usually it's the other way round – but I felt intimidated at that moment, possibly because of their greater numbers. I decided to give way with as good a grace as I could, rather than make them make good on the implied – or perhaps imagined – threat. So I kept my distance as they continued to move forward.

'Ah, you'd best be off,' said the young man.

'I reckon so,' I said. 'Good night to you all.'

I turned on my heel and stalked off with as much dignity as I could muster. A stone bounced on the paved road as I reached it, but I didn't look back, or quicken my pace. Inwardly I was boiling with shame at having been, twice in one evening, faced down by tinkers. I was determined, however, that no one among my friends and acquaintances should know about this – not because of the embarrassment to myself, but because they might feel obliged to engage in some collective counter-intimidation of their own.

It was not a busy night on the square, and I didn't feel like meeting people and talking. In fact I felt like doing some solitary drinking. I bought a bottle of whisky in The Carronade, for a mark, and ducked out without greeting anyone with more than a wave.

Back at my room I found an envelope pushed under the door. It contained a telegram, which I unfolded and read in the ruddy sunset light by the window.

'CLOVIS C/O CATHERINE FARFARER MAIN ST CARRON STOP AM V CONCERNED RE MISSING FILES REQUEST RETURN BY SEALED POST TOMORROW TUESDAY OTHERWISE HANDS TIED RE POSS DISCIPLINARY ACTION ALSO INVESTIGATION IMMINENT STOP YOURS AYE GANTRY.'

On my walk along the shore I had concluded that I was a fool to walk out on Merrial, whatever the provocation; and now I felt this even more bitterly. She had warned me at the beginning that loving her would not always make me happy, and she had been right about that. Learning that she could be a member of a secret society made her refusal of confidence more understandable, even as the basis of that society filled me with dismay. My historical erudition had not disabused me of the vulgar view: that the communists had, in their blundering, bloody way, done much to fight the Possession, but that the final victory had not been theirs, and we could thank Providence that there was not a communist left on Earth. I could not bring myself to believe that Merrial really, in her heart, espoused that evil creed.

Any more than the Deliverer had. Perhaps Merrial, and even the other tinkers in the society, used its rituals and phrases for their own purposes, just as the Deliverer had exploited it to found her republic.

On that happier thought I drank a dram or two and fell asleep on the bed.

The following morning Catherine Farfarer, the landlady, handed me two telegrams. One was from the Disciplinary Sub-Committee of the University Senate, suspending me from membership of the University *sine die*, withdrawing all rights and privileges other than representation at a University court, just before the beginning of the academic year. The other was from Gantry, expressing his sympathy and saying that he would APPL THIS OUTRGS DECN.

And it was outrageous – in effect I was being punished before trial, because my chances of sponsorship or patronage were now non-existent. Even if I were cleared, I would lose at least part of the first year of my project, which as good as meant losing it all. I wired Gantry back, thanking him; but I held little hope that he could do much to help, or that I, with my stubborn closed mouth, deserved it.

Not to my surprise, Merrial was not at work. I got through most of my dangerous day in the arc-lit dark of the platform leg without incident, and was just cleaning my tools (and everyone else's) at a quarter past four when Angus Grizzlyback loomed out of the dim scaffolding and sat down at the crate.

'Clovis,' he said. I looked up. He scratched the back of his head with one hand, and looked away from me and at a piece of paper he held in the other.

'Something wrong?'

Even then, the thought that leapt on me was that he was the unwilling bearer of bad tidings about my parents, or some such family matter.

'Aye, I'm afraid so,' he said. 'I'm going to have to let you go. Pay you off.'

'What for?' I asked, simultaneously relieved and shaken.

'Nothing you've done here,' he assured me. 'It's much against my own inclination, Clovis; for all I've slagged you off you're no bad at what you do, and you're a sound man, but—' He shrugged, and looked down at the paper again. 'It's the Society. They've withdrawn your clearance to work on the project.' He looked up at me sharply, a question in his eyes. 'Some trouble you've got into at the University.'

I put the tools down on the rough table and clasped my oily hands to my head. 'How can they do that?' I asked, but I knew the answer. The University had fingered me to the Society – of which it was, of course, a part – as a risk to the project's security. It all made sense, unjust though it seemed.

'You can appeal, you know,' Angus said. 'I'll back you up.'

I swallowed bile. 'Thanks,' I said. 'I'll bear that in mind. Of course I'll appeal it.'

The only reason I could think of to appeal it was that not doing so would seem like an admission of guilt – and, indeed, I was guilty of plenty, none of which I'd want brought out in a work tribunal. Confident though I was that nothing I'd done could endanger the project, others might not regard being madly in love with a stranger as a sound basis for this conviction.

'Ach, well, I'll set the machinery in motion,' Angus said. 'I'll tell Jondo and he'll take it up with the union.' He forced a grin. 'Have you back in no time.'

'Thanks, Angus,' I said.

'But right now,' he went on, 'I'll have to ask you to leave straight away. It says here I should escort you off the premises, but I'll not do that.'

I was very grateful indeed that he trusted me as far as the gate; but as I turned and looked back on my way out of the yard, I noticed his tiny figure on the outside of the platform, and realised that he'd discreetly watched my every step.

I took an early and almost empty bus back to Carron Town, and went to my room. The whisky bottle, at that moment, felt like my only friend. By morning, it would seem false; we'd have had a severe falling-out, but we'd both know it was only a matter of time before we'd make up. I knew all this perfectly well as I sat under the skylight and tipped myself a generous measure of the malt. Its fortifying fire rushed through my nerves, and I could contemplate my unravelling life with a degree of detachment.

I thought about what I'd lost, and what I hadn't, and determined that what I had left was enough to win me back the rest, if only I could think of a way. So, instead of settling down to some sad solitary drinking, I cleaned up and shaved and changed and went over to The Carronade.

The doors of the pub, heavy with glass and brass, swung shut behind me. After the sunshine the light seemed low. As I walked to the bar my eyes adjusted. At that time, about half past five, it was almost empty. The barmaid was the same girl who'd served us on Monday evening. She was a local girl, tall and thin, with long fair hair bundled up, and strong arms from pulling the pumps. Her name, as I learned in a few minutes of chat as I leaned idly on the bar, sipping at a half-litre of pale ale, was Jeanna Berrymead. She'd grown up on a farm up the glen a bit, at Achnashellach.

Carron Town, before the project had started, was a place where everybody knew everything about everybody else, or at least talked as though they did. Jeanna's knowledge of my meeting with, and parting from, Merrial was elaborate enough to suggest that local gossip was fast catching up with the influx.

'That tinker who was in here—' I said, trying to steer her away from her obvious probing of my side of the story.

'Oh, aye, Fergal.'

'You know him?'

She shrugged and made a mouth. 'To see. He drops in now and again. Bit of an arrogant sod, but he stands his round.'

'Any idea where he works?'

'Aye, in the old power-station up at Lochluichart. It's no' a power-station any more, you understand. But folk still call it that.'

'So what is it now?'

She grimaced. 'Not a place you'd like to go to. It's said the tinkers make their seer-stones there. I've heard tell it feels . . . haunted. A creepy place. Mind you, I've never met anyone who'd been there. Or who'd want to,' she added pointedly.

'Anyone who wasn't a tinker, you mean,' I said. 'Presumably Fergal has mentioned he's been there.'

She shook her head, frowning. 'He's never said a word about it, even when he's drunk. Not that he's drunk often! He can hold his drink, that one.'

'So how do you know that's where he works?'

'Ah, I don't know,' she said, as though impatient to be off the subject. 'It's just – you know – what people say.'

I was about to try to get more than that out of her when another voice joined our conversation.

'Is this you back on the pull, Clovis, so soon after the quarrel with your last lassie?' My workmate Druin sounded amused. I turned and grinned back at him as the barmaid poured him a half-litre. Druin was a local man, married and in his thirties, his weskit showing bare brown arms still oil-stained from his day's work, and scarred from years of work before it too.

'That's not it at all,' I said. 'I thought better of it, as who wouldn't? But she's not to be seen. So I'm trying to find out more about the tinkers.'

He laughed. 'You're a character. The reading makes you funny in the head.' He said this not as an insult but as a charitable explanation. 'Mind you,' he added, 'that's a girl I wouldn't walk out on myself.'

I asked Jeanna for another half-litre and, noticing a temptingly cheap bottle, said, 'Oh, and a couple of shots of the Talisker, please.'

Druin raised his glass. 'Thanks, mate.' He took a sip of the Talisker and asked, 'What's this about you getting the sack?'

'Some trouble with the University,' I said. 'I borrowed some papers, and found I had little choice but to let Fergal take them. The ISS seems to have taken it as a sign I'm not to be trusted. I take that as an insult.'

'As well you might.' He looked at me curiously. 'You don't seem too bothered about it, though.'

I made a twist of my lips, turned my hand over. 'Aye, I'm bothered, but there's no sense letting something like that get to you. I'll appeal it, Jondo's going to take it up. It'll get sorted out. I'm more worried about why Merrial isn't at work.'

'Ah,' he said. 'She isna taking the day off, or suspended or anything like that. She's finished her contract.'

'How d'you know that?'

He tapped the side of his nose. 'Jondo told me, because naturally he asked Admin if she'd been chucked out as well.'

I sighed. 'I suppose that's a relief, in a way. But she said nothing about it to me, even before.'

Druin nodded. 'Aye, they're a close-mouthed lot, the tinkers. So, what is it you wanted to know about them?'

'Well, we sort of take them for granted, right? Some people do one kind of work, and nobody else knows much about it. How did that start? Why can't just anybody follow the path of light? How do people become tinkers in the first place?'

Druin looked at Jeanna, and then at his drinks. He scratched his chin. Jeanna unaccountably blushed a little, and held her hand over a giggle.

'That's a lot of questions,' Druin said. 'To answer your last one first, most people who become tinkers are born into it. They're tinkers because their parents were tinkers.'

'Aye,' I said, 'but look at the tinkers. They're not an inbred people, whatever else they may be. So they must get new recruits, so to speak, but I've never heard of such.'

Jeanna's giggle broke through. She turned away and moved down to the other end of the bar. Druin glanced after her and back at me, smirking.

'Well,' he said carefully, 'it is rumoured that those of the settled people who become tinkers do so through sexual intercourse.' He laughed at the look on my face. 'You might have been well on the way to becoming one yourself, I gather.'

'Oh, come *on*,' I said. 'That's ridiculous.'

Druin shook his head. 'It's no ridiculous,' he said firmly. 'You think about it. A tinker won't settle down without ceasing to be a tinker, and damn few do that. So if you want to be with a tinker, you have to become a tinker yourself. And wander off, and never be seen again, often as not. The tinkers don't stay in the one place more than one or two year, if that.'

'All right,' I said, 'I can see there might be something in that.' My mind was turning over a lot of possible implications, none of which I was in any mood to share with Druin. 'What about the other questions?'

He shrugged. 'As to why they and only they do what they do? I've given that some thought myself, and the only thing I can say is, it goes back to the Deliverance, and it works fine. What more can you say?'

'Oh, plenty,' I said. 'Like whether it's the best way of doing things.'

'Aye, well, like I said. It works.' He leaned closer. 'Here's a bit of tinker cant I picked up: "If it ain't broke, don't fix it." Sound advice, wherever it comes from.'

He drained his mug and knocked back the whisky, then grinned and clapped my shoulder. 'I can see I've given you a lot to think about, but I haven't the time to talk any more. I'm off. Home to the wife and the tea, then out on the hills with the rifle.'

As he slid off the stool and stood up he gave me a canny look and asked, 'You happen to fancy coming along, Clovis?'

'Deer hunting?' Suddenly it felt like something I desperately needed to do to get my head clear. My first inquiries had already given me far too much new information to assimilate.

'Sure,' I said. 'Thanks.'

'Great, well, come along for your tea as well.'

'Oh, I couldn't, your wife's not expecting any—'

'Ach, man, if you saw how much she tries to make me eat, you'd come along out of sheer sympathy. Nah, you'll be welcome.'

'Thanks a lot. See you, Jeanna.'

Druin's wife's name was Arrianne. A calm, solid, dark woman who took my arrival entirely in her stride. We sat around a heavy table in the living-room, under a loud-ticking ancient clock, with the two children: a boy of about fourteen called Hamish, already working at the fish-farm, and a girl of six called Ailey, who unfussily helped her mother to serve the dinner.

The dinner – or 'tea' as they called it – consisted of fresh mackerel, limpets boiled in salt water, new potatoes and carrots and fresh-picked peas. I had to stop at the third helping, but Druin and Hamish went right on through it. This kind of feeding didn't seem to have put an ounce of fat on either of them; Arrianne insisted that I looked undernourished, and she may have been right.

164

After the woman and the girl had cleared away the plates Druin stood up and reverently lifted two rifles down from a rack on the wall. He pushed one across the table to me.

'You know how to handle this?'

Single-shot, bolt-action, scope. I demonstrated my familiarity and safety to Druin's satisfaction.

'Has a hell of a kick,' he warned, passing me a half-dozen shells. 'Still, you'll no get more than one shot in even if we're lucky.'

He said goodbye, and I said thanks to his family, and then he led me out the back and to the side of the house where his pick-up truck was parked. We racked the rifles on the back and climbed into the cab. The seats were leather, the dashboard hardwood and stainless steel, all lovingly polished.

'Fusion engine,' he said proudly as he turned the key and got an instant low thrum in response. 'Eighty years old, and not a thing wrong with it. Been in the family that long. None of your wood-alcohol or methane stinks for us.'

The vehicle purred into the main street and on to the road past New Kelso. Druin caught me craning my neck to look over at the tinker estate, and laughed.

'Ach, you'll find her,' he said.

He turned right at the junction, up the glen. The evening traffic surge had eased off and we made good progress at about forty kilometres an hour.

'Where are we heading?' I asked, as he slowed for the main street of Achnashellach. A small herd of Highland cattle were being walked through the town, for God knows what reason.

'Ah, you'll see when we get there.' He looked at me sideways. 'You can smoke if you want, just make sure the ash goes out the window, and the butt goes in the ashtray.' He hit the horn. 'Ah, move yer fucking arse,' he advised a hairy beast, which looked back at him as though it had heard, tossed its horns and plodded obliviously in front of us for a further couple of minutes.

Clear of the obstruction he speeded up for the long, slowly rising road to Achnasheen, which we passed through about twenty minutes later. The streets of that town climbed high into the forested hills, and its greenhouses across the floor of the glen.

'In my grandfather's day this was all a fucking bog, the way he tells it,' Druin remarked. 'The station, and the hotel, and fuck all else. Aye, we've got the land back and no mistake, just like the Brahan Seer said.'

'Who?'

'Och, some prophet from the old time, he said the people would come back to the glens. The Nostradamus of the North!' He laughed. 'They say he looked at the future through a hole in a stone, and that very stone is at the bottom of a loch somewhere.'

'A seer-stone?'

Druin guffawed. 'You've got tinkers on the brain, Clovis! The Seer lived and died long before even computers. Which he did not foresee. No, it was an ordinary wee stone with a hole in it that he looked through.'

'Do you believe that?'

'I don't think there was anything special about the stone,' Druin said. 'But there may have been something special to the eye or the brain behind it.'

'The second sight?' I said sceptically.

'I don't know about that,' said Druin. 'The Brahan Seer saw the future in his imagination, and so do we all.' He chuckled. 'He was just better at it than most.'

Druin stopped at a wee place called Dark, and, leaving the truck parked off the road, led me up through the pines on the left.

'No smoking,' he said quietly. 'And no talking either.'

I nodded, concentrating on heaving myself and the increasingly heavy rifle up the slope. The thick needle-carpet made for slow, if silent, progress. I had a bit of difficulty keeping up with Druin, and decided then and there that smoking was indeed unhealthy. At the same time, I was feeling a tension that only a smoke could relieve. Something in Druin's manner, and something about our location, was bothering me, but I couldn't think what. We climbed steadily, away from the road and up the hill.

Druin reached the top of the ridge ahead of me, and there paused, hands on one knee, while I caught up. He pointed down through a gap in the trees to where the other side of the ridge sloped back to the road. Looking down, I could see the road, the railway line and a long, narrow loch.

Loch Luichart. I recognised the place with a sudden jolt at remembering that this was where – as Jeanna had told me – Fergal worked and the tinkers made their strange stone computers. The old power-station, at which Druin was pointing, was a large, dark, block-shaped building at the foot of the slope below us.

'What's this about?' I asked Druin, as quietly as I could.

He grinned at me and began walking slowly up the ridge.

'Thought you might want to hunt more than deer,' he said. 'You're after your man Fergal, and your lassie Merrial. Down there might not a bad place to look.'

I gasped, and not with the exertion of keeping up with him. 'We can't just march in there!'

'Why not?' he grunted. 'But anyway, we won't just "march in".' He stopped, and took a few paces off to the right, into a clump of bushes. 'Ah, here it is.'

He'd arrived at a cylindrical structure of weathered, creeper-covered ceramic, about a metre high and a metre across. As I approached he leapt up on top of it and began scraping away the overgrowth with the side of his boot. In a moment he'd exposed a rusty hatch.

Not so rusty it didn't open, though. I looked in and saw a series of rungs disappearing into the blackness. Druin dropped a pebble in and cocked his ear.

'It's only about twenty metres deep,' he told me.

'Good grief, man, you're not talking about going down there, are you?'

'Aye, I am that,' he said. 'It's safe enough, so long as you hang on.'

'But do you know what's at the bottom?' I looked at him suspiciously. 'And how do you know about this, anyway?'

Druin sighed theatrically. 'What's at the bottom is a tunnel – I don't know if it's part of the original hydro-station or something that got added later. This whole hill has been tunnelled and mined; it was used as an underground base by the British army, and by the Republicans during the civil war before the First World Revolution – changed hands a few times, I think. As to how I know about it—' He laughed. 'There's a map and a diagram of it all in the museum at Jeantown! Mind you, I guess the tinkers will have made yon diagram out of date, one way or the other.'

'Looks pretty dark,' I said.

'Ach, there'll be some kind of lighting down there. And I've got a torch.'

'Was this on your mind all along?'

'Aye,' he admitted. 'But I didn't want to tell you beforehand, in case you got cold feet from worrying about it before we even got here. As it is, I'm just beginning to wonder if I was right in thinking you had a spirit of adventure. You've done nothing but raise objections this past five minutes. Do you want to go after this woman, or no?'

'Of course I do,' I said, stung into action – as he no doubt intended – by his hint at cowardice. I slung the rifle across my back and scrambled up and set my feet on the rungs as I lowered myself in. 'You'll be coming too, will you?'

'I'll be right above you,' Druin said.

For the next couple of minutes I concentrated entirely on descending the laddered steps. The rungs looked rust-free, as did their bolts – in fact, the metal and the ceramic of the shaft were both unknown to me. But I could not be sure that every rung had survived the centuries, so I tested each one before putting my full weight on it. The slung rifle made it even more awkward. One upward glance confirmed that Druin was following. Above him the hatch was visible as a small, bright hole.

After what seemed a long time my foot encountered empty air where a rung should have been. After a moment of fright I lowered the foot further, cautiously, and touched a floor. I grunted with relief and stepped down and away from the ladder, still taking care where I placed my feet. Druin completed his descent a moment later and we stood together in dark and silence.

On the descent my eyes had adapted to the diminishing light and even here, at the bottom of the shaft, it was not entirely dark. I became aware, without quite knowing why, that we were indeed in a tunnel and that it sloped fairly sharply. Looking around, I could see a brighter area lower down. I peered at Druin and gestured in that direction. The pale oval of his face made a bobbing motion which I interpreted as a nod. Together we turned and headed down the slope.

After a few steps I stubbed my toe on something hard. 'Damn,' I muttered, pulling up short. Druin bumped into my back and we both swayed dangerously.

'Fuck this for a game of soldiers,' said Druin. He unclipped the torch from his belt and switched it on. A powerful beam of white light illuminated the tunnel in front of us. It revealed that the floor was indeed littered with obstacles – oddly shaped seer-stones of various sizes. It also revealed that the tunnel was full of people.

Druin yelped a curse and brought his rifle to bear in a surprisingly smooth and swift movement. The torch-beam wavered hardly at all. I was still stiff with shock; the instant I recovered from it I looked over my shoulder and saw more figures crowding behind us, dim in the backwash of the torch's light. One such figure was apparently in the act of reaching out for me – I struck wildly at his arm, and almost fell over because my fist passed right through it. Druin whirled around at the same moment, and the torch-beam cast my shadow grotesquely on the figures before me. They responded neither to the shadow nor the light. Druin let out his breath in a gusty gasp, then laughed.

'They're just hollows, man!'

'Ah.' I stood looking at them in amazement. 'Aye, like the tinkers scare children with at fairs.'

'That's it. God, they had me scared enough.'

'No wonder Jeanna said the place was haunted.'

'She said that, did she now?' Druin pondered. 'I'll have another chat with yon lassie sometime. Anyway. Let's go on. Keep the voice down a bit though.'

Neither of us had spoken loudly at all, but the slightest sound seemed magnified by the tunnel's acoustics. We turned again and walked on, the pool of light from Druin's torch enabling us to avoid the stones on the floor, and almost to ignore the apparitions they cast. Almost – for the still faces of the men and women depicted in this intangible statuary were caught in a moment of anguish and alarm, which, as they repeatedly loomed out of the dark and passed us – or passed through us – was enough to inspire, in me at least, a creeping sensation of disquiet. They looked uncannily like the lost souls, the damned of the Christian and Mohammadan superstitions, and it would have taken a stouter faith in Reason than mine to have walked that dark path unshaken. Irrational as it may be, I drew some comfort from the fact – known to any child old enough not to be frightened by the 'ghost tent' at a fair – that hollows have no existence outside the light, and that, therefore, there was not an unseen crowd of them in the darkness behind us.

Presently we passed beyond their eerie company, and closer to the source of light at the end of the tunnel (an expression whose full force I for the first time appreciated). The air smelt damper, and at the same time fresher. We had reached the foot of the slope; the rocky floor of the tunnel here was flat. Druin switched off his torch and we proceeded very slowly and silently for the remaining few metres. The reason for the light's vagueness turned out to be a sharp bend in the tunnel; we crept around it, keeping close to the outer side of the crook, rifles gripped (though not, I recalled at that very moment, loaded).

I nudged Druin and, taking a shell from my pocket, made to put it in the rifle. He shook his head, firmly, and I desisted, reassuring myself with the reflection that the pistols on our belts were ready for immediate use. We rounded the bend and found ourselves looking out at a brightly lit space of great size – at least twenty metres across, I guessed, and ten high. The lighting came from overhead panels, and seemed like sunlight. The walls curved over to the ceiling, all stone; a cavern then, and not a natural one. Its full length was not obvious from where we stood, at one corner of it.

It contained row upon row of stone troughs, connected with stepped open pipes through which rivulets of water trickled; some arranged to feed the troughs, others to carry away waste – or so I guessed, from the fact that no channel that came out of a trough went into another. I could make out half a dozen people working there, moving from trough to trough, making undetectable adjustments to the flow or sifting some powdery material in. They looked like hydroponic gardeners, and I thought at first glance that they were following this familiar trade, possibly for some recondite component of the tinkers' food-supply. Then I noticed the contents of the troughs farther to my right, and – as I quickly realised – of more mature growth. They were growing seer-stones – I could distinctly see the larger ones lined up, five to a trough.

'Well, well,' said Druin, as though thinking, as I was: so *that's* how it's done! He slung his rifle on his shoulder, glanced at me and shrugged.

'No point in creeping about now,' he said.

With that he marched boldly out into the light.

10

Forget Babylon

They made their way back from the ossuary, ducking under arches and through hammered holes in the walls, into the church. Beneath pocked, defaced Orthodox murals a Turkish woman sold silver and jade and crochet. They ignored her gestured pitch, stepped outside, stalked past more stalls. Across the hollow from the hilltop where the church stood, a hillside of streets of empty, roofless stone houses fought the slow green entropy of birch and bramble. The light was blinding, the heat choking, the silence intense. The cicadas broke it, the birds, the skitter of a lizard.

Jason wandered around to the front of the church, traced a date in coloured pebbles on the paving.

'1912,' he said. 'That's when they finished it. How proud of it they must have been. Ten years later, they left. Voluntary population exchange, hah.'

Myra squatted in the sunlight, swigged Evian, sucked Marlboro. 'Worse things have happened since.' The dry, ancient ribs and femurs in the ossuary hadn't disturbed her as much as the fresh bodies she'd seen the evening she arrived.

'No doubt.' Jason shrugged. 'But you know, this place, it makes me feel like I'm a Greek, for the first time in my life. Even a god-damn *Christian*.' He glanced at the hawkers a few tens of metres away, hunkered down beside her and spoke in a low, earnest voice. 'As in, you know, Western. It's a different culture. They don't like us.'

Myra stared at him, shocked. Karmilassos, or Kaya, or Kayakoi, or whatever it was called (the Turks shamelessly called it 'the Greek ghost village') oppressed her too, but the CIA agent seemed to be drawing entirely the wrong moral from it.

'This is what nationalism does,' she said. 'And what that kind of thinking does. No, thank you. I don't buy it.'

Jason looked somewhat hurt. He tilted his hat back and started skinning up a joint. His age – he claimed, and she believed, though who could now be sure? – was twenty-four. The last time she'd been seriously hassled by the CIA had been just over sixty years earlier. There was something awesome about a man following up a file so much older than he was.

(Last time: the man from the Agency had talked to her over lattes in a Starbuck's off Harvard Square, in July 1998 when she was touting for medical aid to Kazakhstan's fall-out victims; the campaign's poster child had a cleft palate. A surgeon she'd met had set up the contact; someone who'd worked at the consulate in Almaty, he'd said, but she wasn't fooled. She brought a tape-recorder, discreet in the pocket of her blouse. She expected someone who looked like a Mormon, a Man In Black. He was young, dark, bright; blueberry T-shirt, baggy camos. Called himself Mike.

They chatted about Britain. Mike was interested in Ulster. The Orangemen were marching at Drumcree. Myra told him nothing he didn't know; he knew more about her than she did, casually name-dropping demos she'd been on in the seventies as he idly turned the foreign news pages of the *Boston Globe*. They took their coffees outside, sat on a low wall while Myra had a smoke.

Mike nodded at the clenched black fist of a faded black power mural high on a wall on the other side of the street, above the map shop on the corner. 'All that's over,' he said. 'No more arguments about the politics, Myra. All of the line-ups are new, now. We aren't asking you to betray anyone, or anything. Just share information. We have mutual interests. You're going to a dangerous place, after all.' (Ah, there it was, the threat.) 'You never know when the right contacts might be crucial.'

'Indeed,' she said. She was staring abstractedly at a teenage girl with pink hair, sure she'd seen her before. She shook her head. 'I'll bear it in mind,' she said. 'Here's my mobile number.'

Mike gave her his, and went away. That night Myra phoned her tape of the whole conversation through to the office of one of the local sections of the FI, and to a reporter on *Mother Jones*. The journalist was dubious, the local cadres – after a quick, panicky consultation – told her to play along.

Two weeks later she was in New York, and met Mike again, leaning on the rail of the Staten Island ferry. The last round trip of a day which had been humid, and was now hazy. Commuters dozed on the benches, tourists posed for pictures of themselves with the Statue of Liberty or the towers of Manhattan, the *apparat* of capital, looming in the background. She agreed to liaise with the consulate when she got back; and in the years that followed, she did, now and then, as she and Georgi clawed their way up the structures of post-Soviet Kazakhstan, through revolutions and counter-revolutions. Mainly she reported on people who were as much her enemies as they were the CIA's; smugglers of drugs and people and arms, dealers in corruption and mineral concessions and resource looting. She told the FI about every such encounter, and nothing came of it, and it all faded out. After the Fall Revolution a lot of files were opened. Myra had idly run searches on her own name and code-names in them, and found that most of the individuals and companies she'd shopped to the CIA were working for the CIA.

But they still had her down as an asset, the bastards, after all those years and changes.

And the girl with pink hair had been on the Staten Island ferry, too. She never did figure that out, and in the end put it down to coincidence.)

Jason passed her the joint, and they smoked it together as they ambled down the steep, rocky path through neglected olive-trees to the foot of the hill, where they'd left their hired jeep. The dingy little settlement there had consisted of newly built concrete houses, and a few of the stolen stone houses in the first street of the long-emptied Greek town. All of them had been gutted years ago, the Turkish families living there slaughtered by Greek partisans in the last war. The blue-and-white ceramic eyes – for good luck, against the evil eye – above the doors were cracked, the timbers blackened. Myra ground the roach into charcoal ashes that still lay inches deep. She didn't feel high, just focused, her sight enhanced as if by a VR overlay. She could *see* why this land was worth fighting over.

Jason got into the driver's seat as Myra climbed in the other side. He looked at her sympathetically, as though half-sorry for having brought her here.

'Sometimes God is just,' he said.

173

'Yeah. In a very Old Testament way.'

Jason started up the engine and swung the jeep around on to the narrow road to Hisaronu. The road climbed, scraping trees, edging precipices. Pine and rock and dry gullies – it was like a hot day in Scotland. Myra remembered a day with David Reid, by a river between Dunkeld and Blair Atholl, that had felt just like this. He had talked about depopulation and forced migration in biblical terms as well, she recalled.

'*Mene, mene, tekel, upharsin,*' she heard herself say.

'What?'

'That thing from the Bible. You know, about the king of Babylon? "Thou art weighed in the balances, and found wanting."'

'I'm aware of the source,' Jason said, keeping his eyes on the road. 'It's the relevance that kind of escapes me.'

'It's the way I feel,' Myra said. She stuck her hand in the air above the windscreen, feeling the cool rush between her fingers.

'That's how you feel about yourself? That's bad.'

'No,' she told him. 'About the fucking *world.*'

'That's worse.'

She laughed, her spirits lifting.

'Anyway,' Jason went on, 'it's just the rejuve talking. People get like that.'

'You would know, huh?'

'Not personally. With me, it's just stabilising, right? With you –' he smirked sidelong at her '– it's got a *lot* of work to do.'

'Thanks.'

'It makes you feel strange. Euphoric and judgemental.'

'Yeah, that's me all right!'

It was the fifth day since she'd swallowed the surgery. The nanomachines had differentiated and proliferated inside her, spreading out through her circulation like an army of sappers, tearing down and rebuilding. She felt their waste heat like a fever, burning her up. Her moods swung from normal to high, she didn't have depressions any more, it was like a biological Keynesianism, except that in the long run she was not going to be dead. She was not immortal, not really – who could tell? The best guess was centuries and in that time something else would come along – but she felt immortal, she felt like people did in their twenties before their cells started running down and their neurons began to die, no wonder she

174

could remember the seventies so vividly, no wonder she was getting so arrogant!

Sex with Jason had been a foregone conclusion, from about the second she saw him. He was an imperialist agent, a strategic enemy even if a tactical ally, and she didn't care, she wanted to seduce him and subvert him herself, turn tricks learned in a lifetime that would curl his toes and grey his dark-copper hair. If he had any inhibitions or revulsion from her still-aged body they had been dissolved in the first evening's first bottle of raki. She'd sucked him rigid, fucked him raw, taught him much and told him little.

The little she told him was about Georgi, and the circumstances of Georgi's death. For reasons which Jason didn't spell out, but which Myra suspected had 'Agency asset – poss future use?' scribbled in their margins, the CIA was conducting its own investigation into that death which had been so deniably convenient for *somebody*.

In the early hours of the mornings, when he thought she was asleep, he would go out to her room's tiny balcony and talk for a long time on the phone. She pretended not to notice and didn't object, instead using these times in murmured pillow-talk on her own, using the eyeband to consult Parvus and to listen to v-mail from her Sovnarkom colleagues about the situation back home. It wasn't good.

Denis Gubanov, in particular, was glum. His summaries of popular attitudes – derived from agents' reports and readers' letters to *Kapitsa Pravda* – indicated what to Myra was a surprising groundswell of opposition to the whole deal with Kazakhstan. All unnoticed, a thick scrub of patriotism had grown up over the years on her tiny republic's thin, infertile soil. Its independence had come to matter to its citizens, far more than it ever had to her. Each night she looked at shots of the growing daily picket outside the government building: red flags, yellow-and-black trefoil flags, pictures of Trotsky. She'd sigh, turn over and pretend to be asleep when Jason came back.

At Hisaronu, a pleasant small town scattered across a hilltop surrounded by higher, distant mountains, they stopped at a pavement café on the main street. They drank Amstel and ate Iskander kebabs, under a striped plastic awning. When they were smoking, and sipping muddy coffee, Myra leaned forward across the table and clasped Jason's hand, letting their fingers intertwine.

'What do you want from me?' she asked.

He clasped back.

'Apart from what I've got?'

'Yeah.'

He disentangled his fingers from hers and pulled from his pocket and unfolded a Mercator projection world-map, furred at the creases. He elbowed aside his drink and a plastic ketchup bottle and spread the map out on the metal table.

She pointed. 'We're here.' She dusted off her hands and made as if to rise. 'Glad to be of help.'

'Sit,' he said, laughing. 'Look.'

She sat down again. 'Who else is looking? If you're about to give me a briefing, wouldn't VR be better?'

Jason waved his hands and looked around. Tourists and soldiers and locals ambled along the noonday street. 'Nobody's looking.' He combed his fingers through his hair. 'And you'll have noticed, I don't have an eyeband.' He shrugged. 'All the networks are compromised anyway, have been for years. That's why I listen to the radio, and read newspapers, and write in a notebook, and carry paper maps.'

'Fair enough,' said Myra, lightly, to hide her cold shock at what he'd just said. Then she realised she couldn't let it pass. 'What do you mean, "compromised"?'

'Insecure, no matter what you do. Codes, hiding the real message in the junk, whatever – there are systems that'll crack every new variant as soon as you set it up. Quantum computation killed cryptography, and there are better methods than that now, implemented on things *nobody* understands. They're out there, Myra. I've seen them.'

She smiled sceptically. 'Things that man was not meant to know?'

Jason nodded vigorously. 'Yes, that's it exactly!' he said, as though he'd never heard the expression before. Perhaps he hadn't. The youth of today. He looked down again at the map, dismissing the subject with a twirl of his hand. Myra let it drop too, but she didn't dismiss it. She was pretty sure he was mistaken, or lying, or had been lied to. And in whose interest might it be for her to distrust her 'ware?

Hah.

Jason jabbed a forefinger on North America, ran it around the Great Lakes and partway down the Eastern seaboard. 'OK, here's my country, was yours. The United States, as we still call ourselves. Not exactly "sea to shining sea" any more. "From St Lawrence to the Keys" never quite caught on, and even that's hard to hold. I mean, we need Maine between us and the Canadian hordes, but, shit. We're holding down major insurgencies everywhere between Baltimore and Jacksonville. And the only reason we hang on to Florida is for Canaveral, frankly, and the only reason they stay with us is they're scared of *El Barbudo*.' He glanced up under his brows, cast her a wry smile. 'You should hear the old boys at Langley kicking themselves about that one. After the Pike Commission put a stop to the exploding cigar capers they just thought fuck it, the bastard's gotta die sometime. Not.'

He opened his fingers like dividers and straddled the continent. 'West Coast . . .' He sighed. 'La-la Land. They got a rival claim in to be the successor state, so diplomatically we don't get on, but between you and me and the *garçon* here –' he absently waved his other hand, snapped fingers, pointed to their glasses '– we're the best of friends.' He brought the heel of his palm down on the middle of America, masking off a large area between the Appalachians and the Rockies. 'Compared with how we get on with the rest. The Mormons, the militias, the fundies, the White Right, the Indians – name it, we lost to it.'

'Yeah, well,' Myra said. 'I had heard.'

'Lucky for us,' he went on, 'they're a bit down on scientists. They got oil and minerals, all right, but with Flood Geology they won't find much more of it. This ain't rocket science. Speaking of which, we and our La-la friends got all the aerospace and comp sci and nuke tech experts. At least, we got the ones who didn't die trying to convince some hick inquisitor with a mains supply and a jump-lead that they really, really didn't know where the alien bodies were buried. Or where the crashed saucers were stashed.'

'You're kidding.'

'I wish. Turned out more people believed in the UFO cover-up than ever believed in the Jewish bankers. When they got their hands on some of yer actual *eevill guvmint scientists* . . . you can imagine the fun they had.' He had a thousand-yard stare, past her, for a moment. 'Some of the scientists confessed. In astonishing detail. Names, dates, places, A-to-Z files.'

The kid serving tables put down another couple of bottles. Myra smiled at him, shoved him a few greasy gigalira notes, waved a cigarette at Jason.

'Any of it true?' She laughed uneasily. 'I've sometimes wondered, like about the diamond ships . . .'

Jason blinked, shook his head. 'Oh, no. Total corroborative hallu-cination. Like alien abductions, or witches' sabbats. *They'd* heard the stories too, see? Hell, maybe some even believed it themselves, who's to say. The diamond ships, nah, that was just black tech from way back. Your basic Nazi flying saucer. Neat idea in principle, but it never was practical until the right materials came on-stream with the carbon assembler.'

Myra leaned back, refilling her glass, wishing she could consult Parvus. 'You're telling me,' she said, 'that East America has border security problems too? Well, let me put your mind at rest. We're not about to embarrass you by asking for *ground troops*. Or even teletroopers.'

'God, if it was that . . .' Jason had the long gaze again. 'No, it's a bit more complicated. You're going to Ankara next, right?'

'What?'

'You're going to ask the Turks for ground troops.'

'I don't know where you got that idea,' Myra said, carefully not denying it. Ankara wasn't on her itinerary at all, but she was very curious to know why Jason thought it was, and what bothered him about it.

'Sources,' Jason said. 'Anyway, that's what I'm here to tell you would be a very bad idea. If you want to get any help from the US, that is.'

'Hmm,' said Myra. She glanced at a soldier trawling a souvenir rack a few metres away. 'I'm just looking at a US-made GI uniform, US KevlarPlus body armour, a US Robotics head-up with Raytheon AI, a US Colt Carbine-14 . . .'

'Yeah-yeah-yeah,' said Jason impatiently. 'Valued customers. Old friends. Doesn't mean we'd be happy to see their standard-issue US Army boots tramping all over Central Asia.'

'Even to stamp on the Sheenisov?'

Jason leaned his elbows on the table, steepled his hands in front of his face to mask his mouth, and spoke quietly.

'Look, Myra, these ain't communism's glory days. I mean, in *our* glory days we'd have been pounding them with B-52s round the clock, for all the good that would have done. I understand your, ah, fraternal allies have tried that in their own inimitable way, with Antonovs. I've been authorised to let you know – off the record, and deniably – that if you come to New York or DC you'll be welcome, and your requests will be listened to sympathetically. But. Our threat assessment of the Sheenisov – where the *fuck* did that name come from? – is pretty low-key. If a motorised horde of Mongols in plastic yurts want to plan their economy with steam-driven computers, that's their problem, and if it turns out to be popular in your country, that's yours.'

Myra stared at him, rocked back. 'Jeez. That's me told.'

'Hey, nothing personal. It had to be me – or someone like me – who told you this, because at the level you're gonna be dealing with in NY or DC it'd be . . . undiplomatic and impolitic to put it to you so bluntly. I'm not saying you won't get anything. You will, just – maybe not as much as you'd like.'

She narrowed her eyes, leaning forward again. He looked so straightforward, so frank. He couldn't know about the nuclear card up her sleeve.

'OK, OK,' she said, as though not too bothered, which she wasn't. 'So, you're more worried about the Turkish Federation expanding than you are about the SSU?'

'You got it. And, well, there are bigger concerns than that. The coup attempt has – let's say it hasn't made things easier for us.'

'How?'

Jason compressed his lips. 'You'll find out,' he said gloomily.

'All right,' said Myra. She swirled her beer, looked in it, divined no clues. She looked up and smiled at Jason. 'Nothing personal, point taken. So let's get back to personal.'

Jason relaxed suddenly. 'Yeah, OK.'

'And it's from the Gaelic, by the way.'

'What?'

'The name – Sheenisov. I think it was David Reid who coined it.'

'Well, whaddaya know.'

'What I want to know,' said Myra, draining her glass and getting up, 'is what's this about them having steam-driven computers?'

'Ah,' said Jason, as they returned to the jeep, 'I can tell you all about that.'

'Should you be driving?'

'Ah, I guess not.' Jason switched the jeep over to autopilot, and as it took them back down the long road to Olu Deniz he told her all about the Sheenisov's strange machines.

*

179

It was a strange machine that took her to America.

On her last morning she woke before Jason did, lay for a while, then reached automatically for her contacts. She was on the point of putting the disposables in when she noticed that she could see clearly, all around the room. A quick look out of the window confirmed that she wasn't myopic any more. She brought her hand within two inches of her face, and it stayed in focus; she didn't have long sight, either.

In the shower she looked down at her body, but apart from seeing her toes clearly she couldn't see any difference. Towelling her head afterwards, she found a loose hair in her hand. She stared at it.

'Jason, lookit that, lookit that!'

'Wha'?' He sat up, looked at her, examined the hair.

'It looks like . . . a hair.'

'No, look at the *end*. No, the *other* end.'

'There's something to see?'

Was he awake? She shook his shoulder again.

'There's a quarter inch of blonde there! Not grey!'

'Oh, Jesus. I'll take your word for it.'

'Hah,' she said. 'Obviously the fix hasn't done anything for *your* eyes. I'd have them checked, if I were you.'

'They're good enough for the road, anyway.'

He helped her load her luggage on the jeep, disappeared politely – probably for another surreptitious phone-call – while she sweated through a final check-up by Dr Masoud, and was waiting at the wheel of the jeep when she skipped out of the clinic and hopped in beside him.

'All set?'

'Yup. All clear.'

'Welcome to eternity,' he said, gunning the engine and slewing the jeep out of the driveway in a spatter of gravel.

'Just don't *send* me there first!'

'Ah, I'll be fine,' Jason said, turning right on to the road up into the hills, towards Fetiye. They climbed and climbed, overtaking taxis and trucks and dolmushes, being carefully polite to the troop-carriers. The valley farms and roadside stalls were almost all worked by astonishingly old people, who looked as though they'd had the basic metabolic rejuvenations but couldn't afford the cosmetic ones. Instead of being small and stooped they were tall and straight, but their faces were like Benin masks, dark and corrugated, with bright eyes glittering out.

So, as Jason remarked, no change there.

They crested a rise and Myra could see again before and below them the impossibly blue, the Windolene-dark sea. A mile or so off-shore, visible even from that distance, that height, was the ekranoplan. Smaller craft buzzed around its hundred-metre length. Beyond them all the naval hovercraft and hydrofoils busily patrolled; still further away, across the strait towards Rhodes, Myra could make out their equally assiduous counterparts, the patrol-boats of the Greek Threat.

They followed the long swooping road down to Fetiye, passing the Lycian tombs in the cliffs and turning right before the mosque and down along the edge of the bazaar to the harbour's long mole and esplanade. They pulled up at the embarkation point, beside a star-and-crescent flag and a glowering statue of Kemal.

The engine spun to a halt. Jason looked across at her.

'Well,' he said. 'Will I ever see you again?'

'If we're both going to live forever,' Myra said wryly, 'probably yes.'

'I'll take that as a no.' Jason stuck out his hand. 'Still. It's been a good few days. Keep in touch. And if the investigation turns up any-thing, *I'll* be in touch.'

She caught his hand, her newly sharpened sight blurring suddenly. 'Oh, don't take it as a no!' she said, dismayed at his casual acceptance of her casual words as a permanent parting. This was like adolescence all over again, this was more than lust, she had a crush on him and she was saying the wrong things. She startled him with a fierce embrace, her lips wet on his, her eyelashes wet on his neck, and all the while thinking this wasn't like her, this wasn't right, she was supposed to be a diplomat and she was falling for a fucking *CIA agent* who had been sent to do a different kind of job on her; this was Not The Done Thing, at all.

They pulled apart, holding each other's shoulders, staring at each other, oblivious to the chattering crowd of small boys around the vehicle.

'Myra, you're amazing,' Jason said. 'I'll never forget you, I'll keep in touch, I'll try to see you again, but we both . . .'

'Yeah,' Myra said. She made a long sniffly nasal inhalation. 'We're both grown-up people, we have jobs, we might not always be on the same side and –' she giggled '– "we only have fourteen hours to save the Earth".'

'Or something. Yes.'

Jason disengaged, with a smile that to Myra still looked like a regretful adieu. They remained awkwardly formal with each other as Jason dismissed the boys' unwanted offers of porterage, helped her take her luggage to the shuttle boat, and shook hands as she stood at the top of the ladder.

As the small boat chugged out across the harbour to the larger craft, Myra watched Jason restart the jeep, turn it around and drive it away, vanishing at a turn off the boulevard.

She sighed and turned around to face the ekranoplan. The vast machine looked even more improbably huge as it loomed closer: an aircraft the size of a ship, with stubby wings. A ship that flew. It was on the regular Istanbul to New York run, which stopped off at Izmir and Fetiye before hitting its stride. The boat steered its way through its competitors and hove to under the shadow of the port wing, where a set of steps extended down to a pontoon platform. Officials officiously tagged the luggage for loading into the cargo hold, and the passengers ascended into the ship.

Myra made her way to the forward lounge, bought a gin and tonic at the bar with her remaining handfuls of Turkish gigalira notes, and took the urgent multilingual advice to sit down before the ship took off.

She'd never before travelled in one of these hybrid vehicles – a Kruschev-era Soviet invention, she remembered with residual pride – and she was suitably stunned by its speed and above all by the *impression* of speed, as the great machine roared across the Med at a mean height of ten metres and a top speed of three hundred miles per hour. It left Fetiye at noon, chased the day across the Atlantic, and arrived in New York fourteen hours later at 6 p.m. local time.

Myra spent most of those fourteen hours relaxing, sleeping, sightseeing and thinking about how to save the Earth.

From the sea, Manhattan had a weird, unbalanced look, the Two Mile Tower growing from the Lower East Side throwing all the rest out of perspective. South Street Seaport was still battle-damaged from the coup, and smelt more than ever of fish. Myra made her way along the duckboarded temporary quay, indistinguishable in the stream of disembarking passengers until she stepped into the waiting embassy limo with its sun-and-eagle pennant and welcoming chauffeur, who had the door slammed before anyone could so much as gawk.

The long car nosed arrogantly into the traffic flow. The driver, a stockily built Kazakh who looked as though he moonlighted as a bodyguard, caught her glance in the rear-view.

'The embassy, Citizen Davidova?'

Myra leaned back in the upholstery. Outside, through the armoured one-way glass, she could see people sitting around fires. 'No, the UN, thank you.'

'Very well, Citizen.'

The car lurched as its front, then rear, suspension coped with a shallow shell-crater. Or maybe a pot-hole, NYC's municipal finance being what it was.

'But I'd appreciate it if you could track my luggage from the ship to the embassy, thank you.'

'You're welcome.' He began talking rapidly in Russian into a phone.

They pulled in at the UN building about ten minutes later, the heavy gates of the compound rolling back for them, closing quickly behind. Myra checked her make-up in a hand mirror, stepped out of the car and checked her jacket and skirt in the bodywork sheen. Everything looked fine; in fact, she felt rather over-dressed for the grotty old place. Puddles on the plaza, repairs on the windows, rust on the structural steel, and the Two Mile Tower overshadowing the glass-fronted obelisk. On a coppice of flagpoles the two thousand, three hundred and ninety-seven flags of the nations of the Earth and its colonies flapped in the breeze like a flock of birds preparing to migrate from some long winter to come.

She took the driver's mobile number, and told him he'd have at least a couple of hours before she called him on it. He thanked her, grinned and walked off briskly. Myra walked slowly past the old late-Soviet sculpture – St George slaying the Dragon of War, in ploughshared missile metal – careful in her Prada heels, around the puddles and across the crumbling tarmac, to the doorway. An expert system recognised her; a guard saluted her.

In the foyer she stood lost for a moment until she remembered that the whole place had been gutted and refurbished, probably several times, since she'd last been here. This time around, it had been done out in the modish retro futurist style, rather like her own office.

The colour-theme was leaves, from shades of green through brown to copper. Soothing, though the people in this calming environment scurried about looking haggard. A huge UN flag, blue ground with stylised globe and olive wreath, hung above the reception desk. Myra registered a momentary shock; it was like seeing a swastika.

Two men approached, their steps light on the heavy carpet. She recognised them both: Mustafa Khamadi, the Kazakhstan UN ambassador, short and dark; and Ivan Ibrayev, the ISTWR's representative, tall and cropped-blond, some recessive Volga-German gene manifesting in his bearing and complexion.

Khamadi shook her hand, his smile showing the gold Soviet teeth he'd kept through two rejuvenations; Ibrayev bowed over her hand, almost kissing it.

'Well hi, comrades,' Myra said, eager to break with formality. 'Good to see you.'

'Well, likewise,' said Khamadi. 'Shall we go to my office?'

Ivan Ibrayev shot her a look.

'Ah, thank you,' Myra said. 'But perhaps for, ah, diplomatic reasons, Citizen Ibrayev's might be . . .?'

'Very good,' said Khamadi.

As they waited for the lift his tongue flicked his lips. 'Ah, Citizen Davidova—'

'Oh, Myra, please—'

'Myra,' he went on in a rush, 'please accept my belated condolences on your former husband's death.'

'Thank you,' she said.

'I only knew him slightly, of course, but he was widely respected.'

'Indeed he was.'

The doors opened. The two men made way for her as they all stepped in. The doors closed.

'I still think those spacist bastards killed him,' Ibrayev said abruptly. He glared up at the minicam in the corner. 'And I don't care who knows it!'

The whoosh and the rush, the slight increase, then diminution of the g-force. Myra felt her knees wobble as she stepped out of the lift into a long corridor.

'Investigations are continuing.' She shrugged stiffly. 'Personally, I don't think Reid had a hand in it, that's all I can say.' She flashed a smile across at Ivan, down at Mustafa. 'I knew the man . . . intimately.'

Ivan's fair face flushed visibly. Mustafa displayed a gold canine.

'It leads to complications, the long life,' he said. 'It makes us all close, in the end. What is the theory, the six degrees of separation?' He laughed harshly. 'When I was very young, I shook hands with a woman who had been one of Lenin's secretaries. Think of that!'

Myra thought of that. 'Come to think of it,' she chuckled darkly, 'so did I.'

But it still hit her, the pang like a blade in the belly: *all my ships are gone and all my men are dead.*

No, no. Not yet. She still had ships, and she might still have Jason.

Ivan Ibrayev's office was small. They sat with their knees up against his desk. The trefoil flag hung on one wall, rocketry ads on the others. The window overlooked the East River. The door was open. A flunkie appeared with coffee and cups, then vanished discreetly. Ivan closed the door and turned on the audio countermeasures. Myra swallowed, trying to make the strange pressure in her ear-drums go away. It didn't.

She swallowed again, sipped her coffee. The two men leaned forward, glanced at each other. Ibrayev gestured to her to go ahead.

'OK,' she said. 'You know why I'm here, right?'

'To negotiate US military aid,' said Ibrayev.

'Yeah, well. East American, anyway.' They laughed. 'I've already been given to understand that not much will be forthcoming. What the person who told me that didn't know, what you probably don't know, is what we have to offer them.' She paused. Their faces showed nothing. 'The ISTWR still has some functioning nukes.'

'Nuclear *weapons*?' Khamadi asked. Ibrayev smirked, as though he'd always suspected that the little state he served still sheathed this hidden sting.

'Weapons,' Myra nodded. 'City-busters, mostly, but a reasonably comprehensive suite – all the way down to battlefield tactical nukes, which –' she shrugged '– aren't that hard to come by. But still.'

'We knew nothing of this,' said Khamadi. Ibrayev nodded emphatic concurrence.

'Chingiz Suleimanyov didn't tell you?'

'*Nyet.*'

'Good,' Myra said briskly. 'Well, that's what I'm here to tell you. Kazakhstan is now a *de facto* superpower, for what that's worth.'

Ivan Ibrayev steepled his fingers. 'How do we use them, that's the question. They're not much direct use against the Sheenisov – no point in nuking steppe, eh?'

Khamadi's eyes brightened, his mouth shaped a shining snarl. 'We could point out that they need not be aimed Eastward . . .'

'Huh!' Myra snorted. 'Citizens, *comrades* . . . I *am* an American, and I can tell you one thing the Americans – East, West or Middle – won't stand for is nuclear blackmail. This is a people whose nuclear strategy involved megadeath write-offs on *their* side. They may have come down in the world a bit, but they're not too demoralised to take us out before we know what hit us if we even try that. No. What the President wants me to do is almost the opposite: offer them – under our control of course, but a public, unbreakable deal – to the US, or the UN, in exchange for a military alliance that can stop the Sheenisov in their tracks.'

The two men pondered this proposal with poker-faced calm. Ivan opened a pack of Marlboros and offered one to Myra. She lit up gratefully.

'It's worth trying,' said Khamadi. 'I must say, between ourselves, I think we may regret giving up the new power which the nukes would place in our hands.'

'It's not much of a power,' Myra said. 'In a sense we are proposing to blackmail the Americans, not with possible use against them but with possible use against someone else without their permission.'

Khamadi refilled the cups, frowning. 'The UN still has some nukes itself, as we've just seen. I suspect their stock has been significantly depleted by their use. So they might just be keen to replenish it.'

Ivan gestured at his wall posters. 'It has occurred to me,' he said, 'that we could go *all the way* back into the old business: selling deterrence to everyone who wants it!'

Myra laughed. 'Deterrence against whom? The UN? I don't see that working for long.'

Khamadi grimaced, as though the coffee were more bitter than he'd expected. 'Yes, I take your point. Perhaps it is for the best. So what can we do to facilitate this?'

Myra drew hard on her cigarette. 'Apart from verifying my authority?' She smiled at them. 'You can arrange – I hope – somebody to represent the other side. I've given this a lot of thought on the way over, and checked through the US personnel here, and I have a suggestion for the right person to approach.'

'Sadie Rutelli,' Ibrayev said.

'That's it! How did you know?'

Ibrayev tapped his eyeband. 'Great expert systems think alike.'

'Oh, well,' Myra said, feeling a bit deflated. 'I guess she's the obvious choice. What are the chances of meeting her?'

Ibrayev rolled his eyes and blinked a couple of times. 'According to her public diary . . . pretty good. She has a blank space between 10 p.m. and midnight, which is when she intends to go home. Would you like me to set up a paging program to arrange a meeting?'

'I sure would,' Myra said.

'It's late,' Khamadi said. 'She'll be tired.'

'Make it the offer of a dinner date,' Myra suggested. 'She can choose, I'll pay. Just the two of us – I hope you don't mind, guys?'

The diplomats dismissed the very idea that they might even have the slightest thought of such a deeply unworthy emotion. Myra and Ivan matched fetches, and their electronic secretaries got busy trying to reach Rutelli's.

'It may take some time to get through to her,' said Ibrayev. 'She's busy.'

Myra stood up. 'Then I'll get a shower and some sleep at the hotel. If somebody says they want me urgently, call my fetch. If Rutelli comes through, call me straight away, direct. Otherwise – call me in the morning!'

'I hope you're not still enough of an ex-commie to be embarrassed about all this,' said Sadie Rutelli. She passed Myra a flute of chilled champagne from the minibar of the limo that had picked her up at the Waldorf.

'Indeed not.' Myra toasted her ironically. She was leaning back in the leather seat and enjoying every second of it. 'I know all about the expenses of representation. It's all in Marx. We ex-commies are all hardened cynics on these matters.'

'It's great to see you again, Myra. It's been a long time.'

'Yeah, what? Thirty-four years. Jesus. And you look like 2025 is when you were *born*.'

Sadie, sitting in the seat opposite, looked quite stunning with her long black hair, sable bolero and indigo evening-dress. Myra remembered her as having been just as stunning in blue fatigues. She'd been one of the UN Disarmament Commission agents who'd stripped the

ISTWR of its nukes after the war. She had done it with tact and determination, and despite the strained circumstances, Myra had warmed to her.

'Oh, you flatter me,' Sadie said. 'I must say you look younger yourself than I remember.'

'Ah, I'm still working on that. Or the little machines are.' Myra stroked the backs of her hands, relishing their now smoother and softer feel, the kind of thing that cosmetic creams promised and nanotech machines delivered.

She felt vigorous, as well – she wasn't experiencing jet-lag (ekranoplan-lag . . .) and her snatched two hours' sleep had refreshed her more than seemed proportionate.

'Still,' said Sadie, 'you can't beat back-ups, if you really want to be sure of living . . . a long time.'

'Oh, really?' Myra tried not to scoff. 'You believe that thing works?'

'To the extent that I've had a back-up taken, yes.'

'Has anyone ever come *back* from a back-up?'

Sadie frowned. 'Not as such, no. Nobody's ever been cloned and had their backed-up memories imprinted on the clone brain. Though there are rumours, about some tests Reid's men did, way back . . .'

'With apes. Yeah, I know about that. How do you tell if a fucking chimp's personality has survived?'

Sadie smiled. 'Ah, Myra. You're still a goddamn dialectical materialist. I was going to say, there have been cases where people have got the backed-up copy to *run*, in VR environments. It's expensive, mind. Latest nanotech optical computers, those things that look like crystal balls. Takes one *hell* of a lot of processing-power, but there are some people who can afford it: rock-stars, film-stars and such.'

'Don't they worry about the competition?'

'No, no!' Sadie stared at her. 'That's the point. The copies do the performances – the originals just retire!'

'Sounds like a raw deal,' Myra said. 'Imagine waking up and finding you're living in a silicon chip, and you have to work for the benefit of your selfish original. Jesus. I'd go on strike.' She struck a guitar-holding pose, sang nasally, 'Ain't gonna play Sim City . . .'

Sadie laughed. 'Until your management reboots you.'

Myra was laughing too, but it chilled her to think of this new way for the rich to desert the Earth, not to space but to cyberspace, with their bank accounts; to live for ever on television, where their faces had always been. And what a laugh it would be if, in their silicon heaven, they were to meet the General . . .

Ah, shit. Back to business.

'Is this car secure to talk?' she asked, suddenly sure that the restaurant wouldn't be.

Sadie waved a languid hand. 'Doesn't matter,' she said. 'I know what you have to offer – the fact that you asked to see *me* kinda gives it away, yeah?'

'Seeing you put it like that . . . but the devil's in the details.'

'We don't need to worry about the details,' Sadie said. 'Not tonight. Just a little discretion and circumlocution, and we'll be fine.'

Myra smiled thinly. Probably Sadie knew a lot of the details. It was still her job to keep track of nuclear deployments. Her eyeband – Myra guessed the fine sparkly band around Sadie's forehead was an eyeband – would show her every suspected tac nuke on Earth and off it. And she'd have a shrewd idea where Myra's strategic nukes were, too.

Myra glanced out of the window. The car was making reasonable speed up . . . Amsterdam Avenue, getting to the high numbers. The old buildings were blistered, the pavements cluttered with nano-built squatter shacks like spider bubbles, linked by webbed stairways and ladders and swing-ropes. Their dwellers, and the people on the street, were in this part mostly white. Office-workers, mostly black and Hispanic, threaded their way among the crowds, ignoring their importunity.

'Middle-American refugees,' Sadie said. 'Okies.'

The restaurant, when they reached it a few minutes later, was well into the Harlem spillover. Black flight had long since changed the character of the area; Myra and Sadie stepped across the stall-cluttered pavement under the incurious, inscrutable stares of Peruvians and Chileans. It looked like an America where the Indians had won. In fact, these Indians had lost everything they had to the Gonzalistas, a decade or two earlier. The Gonzalistas had been defeated, but their intended victims had no intention of leaving the US. Now the former refugees' petty commerce filled the offices and shopfronts and spilled on to the pavements, just as their huge families filled the old public-housing projects.

But still, Myra thought, getting away from the killing peaks at all was winning. The Gonzalistas had been a nasty bunch, even for commies; the kind who would dismiss Pol Pot as a revisionist.

The restaurant was called Los Malvinas. Inside it was crowded, mainly with young old-money Latinos, preppily dressed, snootily confident of their social and racial superiority over the newer immigrants on the streets but exploiting – in their fashion-statements as in other ways – their cultural connection. The air smelt meaty and smoky, the walls had huge posters of Perón, Eva, Che, Lady Thatcher and Madonna. Sadie was welcomed by name by an attentive head waiter who escorted them to a table out the back, in a small yard enclosed by trees and creeper-covered walls.

'Nice place,' Myra said. She looked down the menu. 'Doesn't look like it'll take a big chunk out of the company card, either.'

'Knew you'd like it,' Sadie said. She shrugged her bolero on to the chairback, revealing her bare shoulders. 'Jug of sangria?'

'Good idea.' Myra tapped the menu. 'You'll have to advise me on this. Just as well I'm not a vegetarian.'

They put together an order which Sadie assured her would be both good and huge, and sipped sangria and smoked a joint and gnawed garlic-oil-dipped bread while waiting for it.

'OK,' said Myra. She glanced around, reflexively. Half a dozen Venezuelan oil engineers, in shirts and shorts, were talking loudly around the only other occupied table; she shrugged and shook her head. 'OK. Let's talk. Hope you don't mind me saying, but, hell. You got authority to negotiate at the level we're talking about?'

'Sure,' Sadie told her. 'Don't worry about that. Straight line to the top. Not that this is one of the Boss's top priorities, mind you.'

'How about on the UN side?'

Sadie waved a chunk of bread dismissively. 'That's all squared.'

'No change there then, huh?'

'Changes, yeah, but we've rolled to the top again. For what it's worth.'

'Right, I know what you mean. "For what it's worth" seems to come up in conversation a lot these days. Anyway. Here's the deal. We sell you exclusive rights to the package, you back us up against the commie hordes. Shopping-list to follow, but like you say, later for details.'

The waiter arrived with a hot platter and a couple of dishes; a girl followed with bowls of salad and rice. The main dish was like a salad of meat, in which most possible cuts from a cow were represented, along with the tastier internals and a few of the less tasty.

'Enjoy your meal, ladies.'

'Thank you,' said Sadie. She stubbed out the roach. 'Oh, and another sangria, please.'

Myra was ravenous, her appetite honed even keener by the joint, and spent about twenty minutes in atavistic carnivorous ecstasy and exclamation before slacking off enough to take up the conversation properly again.

'So, Sadie.' She put down a rib, wiped her fingers and chin. 'What do you say?'

Sadie took a long swig of sangria, the ice chinking slushily.

'You know, that guy we sent to speak to you? From the Company?'

'Bit hard to forget him.'

'Uh-huh.' Sadie sighed. 'Well, Myra, sorry about this, but.' She scratched her ear. 'It's still the deal, basically. We can give you some kit, sure, but nothing like what you're asking. Definitely no alliance.'

Myra rocked back. She heard the feet of her metal chair scrape the flagstones.

'That's even *with* what we're offering?'

'Even with.' Sadie picked up something intestinal-looking, dragged it through her teeth. 'Because we can't take it. It's no use to us anyway, frankly.'

'Oh my God. Oh, shit.' Myra reached for her cigarettes. 'Mind if—'

'Go ahead. Yes please.'

'What's the problem with our package?'

'Skill sets and legacy systems, basically.' Sadie looked at the tip of her cigarette, wrinkled her nose and sucked grease from her lips. 'Look above my head. Up. What do you see?'

Myra gazed southward and upward.

'Top of the Two Mile Tower?'

'Right. Know what's in it? Squatters, mostly. Damn thing damn near built itself, like a stone tree. But the builders couldn't find enough businesses to rent work-space in it.'

'That sort of thing's common enough,' Myra said. 'Speculative spectacular buildings are usually finished just before the recession hits, and stay empty until the next boom.'

'If there is another boom . . .' Sadie said gloomily.

Myra remembered Shin Se-Ha's version of the Otoh equations. 'There will be,' she said. One more, anyway, she didn't say. 'What's your point?'

'We're losing people,' Sadie said. 'It's no secret. The coup has succeeded in more ways than it's failed. A hell of a lot of our best scientists and engineers have migrated to the orbital colonies, and they support the faction that Mutual Protection have been running supplies for.'

'The Outwarders.'

'Yeah. Think civilisation on Earth is doomed, and they're getting out. And, more to the point, so is a lot of the big money. Most of the corporations have been headquartered in orbital tax-havens since at least the Fall Revolution. Now they've got the muscle – technical, military – to back that up. And the on-site personnel. They'll finance us, all right, but strictly as user fees, like hiring a defence agency, and only as long as we don't step out of line. You may think of the US as the old imperialist oppressor, but these days we're just another banana republic. The whole Earth is one Third World. Big money and skilled labour are in space, and what's left down below is mostly surplus population.' Sadie smiled wryly. 'And bureaucrats, like you and me.'

'So you're saying the US empire still exists,' Myra said. 'But its capital – in both senses – is now in orbit.'

'Yeah, exactly!'

'Fair enough,' said Myra, 'but how does that affect our offer?'

'Well.' Sadie leaned back, took a short draw, like a sip, on her cigarette. 'Let me draw you an analogy. Suppose, just hypothetically, for the sake of argument, that the US wanted to go back to a strategic nuclear posture. Leave aside the fact that the Third World War did for nukes what the First did for gas. At least in terms of using them on Earth – the UN got away with the Heaviside Layer blasts, but that was a bit of a fluke. Leave aside the fact that the big money in orbit is becoming virtually Green with paranoia about nukes in space, too.'

Aha, Myra thought. She would not leave that aside, at all. This was the crux, however valid the rest of Sadie's points were.

'Leave aside the fact that there simply aren't that many big nukes left around. Suppose somebody came to us with, I dunno, a stash of old post-Soviet city-busters: laser-fusion jobs, long shelf-life, low maintenance. They still wouldn't be any use to us, because our whole military doctrine has shifted away from reliance on nukes. There's a lot more to maintaining a credible strategic nuclear deterrent than maintaining the actual weapons. You need missile and bomber crews, tactical boys, analysts, constant practice. Hell, I should know, I worked hard enough at dispersing the teams and scrubbing the records, back in my disarmament days. We don't have people with the relevant skills any more, and we don't have the people to train new ones. We need all our available skill pool to keep our stealth fighters flying, and our teletroopers, smart-battle tactics and techniques up to scratch.'

'I think I see your point,' Myra said dryly. 'So, by the same kind of reasoning, our offer of, uh, mining rights in Kazakhstan isn't really of interest.'

'You could say that. That is the analogy, yes.'

Myra doubted that their reversal of analogy and actuality would have fooled any snoop for a second, but there was a protocol to be followed on these things. It was, she recalled, illegal for public officials under UN jurisdiction – after the Fall Revolution as much as before – to even *discuss* nuclear deterrence as a serious policy option.

And of course they hadn't. Not in a way that would stand up in court, which was all that mattered.

'There is of course one advanced country that isn't a banana republic just yet . . .' Myra said. 'Never even rejoined the UN, come to that.'

Sadie shrugged. 'Go to the Brits if you like,' she said; lightly, but she acknowledged the implied threat. 'Not my problem. But it will be somebody else's.'

'Just so long as we know where we stand,' Myra said, likewise taking the hint. 'OK. Forget about the package deal. What about ground troops and air support?'

'The latter, maybe. At a pinch. And hardware. Hardware, we got. Troops, no.'

'Oh, come on. Even mercenaries. We can pay good rates.'

'Mercenaries?' Sadie laughed. 'Mercenaries are the best *we* have. We use them to put some backbone into our crack regiments. And the crack troops are about all that's left. It's become just about impossible to raise ordinary grunts. Conscription? Don't even think about it.'

Myra still looked sceptical. 'I'll show you,' Sadie told her.

They chatted amiably for a while longer, agreeing to dump on Khamadi and Ibrayev the detailed work of negotiating what little aid the US had to give; but basically, the discussion was over. Myra settled the bill, left a generous tip and followed Sadie out. As they recrossed the crowded pavement to the limo, Sadie startled Myra by walking boldly up to a bunch of Andean lads hanging around a headware stall. The boys looked her up and down, lazily curious.

'Hi, guys,' she said. 'How're you doin'?'

'Fine, lady, fine.'

'How 'bout work?'

'This our work.' They grinned at the stall's owner, who smiled resignedly back.

'Ever thought of joining the Army? Good pay, great conditions. Tough guys like you could make a good go of it.'

They had to hold each other up, they were laughing so hard.

'Not gone get killed fighting hicks and geeks,' one of them said. The sweep of his arm took in everything from the Two Mile Tower to the stall's bristling headware whiskers. He spat away, on to the pavement.

'You preferred tech to men,' he said. 'Let tech defend you.'

11

The Rock Covenant

I followed Druin out of the tunnel and into the gallery of the seer-stone growers without any idea of what he intended to do. Like him, I had my rifle slung and my hands empty. He strolled across the floor to a central aisle between the ranks of stone troughs and turned down it, walking in the same overall direction as we had been following in the tunnel – downwards, towards the old power-station.

'Hey!'

One of the growers came hurrying up. He was a stocky, dark man with sharp, darting eyes. His overalls were blue, dusted with white powder that caught the light like ground glass. He stopped a couple of metres in front of us and glared.

'What are you doing here?' he demanded. 'How did you get in?'

'We're—'

Druin motioned to me to be quiet.

'We're just passing through,' he said. He gazed around the chamber with an expression of slack-jawed wonder. The other tinkers had stopped work and stood about watchfully. 'It's a fascinating place you've got here, I must say.'

'How did you get in here?' the tinker repeated, taking a step closer.

Druin jerked his thumb over his shoulder. 'Oh, we were out chasing the deer,' he explained casually. 'We came across a kind of –' he looked at me, as if searching for a word '– a manhole, would you call it? In the woods up there. We went down it for a bit of a lark, like, and made our way down through yon tunnel.'

Druin hitched his thumb under the rifle's strap and added, 'So if you don't mind, we'll just be on our way.'

The tinker showed more real amazement than Druin had feigned.

'You came through the tunnel?'

195

'Aye,' said Druin. 'It's got some real eerie hollows in it,' he added, with an appreciative wink. He began to walk forward, and I beside him. To my surprise the tinker stepped aside, with a glance and a small shake of the head to his colleagues. I suspected that no outsider had made it past the cavern's spectral guardians for a long time, and that the tinkers here just didn't know what to make of us.

On either hand of us were the stone troughs; the ones we passed first each contained a layer of tiny stones, gravel almost; subsequent ranks had larger and fewer stones, until we reached the very end, where a trough – or rather, by this point, a large circular tub – might contain a single boulder. On the floor below the troughs were oddly shaped stones, apparently discarded; some of these casualties of quality-control had evidently ended up in the tunnel. However, we saw no hollows in that chamber, and I wondered if I'd misunderstood the implied sequence of events, or if the light in there was too bright for such displays.

Within the stones themselves, queerly distorted by the rippling water, strange fleeting scenes played themselves out with a coherence that increased with the size of the stones. I had no leisure to inspect them, but several times I felt that the faces flickering across these smooth surfaces were faces I had seen in the tunnel.

The walls and ceiling of the unnatural cave converged to an entranceway to another passage, about two and a half metres high and two wide. It continued for about thirty metres ahead of us, beyond which a darker doorway loomed. This corridor was unmistakably artificial, its squared walls and ceiling being made of the same glazed substance as the shaft. Its lighting, too, was subtly different from that of the growing-gallery – though it came from similar glass panels, it had that overtone of yellow which marked it as ordinary electric lighting, if more powerful than usually encountered. Our footsteps rang on the ceramic floor, echoing sharply.

'You carried yourself cool in there,' I said to Druin.

'Ah, it's all bluff,' he said. 'They've got used to folks being scared by *their* bluff. But I reckon we'll soon meet some who're ready for us – our friends back there will have signalled ahead.'

'You're not bothered?'

'Not a bit.'

I was, but I wasn't going to show it. My heart was hammering and my head was buzzing with bewildered images, like the seer-stones themselves, and my hand clutching the rifle's strap was slick with sweat.

The response that Druin had expected – or, possibly, a stronger response – came when we were about two-thirds of the way down the corridor. Fergal and two other men appeared in the exit, barring our way. They carried rifles of an unfamiliar design, not aimed at us but ready for use. We walked forward. He stepped out in front of the others and raised a hand.

'Stop right there!' he ordered.

We stopped.

'What are you here for?' Fergal asked.

I decided it was about time I spoke up for myself.

'I'm here to see you,' I said. 'And Merrial.'

'You're seeing me,' Fergal said. He waved a dismissive hand. 'I'll talk to you later.' He stalked closer, to a few metres away, and stared at Druin. 'I know you,' he said venomously.

Druin shrugged. 'You'll have seen me around.'

Fergal's weapon was instantly aimed square at Druin's gut. My companion made a twitch towards his rifle strap, then raised both hands above his head. The other two tinkers brought their rifles to bear at the same moment.

'I know who you *are*,' Fergal said slowly, 'and what you are. Give me one good reason why I shouldn't kill you now.'

Druin took a deep breath. 'Och, man, if you have to ask that there is no help for you,' he said in a steady voice. I looked at him sideways, frozen except for a severe shaking in my jaw and my knees. 'You see,' Druin went on conversationally, 'if you were to kill me, now, my friend Clovis here would some time soon have to kill you. He would kill you and cut your head from your neck, and carry it to my widow and my weans to prove that you were dead and the matter was at an end.'

He glanced at me. 'You would, aye?'

'I would,' I swore. I had eaten under Druin's roof, and could not well refuse the task, if required. The thought of it made me feel sick, but it didn't shake my resolve. I had no idea why Fergal might want to kill Druin in the first place, and I didn't care. That he was willing to contemplate murder told me all I needed to know about him.

'Well, there you are,' said Druin. 'You could kill Clovis too, I suppose, but that would just double your problem.'

197

I did not find this last consideration quite as definite and reassuring as Druin made it sound.

Fergal's glance flicked between the two of us, his tongue unconsciously touching his lips. He backed off a little.

'Put down your weapons,' he said, then added, as we lowered our rifles, 'all of them.'

As I unbuckled my belt I looked at Druin. He shook his head, almost imperceptibly. I placed my knife and pistol and multi-tool beside the rifle.

'The *sgean dhu* as well.'

I felt naked when I stood up. Quick hands passed over or patted my body.

'They're clean.'

Fergal picked up my gear, and one of the other tinkers picked up Druin's. Fergal jerked his chin at the exit and moved around behind us.

'This way.'

We walked forward to the end of the corridor. Beyond it was the open interior space of the old power-station; we descended a short flight of steps to a concrete floor and were told to halt. Behind us I could hear some low-voiced consultation. We waited for its decision, hands on our heads, and I looked about. The turbine, of course, was long since gone, as were most of the original fittings; all that remained was a haunting afterlife of odours, of flaked paint and rusted metal and antique brickwork. Above these whiffs rose the newer smells of concrete and solder. The whole big cuboidal building, with its long windows, had been turned into a complex factory full of workshops and walkways, noisy and bright with the screech and sparks of metalwork. From the number of people I glimpsed at their benches or hurrying along, I guessed that about a hundred tinkers were at work in the building.

Strangely I felt on safer ground here, amid those scores of busy people, and hard by the road and rail of civilisation. I knew this comfort was delusory, but clung to it anyway. The thought of calling out for help crossed my mind; then I reflected that Fergal and his comrades would hardly be so bold if their actions were unknown to the rest.

Suddenly the tinkers clattered down the steps behind us and we were each roughly jostled away, in opposite directions. I heard a door slam, from the other side of the stair, just before I was pushed through another.

The room into which I stumbled was a few metres square, with an overhead light, a table and a couple of chairs. Along its sides rough stacks of copper piping, coils of cable, sacks and so forth suggested that the room was one that currently didn't have a definite use, and was used indifferently as a store, a meeting-place and – now – an interrogation cell. There was even, as somehow seemed inevitable, a sink and an electric kettle and some grotty opened bags of coffee, sugar and tea.

Fergal stepped past me, spun a chair into place on the opposite side of the table and gestured to the other.

'Have a seat.'

He put the weapons he'd taken off me on the draining-board, keeping his own rifle trained on me all the while. Then he sat down, not at the table but tilting his chair against the far wall, and cradling the black rifle with its odd, curving ammunition clip.

'OK, man,' he said. 'Looks like I underestimated you, Clovis.' I let this flattery pass. He rocked the chair forward again, gazing at me intently. 'You've got yourself into a bit of a mess,' he continued in a confidential tone, 'and the others are pretty riled with you, but I think I can square it with them. We can sort this out.'

I said nothing.

'Do you know what Druin is?'

After waiting a moment for some response, he went on, 'He's a management spy, that's what. He works for the site security committee of the ISS at Kishorn. He reports on union activists, among other things.'

Fergal said this in such a tone of loathing that I was surprised. The minor hassles between the unions and the contractors and subcontractors seemed to me hardly a matter for such moral outrage, let alone death threats. I folded my arms and cocked my head slightly to one side. Fergal leaned back again.

'He pushed to have you sacked, you know,' he said. 'That's why he was in the bar at The Carronade.'

I admit I felt slightly shaken by this, because it was entirely plausible and because it implied that someone in the bar had been watching us, but I still made no reply.

'He has not come here, with you, to spy on us. He's here to spy on *you*, to find out what your real connections to us are.'

199

'If that's what he's doing, it sounds reasonable enough to me,' I said, goaded at last. 'I'm sure none of what you're doing is a threat to the project, anyway. That's why I helped Merrial in the first place. So what's the problem with his being here?'

'Oh, it has nothing to do with that. Merrial told you the truth – we think there's a possible threat to the ship, we're investigating it urgently and if we find evidence for it we'll present the evidence to the project's management. No. Druin – and whoever is behind him – are looking for any stick to beat the tinkers with. He's out to discredit us, and arouse hostility to us.'

I shook my head. 'No – he's never shown any hostility to the tinkers, as far as I know.'

'Naturally,' Fergal said derisively.

'Why should he or anyone want to do that, anyway?'

'God, you are so fucking naïve!' Fergal waved a hand to indicate everything outside the room and inside the building. 'We're a somewhat privileged group, by virtue of our monopoly on skills which, frankly, are not hard to learn. Why should you depend on us to build and run your computers?' He laughed. 'You've seen how we make them. It's an ancient technology, called *nanotech*. We don't understand it, but we can apply it. A farmer could do it, just as a farmer can grow crops without understanding how the molecular genetics and replication work. A competent mechanic, with maybe a skilled jeweller or watchmaker for the fiddly bits, could incorporate the seer-stones, as you call them, into machinery.'

'They'd have to know the white logic.'

'That too is not hard to learn. So what's stopping you?'

'Me?'

'Your *people*,' he said impatiently.

'Funnily enough,' I said, 'I asked Druin that very question. He said it was – well, tradition, you would call it. It works, it goes back to the Deliverance, no point questioning it. That's what he said.'

'No doubt. And it wouldn't have been long before he was complimenting you, saying he'd mulled it over and he thought it was a good question.'

'Do you mind if I smoke?' I asked. I wanted to give the impression of weakening; my craving made it credible.

'Sure, go right ahead,' said Fergal.

I took the materials from my pocket and lit up.

'What I don't understand,' I said, 'is why you're so bothered by his turning up here. You even threatened to kill him. Maybe that was a bluff—'

'It wasn't!'

'But why? Even if he's as hostile as you say, he'll have people searching for him if he doesn't return, and it won't take anyone long to think of looking here.'

Fergal flicked his fingers. 'We could make it look like an accident that had nothing to do with us. It's a dangerous sport, deer-hunting.'

'And I would go along with your story, or join him at the bottom of a cliff?'

'Something like that.'

'What,' I asked, trying to keep my voice from betraying my rage and fear, 'is important enough to justify doing *something like that*, now?'

'Ah.' Fergal frowned. 'He – and you – have arrived at a very awkward moment. We've found something in the files that Merrial retrieved – something we've been missing for a very long time, and which we only recently realised might be stored at the University, of all places. We—'

He paused. 'Let's just say we'd lose a lot if anyone started poking around now. There's obviously an investigation going on, and we really aren't in a position to resist any intrusion in force.' He dusted his palms and stood up, laying the rifle carefully aside across the sink, within his reach and out of mine. 'Which is where you come in, Clovis. Obviously we don't want to kill Druin, or yourself.'

'If you can possibly avoid it.'

'Exactly!' he smiled, damning himself with his grin. 'No need for any of that. You're an intelligent bloke, Clovis, and you can help us. All you have to do is persuade Druin that there's nothing here to threaten the project, and that he should leave well alone.'

'That shouldn't be hard,' I said. 'And Druin shouldn't worry you. Even if he is what you say, he's only doing his job. And speaking of jobs, I've just lost mine and I want an explanation. As well as the files you took, and a chance to speak to Merrial.'

Fergal narrowed his eyes. 'Merrial might not want to speak to you.'

'That's for her to say.'

'As for the files—'

He frowned, considering. I got the impression that he was beginning to feel the files were turning out to be more trouble than they were worth.

'Look,' I said, 'I understand why you feel they're yours. But they're not mine to let you have, or yours to take. The Deliverer left them to the University, not to the Fourth International.'

Fergal jumped up as if he'd sat on a wasp.

'Who told you about the Fourth International?'

I shrugged. 'I'm a historian,' I said. 'It's common knowledge among scholars.'

This double lie deflated Fergal somewhat. He sat back down and eyed me warily.

'So what do you know about it?'

'It's a communist secret society that goes back to before the Deliverer's time.'

'Hmm,' he said. He rubbed an eyelid. 'That's about right. Though "communist" doesn't really tell you what it's all about, these days.' He laughed harshly. 'God, I sometimes feel if we could get *capitalism* back—'

'The Possession?' I asked incredulously.

'Well, you would call it that. Let me tell you, it would be better than this dark age you people have got yourselves bogged down in.'

'This is a dark age?' I laughed in his face. 'We're building a spaceship not fifty kilometres from here.'

'Oh, Christ.' Fergal knotted his fists. 'Aye, building it out of boiler plate. You build everything, up to crude atomics and even fucking *laser-fusion engines* with skills handed down from master to apprentice. Compared to the ancients, you people are complete barbarians. Compared to what you could be—'

He sighed and stood up, and began pacing the room like a beast in a cage. 'You could have a world where nobody has to do any work that isn't like play, where almost any sickness or injury could be mended, where nobody has to die, where we live like gods and fill the skies with our children's children. Instead we have *this*.' He smacked his palm with his fist and looked around with an expression of disgust.

'And who would do the work in this paradise?' I asked, perhaps more offensively than I intended.

'Machines, of course. Every bit of work in the world can be done by machines, linked up and co-ordinated.'

'Oh, right,' I said, disappointed. 'The path of power.'

'It doesn't have to be like that, next time—'

'*Next* time?'

Fergal leaned over the table on his fists, in a manner simultaneously intimidating and confidential. 'That's what the International exists for: the next time. The next chance humanity has to break out of this prison. Our time will come, again. And next time, we'll be ready.'

I shook my head. 'I don't understand.'

He looked at me with some regret, then straightened up and moved back to his seat. 'It's no use trying to explain it to you now,' he said. 'There's so much you need to know to make sense of it, and you have no way of getting—'

He was interrupted by a banging on the door.

'Who's there?' he shouted.

'It's me – Merrial! Fergal, you've got to—'

'Wait there!'

His shouted command came too late. The door burst open and Merrial charged in. She rushed past me and placed something on the table and then snatched her hands back from it as though it were a dish too hot to handle. It was a seer-stone apparatus, and the stone in the middle of it was glowing with colour and alive with movement, forming a tiny scene under the domed surface, a bubble of life startling in its virtual reality.

The scene was of a forest glade, in which a man sat elf-like on a rock. He looked out at us, quite calm and uncanny. He spoke, and his voice came from a speaker in the side of the surrounding apparatus. The volume was too low to make out what he was saying – certainly not above Merrial's shouting.

'You never told me there was a deil in it!'

Fergal had jumped up, and was staring down intently at the stone. He raised a hand, without looking up.

'Calm down, Merrial,' he said mildly. 'This is no deil. It's what you were looking for.'

'What in hell is that?' I asked. I too was on my feet, peering entranced at the amazing, beautiful thing.

'It's an artificial intelligence,' the tinker said, his voice thrilled with awe. He stooped to the seer-stone and placed his ear close to the speaker and listened. Merrial seemed to have noticed me just as I spoke.

'What are you doing here?' she asked. Her eyes were reddened, her cheeks pale with fatigue. She looked scared and puzzled.

'I came here for you,' I said. 'I hoped you might want me to come back.'

'But I thought—'

'You two, please leave now,' Fergal said. He didn't even look up at us. He waved a hand absently to one side. 'Take your weapons and tools, Clovis, take this woman if you want and get the hell out of here with your friend, the company spy.'

Merrial turned and looked down at Fergal.

'You want me to go?' She sounded hurt, but hopeful as well.

'Yes, yes,' Fergal said, impatiently deigning to spare her a glance. 'You've done your job, and very well too. Your skills won't be needed in the . . . next phase. Oh, and Clovis – take the bloody paper files while you're at it. We won't be needing them any more, either.'

Merrial glowered at Fergal for a moment and clutched my hand.

'Clovis, what's going on?'

'I think we'd better do as he says,' I said. I let go of her hand and edged around the table, picking up the rifle I'd carried and the gear from my belt. I buckled them back on, shoved the sheathed dagger back in my boot and took Merrial's hand in my left, keeping the rifle in my right. Together we backed out of the room. Fergal didn't watch us go, or even – as far as I could see – notice. He was talking quietly to the sprite in the stone. I pushed the door shut with my toe.

'Do you want to come with me?'

Merrial blinked. 'Of course I do.'

I hugged her (rather awkwardly with the rifle in one hand, but I wasn't letting go of it again) and then said, 'We better get out before that bastard changes his mind.'

'Or something worse happens. Yes, come on.'

The big work-shop space was still busy, with lights coming on here and there as the evening shadows lengthened – the time, I was startled to realise, was only ten o'clock – and the ambient light reddened. A few people on the overhead walkways glanced down at us curiously, but that was all.

The room in which Druin was being held was only a few quick strides away. I opened the door and walked in, Merrial close behind me. This room had only a chair in the middle, with one very bright light above it. Druin was sitting on that chair with a bored, sullen and stubborn expression on his face, while the two tinkers who'd accompanied Fergal stood, one in front of him and one behind. Their raised voices fell silent as we entered. Their rifles – and Druin's – were propped against the back wall; mine was pointing straight ahead. It still wasn't loaded, but they weren't to know that.

'Fergal says you're to let him go,' said Merrial.

'What have they been doing to you?' I asked.

Druin stood up and stretched. 'Och, nothing to speak of,' he said. 'They have merely been boring me with an account of my sins. I have not yet found it in my heart to confess.' He deftly retrieved his weapons and kit. 'I'll thank you to escort us out, gentlemen.'

One of the tinkers found his voice. 'I want this confirmed by Fergal.'

'You do that if you like,' Merrial said. 'But I warn you, he's not in a friendly mood.'

The tinker opened his mouth and closed it again. He smiled at Merrial in a surprisingly complicit way, which made me suspect that he and Merrial had some shared experience of Fergal's moods. 'Oh, well, it's your responsibility,' he said.

We stepped outside the room.

'Wait a minute,' said Merrial.

She skipped away up a stair-ladder and ran along a walkway, her feet setting the metal ringing. We waited in uneasy silence until she returned, the two file-folders hugged to her chest.

'That's us,' she said. 'All set.'

The two men walked ahead of us down a long central passage through the machine shop to the building's ancient green copper doors, then turned sharply left and showed us out through a rather less imposing wooden door.

'Goodbye,' said Druin balefully.

The tinkers ignored him.

'Are you leaving?' one of them asked Merrial.

'I'm going home,' she said. 'I hope I see you again.'

Druin's truck was just over a kilometre away. We hastened along the quiet road, the late sun in our eyes. Druin strode briskly in front. Merrial's hand was clasped in mine, fingers intertwined. None of us said very much; we had too much to say all at once.

205

At last we reached the truck. Druin stopped and looked at the rifles.

'Och, I forgot, we have some deer to kill.'

He laughed at my face, and took the two rifles and racked them again on the back of the truck. We went around to the cab and climbed in. Merrial shared the double passenger-seat with me; it was comfortably crowded. For a minute we all slumped gratefully. I passed Merrial a cigarette and lit for both of us. The Kyle train clattered past.

'You know,' Druin said reflectively, 'I've never before had a gun pointed at me, thank Providence. It isn't an experience I'd want to repeat.'

'I don't think they'd really have killed either of us,' I said. 'It was us who marched in with rifles, after all.'

'Aye,' said Druin indignantly, 'and I've carried a rifle into The Carronade many's the time, and nobody ever took it ill.'

'Different situation—'

'Fergal could have killed you!' Merrial interrupted. 'If he was in the mood. It was only the possible consequences that stopped him. You did something *stupidly* dangerous going there.'

'Well, we went there to get you, and to get yon papers that Clovis makes such a fuss about,' Druin grinned. 'And that's what we've come out with.'

'What a charming way to put it,' said Merrial, unoffended. I leaned past her and frowned at Druin.

'What about you? Fergal said you were working for site security, spying on the unions and on the tinkers. And that you argued for getting me sacked. Is that true?'

'I don't *spy* on anyone,' Druin said. 'That's just the tinkers' way of putting it, at least those three who caught us. There'll be the deil to pay for that, you know!'

'How?' Druin's non-denials hadn't passed me by, but this was more urgent.

Druin turned the engine on and began to steer the truck back on to the road west. 'False imprisonment!' he said. 'And assault with a deadly weapon, which is what threatening someone with a gun is. You and me, Clovis, we could sue the bastards.' He glanced across at me sharply. 'You haven't any idea, by any chance, why they kept us in the first place, and why they let us go when they did? I mean, with me

206

they just kept banging on about what a scab I was. What did Fergal have to say to you? And, come to think of it, what are you two up to anyway? I know you're up to something, and that it concerns the ship. Which means it concerns me.'

I slid my arm around Merrial's shoulders. She smiled at me, then gazed straight ahead.

'Tell him,' she said. 'Tell him it all.'

So I did, as we pulled out of Dark and drove into the sunset.

'Aye, well,' said Druin, 'you've told me all you know, Clovis.' He sipped his whisky and flicked at a midge. 'Quite a tale! But I haven't heard Merrial's side, and I reckon that's more than half the story.'

We were sitting around a roughly made, age-smoothed table in the broad stone-flagged kitchen of Druin's house, ourselves surrounded by the shelves of crockery, the shining electric oven and a sink with a dripping tap. Arrianne and the children had long since gone to bed. The back door stood open to the warm night, and the smells and sound of the sea-loch. A saucer on the table was filling up with our cigarette-butts. Beside it a bottle of whisky and a pot of coffee were emptying fast.

Merrial rubbed her eyebrows, ran her fingers through the wide swathes of her hair and flicked them back behind her shoulders. She had not expanded on any of my account, beyond the occasional cor-roborative comment or nod.

'Well, all right,' she said. 'From my side there's – well, some of it I'd rather talk about with Clovis – it really is personal, it really is no con-cern of yours, Druin.'

Druin tilted his hand. 'OK. And the rest?'

'Ah, well, it goes back a wee bit, to when I started worrying about . . . stories I'd heard about what happened at the Deliverance. Basically, it was that the Deliverer, Myra Godwin herself, had set off something that physically destroyed the settlements and satellites, and that in doing so she'd not only killed God knows how many people, she'd created a barrier to anything ever getting safely back into space again. Every orbiting platform that was destroyed would have been broken into fast-moving fragments which in turn would destroy others, and so on until there was nothing left but a belt of debris around the Earth – and anything that goes up now would just end up as more debris! Now, Fergal is a well-respected tinker, apart from his being a . . . leading member of the International.' She shot us a glance. 'Which is not as sinister as you think! But that's by the way. Fergal's in charge of the tinkers who're working on the project, though he doesn't work on the site himself. So after getting nowhere with the project management, I took it to him, and he said we should try to investigate it for ourselves. It was myself who suggested we could look for someone who might have access to anything the Deliverer left at Glasgow, and that, well, there were students working on the project for the summer who might . . .'

'So you came looking for me?'

'Aye,' she grinned. 'But I wasn't to know what I'd find. Could have been somebody who was only interested in scholarship, or who would not have gone along with the idea. Anyway, I kept my ears open, and it was not long before I heard about you.'

Druin laughed, as much at my embarrassment as at her account.

'Clovis was not exactly quiet about his interests! He's been bending our ears about the Deliverer and history all the bloody summer. But back to your Fergal. It sounds like he took your worries seriously.'

'Oh, sure,' Merrial said. 'I got the impression that quite a few tinkers have the same idea, and . . . at least some people in the International had even stronger reasons to think it.'

Druin took a sudden wasteful gulp of his good whisky.

'Why would the tinkers – or this International – want to keep that a secret?'

Merrial stared at him. 'Because the Deliverer's reputation, and her last message to the world, is what protects the tinkers! If the ordinary folk, the outsiders – no offence – got to think she was some mass-murdering monster like Stalin, what would they care about anything she said?'

Druin cupped his chin with his hand and regarded her quizzically.

'Is that what you think, or is that what Fergal told you?'

'Both, but, well, yes. I see what you mean.'

'More than I can say,' I said.

Merrial turned to me. 'What he means is, it's something I've accepted as long as I can remember without thinking about it, but when you say it out and think about it, it just doesn't seem very likely.'

'Exactly!' said Druin. 'It's true up to a point, mind, but fundamentally it doesn't explain why the tinkers and the rest of us rub along fairly well for the most part. The story that they're the Deliverer's children, as it's said, is just a symbol, a signpost or landmark, like the statue itself. We don't get on with the tinkers because we respect the Deliverer – we respect the Deliverer and maintain her statues because we get along with the tinkers. And we do that because we need the tinkers, and they need us.'

I looked at the man, astonished. In all my years of study I had never read or heard a hint of anything like that. I had certainly never had such a reflection on my own. That something so self-evidently true – once stated – yet so unobvious and against the grain of what Gantry would have called 'vulgar cant' should come from this metalworker and not from a scholar was something of a shock to my estimation of scholarship, not to mention of myself.

There was no way I could say all this without sounding condescending, so I only said, 'Druin, that's brilliant. Never thought of that.'

He gave me a thin-lipped, narrow-eyed smile, as if he knew my unspoken thoughts. 'Aye,' he said, 'brilliant or no, I'm pretty sure the thought has occurred to our man Fergal. So his secrecy has other aims than that. If you, Clovis, were to publish your great work on the Deliverer when you're an older and wiser man, which proved beyond a shadow of a doubt that she was the most wicked woman who ever walked the Earth, do you think for a minute that folk would start throwing stones at the tinkers?' He laughed. 'No, they'd be throwing stones at you!'

'Where does that get us?' I asked, somewhat defensively.

'It gets us to this,' Druin said slowly, tapping the table with a blunt fingernail. 'Like I said, Fergal's desire for secrecy in this matter is not for the reason Merrial and you thought. In fact, from the way you say he behaved when Merrial found the wee man in the stone, I would say that finding yon thing, whatever it is, was his real aim all along. That was what he sent you both to seek in Glaschu. Now that you've found it for him, he doesn't give a damn about any supposed space debris. And don't forget, Merrial, you raised the matter with the project and the only reason you were slapped down hard is that *of course* the designers have thought of that – whether the Deliverer's doing or no, the stuff that was up in orbit in the past must have gone somewhere! In the old records, such as they are, you could see them like moving stars with the naked eye – is that not so, Clovis?'

I nodded.

'Well, they're no there the now, and our best telescopes – which isn't saying much, I admit, compared to the ones with which the ancients saw the Universe born, but still – can't see a speck up there. And there's no more shooting stars now than there was in antiquity – we know that for sure, because these records were on paper and were passed on. So there's likely no cloud of debris around the Earth, although if the Deliverer did as you said, I guess there could be some heavy stuff up there in the high orbits yet. But even that's unlikely. It's said that in the troubled times the sky fell, and the best scientists' guess is that that was our ancestors' way of saying what they saw when the great space cities, long deserted or filled with dead, were eventually brought spinning down by the thin drag of the air up yon and fell to Earth of their own accord.'

By this time I was beyond being surprised by Druin; his words were just further nails in the coffin of my conceit.

'Did you find anything in the computer files about this?' I asked Merrial.

She shook her head. 'No, there's nothing that goes up to the date of the Deliverance itself. It was when I was searching through them that I opened the file that released what Fergal called the "artificial intelligence".' Her eyes widened at the memory. 'At first I thought it was just one of they faces that appear in the stones.'

'What are those, by the way?' Druin asked.

Merrial waved her hand. 'We don't know. We've found references to things called Help programs, and that seems to be what they are – they're aye spelling out "help", anyway! Just some old stuff that got passed down, I think. But this thing wasn't one of them at all. It looked straight at me, and spoke.'

'What did it say?'

'"Hello",' she said, in an unnaturally deep voice.

We all laughed.

She gave an exaggerated shudder. 'My next thought – when I'd got over the shock a bit – was that it was a security demon, like the one you and me ran across in Glasgow. But it wasn't that, either. It wasn't warning me off – it was inviting me in. That's when I ran with it to Fergal.'

'Who seems to have accepted its invitation,' I said. 'He lost interest in all else as soon as he saw it.'

'Hmm,' said Druin. He stood up and stepped over to the door-way, perhaps to get away from our smoke. The sky, an hour after midnight, was still light – or growing lighter again – behind him. 'Which rather suggests to me that that was his objective all along. As why shouldn't it be?' He turned back to us, his eyes shining. 'Who wouldn't want to talk to an artificial intelligence? The ancients had them, and even the tinkers have lost them – am I right, Merrial?'

'Oh, sure,' she said. 'I've never seen or heard of us having anything like that myself, and I . . . I think I would have.'

'You know,' Druin said, 'this is a relief, really. All right, the two of you were used by Fergal, maybe put through a bit of anguish and inconvenience, but no great harm has come of it. And no, Clovis, I don't count your little difficulties as great harm – you'll have worse trouble than that before you're my age!'

'All right,' I said, holding back some irritation, 'I can see how it might not seem important to you. But Fergal has got hold of this thing, and what's worrying me is what he intends to do with it.'

'What he intends to do with it,' said Druin, 'depends on what it is. Any ideas there, Merrial?'

'No,' she said. 'It was in Myra Godwin's files, and we know that some people had these things back then – it could have been some kind of adviser or counsellor. Maybe Fergal knows what it is, but I don't.'

'I hate to think what Fergal might do with an adviser that has access to knowledge from the past,' I said. Druin shook his head.

'So what if Fergal has found a new toy, or a new friend for all I know? It's none of our damn business, and certainly none of mine – it has nothing to do with the security of the ship, now has it?'

'You've got over your annoyance at being held and disarmed pretty damn quick,' I said sourly.

'Ach!' Druin said. 'Hot words. Forget it. Who would sue a tinker, anyway?'

At that Merrial and I both had to laugh. The futility of 'taking a tinker to court' was proverbial.

'That doesn't solve the problem though,' Merrial said.

'What problem?'

'The problem isn't the thing itself. Fergal is the problem.' She frowned, evidently troubled. 'He's no exactly evil – his intentions are

211

good, in a way, and he can be a very . . . charming man in his way, on a personal level; but he's very . . . single-minded, you know? He has a tendency to focus on one thing at a time, and to over-ride anything and everybody else.'

Druin snorted. 'Hah! I don't know Fergal, but I know the type. More by repute than experience, thank Providence.' He chuckled. 'Mind you, if ever I run across a manager like that, he tends to have a short career thereafter. As a manager, anyway.' He stomped over and sat down again. 'But still – that's a problem for your lot, no for mine. I still say we'd best let the matter drop. The project's getting awful close to completion, we're actually ahead of schedule, and there's big bonuses riding on getting the platform out the yard before the end of August – which could make the difference between getting it out before the winter and having to wait till the spring. That's no small thing, and trouble wi the tinkers is the one thing that could blow it at this stage.'

'What worries me about Fergal,' I said, 'is not so much his personality as his beliefs. I know you're not that kind of person, Merrial, but communism is notoriously susceptible to characters who are . . . who can twist it into a reason for doing what they'd like to do anyway, which is living outside the covenant.'

'What do you mean by "the covenant"?' asked Druin.

'Och, what you said – when Fergal seemed to be threatening to kill you. Blood for blood, death for death – that's the covenant, the rock. Or what you said about us and the tinkers, having to live together – same thing, on the side of the living.'

'Fergal sometimes says things like that,' Merrial interjected hastily. 'That so-and-so ought to be shot, or whatever. He doesn't mean it, it's just hot words, as Druin put it.'

Druin made a conciliatory gesture. 'What you're both saying may well be true enough,' he said mildly. 'The covenant is strong in our days, for reasons which – och, we all know the reasons! So a man like Fergal can rant and rave, but he can't do much harm. How many of the tinkers would you say follow his ideas, as opposed to, say, respecting him as a man and an engineer?'

'Not many,' said Merrial cautiously.

Druin leaned back and took a sip of whisky, then topped up our coffees.

'Well, there you are,' he said in a relaxed and expansive tone. 'Like

212

I said, no business of mine.' He leaned forward, becoming more concentrated in his expression, fixing us both with his gaze. 'As to what my business is, Fergal and his two sidekicks were right in one respect – I do have a place on the site security committee. I'm no spy – I was put there by the union, dammit! And I did push for having your clearance revoked, Clovis. What else could I do, with the information I had? But I can equally well push to have it restored, and I will. You'll be back at your job in a day or two, if you want it, whatever your University decides about you.'

'That's –' I shook my head '– that's great, that's what I want. Thanks.'

'But before you return yon files to the University, have another look through them, and try to see if there *is* anything in them about what happened at the Deliverance. Or anything about this artificial intelligence. Tell me what you find, even if it's nothing, just to put my mind at rest. Put that couple of days to good use, you and Merrial.' He grinned slyly. 'I don't need to tell you to do the same with the nights. Speaking of which, I'm off to my bed. And meanwhile, not a word about all this. Keep the peace with the tinkers, and we'll get this show on the road.'

'The sky road,' I said, quoting Fergal.

'Aye. Everybody happy?'

We walked to Merrial's house, and on the way we talked.

'I thought,' she said, 'that you were too committed to your history, your research and your old papers, to be willing to stay with me. That was what I was upset about, not your questions.'

'Ah,' I said. 'And I thought you were too committed to the secrets of your society to trust me.'

'Aach,' we both said at once.

I told her what Druin had said, about the tinkers' methods of recruitment.

She laughed, clinging to my arm and swinging away out on it, looking up at me and looking away, giggling.

'It's true!' she said. 'It wasn't what I'd planned.'

'So you—'

'Fell for you and hoped you'd join us, yes.'

'Ah-ha-ha! Become a tinker!'

'Well, why not?'

213

She swung around and caught me by both elbows and looked me straight in the eyes.

'Why not?' she repeated.

I thought of what I'd seen and felt – and smelt – in the library when I went there with Merrial, and I thought of what I'd seen in the old power-station. This was history, this was the real thing, not dead but living, a continuity with the past and an earnest of the future, the sky road indeed. But who's to say it was those considerations that weighed with me, and not the sight of Merrial under the stars, on her way to a bed I could share for all the nights of my life?

Not me, for sure.

'Why not,' I said. 'Yes.'

12

Dark Island

Coming in from the West on the M8, the taxi hired by the Kazakhstani consulate to take Myra from Glasgow Airport was hit by small-arms fire just as it came off the flyover at Kinning Park.

Myra saw white starry marks pock the smoky armoured glass, *did-did-did*, heard the wheels' *whee* of acceleration; her hand went reflexively to the shoulder holster under her coat and got caught in the strap of the seatbelt. For a moment, as she looked down at her recently, newly smooth and now suddenly white hand, she thought death had found her at last – that she was going to die old and leave a good-looking corpse.

Then they were out of it, smoothly away, swinging around up and on to the Kingston Bridge over the Clyde. Myra twisted about and looked back and to the left, where the standard-practice burning-tyres smokescreen rose somewhere among the office-blocks and high-rises into the pale-blue late-May morning sky. A helicopter roared low and fast above the motorway, making the big car rock again, and flew straight at one of the tall buildings. A diagonal streak of punched square holes was abruptly stitched across the reflective glass of the building's face. The helicopter paused, hovering; the car swooped from the brow of the bridge, and the scene passed out of sight.

'Jesus,' she said, shaken. 'What was all that about?'

The speaker in the partition behind the driver's seat came on.

'Greens,' the man said. 'They sometimes shoot at traffic from the airport.' She saw his reflected eyes frown, his head shake. He wasn't wearing a peaked cap. He was wearing a helmet. The car slowed as the traffic thickened. 'Sorry about that.'

'Can't be helped, I guess,' Myra said. 'But –' she put on her best ignorant-American tone '– I thought you folks had that all under control. In the cities, anyway.'

Not what she'd call a city – there were taller buildings in *Kapitsa*, for fuck's sake! Even with its hills Glasgow looked flat. She could see the University's bone-white tower above the stumpy office-blocks. The place had changed considerably since the 1970s, but not as much as she'd expected, considering all it had been through: the 2015–2025 Republic, the Third World War and the Peace Process; then the Restoration and the guerilla war against the Hanoverian regime, and the Fall Revolution and the New Republic, itself now in its four-teenth year of (what it too, inevitably called) the struggle against terrorism. The blue, white and green tricolour of the United Republic and the saltire of the Scottish State flew from all official or important buildings.

'No, I'm afraid it's not all under control at all,' the driver was saying. 'They're right here in the towns now, and there's bugger all we can do about them. Apart fae bombing the suburbs, and it's no that bad yet.'

'Just bad enough to be strafing tower-blocks?'

'Aye.'

Myra shivered and settled back in the seat. Her not very productive mission to NYC had taken up less time than originally scheduled, leaving her a couple of days before her pencilled-in meeting with someone from the United Republic's Foreign Office. She was begin-ning to wish that nostalgia – and an itch to personally sort out the disposal of her archive – hadn't made her decide to spend that Saturday and Sunday in Glasgow.

The United Republic, though not her first choice of possible allies, was still the next best thing to the United States. It was politically opposed to the Sheenisov advance, but hadn't done much to stop it because it had a healthy distaste for entanglements in the Former Union. On the other hand, thanks to shared oil interests in the Spratly Islands it was a strong military and trading partner of Vietnam, which was standing up pretty well against the Khmer Vertes, which . . . after that it got complicated, but Parvus had the story down to the details. The upshot was that with an actual state on offer as a stable ally, the UR might well be interested in a deal, nukes or no nukes.

The taxi exited the motorway and took a few sharp turns to arrive at the western end of St Vincent Street, slowing down just across from the New Britain Hotel, where she had a room booked.

'Bit ay a problem . . .' said the driver.

A crowd of a couple of hundred was outside the hotel, almost blocking the pavement, and spilling over on to the street. It consisted of several small and apparently contending demonstrations; three separate loud-hailer harangues were going on from perilous perches on railings and ledges of next-door buildings; lines of Republican Guards segmented the groups. The reverse sides of placards wagged above bobbing heads.

'Ah, no problem,' Myra said. 'Just a lefty demo.'

Probably protesting the presence of a representative of some repressive regime, or possibly an unpopular government minister staying at the New Brit. As the big car described a neat and illegal U-turn and glided to a halt a few yards from the left flank of the demonstration, Myra idly wondered what specimen of political celebrity or infamy she'd be sharing residence with.

The driver stepped out – on the wrong side, as she momentarily thought – went around the rear, pinging the boot open on his way, and opened the door for her. She gave him a good flash of her long legs as she swung them out and emerged, in tall boots, short skirt, sable hat and coat. The rejuvenation was definitely making her legs worth seeing again; she'd have to rethink her wardrobe . . .

The driver lifted her two big suitcases from the boot; she waited for a moment as he clunked it down and closed the nearside door, then she walked towards the hotel entrance, looking curiously at the demo as she hurried past it. There was about three yards of clearance between the shopfronts and the half-dozen or so Republican Guards deployed along the pavement to demarcate the front line of the demo. Behind the Guards the crowd was jumping up and down and yelling and chanting.

She glanced up at a placard being waved above her and saw at the centre of it a blurrily blown-up newsfeed-clip picture of her own face. Suddenly the contending chants became clear, like separate conversations at a party.

'Victory to – the SSU!'

That one was in a battle of the soundwaves with, 'Sheenisov – hands off! Viva – Kazakhstan!'

Above them both, not chanted but being shouted repeatedly

through one of the loud-hailers, 'Support the political revolution in the ISTWR!'

A competing loud-hailer was going on in a more liberal, educated and educational tone about the crimes of Myra Godwin's regime – she caught the words 'nuclear mercenaries' and 'shameful exploitation' in passing.

For a moment Myra stopped walking; she just stood there, too shocked to move. Her gaze slid past the reflecting shades of a Guard to make eye-contact with a young girl in a tartan scarf. The girl's chant stopped in mid-shout and Myra couldn't look away from her disbelieving, open-mouthed face. Then the girl reached over the Guard's shoulder and pointed a shaking finger at Myra.

'That's *her*!' she squealed. 'She's here!'

Myra smiled at the girl and looked away and walked steadily towards the steps up to the hotel door, now only about ten yards away. The driver puffed along behind her. The chants continued; it seemed she was getting away with it.

And then a silence spread out, just a little slower than sound, from the girl who had identified her. The chants died down, the loud-hailer speeches ceased. The crowd surged through the wide gaps between the Guards, blocking the pavement. A young man, not as tall as Myra but more heavily built, stood in front of her, yelling incomprehensibly in her face.

Her old understanding of the Glasgow accent restored from memory.

'Ah despise you!' the man was shouting. 'Yi usetae call yirsel a Trotskyist an yir worse than the fuckin Stalinists! Sellin nuclear threats and then sellin slave labour! And noo yir fightin agin the Sheenisov! They're the hope o the world and yir fightin them for the fuckin Yanks! Ya fuckin sell-out, ya fuckin capitalist hoor!'

He leaned in her face ever more threateningly as he spoke. His fists were balling, he was working himself up to take a swing at her. Three yards behind his back somebody holding up a 'Defend the ISTWR!' placard was pushing through the press of bodies. Myra took one step back, bumping into one of her suitcases – the driver was still holding it, still behind her. Good.

She slipped her right hand inside her coat. The yelling man's clamour, and forward momentum, stopped. Another silence expanded around them. Myra reached into a pocket above her thumping heart

218

and pulled out her Kazakhstani diplomatic passport. She thumbed it open and held it high, then waved it in front of the nearest Guard's nose.

'Officer,' she said without turning around, 'please escort my driver into the hotel.'

'Aw right, ma'am.'

'Thanks!'

The driver passed by on her left surrounded by uniforms. Myra took advantage of the accompanying flurry of distraction to dive behind the man who'd yelled at her, and to push herself into the small huddle of pro-ISTWR demonstrators. She glanced quickly around five shocked but friendly faces, noticing lapel badges with a flashed grin of recognition and pride – the old hammer-and-sickle-and-4, a solidarity-campaign button with the ISTWR's signature radiation trefoil, sun-and-eagle stickers ...

'Comrades,' she said, 'let's go inside.'

The comrades clustered around her and together they stepped back on the pavement. The angry man was being restrained by some of his own comrades, but still denouncing Myra at the top of his voice. Myra's group marched up the steps and through the hotel's big swing doors into the now crowded foyer. White marble floor, black-painted ironwork, fluted mahogany at the reception and stairwell, a lot of flowers and stained glass. The militiamen and the driver were standing off to one side, some hotel-management chap was hurrying up with a politely concerned look and a mobile phone, and – looking back – she saw that everyone was inside and the steps were clear and the door was being secured.

'Jesus H. Christ,' she said. By now she was thoroughly rattled. She reached inside her coat again. Everybody froze.

She stayed her hand, and looked around; smiled grimly.

'Anybody else need a cigarette?'

The iron fire-escape door was spring-loaded and would clang if she let it swing back, so she closed it slowly, letting go of its edge at the last moment.

It clanged.

Myra looked up and down the fire-escape and around the back yard of the hotel. Dripping pipes, rattling ventilation ducts, soggy cartons; moss and lichen and flagstones. She padded down the steps,

219

almost silent in her battered sneakers, old jeans, sweater and padded jacket. At the bottom she pushed her eyeband under the peak of the baseball cap under which she'd piled her still-grey hair, jammed her fists in the deep pockets, feeling the reassurance of the passport and the gun, and strolled across the yard, through another one-way gate, along an alley to Pitt Street then down on to Sauchiehall.

She caught her reflection in a shop-window, and smirked at how like a student she looked. It wasn't a perfect reflection, so it also made her look flatteringly young – like she'd look in a month or two, she hoped. And she already had the bearing, she could see that as she glanced sideways at the reflection of her walk, jaunty and confident. Her joints didn't hurt and her heels didn't jar and she had so much energy she felt like running, or skipping, or jumping about just to burn some of it off. She couldn't remember having felt this good when she really was young.

And things were coming back, memories of an earlier self, earlier personal tactics, like, before her rejuve, if she'd got caught up in a situation like that outside the hotel she'd have turned to the Guards to protect her, as though by reflex, and no doubt sparked a riot right there; not now, it had been a lightning calculation that the demonstrators, however hostile to each other or to the militia, would not attack an innocent minion like the driver and would not attack her while she was shielded by the comrades. No violence in the workers' movement, no enemies on the Left – it didn't work all the time, but by and large the truce was honoured; mutual assured deterrence, perhaps, but then, what wasn't?

Sauchiehall, Glasgow's main shopping street, had been de-pedestranised since she'd last been here and it thrummed with through traffic, electric mostly but with a few coughing old internal-combustion engines and speeding cyclists and, jeez, yes, cantering horses among them. Myra raced the red light at the end of the street, kept up her jog as she crossed the pedestrian bridge over the howling intersection above the M8 and up into Woodlands Road. There she slowed and strolled again, relishing the old patch, the familiar territory, the nostalgia pricking her eyes. (God, she'd flyposted that very pillar of that overpass for a *Critique* seminar in 1976!)

But the area was posh now, full of Sikh men in suits – bankers and lawyers and doctors – and women in saris accompanied by kids and often as not a Scottish nanny; pavements over-parked with expensive, heavy Malaysian cars. Not like old times, not at all, except for the occasional curry aroma and the feel of the wind and the look of the scudding clouds above.

Talking to the comrades in the New Brit, *that* had been like old times. It had been like fucking *time travel*, and far more like home-coming than any encounter she'd had in New York. After she'd thanked the militia officers, flatly refused to press assault charges, and insisted on giving a huge tip to the driver, she'd retired to the hotel's café for a coffee and a smoke with the five young people who'd escorted her in: Davy and Alison and Mike and Sandra and Rashid, all proud members of the Glasgow branch of the Workers' Power Party, an organisation much fallen-back from its high-water mark in the 2020s under the old Republic but still struggling along, still recruiting and still the British section of the Fourth International.

And they really were young, not rejuvenated old folks like her; she could hardly understand it, because she'd been thinking of the International, for decades now, as a club of ageing veterans. But then she thought of how the most formative and exciting experience of their childhoods had been a revolution – the British section of the Fall Revolution, yes! – and how that might have given them an idea of what the real (that is to say, ideal, never-actually-existing) Revolution might be like.

They'd regarded her, of course, as an old comrade, a veteran revo-lutionary who'd actually made a revolution, and actually ran a workers' state; but they'd soon lost their reserve, perhaps uncon-sciously misled (she fancied) by her increasingly believable apparent youth; and told her in more detail than she needed to know of the inevitable rancorous rivalries that had pitted them against, and the rest of the local Left for, her regime's liberal critics and/or Sino-Soviet communist foes.

She was grateful for their support, of course, and told them so; but she thought their ingrained acceptance of far-left factionalism was blinding them to the depth of genuine hatred and moral outrage she'd aroused, and indeed to its justification. There had been nothing in the angry man's diatribe which she hadn't at one time or another said to herself.

You fucking sell-out, you fucking capitalist whore. Yes, comrade, you have a point there. There may be something in what you say.

At the same time she found that the comrades were over-solicitous, certain that she'd be in danger if she wandered around on her own in Glasgow. They urged her to contact the consulate, and to travel officially. Myra had demurred, pointing out that that was exactly what had got her into this trouble in the first place. She hadn't told them what she did intend to do, however – *somebody* must have leaked the news of her unheralded and early arrival, and she had no reason to suppose it might not be one of them.

She passed the old church, St Jude's, which still looked much too grand, too *catholic* for the tiny denomination it served, and opposite it the Halt Bar where she'd drunk with David Reid and with Jon Wilde, separately and together, during and after the brief, intense affairs that had nudged all their lives on to their particular paths.

And thus, the lives and deaths of countless others. Jon had virtually started the space movement, and founded Space Merchants. Reid had built up Mutual Protection, and Myra the ISTWR. All from small beginnings, inconsequential at the time, all eventually affecting history on a scale usually attributed to Great Men.

Perhaps if they had not, there would have been some other Corsican . . . but no. Chaos reigned, here as elsewhere.

At the green bridge over the Kelvin she paused, gazing down at the brown spate and white swirl. How trivial were the causes of the courses of any particle, any bubble on that flow. No, it was wilder than that, because the water was at least confined by its banks: it was more like how the whole course of a river could be deflected by a pebble, by a grain of sand, a blade of grass, at its first upwelling; where the great forces of gravity and erosion and all the rest did minute but momentous battle with the surface tension of a particular drop. History was a river where every drop was a potential new source, a fountainhead of future Amazons.

She walked on, past the salient of Kelvingrove Park on the left and up the steepening slope of Gibson Street, and turned to the right along the still tree-shaded avenue to the Institute. She rang the bell, smiling wryly at the polished brass of the nameplate. Once the Institute of Soviet and East European Studies, then of Russian and East European Studies, then . . .

The Institute for the Study of Post-Civilised Societies, was what they called it now.

*

The woman who opened the door looked very East European, in her size (small) and expression (suspicious). Her dark eyes widened slightly.

'Oh, it's you,' she said. 'Godwin.'

'Yes, hello.' Myra stuck out her hand. The woman shook it, with brief reluctance, tugging Myra inside and closing the door at the same time.

'This place is watched,' she said. She had black bobbed hair; her age was hard to make out. Her clothes were as shabby as Myra's: blue denim smock, black jeans grey at the knees. 'My name is Irina Guzulescu. Pleased to meet you.'

They stood looking at each other in the narrow hallway. Institutional linoleum, grey paint and green trim, black stairway. The place smelt of old paper and cigarette smoke. Posters – shiny repro or faded original – from the Soviet Union and the Former Union: Lenin, Stalin, Gorbachev, Antonov, solemn; Gagarin, smiling. The Yeltsingrad Siege: heroic child partisans aiming their Stingers at the Pamyat Zeppelins. The building was completely silent and there was nobody else around.

'I was kind of expecting more people here,' Myra said. 'I left a message.'

'Like I said.'

'Oh.' Myra felt baffled and miffed.

'Your cases arrived safely,' Irina said, as though to mollify her. She escorted her up the narrow black-bannistered stairs to the library. The stair carpet was frayed to the point of criminal negligence. The library itself was cramped, a maze of bookcases through which one had to go crabwise. Several generations of information technology were carefully racked above the reading-table. Myra's crates were stacked beside it.

'I'll leave you to it,' Irina said.

'Thanks.'

Myra, alone, pulled down her eyeband, upped the gain, looked down at the crates and sighed. They were still bound with metal tape. She clicked her old Leatherman out of its pouch and got to work opening them, coiling the treacherously sharp bands carefully into a waste-paper basket. Then she had to pull the nails, like teeth. Finally she was able to get the files out.

She sorted the paper files into stacks: her personal stuff – diaries and letters and so on – and political, sorted by time and organisation, all the way back from her ISTWR years through to internal factional documents from that New York SWP branch in the 1970s. These last still made her smile: had there really ever been anyone daft enough to choose as his *nomme de guerre* for a debate about the armed struggle 'Dr Ahmed Estraguel'?

She worked her way, similarly, through the formats and conversions from Dissembler through DoorWays to Linux to Windows to DOS, and through storage media from the optical disks and bubble-magnetic wafers and CD-RWs ('CD-Rubs', they used to be called) to the floppy disks, almost jumping out of her seat at the noise the ancient PC made when it took the first of those. In the quiet building, it sounded like a washing-machine on the spin cycle.

After about an hour and a half, which passed in a kind of trance, all her optical and electronic files were copied to the Institute's electronic archive. She blinked up her eyeband menu, and invoked Parvus.

'Hi,' she said.

'Hello,' he said.

She felt almost awkward. 'Do you mind having a copy taken, and its being downloaded?'

The entity laughed. 'Mind? Of course not! Why should I mind?'

'OK,' Myra said. She uncoiled a fibre-optic cable from the terminal port and socketed it to her eyeband. 'I want your copy to guard this collection of files –' she ran her highlighting finger over it '– and anything you've got with you right now, applying the kind of discretionary access criteria that your existing parameters permit. Give the scaling a half-life of, oh, fifty years. Got that?'

'Yes.' Parvus smiled, doubled, then one of him disappeared dramatically like a cartoon genie swooshing back into a bottle.

'Done,' he said. It had taken longer than she'd expected – she must have had more files on her personal datadeck than she'd realised.

'Thank you,' said Myra. 'Anything to report, by the way?'

Parvus shrugged expansively. 'Nothing that can't wait. Except that Glasgow Airport is closed.'

'What?'

Surely not a coup, not here—

'Fighting on the perimeter. Damage to the runways. Just Green partisans, nothing serious, but there's no chance you'll get your flight on Monday.'

'Oh, shit. Book me a train. For tomorrow, OK? Catch you later.'

She disengaged the cable link and let it roll back. Then she got to work labelling the stacks, dating the paper folders and making notes for the Institute's archivist.

Somebody clattered up the stairs, strode into the library and flicked the light on. Myra turned around sharply and met the surprised gaze of the girl who'd identified her at the demo.

'Oh!' said the girl. She slowly slid her tartan scarf from around her neck and flicked her long, thick black hair out from under her denim jacket's collar. 'What – what are you doing here?'

Myra straightened up, feeling irrationally pleased that she was marginally taller than the younger woman.

'I was about to ask you the same question,' she said.

'I work here! I'm a post-grad student.'

She said it with such confusion of face, such a widening of her big brown eyes, that Myra couldn't help but smile.

'And a political activist, too, I understand.'

The girl nodded firmly. 'Aye.' The comment seemed to have allowed her self-confidence to recover. She stepped over to a chair and sat, stretching her legs out and propping her boots on a book-caddy. Myra observed this elaborately casual behaviour with detached amusement.

'I was an activist myself, when I studied here,' Myra said, half-sitting on the edge of the table.

'I know,' the girl said coldly. 'I've read your thesis. *Detente and Crisis in the Soviet Economy*.'

Myra smiled. 'It still stands up pretty well, I think.'

'Yeah. Can't say the same about your politics, though.' She frowned, swinging her feet back to the floor and leaning forward. 'In a way it's nothing . . . personal, you understand? I mean, when I read what you wrote, I like the person who wrote it. What I can't do is square that with what you've become.'

That was laying it on the line! Myra felt a jolt of pain and guilt.

'I don't know if I can, either,' she said. 'I changed. Real politics is more complicated than – ah, fuck it. Look – uh, what's your name?'

'Merrial MacClafferty.'

'OK – Merrial. The fact is, the Russian Revolution got defeated, and never got repeated – perhaps because the defeat was so devastating that it made any subsequent attempt impossible.' She laughed

225

harshly. 'And like the man said, it's gonna be socialism or barbarism. Socialism's out the window, it was dead before I was born. So barbarism it is. We're fucked.'

Merrial was shaking her head. 'No, nothing's inevitable. We make our own history – the future isn't written down. "The point is to change it." Look at the Sheenisov, they're building a real workers' democracy, they've proven it's still possible – and what do you do? You fight them! On the side of the Yanks and the Kazakhstani capitalists.'

'Like I said,' Myra sighed. 'Real politics is complicated. Real lives, mine and those of the people I've taken responsibility for. The future may not be written but the past bloody well is, and it hasn't left me with many options.'

'You mean, you haven't left *yourself*—'

'Tell you what,' Myra said, suddenly annoyed. She waved at the stack of cardboard and paper around her. 'Here's my life. There's a lot more on the computer.' She jerked a thumb over her shoulder. 'Password's "Luxemburg and Parvus" for the easy stuff. You're welcome to all of it. The hard stuff, the real dirty secrets, I've put a hundred-year embargo on, and even after that it'll be the devil of a job to hack past it. If you're still around in a couple of centuries, give it a look.'

'This is what you're doing?' Merrial asked. 'Turning over your archives to the Institute? Why?'

Myra could feel her lips stretch into a horrible grin. 'Because here it has a very slightly better chance of surviving the next few weeks, let alone the next few centuries. You want my advice, kiddo, you stop worrying about socialism and start getting ready for barbarism, because that's what's coming down the pike, one way or another.'

Merrial stood up and glared down at Myra. 'Maybe you've given up, but I won't!'

'Well, good luck to you,' said Myra. 'I mean that.'

The young woman looked at her with an unreadable expression. 'And to you, I suppose,' she said ungraciously, and turned on her heel and stalked out. Whether automatically or deliberately, she switched off the light as she went. Myra blinked, fiddled with her eyeband and got back to work.

'Everything all right?' Irina Guzulescu was limned in the backlight of the library doorway.

Myra straightened up and dusted off her hands.

'Yeah, I'm doing fine, thanks.' She laughed. 'Sorry about the dark, I was using my eyeband to see with, instead of putting the light on.'

'Probably just as well,' the small woman said. She advanced cautiously into the room, past the opened crates and labelled stacks of Myra's archives. 'Some of the books in here are so fragile, I fear sometimes one photon could . . .' She smiled, and handed Myra a mug of coffee.

'Oh, thanks.' It was cold in the library's still, stale air. She clasped her hands around the china's warmth. 'Is there anywhere I can go for a smoke?' she asked.

'Oh, sure, come on down to the basement.'

The basement seemed hardly changed; the big table that took up most of the room brought back memories – the long discussions and arguments around it, the adventures planned there, the afternoon she'd talked with Jon and Dave, and gone with Jon.

Along the way, Irina had picked up her own mug at the kitchenette cubby-hole. She sat down opposite Myra and shoved an ashtray across the table. In the unforgiving light she looked older; she'd obviously had the treatments, but the weight of her years still pulled at her face; it didn't sag, but it showed the strain.

'Well,' Myra said, lighting up, 'uh, that thing you said? About the place being watched? Why's that?'

Irina moved her hand as though flicking ash. 'Police mentality,' she said. 'Obviously if we study the post-civilised, we're potentially sympathetic to them, and to the enemy within.'

'The what?'

'The Greens.' Irina laughed. 'The FU and the Greens, it's like it used to be with the SU and the Reds. In the good old days of the Cold War, being interested in the other side at all was suspect, no matter how useful it might be. And of course the same on the other side.' She smiled. 'I worked at the Institute of American Studies in Bucharest. *Securitate* on my case all the time.'

'Jesus. You must be nearly as old as I am.' Myra thought the remark tactless as soon as it was out of her mouth, but Irina preened herself at it.

'Older,' she said proudly. 'I'm a hundred and ten.'

'Wow. Hundred and five, myself. Had the earlier treatments, of course, but I've just had the nano job.'

227

'Ah, good for you, you won't regret it.' She smiled distantly. 'You know, Myra Godwin, you are part of the history. Of this Institute, and of the societies it was set up to study. I supervised a student a few years ago in a PhD thesis on the ISTWR.'

'Never thought I'd end up in charge of my very own deformed workers' state.' A dark chuckle. 'Not that I ever believed that's what it was, or is,' Myra hastened to add. 'Or that such a thing could exist. Ticktin cured me of that delusion a *long* time ago.'

'Hmm,' said Irina. 'It was Mises and Hayek for me, actually. Ticktin didn't rate them very highly. Or me.' She laughed. 'Used to call me "Ceauşescu's last victim".'

'Well, yes,' Myra said. 'Never found the liberals terribly persuasive myself, to be honest. The question that always used to come to mind was, "Where are the swift cavalry?"'

Irina shook her head. 'I'm sorry?'

'Oh, it was something Mises said. If Europe ever went socialist, it would collapse, and the barbarians would be back, sweeping across the steppe on swift horses. Well, half Europe was – not socialist as I would see it, but as Mises would see it – and where are the swift cavalry?'

Irina stared at her. As though unaware of what she was doing – the reflexes of a habit she must have thought was conquered coming back – she reached across the table for Myra's cigarettes and lit one up.

'Oh, Myra Godwin-Davidova, you are so blind. Where are the swift cavalry, indeed.' She paused, narrowing her eyes against the stream of smoke. 'What mode of production would you say exists in the Former Union?'

'The post-civilised mode?'

'A euphemism.' She waved smoke. 'What would your Engels call a society where cities are just markets and camps, where most people eat what they can grow and hunt for themselves, where almost all industry is at the village level, where there is no notion of the nation?'

'Well, OK, it's an old-fashioned term,' Myra said, with half a laugh, 'but I suppose technically you could call it barbarism. Technologically advanced barbarism, but yes, that's what it is.'

'Precisely,' Irina said. She looked at her cigarette with puzzled distaste and stubbed it out. 'There are your swift cavalry. Look outside our cities, at the Greens. In fact, look inside our cities. There are your swift cavalry!'

Myra really had never thought of it like that.

'The only swift cavalry I'm worried about,' she said bitterly, 'are the goddamn Sheenisov.'

To her astonishment and dismay, Irina began to cry. She pulled a grubby tissue from her pocket and sobbed and sniffled into it for a minute. On a sudden impulse, Myra reached across the table and grasped her hand.

'Oh God,' Irina said at last. 'I'm sorry.' She gave a long sniff and threw the tissue away, accepted Myra's offer of a cigarette.

'No, *I'm* sorry,' Myra said. 'I seem to have said something to upset you.'

Irina blinked several times. 'No, no. It's my own fault. Oh, God, if you just knew. I stayed here to see you, not just to let you in.' The cigarette tip glowed to a cone, she was sucking so hard. 'Nobody else wanted to come in this morning and meet you. They think you are a terrible person, a monster, a criminal. I don't.' She blinked again, brightening. 'I go back, you know. To Romania, and to . . . other "post-civilised" countries. All right, to the Former Union. And you know what? People are happy there, with their farms and workshops and their local armies and petty loyalties. The bureaucrats are gone, and the mafias have no prohibitions to get rich on, and they are gone. The provinces have their small wars and their feuds, but –' she smiled now, sadly '– I sound like a feminist, if you remember them, but the fact is, it's just a testosterone thing. Young men will kill each other, that's the way of it. For a woman, Moscow – hell, any provincial post-Soviet town – is safer than Glasgow.'

Oh, not another, Myra thought. A Green fellow-traveller, a political pilgrim. I have seen the past and it works.

'And when I see something like communism coming *back*,' Irina went on, 'when I see the goddamn Sheenisov riding in their tanks, collectivising again, assimilating all those little new societies, I want to see them stopped.'

She looked straight into Myra's eyes. 'You can do it, you can stop them. You must fight, Myra. You're our only hope.'

Myra felt like crying, herself.

The Brits just didn't *do* trains.

They'd invented them. They had a couple of centuries' experience with them. They had more actual enthusiasts for trains per head of

229

the population than anywhere else. They'd invented *trainspotting*. And they still couldn't seem to figure out how to make trains *run on time*.

So here they were on a bright, cold Sunday morning, somewhere south of Penrith, and under traction from one electric engine that sounded like it came from the sort of gadget you would use for home improvements. Wooded hillsides slid slowly past. At least she had a seat in First Class. The train's guard was just wandering through the adjoining Second Class, where all the screaming kids were, and the refreshments trolley was being trundled along behind him.

Myra lit a cigarette and gazed out. She felt relatively content, even with a long journey, made longer by bloody typical Brit inefficiency, ahead of her. She had plenty of reading to do, right there in her eye-band. Parvus had prepared her a digest of recent British foreign policy, last time she'd done a download. About 100 kilobytes, not counting hyperlinks and appendices. Stacks of v-mail to catch up with.

Not to mention the news. By now there was a regular CNN spot, on the world-affairs specialist newsfeed, dealing with the ISTWR. The demos opposing the policy of federation with Kazakhstan had grown to a daily assembly of two thousand or so, with a couple of hundred people braving the chilly nights in tents in Revolution Square. Some of their banners were what Myra would've expected from her local ultralefts, the sort of folks she'd tangled with outside the New Brit. Others were liberal – pro-UN – or libertarian, with a pro-space, pro-Outwarder undertone.

Nobody on the street – or on the net – seemed to have yet found out about the nukes; a small mercy, but Myra suspected that some at least of those behind the various demonstrators knew about them. Reid, for one, certainly did, and she thought it possible that his hand was reaching for them through the ISTWR's home-grown space-movement militants.

Myra had spent the first hour or so of the journey at her virtual keyboard, writing out reports back and instructions and advice for her commissars, Denis Gubanov in particular. She wanted every chekist he could spare to get busy infiltrating and investigating these demos.

The partition doors hissed and thunked open. The guard came

through, a tall, stooping man in a uniform, with a holstered pistol on his hip.

'Tickets from Carlisle, please.' He had a slightly camp voice, gentle and pleasant. He smiled and checked the tickets of the business executive sitting opposite and across from Myra.

''Scuse me,' the steward sang out, behind him. The steward was a small, scrawny youth in a white shirt, tartan bow-tie and trews. Spiky black hair.

The trolley rattled and jangled into the compartment. The guard stepped aside to let it pass. As he did so the train lurched a little, setting the trolley's contents ringing again, and the brakes squealed as the train came to a halt.

There was a crackly announcement, from which Myra could only make out the words 'trees on the line'.

A ripple of derision ran through the carriage. Myra added her hoot to it, and glanced out of the windows. There were trees beside the line, to the right, but they were about a hundred yards away, across a puddled meadow. On the other side, a sharp slope, with trees above the scree.

She heard a gasp from the steward, and a sort of cough from the guard. A large quantity of some red liquid splashed across the table she was sitting at, and some of it poured over the edge and on to the lap of her skirt. Myra recoiled, looking up with a momentary flash of civilised annoyance – her first impression was that somehow the steward had spilled a bottle of red wine over her.

The guard fell sideways across the table with a shocking thud. His throat gaped and flapped like a gill-slit, still pumping. She could see the rim of his severed windpipe, white, like broken plastic. His mouth was open too, the tongue quivering, dripping spittle. His eyes were very wide. He raised his head, and looked as though he were trying to say something to her. Then he stopped trying. His head hit the table with a second thump, *diminuendo*.

The steward was still standing, clutching a short knife in one hand and an automatic pistol, evidently the guard's, in the other. His shirt-cuff had blood on it, as did the front of his shirt. It looked like he'd had a nose-bleed which he'd tried to staunch on his sleeve. It was surprising how thin a liquid blood was, when it was freshly spilled, still splashy, a wine-dark stream.

The steward flicked his tongue across his lips. He waved the pistol

231

in a way that suggested he was not entirely familiar with its use. Then, in a movement like a conjuring trick, he'd swapped the knife and the pistol around and worked the slide. Lock and load; he knew how to use it, all right.

'Don't fucking move,' he said.

Myra didn't fucking move. She'd stuck her small emergency-pistol in the top of her boot when she'd taken off the holster with the Glock, which was now lying under her jacket on the luggage-rack above. There was no way she could reach either weapon in time. Nor could she blink up a comms menu on her eyeband – the phone was in her jacket, too. The other passenger, who was sitting across the aisle and facing the opposite direction, didn't move either. Somebody, not a child, in the Second-Class compartment was screaming. The steward had his back to that compartment, and at least several people in there must have been aware of what had happened. Without moving her head, or even her eyes, Myra could see white faces, round eyes and mouths, through the glass partition.

She was thinking *why doesn't someone just shoot this fucker in the back?* Then, out of the corner of her eye, she saw movement outside, along both sides of the train. Men and women on horseback. Long hair; feathers and hats; leather jerkins and weskits; rifles and cross-bows brandished or slung. Like cowboys and Indians. Green partisans. Barbarians.

Far behind her, near the back of train she guessed, there was a brief exchange of fire and a distant, thin screaming. It went on and on like a car alarm.

Every door in the train, internal and external, thunked open. OK, so somebody'd got to the controls. Myra felt a cold draught against the warm and now sticky liquid on her knees. The colour washed out of the world. Myra realised that she was about to go into shock, and breathed hard and deep.

Some of the horsemen, dismounted, leapt aboard the train. At the end of each carriage, a pair of them faced opposite ways, covering the passengers with rifles. The man who landed facing Myra filled the partition doorway. 'Barbarian' was not an epithet, applied to him; he was tall and broad, he had a beard and pony-tail gleaming with grease, and his jacket and chaps bore smooth-edged, irregularly shaped plates of metal attached to the leather with metal rings, a crude and partial armour.

232

'Hands on heads! Everybody outside! On to the track!'

Myra put her hands on top of her head and stood up and shuffled sideways into the aisle. The steward-punk who'd murdered the guard still had her covered, and was backing out past the big fellow, whom he obviously knew. The businessman, standing up, had a curiously intent look on his face. Myra guessed instantly that he was about to make himself a hero, and in a fortuitous moment of eye contact she shook her head. His shoulders slumped slightly, even with his hands in the air; but he complied with the shouted command and the minutely gestured suggestion, jumping out to the right and landing on the permanent way on his feet and hands, then scrambling up and running across the adjacent track to the low bank with the fence by the flooded meadow.

Myra raised her hands and stepped over the guard's buckled legs, edged past the barbarian and the steward and jumped out. She landed lightly, the impact jolting her pistol uncomfortably but reassuringly deeper down the side of her boot, and walked across the track and up the bank, then turned to face the train.

People were all doing as she had done, or helping kids – silent now – down to the broken stones. The Greens strode or stood or rode up and down, yippeeing, all the time keeping their rifles trained on the passengers. There were at least a score of the attackers on each side of the train, probably more. About a hundred people, passengers and crew, had come off the train. Somebody was still on the train and still screaming.

Myra stood with her hands on her head and shivered. The sight of so many people with their hands up made her feel sick. The barbarians probably intended to loot the train – they must know that some at least of the passengers would be carrying concealed weapons, but they weren't as yet even bothering to search for them. The hope that they would be spared would be enough to stop almost anyone from making an inevitably doomed attempt to fight. It might just stop them until it was too late. If the Greens intended a massacre they would do it, of that she was sure, just when least expected. The Greens would manoeuvre inconspicuously so that they were out of each other's lines of fire, and the fusillade would come. Then a bit of rape and robbery, and a few final finishing shots to the head for the wounded if they were lucky.

One tall man in a fur cloak and leather-strapped cotton leggings

233

was stalking around from one group of passengers to another, peering at and talking to every young or young-looking woman. When he reached Myra he stopped on the slope just below her, rested his hand on his knee and looked up, grinning. He was clean-shaven, with long sun-bleached red hair tied back with a thong around his brow. On another thong, around his neck, hung a whistle. Beneath his fur cloak he wore a faded green T-shirt printed with the old UN Special Forces motto: SORT 'EM OUT – LET GOD KILL 'EM ALL.

'Ah,' he said, '*you* must be Myra Godwin!'

He had a London accent and a general air of enjoying himself hugely. Myra stared at him, shaken at being thus singled out. He recognised her, and she had a disquieting feeling that she'd seen him somewhere before.

'Yes,' she said. 'What's it to you?'

'You got any proof of that?'

'Diplomatic passport, jacket pocket, above the seat I was in.'

'I'll check,' he warned, eyes narrowing.

'Oh, and bring my fucking Glock as well. You are in deep shit, mister.'

'We'll see about that,' he said. He turned around and yelled at the big man who'd emptied her carriage; he was still standing in the doorway, rifle pointed upward.

'Yo! Fix! Get this lady's stuff out. From above her seat.'

He didn't take his eyes off her as the big man passed him the folded jacket and he fingered through it. One quick glance down at the opened passport, and he put the whistle to his lips and blew a loud, trilling note, twice.

'Right, Fix, spread the word,' he said. 'We got her. Tax them and leave. Let's get outta here before the helicopters come.'

The other man jogged off, shouting orders. In a minute, out of the corner of her eye, Myra could see the tax being organised: the people from the train had all been herded into one group, and a man with a shotgun and a woman with a sack were going around, taking money and jewellery and small pieces of kit and personal weapons. People handed their stuff over with a sickeningly eager compliance.

'Want your jacket back?'

Myra nodded. He tossed it, still folded, to her; held on to the holstered automatic, the passport and the uplink phone.

234

'You'll get these back later,' he said.

She put the jacket on. It was a thin suit jacket and didn't do much to keep out the chill.

'What do you mean, "later"?' she asked.

He laughed at her.

'You're coming with us. We'll let you go soon.'

The wind just got colder.

Myra gestured at her blood-spattered blouse and blood-soaked skirt.

'Excuse me if I don't believe you.'

'War is hell, init?' he agreed brightly. He moved his hand as though tossing something light away. 'The guard was a spy, anyway.'

Myra said nothing.

'OK, youse lot!' some guy on a horse was shouting. 'Get back on the train and stay there. Don't try chasing us, don't anyone try shooting after us. 'Cause if you do, we'll come back an' kill youse all. And don't leave the train after we're gone, neither, or the choppers will pick you off in the fields.'

The group filed into the train through one of the doorways. Myra could see them dispersing along the carriages.

'That's all you're going to do?'

The red-haired man nodded. 'This time.' He jerked his thumb over his shoulder. 'I mean, I feel sorry for these people, but not sorry enough to kill them. And I'm not going to waste time searching the train for valuables. No point in being greedy, otherwise the trains would just stop coming through. Just enough tax to cover the op, you know.'

'What op?'

He stared at her. 'Getting hold of you.'

Oh, shit. She'd thought that was what he'd been driving at. She blinked rapidly, recording his image, and triggering a search protocol on her eyeband, to see if this knowledgeable bandit was known himself.

'You did all this just to get me?' She smiled sourly, over chattering teeth. 'How did you know I was on the train?'

The man looked at her scornfully. 'That wasn't difficult,' he said. He waved a hand expansively but evasively. 'We're everywhere.'

'Seems a bit excessive.'

'Some things you just can't say in a phone call,' he said idly. Then he shifted his feet and straightened up, grinning. 'Besides, raiding is such fun.' He drew in a long breath of fresh air as though inhaling a drug. 'It's a lifestyle thing.'

A slender, dark-skinned woman with curly, wavy blonde hair down to her waist rode up on a big black horse, leading a similar horse and a dun mare. She smiled at the tall man, and turned a colder smile to Myra.

'You know how to ride?'

In a moment everyone was mounted. Myra tugged up her bloody skirt as she settled in the saddle. The tall man waved and whistled three blasts. Suddenly the Greens were dispersing away from the train, diagonally up the scree-slope to the trees or, as those around Myra did, straight across the wet meadow. She found herself on a hell-for-leather gallop behind Fix, with the blonde-haired woman and the red-haired man on either flank. Over a hedge, down a path, into a narrow wooded dell.

Somewhere far away, the sound of a helicopter. Then some short machine-gun bursts, though at whom they were aimed, Myra did not wish to guess.

Myra rode silently like the others, but in the spectral company of Parvus; the AI was murmuring into her bone-conduction earclip and flashing Grolier screens up in front of her eyes. Nothing more current was available without the uplink phone. He'd provisionally identified the man who'd captured her, but it wasn't very enlightening – the latest pictures of him were from about twelve years ago, and he hadn't been a land-pirate then. He had been a net commentator, and – before that – a minor agitator in the Fall Revolution. The television clips of his rants explained why he looked vaguely familiar – she'd watched the British national democratic revolution in the time she'd been able to spare from following the Siberian Popular Front's assault on Vladivostok.

The dell opened to a larger valley, thickly settled. Old stone houses, geodesic domes, wattle huts, new thatched cottages, a few nanofac-tured carbon-shell constructions. A lot of cattle and sheep in the fields; kids running everywhere. The path became a gravel road which widened, at the centre of the main street, to a small cobbled square. In the centre, just by a verdigrised copper statue of a Tommy with a fixed bayonet, memorial to the fallen of three world wars, was an outdated but still effective anti-aircraft missile battery. No higher than the statue itself, it held a rack of a dozen metre-long rockets. Myra could read the small print of what they were tipped with: laser-fuser tactical nukes.

People crowded around, welcoming the returning raiders. They called the red-haired man what she thought at first was 'Red', which made sense; then realised it was 'Rev', which made no sense at all. It certainly wasn't the name her search had come up with. The kids were cheering and doing the high-stepping, high-jumping Zulu war-dance called *toyi-toying*.

Fix reined in his horse in front of a large stone building which had a low-ceilinged front room open to the street: a café. Myra followed suit, dismounted and was led through into a back room with a fire, and high leather chairs around a table. The room smelt of woodsmoke and alcohol and unwashed humanity and damp dogs.

'Have a seat.'

Myra sat and the two men and the woman sat down opposite her. They regarded her in silence for a moment. She decided to hazard the Grolier's guess.

'Jordan Brown,' she said. 'And you must be Cat Duvalier.' That name was in the entry's small print as Jordan Brown's wife.

'Well done,' the man said, unperturbed. 'Nifty little machine you've got there.'

Myra flipped the eyeband back. 'Yes. So tell me, Mr Brown, what it is you want.'

'It's *Reverend* Brown,' he said. 'First Minister of the Last Church of the Unknowable God.' He smiled. 'But please, call me Jordan.' He looked over his shoulder and shouted an order. 'Beer and brandy!'

He slung his cloak over a chair; without it, leaning over the table in his T-shirt and wild hair, he looked somewhat more intimidating. Some absence in his gaze reminded Myra of *spetznatz* veterans, or old Afghantsi. The Blue Beret slogan on the T-shirt just might not be ironic, she thought. A boy padded in carrying glasses and bottles.

'All we've got at the moment,' the woman called Cat said. 'What'll you have?'

'I'll have a beer.'

She accepted the drink without thanks, and lit a cigarette without asking permission or offering to share. Damned if she was going to act as though she was enjoying their hospitality.

'You were saying, *Reverend*.'

Jordan Brown spread his hands. 'Just to talk things over.'

'You've gone to a lot of trouble to do that.'

'I sure have,' he said. 'I've risked the lives of my fighters, I've exposed one of my agents, I've had a man slaughtered like a pig – which he was, but that's nothing to you – and had another train guard shot in the belly just for trying to do his job. Quite possibly, some of the passengers have already fallen to friendly fire.' He shrugged. 'And I would have killed more, if I'd had to. The point is, I'll get away with it.' He waved his hand above his head. 'We all will. The helicopter was the worst the British can do against us.'

Myra looked straight at him. 'Like I care. You might not get off so lightly when this gets back to the Kazakhstani Republic.'

Jordan nodded soberly. 'No doubt I'm trampling all over diplomatic niceties. But it's you that came to Britain to get help, not the other way round. So you'll forgive me for not worrying too much.'

'Hah!'

'Anyway,' Jordan went on, 'I've no wish to get into a pissing-contest. I have something more important to say to you. So. Are you willing to have a serious conversation?'

Myra shrugged, looking around theatrically. 'Why not? I don't see any better entertainment.' She poured a brandy chaser, again without false courtesy.

Jordan Brown leaned forward on his bare forearms, took a swig of brandy and began to speak.

'You've come to Britain to get military aid against the Sheenisov. You might even get it. What I want to tell you is two things. One, don't do it. It won't do you any good. You can't fight communism with imperialism. It's just throwing napalm on the fire.'

Myra favoured him with a look that said she'd heard this before. 'If you say so. And what else do you have to tell me? Try and make it something that's news to me, how about that?'

'You're in worse trouble than you think,' Jordan said. 'The entity you call the General is working for the Sheenisov.'

Myra almost choked on her sip of brandy. She coughed fire for a moment. She felt totally disoriented.

'*What?* And how the hell would you know?'

'Strictly speaking,' Jordan Brown said, 'the Sheenisov are working for *it*. As to how I know . . .'

He held out a hand towards Cat. She leaned forward as Jordan leaned back.

'Myra,' she said earnestly, 'I may be a barbarian now, but I used to be like you. I used to be in the International.'

'Oh, Jesus!' Myra exploded. 'Half the fucking world is run by ex-Trots! Tell me something I don't know, like how you heard about the FI mil org – the General.'

'I was coming to that,' Cat said, mildly enough – but Myra could read the younger woman's face like a computer screen, and she could see the momentary spasm of impatient rage. This barbarian lady was someone who'd got dangerously used to not being interrupted. Cat forced a smile. 'I still hear rumours.'

'Rumours? That's what you're relying on?'

'It seems you've just confirmed one,' Jordan said, dryly.

Myra acknowledged that she had. But it seemed a situation where stonewalling would be less productive than admitting that the General existed, and trying to find out where the rumour came from. Parvus hadn't spotted anything like that . . .

'Did you pick this up off the net, or what?'

Jordan looked at Fix and Cat, and all three of them laughed. To Myra, it sounded like a mocking laugh.

'God, you people,' Jordan said. His tone changed as he went on, becoming an invocation, or an imprecation. 'You have a screen between you and the world all the time. We have the human world, and the natural world. We have the whole world that you call marginal, the scattered society of free humanity. We have the whisper in the market, the gesture on the road, the chalked mark on the pavement. The twist of a leaf, the turning of a twig. We have the smell carried on the wind. We have the night sky and the names of all its fixed and moving and falling stars. We have our friends in all your cities and camps and armies. We have the crystal radio that receives and the spark-gap that transmits, in codes you have forgotten, on wavelengths you no longer monitor, in languages that you disdained to learn.'

He tipped his head back and began glossolaliating in Morse code, *da-da-dit-di-da-didididah* . . . Cat and Fix cocked their heads, listening, and after a minute grinned and guffawed.

Jordan looked a little smug at this demonstration. 'See, I can joke in tongues. We have our own Internet, and our own International. Don't bother looking for a leak from yours.'

'Besides,' said Fix, speaking up for the first time, 'we know this thing from way back. Jordan and Cat fought in the revo, and so did it. It was called the Black Plan, and it was used by – or it used – the Army of the New Republic. We've all encountered it, and we know where it went. To New View, your commie-cult commune in space.'

'And we know how it thinks,' said Cat. 'We can see its hand in what the Sheenisov are doing, in their tactics and in their strategy. It's not exactly malevolent, but it is . . . ambitious.'

'So?' Myra shrugged, trying hard to stay cool, and to reassert her control over the conversation. 'We – that is, my country, Kazakhstan –' there, she had said it, and the words *my country, Kazakhstan* could not be unsaid '– we are not relying on this thing. We take no orders from it, not since – well, it got on the wrong side of me, put it that way. I don't say I believe you about its taking the side of the Sheenisov, but – let's say I wouldn't put that past it. If you're so worried about it, why do you object to my getting help to stop it?'

'Because,' said Jordan, emphasising each word with a chop of the hand, '*it can not be stopped*. Not by fighting it. If it finds itself on the losing side it will change sides, or work for both sides, and it will win. Its only real enemies are rival AIs, such as those of the space move-ment, and those strange ghosts of genius that some of the spacers are trying to turn into. It will defeat them, or absorb them, and then it will be content in its . . . singular godhood, spreading with humanity to all the worlds to come. It will look after our best interests, whether we like it or not.'

'Hah, come on. you can't possibly know that.'

Jordan sat back and looked at her with an ironic expression. 'Oh, yes I can, but call it an educated guess if it makes you feel better. If the British Republic were to come in on your side, I'm sure they'd be delighted to get their old planning-system back. They'd jump at any offers it made them. Or they would accept similar Greek gifts from the space movement's AIs. So whoever wins – the Western powers, the space movement or the Sheenisov – humanity will be living inside some machine or other, for ever.'

'Would that be so bad?'

'No,' said Jordan. 'That's what I'm afraid of.'

He jumped up. 'But what the hell. You do as seems best. If you still want to ally with the British when you get to London, go right ahead. Much good it'll do you.'

He downed his remaining brandy and looked around at the others, then at Myra. 'Come on,' he said. 'I'll take you to the road.'

She rode along beside the red-haired man, troubled but unconvinced by his strange tirades. Wet branches of beech and birch brushed past them, making her duck and blink. The stony path led up the side of the hill above the settlement. Myra looked back down at it before it passed from view.

'How do you people live?' she asked. 'You can't live just on raiding, and some day soon, according to you, there'll be nothing left to raid. Like, who pays for these anti-missile missiles?'

'We all do,' Jordan said. 'We don't have taxes, that'd be a laugh. We – not just this village, all of the free people – have a couple of simple economic principles that have been applied in communities like this for nearly a hundred years now. One is that we don't have rent, but land ain't free – God ain't making any more of it, but we keep right on making more people. So we apply the equivalent of rent to community purposes, like defence. The other is that any individual, or any group, can issue their own currency, backed up at their own risk. No landlords, no usurers, and no officials.'

'Oh, great,' said Myra. 'A peasant's idea of utopia. Single tax and funny money! Now I've heard everything!'

'It does work,' Jordan said. 'We, as you can see, flourish. We're the future.'

'Jordan,' she said, 'you know I found some clips of you on my encyclopaedia? Well, from them I'd never have figured you for going over to the Green Slime. Or for a preacher, come to that.'

Jordan laughed, unoffended. 'The world will fall to the barbarians or to the machines. I chose the barbarians, and I chose to spread some enlightenment among them. Hence the preaching, which was – to begin with – of a kind of rationalism. I can honestly say I have led many of my people away from the dark, heathen worship of Gaia, and from witchcraft and superstition. But I also found, like many another missionary, that I preferred their way of life to the one from which I'd come. And along with loving nature, I came to love nature's God.'

'You were an atheist.'

'So I believed. I later realised that I was an agnostic. A *militant* agnostic, if you like. All theology is idolatry, all scripture is apocrypha. All we can say is that God is One. God encompasses the

241

world, there is nothing outside him, and nothing opposed to him. How could there be? So God approves of all that happens, because all that happens is his will. God loves the world, all of it, from the Hubble to the Planck, from the Bang to the Crunch. God is in the hawk hovering up there and in the mouse that cowers from its claws in yonder field. God is in the sickle and the sheaf, the hammer and the hot iron, the sword and the wound. God is in the fire and in the sun and in the holocaust. God was in the spy I had killed today, and in the man who killed him.'

Antinomianism was, Myra knew, a common enough heresy in periods of revolution or social breakdown. Four hundred years ago, these same words could have been ranted forth on those very hills. There was nothing new in what Jordan said, but Myra felt sure it would not disturb him in the slightest to point this out. He had probably read Winstanley and Christopher Hill for himself.

'You seem to know a lot about this unknowable God of yours.'

'That I do.'

'Is God in the machines, in the AIs that you fear?'

'That too, yes.'

'What's the difference between a God who makes no difference and takes no side and no God at all?'

They had reached the crest of the hill. Jordan reined in his horse. Myra stopped too, and looked down the hill at the grey ribbon of the motorway and the white blocks of a service-station.

So close, all the time.

'You can walk from here,' Jordan said dryly. He took her horse's reins as Myra dismounted. He soberly returned her holstered weapon, her passport and her phone.

'Oh, and to answer your question. There is no difference, in a sense. But to believe that God is in everything, and is on your side whatever you do and whatever happens, gives one a tremendous access of energy.' He grinned down at her. 'Or so I've found.'

And with that, the agnostic fanatic was gone, swift on his horse.

Myra slogged down the hill to the service area, cleaned up, made some phone calls while she ate in the cafeteria, and hired a car to take her to London.

She arrived, through all the obstacles thrown up by the small battles on the way, on the evening of the following day. She had long since missed her appointment with the Foreign Office; she had told

242

them that in advance, and they'd asked her to call back when she arrived, to make another.

But, after all she had seen along the way, and all she had not seen – such as any evidence that people like Jordan's band, and worse, operated with anything other than insolence and impunity, give or take the odd gunship attack – there didn't seem to be a whole hell of a lot of a point.

13

The Sea Eagle

Rain drummed on the roof of Merrial's house. The view outside was dreich. I'd looked out the window earlier, down the glen and the loch; ranks of cloud were marching in off the sea, and one after another shedding their loads on the hills. Inside, it was warm: we sat huddled together, backs to the piled-up pillows, sipping hot black coffee.

'No work today, thank Providence,' I said.

'Not at the yard anyway,' said Merrial. She waved a hand at the soldering-iron and seer-stones and clutter in the corner of the room. 'You start learning a different work, here.'

'Aye, great,' I said.

'What is this Providence you talk about, anyway?' she asked.

'Um.' I stared at the slow swirl of the coffee. 'It's . . . the helpful side of Nature, you might say. When things work out as we would wish, without an apparent cause.' I looked at her. 'You must know that.'

'But that's just coincidence,' she said. 'All things come by Nature.'

'Some things are more than coincidence, and Nature is more than—' I was going to say 'more than Nature' but stopped and laughed. 'You really don't know any Natural Theology?'

'No,' she said cheerfully. 'I've always just taken for granted that the outsiders have strange beliefs. Never gone into the details.' She put her empty mug down at her side of the bed and snuggled up to me. 'Go on. Tell me the details.'

'Oh, God. All right. Well, the usual place to start is right here.' I tapped her forehead, gently. 'Inside there. From the outside we see grey matter, but from the inside we think and feel. We know there are billions of cells in there, processing information. So thinking and feeling – consciousness – is something that information does. It's what

244

information is, from the inside, its subjective side. Where there's information, there's consciousness.'

'But there's information everywhere,' she said. 'Wherever anything affects anything else, it's information. The rain falling on the ground is information.'

'Exactly!' I slid my arm around her shoulders. 'You've got it.'

'Got what? Oh.' She shifted a little and looked straight at me. 'You mean there's consciousness everywhere?'

'Yes! That's it!'

'But, but—' She looked around. 'You mean to tell me you think that clock, say, has *thoughts*?'

The ticking was loud in the room as I considered this.

'It has at least one,' I said cautiously.

'And what would that be?'

'"It's later . . . it's later . . . it's later . . ."'

She laughed. 'But the whole universe—'

'Is an infinite machine, which implies an infinite mind.' I put my hand behind her head, cradling the container of her finite mind. '"And this all men call God",' I concluded smugly.

Merrial punched me.

'And the computers, I suppose you would say they are conscious too?'

'Aye, of course,' I said.

'What a horrible thought.'

'They may not be conscious of what we see from the outside,' I said. 'They may be thinking different thoughts entirely.'

Merrial gazed abstractedly out of the window.

'What thought is the rain thinking?'

'Can't you hear it?' I said. 'It's thinking "yesssss".'

'Hmm,' she said. 'Now *there's* a coincidence . . .'

We used the couple of days before my reinstatement in my job at the yard for the beginnings of an education in fine soldering and in programming, the latter subject being simultaneously fascinating and maddening. We also made a painstaking study of the Deliverer's documents, which continued – after we'd returned the originals to Gantry, and I'd returned to work at the yard – with the photocopies, but they yielded no information relevant to the ship's mission. The folder from the 2050s reinforced, in its casual references and

245

assumptions more than its explicit statements, the staggering extent of the orbital activity of pre-Deliverance humanity. But it contained no hint of the Deliverance itself.

There was one moment when I thought I had won a real historical insight, albeit one tangentially relevant to our immediate concerns.

I looked up from the stack of papers on Merrial's broad table. Every evening after work, I'd slowly sifted through them, as now, in the late sun.

'Merrial?' I said. She turned from the seer-stone apparatus on which she was working, and laid down her soldering-iron.

'You found something?'

'No, just – realised something. These Greens she talks about in some of her articles, the marginal people who lived outside the cities. She makes the point here that they had a lot more practical skills than folk gave them credit for, that they weren't just ignorant barbarians but farmers and smiths and electricians and so on.'

'Yes,' she said, with a mysterious smile. 'That was true.'

'Well! These people, the Greens, they must have been the ancestors of the tinkers!'

'Here,' she said, passing me a cigarette. 'You're going to need this.'

'Why?' I asked, lighting up.

'Because – oh, *Dhia*, how can I break this to you gently? You've got it the wrong way round entirely! Why do you think we call the settled folk "the outsiders"?'

'What?'

'Aye, the Greens, the barbarians, these are not our ancestors, Clovis. They're – I was going to say yours, but I can't say that any more, *mo gràidh*, now you're one of us. They're the ancestors of the outsiders! We are the survivors, the descendants, of the city folk!'

'So how is it that we – I mean the outsiders – live in the cities now?'

She stood up then, walking around the small room like a lecturer, gesturing with her cigarette. 'Oh, but your face is a picture, colha Gree! They live in the cities now because they invaded them, they moved in at the Deliverance when the old civilisation and city life had broken down. And they're still there, bless them, blundering around like the barbarians they are, in the borrowed costumes of the past. All these scholars that you wanted to emulate, they're just rummaging about in the ruins, reading books they misunderstand so badly it isn't funny. You're well out of that, my love, you'll learn more from us in a year than in a lifetime at the University!'

Indeed.

A huge cheer went up, almost drowning the inrushing roar of water, as the sluice-gates opened. The water poured over the edge of the drydock in a saline Niagara that went on and on, until it seemed that the loch itself would be lowered before the deep hole was filled. Faster than a tide, the water crept up the legs and pontoons of the platform.

Merrial's hand gripped mine as we made our way through the crowd, pushing to the front like children. The entire accessible part of the cliff-edge around the dock was lined with people. Everybody who'd worked at the yard, on the platform or the ship, was certainly there, along with casual visitors from the surrounding towns, keen sightseers from all over the Highlands, and outright enthusiasts from even farther afield. A couple of hundred metres around the cliff and inward, officers of the International Scientific Society, project managers and exemplary workers made speeches from a wooden stage with a raised dais and an awning. Nobody farther away than fifty metres, at the outside, could make out a word these dignitaries said, particularly not from the PA speakers strung out like fairy-lights on catenaries of cable all over the place. Squawks and howls and crackles worthy of a railway station echoed around the cliff-faces.

I ducked in between a couple of workers at the front who'd incautiously allowed a quarter of a metre to open up between them. Merrial followed with, no doubt, a smile at both of them which made them feel they were being done a favour.

And then we were there, a metre or two from the crumbling, tussocked edge. The platform and the spaceship loomed startlingly close. At that moment another cheer went up, as though to acclaim our arrival, and I realised that the capsule at the tip of the probe was, minutely but perceptibly, swaying. The platform was afloat.

'Hoo-rrayy!' I shouted, joining enthusiastically in the applause. Merrial yelled something almost too high to hear beside me; I could hardly hear myself. Though a less spectacular moment than the flooding of the dock, it was freighted with greater significance: the beginning of the *Sea Eagle/Iolair*'s journey, which would end in space.

It was a strange launch vehicle, simultaneously more primitive and more advanced than anything sent into space in the first age of space exploration. The ancients could, no doubt, have built a fusion torch-ship, but they didn't. They went straight from massive liquid-fuelled rockets to the nanotech diamond ships of the last days. In our time, with chemical fuels relatively expensive and nanotech (other than the tinker computers) quite beyond our reach, and the secret of controlled fusion still extant, the fusion torch is a logical choice.

But, as Fergal had implied, building it out of boiler plate was a trifle inelegant. On the other hand, the skills were there, locally available from shipbuilding; and the weight – given the immense power of the engine – was not a significant constraint. And say what you like about red-leaded steel plate, it is reliably resistant to sea-water. There was, of course, no question of launching such a monster from any-where on land, which is less forgiving – of intense heat, high-energy particles and unstable isotopes – than the sea.

Its mission, too, was primitive, or at least simple: to launch into orbit an experimental communications and Earth-observation satel-lite. That payload had required the co-operation of scientists and engineers (tinkers or otherwise), lens-makers and photographers, from all over the civilised world. Its electronic and electrical systems strayed suspiciously close to the path of power – even deploying, if you wanted to be awkward, a system very like television. But after much soul-searching and acrimony, the majority of the most respected practitioners of Natural Theology had, with some reluctance, nodded their long-haired heads. Television, they gravely pointed out, had been destructive only as a mass medium. To object to it as a method of communication from a satellite to a ground station would, they averred, be crass superstition, unworthy of this enlightened age.

Needless to say, a minority of their equally respected, though (it has to be said) usually older, colleagues insisted that this was the first step on a slippery slope at the bottom of which lay a population reduced to a passively rotting mass of mental and physical wrecks. With equal inevitability, given the nature of Natural Theology, a much smaller (and, yes, younger) faction were pointing out that the sort of abject helotry described and decried by their conservative colleagues were in fact the peoples better known as *the ancients*, who had watched tele-vision assiduously and had an achievement or two to their credit before they fell. To which, of course . . . but the argument's further iterations would be tedious to elaborate.

Merrial walked forward more boldly than I would have and sat down cheerily on the very lip of the cliff, her legs dangling over and her skirt elegantly spread on the heather to either side of her. I sat beside her and tried not to look down at a drop to the sea, direct and vertical except where it was interestingly varied by jutting rocks. We had found ourselves a viewpoint slightly in front of the platform, between its foremost extension and the open gates of the dock.

The shouting and cheering had stopped now, replaced by the susurrus of conversation, the continuing surge of the rising sea and the deep whine of the platform's turbines as they laboured to move the gigantic structure. Very slowly, the mast-like rocking of the ship's shaft was intersected by a net forward motion. Slow though it was, this set up a noticeable bow-wave at the front, clashing and splashing against the incoming waves. Complex interference patterns formed as the waves rebounded off the sides of the dock and the platform itself, and the sun, already past the zenith and dipping towards the west, made spectra in the spray.

Even at five kilometres per hour, the platform didn't take long to pass us, to the sound of further cheering, and waving to and from the operational crew down on the decks. Another significant moment, duly registered by another round of applause, came when the platform passed through the gates and into the open sea – or at any rate Loch Kishorn. After this there was really nothing to see except the slow departure of the rig, and people began to drift away. The platform had a long voyage ahead of it, out of the loch and into the Inner Sound, from whence it would pass the headlands of Rona and Skye before heading out into the Atlantic. Barring any serious mishap – and the weather forecasts were optimistic – it would proceed for seven more days before it was far enough out in the ocean to hold a position for the launch of the ship itself. The onboard crew would transfer to an escort vessel and stand off on the horizon, triggering the launch by radio control when the scientists and engineers had determined that the conditions were right. Given the robustness of the *Sea Eagle* and the power of its drive, little short of a severe storm could stand in its way. Only the platform was, in theory, vulnerable to the wind and the waves – so the chanciest part of the whole venture, the part which could literally sink it, was the one that had just begun.

Unless Merrial's fears about the orbital debris were borne out.

Nothing more had been heard about this from Fergal or any other tinker, according to Druin, and he could be trusted on such a matter, according to Merrial. Although her own contract on the project had come to an end, those of other tinkers working on mission-critical systems (as the cant had it) had not; and she was still well up on the latest tinker gossip – as, increasingly, was I.

In the weeks between our reconciliation and the floating of the platform we had had an interesting time, in which our joy in each other was countered – though not in any way diminished – by the reactions of other people to it. At the yard, I daily endured the merciless mockery which my mates seemed to think entirely compatible with continued friendly relations in other respects. In the softer circumstances of my previous experience – in childhood, schooling and University – some of their insults and abuse would have occasioned life-long, smouldering enmity, if not immediate physical violence. Here they passed as light-hearted badinage, and it was their ignoring rather than avenging that was taken as a token of manly honour.

The stand-offish attitudes of the tinkers at the camp were harder to take, but Merrial insistently reassured me that they were a similar test, of the strength of my commitment to their ways, and to her. As the days and weeks passed their reactions to me had gradually warmed to the point of a frigid, prickly politeness.

Merrial and I were, by tinker custom, bundling – trying out the experience of living together before making a public commitment. I was enjoying the experiment and I was as committed as I could ever imagine being, and so was Merrial, but neither of us was in any hurry to move our relationship on to a more formal basis. A tinker marriage is a serious matter, involving among other horrendous expenses – seamstresses, cooks, musicians – that of keeping hundreds of people drunk for a week.

Merrial looked over at me.

'Time to go?'

'Aye.'

We stood up and made our way back, easier now, through the thinning crowd. For obvious reasons, alcohol was strictly banned from the site, and from this day's event. Everybody was heading back for the towns, starting with the nearest, Courthill. The end of the project, and the final pay-packets and bonuses, would be celebrated by drinking the pubs dry over the course of the afternoon and evening.

We wandered along the path back to the main road, occasionally greeting people we knew. The stage from which the speeches had been made stood empty, and was already being dismantled. The various dignitaries were moving down the path in a compact group, and I hurried a little to overtake them on the grass, eager for a closer glimpse of the famous men and women who had travelled far to honour our achievement. Merrial observed this behaviour with sardonic toleration.

I was pointing out a renowned Russian astronomer and an English spacecraft engineer to Merrial when we both noticed Fergal towards the rear of the procession, walking alone among them all. I was surprised to see him, then realised that I shouldn't be – he had been the project manager on the guidance system, after all. At the same moment, he noticed us. He beckoned us over.

Merrial glanced at me. I shrugged. We went over and joined him, I making sure that I walked between him and Merrial. I felt uneasily that we had no place there, but the rest of the dignitaries politely paid us no attention whatever, to the extent that they noticed us at all, and weren't simply caught up in their own deep conversations.

He looked at us sidelong, without hostility. Our confrontation might as well never have happened, for all that he showed of bearing any grudge. For myself, it was different.

'How have you two been getting on?' he asked. He'd obviously heard of our bundling.

'Oh, fine. Great!'

Merrial caught my hand and swung it. 'This one's no an outsider any more, I'll tell you that.'

'Good.' He smiled, and changed the subject. 'It's a great day for us all.'

'Aye,' I said. 'But I'll not be sure of it until the ship's in orbit.'

'Oh, I wouldn't worry about that,' he said. His gaze flicked to Merrial's eyes. 'The ship is safe.'

'How are *you* getting on?' I asked boldly. 'With your new friend?'

'Who – oh, the AI!'

'What?'

'Art-if-icial In-tell-igence,' Fergal and Merrial articulated at the same moment. I glanced from one to the other and laughed.

'I have to learn that sort of thing sometime!'

'Indeed you do,' said Fergal indulgently. 'Still, you have plenty of centuries ahead to learn it.'

251

'Well, I suppose two is plenty, at that,' I replied, puzzled at this odd remark.

Fergal stopped, then hastened on as others trod on our heels.

'She hasn't told you?'

Merrial was looking at him and at me with a mute appeal that somehow seemed to mean something different for both of us. Fergal firmly shook his head.

'Well, she bloody should have.'

'I didn't want to—' began Merrial.

'Give him an improper inducement? Or scare him off?' Fergal smiled sourly. 'Like it or not, Merrial MacClafferty, it's a bit late for either now, wouldn't you think?'

'Oh, I'm not sure he's ready—'

'Will you two,' I said, 'please stop talking as if I wasn't there?'

Fergal glanced over his shoulder, looked ahead, then turned his gaze to the ground and spoke in a low voice.

'Do you know why people today live longer than they did until some time before the Deliverance?'

'Aye,' I said. 'I found references to it in the Deliverer's papers. Life-extension treatments. I suppose in some way the effects must have persisted, and become hereditary.'

'Close enough,' he said, evidently resisting an impulse to quibble. 'Well, the people who became the ancestors of the tinkers had a better treatment.'

My heart thudded. 'How much better?'

He looked around again. A couple of metres separated us from the others on that path, before and behind.

'So much better that we don't know how much better it is.'

I looked at Merrial, feeling the blood drain from my face, and then rush back. I squeezed her hand.

'Well, if you'll have me, I don't care if you do outlive me, and stay young while I grow old.' Easy enough to say, when you're twenty-two and don't believe that ageing or death have any personal application in the first place. But to my surprise, Merrial laughed.

'This one isn't genetic, any more than the other,' she said. 'It's—'

'Infectious,' said Fergal. 'Or is it contagious? I can never remember.'

'Whatever,' said Merrial. 'It's, um, sexually transmitted.'

She sounded almost embarrassed.

*

252

Fergal, it seemed, was still welcome in The Carronade, and even Druin, when he passed him at the bar, was affable towards him. I guessed, myself, after my third litre and sixth whisky, that the tinker Internationalist was anxious to show us his friendly side. I remained unpersuaded by it, but decided to make the most of it while it lasted. I had still not assimilated the news that I could expect to live longer than I'd ever expected, and it would take me long enough to do it.

'So what,' I asked him, at a corner table in the security of the raucous din around us, 'was that thing Merrial found? The AI?'

'It's . . . a planner,' he said. 'A mind that can co-ordinate an entire economy. Something we're going to need, some day.'

'After your glorious revolution?'

'Yes, and maybe before. It's a revolutionary itself.'

'So what are you going to do with it?' I asked.

Fergal might have been, as Jeanna had said, able to hold his drink. He may well have not done or said anything without calculating its effect on the vectors of his purposes. But I'm sure it was a reckless impulse that made him say what he said next.

'It's on the ship. Well, a copy of it, anyway.'

He was looking at me, not at Merrial, as he spoke. He didn't see what I saw: the momentary flash of triumph and delight on Merrial's face. That glimpse, as much as his words, must have drained the colour from mine. And then – I could see her dissembling – by the time Fergal turned to her, she looked even more shocked than I felt.

'Why the hell did you do that?' she asked.

Fergal leaned in and lowered his voice. 'I learned a few things from the AI,' he said. 'Its memories go right up to a few days before the Deliverance. It knows nothing about what happened but it does know that the Deliverer had control of nuclear and other weapons in space. So the possibility that – you know, what we feared – was true is too strong to ignore. But at this stage – hell, if the mission were aborted, or if the ship were destroyed, God alone knows how long it'd be before we'll see another. There was only one way to do it, and that was to make a copy and let it into the ship's own seer-stone control systems. Out of sheer self-preservation, the copy would be forced to take the kind of fast-reacting control over the ship's drive that would let it dodge through any debris that's still there.'

253

'Would that work?' I asked Merrial, who was staring at Fergal as though seeing past him.

'Oh, aye,' she said, without looking around, 'we couldn't do that ourselves, but an AI would be in with a chance, I reckon. But what happens once it's up?'

Fergal grinned. 'It just sits in the centre of a new communications web, that's all. A useful thing to have.'

'Bloody dangerous, you mean!' I said.

'Don't worry,' said Fergal, realising he'd gone too far. 'It's not going to interfere with the satellite. It'll just . . . gather information. For the future.'

'Oh God!' Merrial exclaimed. 'You're out of your fucking mind! That thing is a deil! It'll have the world in a new Possession before you know it!'

'It'll be our Possession,' Fergal said.

'Yours, you mean!'

Fergal stretched out his legs.

'And what would be wrong with that?'

He looked at our appalled faces and burst out laughing.

'Don't be stupid,' he said. 'There's no way it can do anything without having people to work with, and there are no such people yet.' He placed a thumb on Merrial's chin for a moment. 'As you fine well know.'

She smacked his hand away, none too gently.

'That was not funny,' she said. She got up with unsteady dignity. 'I'm going for a piss.'

Fergal watched me watching her thread her way through the throng. If he detected the tumult in my thoughts he gave no sign.

'No chance of persuading you, Clovis?'

'Not a chance in hell,' I said, still distracted. His casual banter fooled me for not a second; this was a man who wanted power, Possession indeed, and his current scheme with the AI would not be his last. He was a man I would have to watch, and might one day have to kill.

'Oh, well,' he said. 'Our day will come, and you'll see it.'

I was about to contest this when I felt a hand on my shoulder.

'Oh, hello, Catherine.'

My former landlady smiled down at me; like everyone here, she was already a bit drunk. She nodded at Fergal and looked back at me.

'Hi, Clovis. I hope you like your new accommodation.'

'Oh, aye.'

She reached into a pouch on her hip. 'I've got something for you,' she said. 'A letter that arrived a few days ago, I didn't get round to—'

'That's all right,' I said, taking the bulky envelope. 'Thanks.'

Fergal, perhaps subdued by his rebuff, was moodily studying his drink, or tactfully respecting my privacy, as I opened the package. From the handwriting of the address, I knew it was from Gantry. It contained a letter and a thick booklet. The letter was neatly typed. I glanced down the predictable hand-wringing about my expulsion from the University (the trial had been a farce, not that I cared any more) and about my choice of tinkering as a career; then turned over to the next sheet.

> However, Clovis, and just as a little reminder of the joys of historical research – you may remember I looked a little puzzled when you introduced your girlfriend, Merrial? The reason was that I thought I recognised her from somewhere. Actually, of course, I hadn't – but I'd come across a picture of what may be an ancestor of hers by the same name, in one of the Institute's old yearbooks – 2058, in fact. You may even have glanced through this once yourself. Have a look at page 35 – the resemblance is quite striking.
>
> (Needless to say, I expect you to return . . .

I almost dropped the papers as I fumbled open the booklet and turned to the page. It showed – in much sharper detail and better colour than in modern photographs – some kind of social occasion. People were sitting, smartly dressed, at long tables, clapping their hands as others in their company danced. In the immediate foreground was a girl, caught in mid-twirl, her thick black hair swaying around behind her head, one hand swinging her long, layered skirt out to the side, her bare feet lightly, precisely placed. A fine dancer. Merrial.

She was even named, in the small print of the caption.

It could be an ancestor, I tried to tell myself, as Gantry thought. But I knew it was not so. If anyone could be identified from a photograph, Merrial could. She looked, in the picture, no different from how she looked this day.

I had, from the first moment I'd seen her, thought her younger, fierier, fresher than myself, and attributed her occasional ironies and unreasonably intelligent remarks to her native wit, which I was quite unenviously happy to regard as greater than my own. It was a shock to realise that they were the wisdom of age. Dear God, how old was she? She had lived since the Deliverer's time! The thought was enough to make me feel dizzy.

Gantry was right about one thing – I had seen this picture before, on an idle trawl through the Institute's public-relations archive. And, as I had anticipated, the memory of seeing it did come back. It had only been a few seconds' pause as I'd turned the pages, a couple of years earlier, my attention momentarily caught by this pretty image from the past.

Fergal's voice broke into my appalled reflections.

'Bad news from home?'

I shook my head, folding the letter around the booklet again, inserting the sheets in the envelope and slipping it into my pocket.

'No, no,' I said, forcing a smile. 'Nothing like that. It's just – I feel faint, I think I've had too much to drink, on an empty stomach, you know?'

I clapped my hand to my mouth.

'Oh God.' I swallowed. The tinker's sardonic, sceptical eyes regarded me. I realised that I had still to decide what to do about another shock, delivered only minutes earlier: that he – apparently with Merrial's expectation – had put the AI on the ship. All it would take to expose him, and blast whatever schemes either or both of them had hatched, would be a word to Druin . . .

'You sure you're all right?'

'Yeah, I'll be fine. I just need some fresh air. I'm going out. Could you tell Merrial to come out too?'

'Sure,' he said, already scanning the crowd for other company. 'Where'll you be?'

'In the square,' I said. 'At the statue.'

14

Final Analysis

To Almaty then, and apple-blossom on the streets, smoke in the air, and the Tian-Shan mountains beyond; so high, so close they were improbable to the eye, like the moon on the horizon. Myra almost skipped with relief to be back in Kazakhstan.

President Chingiz Suleimanyov's office was a lot grander than Myra's. She felt a tremor of trepidation as she walked past the soldier who held the door open for her. A ten-metre strip of red carpet over polished parquet, at the end of which was a small chair in front of a large desk. The chair was plastic. The desk was mahogany, its green leather top bare except for a gold Mont Blanc pen and a pristine, red-leather-edged blotter. Glass-paned bookcases on either side of the room converged to a wide window with a mountain view. The room's central chandelier, unlit at the moment, looked like a landing-craft from an ancient and impressive alien civilisation making its presence known.

The President stood up as she came in, and walked around his intimidating desk. They met with a handshake. Suleimanyov was a short, well-built Kazakh with a face which he'd carefully kept at an avuncular-looking fiftyish. He was actually in his fifty-eighth year, a child of the century as he occasionally mentioned, which meant that he'd grown up after the Glorious Counter-Revolution of 1991 had passed into history. The reunification of Kazakhstan in the Fall Revolution had been his finest hour, and he always called himself a Kazakhstani, not a Kazakh: the national identification, not the ethnic. He didn't have any of Myra's twentieth-century leftist hang-ups. He had never had the slightest pretension to being any kind of socialist. However, he followed Soviet tradition by wearing the neatest and most conventional business-suit that dollars could buy.

'Good afternoon, Citizen Davidova,' he said, in Russian. She responded similarly, and then he waved her to her seat and resumed his own. The soldier closed the door.

'Ah, Myra my friend,' Suleimanyov said, this time in BBC World Service English, 'let's drop the formality. I've read your reports on your mission.' He gestured with his hands as though letting a book fall open. 'What a mess. Though I must say you are looking good.'

'I'm sorry that I was not more successful, President Suleimanyov—'

'Chingiz, please. And no need to apologise.' He pinched the bridge of his nose, closing his eyes for a moment. He looked tired. 'I don't see how anyone else could have done better. Your action in leaving Great Britain was perhaps . . . impetuous, but even with hindsight it will probably turn out to have been for the best. What a long way down they've come, the English. As for the Americans – well, what can I say?' He chuckled, with a certain *schadenfreude*, and gazed upwards at the crystal mother-ship. 'Fifteen years ago they were stamping their will on the whole planet, and now a few nuclear weapons are too hot for them to handle. In my father's time they were willing to contemplate taking multiple nuclear hits themselves.' He looked back from his reminiscence to Myra. 'Sorry,' he said, suddenly abashed, 'no offence intended. I forget sometimes that you were – *are* – an American.'

'No offence taken,' Myra said. 'I entirely agree with your assessment. What a crock of shit the place is! What a pathetic lot they are! The chance of a long life has only made them more afraid of death than ever.'

The President's bushy eyebrows twitched. 'It has not done that for you, then?'

Myra shook her head. 'I can see the rationality of it – people think they have more life to lose if they have a long one to look forward to – but I think it's a false logic. A long life of oppression or shame is worse than a short one, after all.'

She stopped, and looked at him quizzically. He smiled.

'True, we are not here to discuss philosophy,' he said. 'Nevertheless, I'm happy that you think it better to die free than to live as slaves. We may get the chance some day, but let's try to delay our heroic deaths for a bit, eh?'

'Yes indeed.' She wanted very badly to smoke, but the President was notoriously clean-living.

'Very well,' said Chingiz. 'Something I did not tell you before . . . I arranged for other cadres with similarly relevant experience to make similar approaches to the governments of France, Turkey, Brazil and Guangdong. They have encountered a similar lack of interest. So we have to face the Sheenisov on our own. I need hardly tell you that we don't stand much of a chance, over anything but the short term.'

'I have a suggestion,' Myra said. 'If the West is unwilling to assist us, then to hell with them. Let's cut a deal with the Sheenisov! All we want is our territorial integrity, their withdrawal from Semipalatinsk and access to the markets, trade routes and resources of the Former Union. What they want, presumably, is a passage across or to the north of Kazakhstan, as they make their way west to the Ukraine, which is the nearest soft target but still one that will take them many years, perhaps decades, to assimilate. I don't think they're ready to take on Muscovy or Turkey just yet. It strikes me that these aims are not incompatible.'

'Yes, yes,' Chingiz said, 'the option of our switching sides has occurred to me, and to my Foreign Secretary. The difficulty is that no one has ever "cut a deal" with the Sheenisov. They have no leader, or even leadership – at least, none that the world knows. They are indeed a horde, without a Great Khan like my namesake. That makes them difficult to deal with – in every sense.'

'Ah, come on,' Myra said, feeling bolder. 'Even the anarchists had their Makhno. I don't believe a leaderless horde could accomplish what they have, even in military terms. It's applying guerilla tactics at the level of strategy and of main-force confrontation – that is novel, but it requires precise co-ordination. There is nothing random going on here.'

Chingiz's lips set in a thin line for a moment. He shook his head. 'A system without a centre can achieve more than we may intuitively expect, Myra. That after all is the lesson of the twentieth century, no? It works in economics, and in nature, and to some extent in military affairs too.'

'Good point,' Myra said. She didn't want to bring the deranged Green rumour about the General into this level of conversation. 'Let's assume they have no leadership. In order to have the co-ordination they display, they must have horizontal communication between the units, and some method of arriving at a common response . . . even if it's only some social equivalent of excitation and inhibition in a neural

259

network. In that case, any offer made to a sufficiently large unit would be spread through the rest, as would a response. It would still be worthwhile contacting them.'

'Hmm,' said Chingiz. He steepled his fingers. 'And what do you propose? Walking towards them until they take notice, then talking to the first person able to understand you?'

'That's about it.'

'It sounds dangerous, apart from anything else.'

'Actually, I propose announcing my intention beforehand, through whatever channels we have, then heading for Semipalatinsk.'

'Come, come,' said Chingiz. 'Things are not that bad, not yet. You can still fly in, direct.'

'And out?'

'Oh, yes. Air-traffic control is still functioning. As are radio and television, on selected channels. It's only computer interfaces that are being blocked – by physical cutting of landlines or by electromagnetic jamming. It's incredibly differentiated stuff – very clever. We couldn't do it.'

She peered at his calm face.

'What reports are we getting?'

'About life under the Sheenisov? Hah. In some respects, life goes on as normal. There are certainly no democidal activities. There are what the Sheenisov call *reforms*. Workplace democracy, and so forth. They are very insistent about that. Many businesses dependent on the net are failing – they either re-orient to the Sheenisov internal communications system, whatever that is, or they pick up sticks and go, or they are expropriated on the grounds of abandonment.' He rubbed his hands. 'Needless to say, this is giving our republic a temporary influx of people, of capital, and of comms gear and computer capacity. Some refugees are destitute, but not many.'

'Any willing to join the fight back?'

'No mass rallying to our armed forces, I must say. The usual *dashnik emigré* diversions – plotting, pleading, mounting sabotage expeditions, low-key terrorism. We don't encourage it.' He rubbed a finger up and down the side of his nose. 'Naturally, we try to prevent it . . . to the best of our ability, but our resources are quite inadequate for such a task.'

'But of course.' Myra smiled. 'Could you raise me some *muj*? Two or three good men, not fanatics, not suicidal, but willing to take a risk and have a go if necessary. I'm still deeply reluctant to fly into Semey. Too much opportunity for an opportune mechanical failure – frankly, I'm getting a little paranoid about anything that's computer controlled, on either side. So, if I may, I'd like to drive, with bodyguards.'

Chingiz raised his eyebrows. 'Drive all the way?'

'No, no. Fly to Karaganda, announce what I'm doing, then drive to Semey, bypassing the ISTWR.'

'Ah, yes.' He teased some of the hairs in one shaggy eyebrow back into place. 'A little local difficulty there.' He sounded reproachful.

'The situation's under control,' Myra said.

'Perhaps. But, on balance, I would suggest that you don't go back there, or even bypass it by truck or jeep through the Polygon. Far more dangerous than flying.' He raised a hand, stilling her incipient protest. 'I know what you mean about the computers, and flight control. I too have thought about this. You will get your bodyguards. You make your announcement, fly to Semey, then wander where you will until someone makes contact – which, as you say, someone surely will. You will pass on the proposals and await developments. Then you will fly from Semey back to Kapitsa, and either declare the conflict settled, or rally your people for their part in the common defence.' He smiled thinly. 'Either way, your internal political problems will be over. Externally, however, it may turn out that the Sheenisov are not our most immediate problem . . .'

'Ah, yes,' said Myra. 'The next move. Presumably at least one of the countries we made our offer to will start to worry about what we're going to do with the nukes, and the option of disarming us will move up the agenda pretty damn quick.'

'Precisely,' said Chingiz. 'The US-spacer nexus is the one we probably have to worry about most – as your friend in New York said, the space industrialists and settlers are understandably edgy on the subject.'

'They're your nukes now,' Myra said. 'We'll go along with anything you say. Presumably you'd want us to stand them down and turn over the operational codes.'

Chingiz slammed his fist on his massive desk, making Myra jump.

'No!' he said. 'We are not going to be pushed around. We are not going to give up our nukes without guarantees of military aid. And we are willing to threaten nuclear retaliation against any attack.'

'So you're ready to go to the wire on this one?'

261

'Absolutely,' said Chingiz. 'To the wire. But not beyond.'

'All right,' said Myra. 'We'll go with you. We'll see who blinks first.'

'Thank you,' said Chingiz. His face relaxed a little. 'It's a high-risk strategy, I know. But the endgame is upon us, and I for one am not going into it defenceless.'

Myra nodded.

'The best thing you can do,' she said, 'is act as though you're ready to wash your hands of us – of the ISTWR. Denounce and disown us – privately of course, on the hotline – and urge the UN or US or who-ever to negotiate directly with us. That should buy us some time.'

'Only if they believe you're mad enough to do it.'

Myra bared her teeth. 'They will.'

Semipalatinsk, or Semey, was a pleasant enough town, whose steppe location had let it spread out so much that even its taller buildings looked low, even its narrower streets wide. There was room in those broad streets for trees whose dusty leaves had been an object of sus-picious Geiger-counter monitoring on her first visit, in the late 1980s. The good old days of the Nevada-Semipalatinsk Association against nuclear testing. Of all the betrayals she'd perpetrated against her youth, this one stung the most. Marxism, Trotskyism and socialism could go hang; it was the implacable naïve humanist internationalism of that protest, its irrefutable medical and statistical basis, its sheer bloody outrage rooted in biology rather than ideology, which had been her purest, fiercest flame. She had thought nuclear weapons the vilest work of man, whose very possession contaminated, and whose mere testing was murderous.

Nurup Kerbayev and Mustafa Altynsaryn, her proudly counter-revolutionary bodyguards, strolled a polite step or two behind her, beards and bandoliers bristling, Kalashnikovs slung on their shoul-ders. Nurup was ethnically Kazakh-Russian; Mustafa looked more Mongoloid, almost Han Chinese. With their AKs and baggy pants and scuffed boots and bulging jackets they both looked just like counter-revolutionary bandits. They also looked like Sheenisov sol-diery or the local population, whom the Sheenisov had encouraged to carry arms as a deterrent to counter-revolutionary banditry.

They walked down the streets and across the squares quite unchal-lenged, though one or two people gave Myra a curious glance, as

though recognising her from her television appearance the previous evening. Apart from the parked tanks on the street-corners, around each of which a curious crowd, mainly of children and young people, fraternised with the relaxed-looking crew, the town so far showed little sign of being caught up in a social revolution. It was the weird fighting-machines that were alarming. They stalked and lurched about like Martian invaders; but the locals treated them with casual familiarity, like traffic or street-furniture. Perhaps, Myra thought wryly, it was the absence of searing heat-rays and writhing metal tentacles that did the trick.

As well as those combat drones, big clunky calculating-machines were being installed, indoors in shop-fronts and factories, outdoors in the squares. Gears and teeth and crystal spheres, building to frenetic orreries of some alternate solar system, Copernican with Ptolemaic epicyles. Nanotech dripped and congealed around the brass and steel, like epoxy that never quite set. Around noon Myra and her companions watched one being winched off a flatbed truck and placed carefully in a plaza below a cosmonaut monument.

'Fucking bizarre,' said Myra, half to herself, as a Sheenisov cadre clambered on to the plinth and began an explanatory harangue in Uzbek, not one of her languages.

'With this they will replace the market,' Nurup scoffed, under his breath. 'God help us all.'

A lively market in soft drinks and hot food was already forming around the strange device. Nurup and Mustafa bought her Coke and kebabs, and themselves a hotdog each. Both talked quietly to the stall-keepers. Taking the food, they sat down on a bench and ate.

'There is much discontent,' Mustafa said eagerly.

'Bazaar gossip,' Nurup said. 'Stall-keepers will tell you anything. They will tell the Sheenisov they love them.'

The two men argued obliquely but intensely for a few minutes about the prospects for terrorist action against the Sheenisov.

'We're not here for that,' Myra reminded them. She shared out cigarettes, then together they walked out of the square. Neither of the men raised any questions about her random following of the streets, until they ended up at the bank of the broad Irtysh river. Flats on the opposite bank, a riverside walk on this. A small pleasure steamer chugged downriver, ferrying a calculating-machine on its promenade deck.

Myra leaned against a railing, gazing into the river. The two men leaned against the railing, looking the other way. People passed. After a few minutes of this Mustafa asked what was going on.

'Nothing,' said Myra, not turning around. 'Or maybe something. I'm assuming we've been followed, or watched. I'm quite prepared to wait here for at least an hour. Make yourselves comfortable.'

But they were too edgy and too alert to be comfortable. The most they did was light another of her Dunhills. Myra slipped her eyeband down and was at once struck by a sense of *déja vu*, as the whole scene around her hazed over, sleeted with grey flecks. After a moment she realised the source of that sense of recognition – it reminded her of how she'd first seen towns like this, back in the 90s: through their Soviet pollution haze. She blinked, moved the eyeband up and down, tried to pick up the nets. Nothing but the grey snow. Even Parvus, summoned from memory, looked frazzled by it.

Sheenisov jamming. Shit.

She'd just given up this experiment when she heard her name called. She turned. Shin Se-Ha and Kim Nok-Yung walked side by side up the pathway, waving to her.

'It's all right,' she told her swiftly tense bodyguards. 'I know these guys.'

She shook hands, smiling, with the Korean and the Japanese; introduced them to the Kazakhstanis. Discreet compliments on her rejuvenated appearance were exchanged with her admiration for their now healthier physiques. Even their relatively humane imprisonment had marked them, weighing them down with something which their new freedom – if freedom it was – had enabled them to shrug off. They walked taller. They confronted the Kazakhstani *emigrés* unabashed.

'So, you are *Sheenisov*,' said Mustafa, in a disgusted tone.

'Lay off,' said Myra. 'They're OK. We have to talk.'

'Yes,' said Nok-Yung. 'We have to talk.'

It was a mild day, for the time of year. Not shirt-sleeve weather, but comfortable if you dressed warm, as they all had. Myra indicated a semi-circle of benches in a concreted picnic area along the bank a little. The two ex-prisoners shrugged, then nodded.

Nok-Yung and Se-Ha sat on either side of her, the two bodyguards on separate benches a few metres away. Children, snug-wrapped in quilted satin bomber-jackets and padded trousers, capered about and yelled, oblivious to the adults.

'So how are you getting on, in this brave new world?' Myra asked.

'We're fine,' said Nok-Yung, his comrade nodding emphatically. 'Our families are joining us soon, and in the meantime we have much to do.'

'You both got jobs?' Myra smiled.

'There are no *jobs*,' Se-Ha said primly. 'There is work. We have been . . . co-opted, and we have been sent to talk to you.'

'Well, I had guessed this was hardly a coincidence,' Myra said. 'But I had not expected to see you as Sheenisov cadre already.'

'It's an open system,' Nok-Yung said. 'Interesting contributions are quickly taken up; amplified; discussed.'

'The opposite of the nets, then,' Myra said. They laughed.

'And the opposite of the Leninist system,' Nok-Yung said earnestly. 'Once you are in, you are *in*, there is no . . . apprenticeship? No candidacy, no working your way up. Past experience,' he added rather smugly, '*counts*.'

Myra flashed her eyebrows. No doubt the militant and the Marxist mathematician had found their niches quickly. 'I'm sure that's all fascinating,' she said. 'But I'm here to put a diplomatic proposal to the Sino-Soviet Union as a whole. Can I do that, just by talking to you?'

'Yes.'

'Very well.' She put it to them, straight: the deal, the crossing corridors. Let the revolutionary horde flow around Kazakhstan, like a flood around a rock, and they could swamp the rest of the world, for all she cared. (Could and would run into the sand, she did not say, but that was what she expected.)

They listened politely, now and then asking for clarification, making notes and doodling maps on hand-held slates that – while obviously information-retrieval devices – looked as though they were made of . . . slate. Se-Ha stood up.

'I must consult,' he said, nodded, and walked briskly away. Nok-Yung accepted a cigarette, and leaned back luxuriantly, sprawling out with his elbows on the back of the bench. He regarded Myra through narrow eyes and curling smoke.

'Why do you resist the SSU, Myra?' he asked mildly. 'It is only democracy. It is only socialism. A means – and an end, compatible at last, after all the disasters and crimes done in the name of both.' He spread his hands. 'There are no secrets here, no deceptions. When you were as young as you look –' he smiled '– you would have thought this revolution, this liberation more wonderful than your wildest dreams.'

'Don't let my *mujahedin* friends hear you say that!' she warned, half in jest. She glanced over at Nurup Kerbayev. He smiled back, eyes and teeth flashing like knives.

'But you're right,' she went on. 'Let's just say . . . I may look young again, but I've had a long, long life in the meantime. I've come to believe in myself, and in . . . my country, Kazakhstan. And I will not be assimilated, and nor will we.' She waved a hand around. 'These people, they may seem . . . happy enough to wait and see. But deep down, no – just below the surface – they are seething with suspicion. They are not your Mongolians or Siberians, who God knows had it bad enough under Stalinism but who found everything since was worse. To the Kazakhs socialism means "the tragedy" of the 1930s: the forced settlement, the famine. It means the nuclear tests, the cancers, the birth defects. They don't want to be the subjects of any more experiments. And if you want to point to the ISTWR as a counter-example – that was a special case. A self-selected minuscule minority. Our socialism was always a joke, more black humour than Red. Trotskyism in one country – what a laugh!'

What a laugh she gave. She frightened herself. One of the scampering children playing around them stopped, put his thumb in his mouth and ran away.

'We ran a benign state capitalism, nothing more,' she went on. 'In your case, my friend, it was not even that. God, I feel disgusted with myself that we did it, that we ever allowed ourselves to be compradors for Reid's goddamn private gulags.'

Nok-Yung stared at the sky for a moment. 'I don't know what to say, Myra,' he said at last. 'Your regret over the Mutual Protection camps is . . . well taken. But about the other matters – you must surely know that none of what you have been talking about, the USSR and so on, is socialism as we understand it, and as you understood it. So stop confusing the issue.'

'Oh, I'm well aware that you are different. That you may well be the genuine article: Marx and Engels, Proprietors. And you know what? I don't care. I don't want it, for myself or for anyone.'

'Why not?' Nok-Yung sounded more puzzled than offended.

Myra pointed across the river to the insectile shape of a fighting-machine, patrolling the water's edge with heron-like steps.

'Because of those damn things,' she said. 'And the calculating-machines.'

'What!' Nok-Yung's eyes creased up in amusement. 'Luddism is not your true ideology, Myra. I cannot believe this. These machines are one of the most marvellous achievements of the Sheenisov – a whole alternative nanotechnology, worked out quite independently of the West. You know how the machines scale down, all the way to the molecular scale, and are all mechanical and chemical and optical, with no need for electronic interfaces? That's their – our – secret weapon, an open secret. A computer system that the enemy cannot penetrate, but that everyone can understand and access. I've just begun to use it, and I tell you, it has the most intuitive interface I've ever come across. The capitalists would kill for it. Or rather, they would kill to be able to monopolise it. But it's free, so they can't.'

'I know about your strange machines,' Myra said. 'The CIA told me all about them.' She tapped her temple, smiling ironically. '"I have detailed files."'

Nok-Yung caught the allusion. 'It is not *The Terminator*, you know! Not – what was it in the films? – Skynet. It is not . . . inimical.'

'Not now, perhaps. But what will it do, when it – or you – have covered the world, like a banyan tree?'

Nok-Yung spat a puff of air and smoke. 'More Luddism! The machines will form a benign human environment, a second nature, within which human nature can flourish, truly, for the first time.' He leaned forward, speaking confidentially. 'Let me tell you what we have done, something that no other system would have dared to do. We have nanofactured a virally distributed, genetically fixable version of the anti-ageing treatment. It spreads before our migrations like a benign plague. You may be already infected, yourself. A gift.'

'God, that is *so* irresponsible!' Myra jolted rigid. 'Viruses *mutate*, dammit, in case you hadn't heard!'

Nok-Yung made a planing motion with his hand. 'Not this one. It has self-repair built in. It has tested stable through a million virtual generations.'

'*Virtual* generations, yes! Man, you did enough design work in the camp to know what *that's* worth in the real world!'

'Different system, different design philosophy,' he said, with infuriating complacency. 'Our testing kits are themselves *part* of the real

267

world. It's like the difference between a working scale model and a simulation. There is simply no comparison. And the computing resources are vast, vaster even than anything the spacers have yet built.'

Myra felt her gaze sinking into the bottomless pool of his self-confidence. It was truly terrifying; it was, she realised, what she most feared for herself – to be so sure. To be absolutely certain that she was right would, as far as she was concerned, be the end of her. Doubt was her only hope, her comfort and companion since childhood, her scepticism her sole security.

Shin Se-Ha returned and sat down, affecting not to notice their frozen moment of mutual incomprehension. He looked at Myra, gravely, and shook his head.

'No deal, I'm afraid.'

Myra could scarcely believe it.

'Why ever not? The alternative is to fight your way through Kazakhstan! All you have to do instead is not fight us! What more can you ask of us?'

Se-Ha shook his head sadly. 'It is not that, Myra,' he said. 'It is not aggression, or animosity. It is simply the imperative of our mode of production. It will be global or it will be nothing, as your Trotsky always said. We have to keep running, or fall over, until we meet ourselves, on the other side of the world.'

He saw this wasn't getting anywhere with her. 'More concretely,' he continued, 'we can't have . . . unassimilated areas within the Union. It would be too much of an opportunity for our enemies. And we can't stop for long, because that would force us to engage in internal class struggle, particularly with the small-property owners, which we do not want.' He smiled. 'To put it mildly! We have so far been able to avoid the whole dictatorship of the proletariat scenario by simply carrying the remaining small and large businesses along with us. The machine-based common-property economy expands, and they expand in its interstices. They can live like nits in our hair, as long as we are running. If we stopped, the itch would be intolerable. We would have to . . . *scratch*.'

'Oh, come on,' said Myra. 'You can run a mixed economy indefinitely. We've been doing it in Kapitsa for years.'

'A mixture of state capitalism and private, yes,' said Nok-Yung, 'as you've just reminded me. A mixture of a real non-commodity economy and a market is much more unstable. Conflicts arise very rapidly – if they're both confined to the same economic space.'

An unstable system, that had to expand at just the right speed to stop itself falling over; not too slow, or too *fast* . . . there were plenty of natural and artificial and social analogies to that. Myra almost giggled at the thought of what would happen to them if Kazakhstan just surrendered, if the Sheenisov suddenly found themselves pushing at an open door and fell flat on their collective faces.

But that wasn't an option. She looked around, checking that her guards were still bored and watchful, then back at the two new recruits to the Sheenisov. The absurdity of the situation struck her – she was doing diplomacy by just talking to two guys on the street. For all she knew they could be as deluded as UFO contactees, and not really ambassadors from an alien intelligence at all. Again she felt the urge to giggle – it was just another silly idea; she was feeling lightheaded, flighty, as though her problem had been solved. She couldn't *see* any solution. She was in deeper trouble than ever, but still she felt relieved.

'There is a certain urgency to it,' Se-Ha was saying, a little apologetically. 'Green factions are experimenting with plague vectors. The spacer groups, the Outwarders, have a radically post-human vision. Between them, they threaten humanity with extinction. Our advance is in essence defensive . . .'

She looked sharply at him. 'Tell me, Se-Ha,' she said, 'just who it was you consulted, back there.'

He looked uncomfortable. 'It was . . . a distributed decision. A consensus.'

'Bull*shit*!' she snapped. 'Don't give me that. I didn't see a vote being taken in the streets around here. Did you? So there must be a leadership somewhere, a council. I want to talk to it.'

'You are talking to it,' he said, 'when you talk to us. To the extent that it exists. The policy parameters have indeed been set democratically, but the implementation, the . . . administrative decisions, are made . . .' He chewed his lower lip. 'It's hard to say,' he finished lamely.

'Let me guess,' said Myra, standing up. 'Expert system. AI.'

Se-Ha looked up at her, eyes dark and blank under his thin black brows. 'That is possible, yes.'

Myra straightened and sighed. She was convinced, paranoically perhaps, that the mad preacher Jordan had been right: the General, the Plan, was at the bottom of all this, that it had implemented itself on the Sheenisov's machine ecology and was in the process of taking over the world. With the best intentions, no doubt.

'God, yes, you're right,' she said. 'It's you or the Outwarders. Both sides are like the fucking Borg. "You will be assimilated" – isn't that what you're telling me?'

Nok-Yung shrugged. 'It's not something sinister. We all live in the world machine. Why not live in a world machine that is on our side?'

Myra had to smile. 'You want me to imagine the future,' she said, 'as socialism with a human face – for ever?'

'Yes!' they both said, pleased that she'd got the point at last.

It really would be hard to end this conversation politely, but she would try.

'I'll take your message back to President Suleimanyov,' she said. 'No doubt you will await our response.'

Se-Ha and Nok-Yung stood up and shook her hand gravely.

'Goodbye,' she said.

'Goodbye,' they both said.

Se-Ha smiled mischievously. 'I hope I see you again.'

They'd rented the plane, an executive jet that had seen better days, in Almaty. Just as well; Myra could not have borne to displace any passengers on the commercial flights out of Semipalatinsk, standing room only and a strict baggage allowance.

As soon as they were beyond Sheenisov airspace – and Sheenisov jamming – Parvus made a priority over-ride and poked his virtual head over the back of the seat in front of her.

'Sorry about this, Myra,' the AI murmured. 'Urgent messages.'

'Patch 'em through,' she said.

The message queue consisted of calls from Suleimanyov, Valentina Kozlova and someone with an anonymous code identifier. She worked through them one by one.

As soon as she blinked on the President's identifier, he was through, live from his office. Various aides and ministers hovered in the periphery of the shot.

'Hello,' he said. 'Results?'

Myra grimaced. 'They're adamant that they won't accept it. I was as surprised as you are. In fact, I was shocked. I have a suspicion that the secret of their military and economic co-ordination is a military AI, and that it is . . . calling the shots.'

Chingiz took this with unexpected aplomb.

'It was worth trying,' he said. He waved his hand, downwards. 'However, the Sheenisov are no longer our most immediate problem.'

'What's happened?'

He smiled wryly. 'As we expected. It's all gone public now – everyone knows about the nukes. Our generous offers to the United States, and to other countries, have been referred up to the UN – and referred back to the Security Council, for immediate action. We are to turn over our nuclear weapons to forces under UN authority within twenty-four hours – twenty-three and a half, now – or face aerial and space attack. Specifically, on Kapitsa, which they have rightly identified as the focus of the problem. After Kapitsa, Almaty.'

Myra thought for a moment that the virtual view had gone monochrome, and that the plane had turned over. Then everything was normal again.

'If they carry through their threat against Kapitsa – well, I would hope for air support.' She smiled wanly. 'But please, Chingiz. Don't let them ruin Almaty.'

'I have no intention of letting them do that,' he said. 'I suggest you return to Kapitsa. You have problems of your own. Evacuate the town, if you can. Let them hit an empty shell. We'll send transport and cavalry.'

'Cavalry?'

'For . . . internal security. The stand-off around the government building is very tense.' He glanced away. 'Your own Defence Minister is trying to get through to you. She can explain the situation better than I can. Goodbye for now.'

'Goodbye, Chingiz.'

Before taking the next call, Myra turned to Nurup and Mustafa.

'We're diverting to Kapitsa,' she said. 'I may be going into a very volatile situation. Street violence, at least. And possible bombing, maybe up to nuclear level. This is not what I hired you for. We can drop you off at Karaganda first, if you wish.'

The two *mujahedin* looked deeply offended.

'Our job is to keep you safe until you return to Almaty, or until you tell us to go,' Nurup said.

'OK,' she said. 'I'm telling you to go.'

271

She reached for the intercom toggle. Mustafa was out of his seat in an instant, and placed a hand across the switch. His expression and tone were apologetic. 'We stay,' he said. 'It's God's will.'

And a matter of honour too, she guessed.

'Kapitsa it is, then,' she said.

The two men beamed at her as though *she* had done *them* a favour. Perhaps she had; they probably believed she'd just issued them two free passes to heaven. There were times when she envied the devout.

As the plane banked around she took the call from Valentina. This one was v-mail, recorded in one of the offices in the government building. Behind Valentina, men with Kalashnikovs lurked at windows. Bureaucrats turned desks into makeshift barricades. Somebody was operating a byte-shredder, wiping computer memories, setting up a blizzard of interference.

'Hi, Myra, hope this gets through. Jesus, did you hear that the nuke thing's all over the media? We've got news collectors – warm bodies as well as remotes – coming in all the time, and the demonstrators are acting up for them so they can watch themselves being heroic on CNN. Fucking classic media feedback howl. The nuke thing has really freaked a lot of them out – in all the factions, the lefty headbangers and the pro-UN types and the fucking spacists. Not to mention our very own patriots. Our agents in the crowd – hell, even the reporters – are picking up talk about storming the building. We want you back as soon as you can; we'll have a militia driver on standby at the airport.'

The message was time-stamped at 1.35 p.m., and it was now 2.50. Myra blinked up a split-screen of television news channels while taking the third call. The seatbelt light came on; the aeroplane was beginning its descent to Kapitsa. Thank God for ultra-precise radio tuning – Myra could remember when you couldn't even take a call in level flight. The pilot's voice was raised slightly as he argued with air-traffic control for precedence, throwing diplomatic weight and Kazakh curses about equally. Myra looked out of the window. More aircraft than usual – hastily hired jets, she guessed – were parked beside the runways. The media circus was in town.

Her anonymous caller flickered into view.

'Jason!'

The CIA agent gave her a tense smile, but warm around the eyes.

272

'Hello, Myra. Good to see you. Wow, you look amazing. Just in time for your global stardom, huh?'

'Hah!'

'Almost as much excitement as the coup. Anyway . . . I'm here to tell you that we've got somewhere with the investigation.'

Undercarriage down, thump.

'What – oh, Georgi's—'

'Yup. I'm sorry to have to tell you this, Myra, but – shit, we got this out of the black labs, it's bleeding-edge stuff. We did an autopsy on a goddamn *cell sample* – don't ask how we got it.'

A bump, a rocking forward, another bump, and the incline of deceleration.

'The point is, Myra, we found traces of a very specific, very subtle bit of nanotech. It's not exactly a poison, that's the clever thing. It builds up into a little machine, then disintegrates when it's done its job. We found a few gear trains, but that was enough.'

The aircraft came to a halt and the seatbelt light went off. The door banged open and the steps angled down. Myra stood up and shuffled forward, behind Nurup and in front of Mustafa, still talking and listening. She waved absently to the pilot, left him a handful of gold coins as a bonus. She was thinking ahead.

'Enough for what?'

'Enough to identify it. It's a spacer assassination weapon. A heart-stopper.'

A heart-stopper. Yes. It was that.

She blinked away the floating image of Jason to concentrate on her surroundings. No signs of actual incoming fire. She followed Nurup towards the terminal building, about a hundred metres away. Jason's voice in her head continued.

'So there's no doubt any more – it was murder. Now, there's no *proof* the space movement had a hand in it, beyond supplying the weapon, but the circumstantial evidence is kind of strong.'

'You could say that,' Myra agreed, making a conscious effort to unclench her jaw. Having her suspicions confirmed after all this time of indulging then dismissing them was a shock.

Fucking heart attack . . .

'They don't exactly throw that sort of kit around,' she mused aloud. 'Too easy to reverse-engineer, for one thing. But why would they do it?'

Through the long corridor, letting Nurup and Mustafa do the lookout. Out of the corner of her eye she could see the adjacent, outbound corridor, packed from end to end with a slow-moving queue.

'Well, the obvious motive would've been to stop him making the offer to the Kazakhstanis.'

'And how do you know about that?'

'Uh, that's classified.'

Myra had to laugh.

'But how would they have known about it, I mean before—?'

'You tell me.'

They'd reached the concourse. It wasn't quite as crowded or frantic as she'd begun to expect; most of those intent on leaving must have already left, or at least be in the exit queue. Much to her relief, no newshounds or reporters had spotted her yet, though she identified one or two by their flak-jackets and communications clutter and vaguely familiar faces. Scanning the crowd, she saw a man in the uniform of the Workers' Militia, who caught her eye, saluted and started pushing towards her.

'It was as much of a surprise to everyone else in the government as it was to me,' she said. 'We figured it was Georgi's own bright idea, which he'd spring on us once he'd got some provisional – oh!'

Mustafa bumped into her back.

Jason waved to her, over heads.

'You never told me you were *here*!'

'Yeah, well . . . thought I'd surprise you.'

It was strange seeing his lips move, and hearing the words, beyond earshot. Like lip-reading, like telepathy.

'Who is that guy?' Nurup asked suspiciously.

'He's OK,' said Myra. She wasn't sure whether introducing Jason as a CIA agent would be a good idea, so she didn't.

And then they met up, and to everyone's surprise she and Jason met in a long embrace.

'Jesus, man!'

She broke loose and turned to the militia driver.

'Thanks for coming. Room for these three guys?'

The driver nodded. 'This way please.'

He led them to a service door which Myra knew she must have passed hundreds of times and never seen. Their progress was less inconspicuous – the two *muj* weren't the only armed passengers, but

274

they were the most noticeable. As the driver fiddled with the push-bar latch Myra noticed heads bob and a little buzzing camcopter swoop from the concourse's rafters.

They hurried along a passageway of corrugated iron and unplaned, splintery joists, and emerged beside a jeep in a small bay of the car park.

'Ah, now that's sensible transport,' Myra said as they all piled in. The Militia jeep had a light machine-gun mounted on its rollbar. Mustafa made that his post. Nurup sat in the front with the driver, rifle propped in the crook of his elbow, pointing up. Myra and Jason sat in the back, with Mustafa's legs and the ammo belt between them. As the jeep careered out of the carpark and swerved on to the main road into town, Jason leaned over and said, loud above the noise and the slipstream, 'You were saying?'

'About Georgi's great plan, yeah. As far as we can tell he never told anyone else, not even Valentina. That was him all over – he was a bit of a Kazakhstani patriot, and he *still* tended to act like this whole place was his personal fief. Which it once was!'

The jeep was making good progress – most of the traffic was in the other direction, towards the airport or – judging by the amounts of luggage and household goods piled on top of cars and trucks – towards Karaganda. Her relief at seeing the evacuation already under way was dampened by flashback images of other roads, other columns of vehicles: the road to Basra, the road out of Warsaw, the perimeter of Atlanta . . .

But no, not here! They had their own air cover – Kazakhstan's elite aerospace defence force would surely shield these refugees. She thought briefly of setting up a conference call with Valentina and Chingiz, but decided against it. This conversation with Jason was the most urgent she could have right now, for reasons that were more than personal.

'OK,' Jason was saying, 'as to the motive, right, did anyone *else* approach you for some kind of similar deal, after Georgi's death but before the coup?'

'Only the fucking space movement!' She swallowed hard. 'David Reid himself, at Georgi's funeral.'

'Jesus H. That kind of fingers them, doesn't it?'

Myra found the question of *who knew about what* bugging her.

'Well, there's a problem with that,' she said. 'Whoever killed

Georgi, or had him killed, *must* have known that that would make us suspicious of the spacers. I mean, even before you found the evidence, I had them in the frame. And it's a bit hard to reconstruct now, you know how it is, but when I refused to give Dave any hands-off guarantees, let alone any more . . . active support, well, that suspicion must have been in the scales. Might even have tipped them.'

Mustafa shouted something and brought the machine-gun down and around to the rear. Myra shifted her legs smartly away from the ammo belt and twisted her head around. Five hundred metres behind them was a small, jockeying pack of cars and jeeps, in front of a cloud of dust and beneath a halo of camcopters. She clapped Mustafa's thigh.

'Leave them alone!' she yelled.

He replied with some Uzbek profanity, but desisted, swinging the machine-gun muzzle skyward again.

'So you're saying killing Georgi was counter-productive for the spacers?'

'Damn right!'

'OK.' Jason leaned back in the cramped seat and closed his eyes for a moment. '*Cui bono?* Who benefited?'

'Ah, shit,' said Myra, realising, just as the jeep turned the corner into Revolution Square, and stopped. Myra grabbed the rollbar and pulled herself up. Long practice in estimating the size of demos clicked into place automatically, like eyeband software.

About ten thousand.

'Oh, Jeez,' she said.

It was not a particularly militant or angry crowd, at that moment. Tents and shelters and stalls had been set up, and many of the banners were propped against them or leaning on street furniture, or stuck in the patches of now trampled grass or beds of flowers that chequered the square. People stood or sat about, in small groups, chatting, drinking coffee, reading news off broadsheets or eyebands or handhelds, listening to speeches and songs, arguing with each other or with the scattered ones and twos of the Workers' Militia. Some were dressed casually, others in their best outfits or in national costumes or street-theatre radiation overalls.

'Looks pretty dangerous,' said Jason.

She gave him an appreciative nod. 'Yeah, that's a *mass* demo if ever I saw one. Not to mention a big fraction of the remaining population. Shit.'

The kids back in Glasgow had been right: her small state was having a big political revolution. The two *mujahedin* glowered uncomprehendingly at the mingled banners of Kazakhstan, the ISTWR, the old Soviet Union, the International, the red flags and the black.

She ducked and placed a hand on Nurup's shoulder.

'Stand up,' she ordered. 'Look cheerful. Wave your rifle high above your head. Mustafa, for heaven's sake *smile*, man, wave your arms and keep your hands off the LMG. *No matter what*, you got that?'

To the driver, 'Around the inside edge of the crowd, towards the entrance. Slow and careful.'

She lifted herself up, swung her ass around and perched on the rollbar, feet on the back of Nurup's seat. The driver engaged first gear, then second. The jeep rolled towards the corner of the front of the building. It had about fifty metres to go, then another fifty when it would have to turn right and inch along to the entrance. They went unremarked for about half a minute. Then the people stepping out of their way started calling and pointing. A moment later the pursuing reporters caught up and all chance of discretion was gone.

She could see the news of her arrival spread through the crowd like a gust of wind on a field. The camcopters circled at a safe distance, zooming in on her and on reaction shots of the people looking at her. Their only chance, she'd decided, was to look confident and triumphant. She grinned and waved, meanwhile blinking up a call to Valentina.

'You can see us?'

'Yeah, we've got you covered. We'll open the door for you when you reach it.'

Cheers and jeers echoed off the government office's glass and concrete walls. No organised chanting or coherent mood as yet – people were still unsure what to make of her return. She smiled desperately at every individual face that came into focus, and quite a few smiled back. The hovering camcopters had their directional mikes aimed at her, but she didn't speak to, or for, them.

'It's all right, folks, comrades, we're getting it all sorted out, we've got a strong alliance with Kazakhstan, we're negotiating with the UN and we'll hold off the Sheenisov, I'll be talking to you all soon, once I've had a chance to consult—'

The jeep came to a gentle halt outside the main door. Myra glanced

277

sideways, saw a couple of militiamen holding it, ready to open, their rifles in their other hands.

'Go in, guys, all of you, I'll keep talking.'

They hesitated.

'Go go go!'

One by one they ran up the steps and disappeared inside. Myra stepped from the seat-back to the dash, over the windshield and on to the engine hood, then hopped backwards on to a step, keeping in view all the time. She backed up the steps, smiling and waving, and through the doors.

Jason's arms wrapped around her from behind.

'Well done.'

She leaned against him for a moment, tilting her head back on his shoulder, then straightened up and stepped away, turning to smile.

'That was scary.' She laughed. 'It's weird being the *target* of a demonstration – I feel I should be out there helping to organise it.'

Jason's eyes narrowed. 'That,' he said, 'might become an option.'

'Ah, fuck off, you Machiavellian spook!' She caught his hand, swept an encircling arm at Nurup and Mustafa. 'Come on, guys, let's sort out this mess.'

They held the emergency meeting in Myra's office whose broad window overlooked the square. Denis Gubanov had suggested using the Sovnarkom room, but Myra had dismissed the security man's idea. No way did she want to be in a windowless room.

Everybody was sitting on or lounging against inappropriate furniture – desks and filing cabinets and comms junctions. Myra perched herself on the highest convenient surface, the top of a book-case full of unread yellowing hardcopy. She cradled her Glock in her lap. Somehow sitting in a chair seemed frivolous. Two militia guards stood watchfully at the sides of the windows, using their eyebands to sample camcopter views from the news services. Andrei Mukhartov, Valentina Kozlova and Denis Gubanov all looked sleepless and unkempt: the men unshaven, Val's collar and tie loosened, her uniform rumpled.

Myra introduced the two *mujahedin* and Jason. Denis raised his eyebrows, but made no comment. Myra unobtrusively made sure that her three men were in a position to protect her – she wasn't at all sure who, if any, of those present were leaving the room alive, whether or not the room was stormed by an angry mob. She'd once

interviewed an unrepentant old Stalinist who'd been in the Budapest
Party offices in October 1956 . . .

'OK, comrades,' she began. 'First things first. You know the
Western powers have refused our offers. I've just today been on the
shortest diplomatic mission *ever*, and I can tell you the Sheenisov
aren't interested in a deal either. So it's only a question of time before
they're rolling down the road from Semey. But that's just background.
We have some urgent matters to discuss.

'I'm going to start with something that may not seem like the first
item on the agenda, but bear with me.' She waved a hand at the
window. 'These people can wait. It's about Georgi's death. Jason
Nikolaides here has told me the results of a CIA investigation – murder,
using a spacer nanotech weapon. Hard to detect traces, but Jason says
they've done it, and I believe him. What I don't believe is that the
spacist bastards did it. Whoever did it wanted two things – one, that
Georgi's offer didn't get through to the Kazakhstanis *before* the coup.
Two, that we wouldn't co-operate with the space movement *in* the
coup. Now, seeing as nobody except Georgi knew he was planning to
make that offer, our range of suspects is a bit narrow. Basically, it has to
be someone that Georgi would run the idea past, someone outside the
government information loop – maybe in the Sovnarkom, maybe not.'

She looked down, playing with the Glock's slide for a moment,
then looked up. She'd been thinking aloud, she hadn't had time yet to
go through all the possibilities.

'*Val!*' she shouted. Everybody jumped. 'If I thought it was you, I'd
slam you against the wall till your teeth rattled to get the truth out of
you. You and Georgi were both in the Party, unlike anyone else here.'

She smiled, pleased to see her colleagues off balance. 'But as it
happens, I trust you. Same with Andrei, who's never been into that
sort of shit anyway. Denis, now—'

The secret policeman looked up and moistened his lips.

'I swear, Myra—'

'It's all right,' Jason interrupted. 'The Company checked him out.
He's clear.' He glanced at Myra, then grinned at Denis Gubanov. 'Bit
of a commie son-of-a-bitch, but he's on your side.'

'Good,' said Myra, winging it. 'I'm going through this to *confirm*
that nobody here is a suspect. That leaves only one possibility. Georgi
must have shared his idea with somebody, and it can only have been
the FI Mil Org. The General.'

She let them think about that while she explained to Jason, Nurup and Mustafa about the nukes and the AI.

'It has its own agenda,' she concluded, addressing everyone again. 'And it's working through the Sheenisov. It wants those nukes, very badly. So do the spacers. Whether they used each other – the information on one side, the weapon from the other – knowingly or not, Georgi's murder was a move in that rivalry. Whoever controls these weapons has a gun at the head of everyone and everything in Earth orbit and at Lagrange – which adds up to about ninety-five percent of the human space presence. And I would remind you that, thanks to the coup and counter-coup, the General controls most of the Space Defense battlesats. Now, this has a bearing on what we do about the UN ultimatum. Which is –' she grinned ferally '– the *second* item on the agenda.'

'Excuse me,' said Jason, standing up. 'Just who does control these nukes, at the moment?'

'We do,' said Valentina and Myra, at the same time. Myra gave Val an especially warm smile, hoping that her apparent – and partly paranoically real – earlier suspicion hadn't wounded their friendship beyond repair.

'It's dual key,' Valentina explained. 'Defence Minister and Prime Minister have to go into the command-centre workspace at the same time.'

'And, well, it's not hardcoded in, but right now obviously we have a treaty commitment to give the President of Kazakhstan the final say,' Myra added. 'And his strategy, at the moment, is to stonewall until the last minute, to try and get some military aid concessions out of the Western powers and/or the UN against the Sheenisov.'

'So he intends to turn them over eventually?' Jason asked.

Myra hesitated. 'OK,' she said at last. 'This doesn't go beyond this room, and that goes for everyone here. You guys at the window, too – military discipline, death penalty under the Freedom of Information Law if you breathe a word of it. Everybody clear?'

They all were.

'All right then – yes, he does intend for us to turn them over, eventually. What else can we do?'

'We can use the weapons,' said Denis. 'In space.'

Val's lips set in a thin line. Myra shook her head.

'Massacre,' she said. 'I won't do it, except as a last resort.'

'You're all missing the point,' said Jason. He looked around at all of them, as though unsure whether he had a right to speak.

'Go on,' said Myra.

'OK,' said Jason, 'I'm just speaking for myself here, not for the CIA or East America. I don't know if I'll ever get back to either of them. Anyway . . . the point you're all missing is: *who* are you going to surrender your weapons *to*? Formally, no doubt, it'll be the UN. But physically, somebody's gonna have to dock with them, bring them in, disarm them. Space Defense, and maybe some of the space settlers, have the equipment and expertise to do that. There must be ways of getting past the software of your controls – there always are. Believe me, there are no uncrackable codes any more. Your co-operation would be useful, but it's not essential.'

Myra lit a cigarette. 'OK,' she said. 'So?'

Jason paced over to the window, peered out. 'Still quiet,' he said. He glanced at his watch. 'We've been in here, what? Half an hour? Soon be time to talk to the people, Myra.'

'That's cool,' Denis said. 'We've got agitators out there, they're keeping people more or less up to speed. The line is that the President is negotiating.'

'As I'm sure he is,' said Jason. 'But what does either side have to negotiate? Both sides have hit the bottom of the tank. You have nothing to offer, and the West has nothing to offer you. They will not save you from the Sheenisov. So if I were any of the other players – in particular, the spacers and your FI Mil Org, rogue AI or not – I'd be working very fast right now on two objectives. One is taking you guys and your wonderful dual-key command-centre out physically. The other is lining up rendezvous with the nukes in space. You can bet that while you think you're smart, stringing them along, *they* are stringing *you* along, and they're both going after the same things.'

He looked around again, more confident now. 'This is endgame. Not just for us, but for them. One side or the other – the West-stroke-spacers-stroke-Outwarders, or the East-stroke-the-General-stroke-Sheenisov – is going to grab these weapons and *use* them, sooner rather than later.'

'But—' shouted Val, shocked. 'The ablation cascade!'

'Not a problem for either of them, at the level we're talking about. The Sheenisov's horizons are strictly Earthbound, for the next few centuries. And their computers are invulnerable to EMP hits – they're

281

mechanical, not electronic. As to the spacists and the Mil Org, neither of them is dependent on going back to Earth, or on anything else getting off. And each unit of these forces probably calculates that they can cut and run for a higher orbit, or Lagrange. Of course, they'd rather avoid it, but if they have to they'll take it on the chin.

'So my advice to you all,' he concluded, 'and to those people out there, is get the hell out. And warn everybody that at the first sign of any messing with you, or Kazakhstan, or the nukes – you'll blow them all to hell. Use the nukes against battlesats or detonate in place – either way you'll set off the ablation cascade.'

'Christ,' said Myra, shaken. 'That means the end of satellite guidance, global positioning, comsats, the nets, everything! It'll be like the world going blind!'

'Yeah,' said Jason grimly. 'And every army in the world, too. They're so dependent on space-based comms and sims that they'll be fucked. Except for the marginals, the Greens, the barbarians and the Sheenisov.' He laughed. 'If that doesn't scare them, nothing will.'

The guards at the window were moving from the sides to the centre, gazing out with complete lack of concern for cover. One of them turned around.

'The cavalry has arrived,' he said.

For a moment Myra thought he meant the Sheenisov. Then she realised that Chingiz had come through on his promise, and that the cavalry was their own.

The steppe at nightfall was a moving mass of vehicles and horses. As far as Myra knew, every last person in Kapitsa was moving out. She rode somewhere near the front; she tried to ride at the front, but she kept being overtaken by people in vehicles faster than her black mare. The Sovnarkom rump, and Jason and her *mujahedin*, rode in jeeps beside her. With her eyeband image-intensifiers at full power she could see the Kazakhstani cavalry – horse and motorised – outriding either flank of the evacuation, or migration. The scene was biblical, exodus and apocalypse in one. Banners and flags from the Revolution Square demonstration floated above the crowd, used as rallying points and mobile landmarks. The news remotes and reporters were following the process in a sort of stunned awe, not sure whether the angle was *Road People* (refugees, pathetic) or *Kazakh Rouge* (menaces, fanatic).

Something similar, though not as yet so drastic, was happening in Almaty and other towns across the greater Republic. Chingiz Suleimanyov had pitched the appeal to evacuate as the ultimate protest march, against the West's threats and its refusal of aid against the Sheenisov. If they were to be abandoned to the communists, they had nothing to lose by fleeing in advance to a place that claimed it would be defended. The threat of this avalanching into an unstoppable migration was already spreading panic in Western Europe. Northward, in the Former Union, regional and local chiefs were conferring on their own fragmentary networks, bruiting inflammatory talk of joining in.

'Come in, come in, ya bastard,' Myra muttered. She was riding in a hallucinatory ambience of virtual images, some of them pulled down from CNN and other services, others patched up from the command-centre, whose hardware they'd stripped from the offices and jury-rigged in the back of the Sovnarkom jeep. She could see a satellite image of herself from above – she could wave, and with a second's delay see one of the dots on the ground wave back. (The reassuring thing was that it was the wrong dot, a hologram fetch of herself and her surroundings seamlessly merged with the images from several kilometres distant.) She could see her own face, projected to visual displays around the world by the camcopter hovering a few metres in front of her.

Right now she was trying to raise Logan. A residual loyalty to her former comrades in space impelled her to warn them of the probable imminent disaster. The scanning search of the Lagrange cluster wasn't picking up New View. At length, frustrated, she switched to a broader sweep, and to her surprise connected almost immediately.

'Jesus fuck, Myra,' Logan said, without preliminary pleasantry. 'This is your biggest fuck-up since the Third World War.' He didn't make it sound like an accusation.

'Thanks for the reminder, comrade,' Myra snarled. 'I'm going against my better judgement telling you this, but I've fallen out with your General. That little electric fucker has had the bright idea of making his own bid for world revolution, and I don't intend to wait around to see how it all works out in practice, thank you very much.'

'Yes, I had heard,' Logan said heavily. The delay seemed longer than usual; Myra guessed because she was strung out, running on

283

stretched time. 'You called to say that?' He sounded distracted. A very pretty black girl who looked about ten years old stuck her face past his, grimacing at the camera, filling its field with her microgravity sunburst of frizzy hair. Logan shoved at her.

'Oh, push off, Ellen May,' he said, not unkindly. 'Go and pester your mum, OK? Or Janis. She'll have something for you to do, you bet.'

The girl stuck out her tongue, then flicked away like a fish.

'Kids,' Logan grinned, indulgent despite himself.

'Yeah, they're great,' Myra said, with a pang. 'What I called you for is about that, actually. If that kid's gonna have a future, you guys better get your ass out of Lagrange.'

'We have,' said Logan, five seconds later. 'We raced through our preparations after the coup. We haven't got as much gear as we'd like, but the asteroid miners are going to swing in and join us there. We finished the burn twelve hours ago.' He looked about. 'Made a real mess of stuff I didn't have time to lash down,' he added sadly.

'You're on your way to *Mars*?'

'Yes, at last.' His grin filled the screen. 'Free at last!'

'What does the General think about this?'

'Ah,' said Logan. 'When I found it was bidding to use your orbital nukes in the coup, I figured the same as you did. Not safe to stick around. You remember I said we'd have to leave a few hundred tons behind? Well, it's among them, still in the clutter at Lagrange. We ditched the bugger.' His triumphant smile faded to a bleak inward gaze. 'I hope.'

'Is it still in control of the Mil Org?'

'I guess so. We couldn't do anything to it, beyond discarding the section the hardware was in. Its software is a different matter, it gets everywhere, but, hell—'

'What do you mean "it gets everywhere"? I've got a suspicion it's downloaded to the Sheenisov's weird Babbage engines, but—'

Logan nodded. 'Yeah, and it's probably copied its files to anything of yours that's been in contact with it, like your phone, but it's just the source code, it can't do any harm so long as you don't open the file—'

At that point the connection ended.

Myra took her phone from her pocket and was about to jerk its jack from her eyeband, just in case, when she realised the precaution was irrational. If the bugger was actually running on her phone they were doomed already. She thought about the time the General had appeared right in her own command-centre, and could only hope that Logan was right, and that only its source code, and not its live program, had been secreted there. And in other places . . .

Someday, somebody would open a file stored in the Institute at Glasgow, and find Parvus, and the General behind him. She wished that person luck. Then she remembered Merrial MacClafferty, and realised she'd have to do more.

She had just finished rattling out her urgent message when she heard a dull, distant bang behind her, and turned. Through the eye-band's night vision she saw on the horizon the expanding green glow of the first cruise missile to hit Kapitsa.

It was not the last.

Hours later, in the twenty-below midnight, when most of the migration had camped around fuel-dump fires, Myra was sitting with Jason in front of a portable electric brazier, in the shelter of the dozing horse. She was simultaneously in the command-centre with the others, and with Chingiz. The UN and US had never intended to negotiate, and even the pretence had been dropped.

The Kazakhstani airforce was expending missiles, planes and lives above Almaty now. From space the command-centre was pulling down images of moves from the battlesats. Tiny, manned hunter-gatherer probes were burning off, matching orbits and velocities with the cached nukes. They had hunter-killer escorts, and they were obviously from opposed coalitions – already their exchanges of fire were being replayed on CNN, now that the Kapitsa bombardment had stopped for lack of remaining targets.

'. . . no choice,' Chingiz was saying. 'Our first responsibility is to defend our people, the people we've taken on the duty to protect, even if that means killing more innocent people on the other side than would die on ours if we don't.'

That's talking, thought Myra, that's the way to look at it, that's right. Screw the greatest good of the greatest number. Or maybe not.

'That's the end of the world,' said Valentina.

'It's ending anyway,' Myra said. She looked up from the fire. 'That's my final analysis! We may even save lives in the long run, if we blind and cripple the forces that are getting ready for the last war.' She laughed bitterly. 'In both senses of the phrase.'

An officer leaned into the visual field around Chingiz, and spoke urgently in his ear. Chingiz nodded, once, then raised his hand.

'This is it,' he said. 'Some of the space settlers' diamond ships have just entered the atmosphere. They're heading for—'

Connection lost.

Myra jumped up, and to her utter horror and amazement she saw them, jinking and jittering through the sky towards her. Their infrared radiation signature was arrogantly clear – they didn't need to bother with shielding, unlike the stealth fighters they resembled. One moment they were dots on the horizon, the next they were discs overhead, swooping past at a thousand metres. Their laser lances slashed the vast encampment, and were countered seconds too late by futile fusillades of skyward machine-gun fire. Then they were at the other horizon, and –

– banking around for a second run –

– screams of people and beasts in the night, dying under the laser beams and the humming rain of their own misdirected, falling ordnance –

Earth versus the flying saucers! Way cool!

Myra shook off that mad thought and reached for the command-centre controls as though through thick mud. Valentina's eyes shone in the firelight for a moment, and Myra saw in them a reflection of her own resolution. Then she and Valentina stooped together to their task. As Myra rattled through the codes, she waited for the laser's hot tongue on her neck.

The diamond ships were far too fast for human control, or even for their enhanced, superhuman occupants. Their main guidance systems were real-time uplinks to the space stations, which a few good nuclear explosions could disrupt.

The sky went white, and the black discs fell like leaves.

The ablation cascade did not happen all at once. Lagrange went to eternity instantaneously, in one appalling sphere of hell-hot helium fusion, but Earth orbit was a different thing. Hours, perhaps days, would pass before the last product of human ingenuity and industry was scraped from the sky. Even so, the comsats were among the first to fail. Most, indeed, were taken out by the electromagnetic pulses alone. Riding into the first dawn of the new world, Myra knew that the little camcopter dancing a couple of metres in front of her might well be relaying the last television news most of its watchers would ever see.

Behind her, in a slow straggle that ended with the ambulances and litters of the injured and dying, the Kazakh migration spread to the horizon. The sun was rising behind them, silhouetting their scattered, tattered banners. There was only one audience, now, that was worth speaking to: the inheritors.

'Nothing is written,' she said. 'The future is ours to shape. When you take the cities, spare the scientists and engineers. Whatever they may have done in the past you need them for the future. Let's make it a better one.'

The camcopter spun around, soared, darted about wildly and dived into the ground. The horses' hooves, the worn tyres of the vehicles, crushed it in seconds. Myra wasn't worried; she could see her own image, with a few seconds' delay, appearing in the corner of her eye-band where CNN still chattered away. The rest of the field was filled with bizarre hallucinations, the net's near-death experience.

God filled the horizon, bigger than the sunrise.

15

The Hammer's Harvest

I sat on the plinth of the statue of the Deliverer, and smoked a cigarette to fight my stomach's heaves. Gradually my mind and my body returned to some kind of equilibrium. The din of the launch celebrations, the lights of the houses and pubs, became again something I could regard without disgust and hear without dismay. I stood up, and the ground was steady under my feet. I looked up, and the sky was dark and starry above my head.

I walked a few steps from the statue and turned around. The Deliverer on her horse reared above me. Merrial had told me, a couple of weeks earlier, the reason why the Deliverer's features varied on all the statues I'd ever seen. She was a myth, a multiplicity. Her hordes had never ridden from far Kazakhstan to Lisbon's ancient shore, as the songs and stories say. They had never swept all before them. Instead, each town and city had been invaded by a horde raised closer to home, on its very own hinterland. How many hundred, how many thousand towns had met the new order in the form of a wild woman on a horse, riding in at the head of a ragtag army to proclaim that the net was thrown off, the sky was fallen, and the world was free?

It was that final message, the last ever spoken from the net and the screens, that had identified them with that singular woman, the Deliverer. I leaned forward, to read again the words chiselled on this plinth, as it is on them all, from far Kazakhstan to Lisbon's ancient shore:

NOTHING IS WRITTEN. THE FUTURE IS OURS TO SHAPE. WHEN YOU TAKE THE CITIES, SPARE THE SCIENTISTS AND ENGINEERS. WHATEVER THEY MAY HAVE DONE

IN THE PAST YOU NEED THEM FOR THE FUTURE. LET'S MAKE IT A BETTER ONE.

The last words of the old world, and the first of the new.

I thought of Merrial, and took another step back, still drawing on my cigarette. She was older than I had ever imagined possible. But she was also, I realised, still as young as she'd seemed when I'd first seen her. Nothing had changed, nothing could change that lovely, eager, open personality. She was not old, she had merely . . . stayed young.

As I would.

What did I have to complain about?

I laughed at myself, at my own youthful folly. In the long view of history, in the promise of a long life to come, the difference in our chronological age, however great, could only be insignificant.

A step, a swish, a scent. Her warm, dry hand clasped mine.

'Are you all right, Clovis?'

I turned and looked at her, and drew her towards the plinth. We sat down.

'Merrial,' I said, 'I know who you are.'

'Oh,' she said. 'And who am I?'

I handed her the booklet, open at the page.

She sat for a long moment looking down at it, with a slight smile and a slowly welling tear.

'Ah, fuck,' she said. 'Everybody else there is long gone, as far as I know. But maybe I wouldn't know, as they wouldn't know about me.' She sniffed, and handed the booklet back. 'So now you know. I never wanted to be what people would expect of me, if they knew.'

'But you are,' I said. 'You knew about the AI, and you expected Fergal to do what he did. I saw your face when he said it, and it was like you'd just cracked a piece of white logic.'

'Or black! Aye, I knew. The Deliverer told me about it herself, just before the end. She warned me that it was a dangerous thing, though benign according to its lights. Like Fergal!'

'But *why* did you give it to him?'

Merrial leaned back and looked up. 'Because the deadly debris is up there, colha Gree. I *know* what happened at the Deliverance, because I lived through it. I saw the flashes. I was there when the sky fell. I knew the ship would never get through without a much better guidance system than the one I was working on – well, I knew by the time I'd finished testing it, which was not that long ago. I needed someone to find the AI under cover of seeking something else, and I needed someone who'd put it on the ship – for good reasons or bad.'

She lowered her gaze and smiled. 'So here we are. And now it's you who has to decide, *mo gràidh*. That ship's success will stimulate others, from other lands as well, from the Oriental and the Austral states. Competition between companies and continents, great revolutions to come, and the sky road before us. If it's not launched, or its new mind is ripped out and it fails, or if indeed the AI is not smart enough to save it, then it'll be a long time before it's tried again. And the next to try might not be as benevolent as the International Scientific Society. It could be an army, or an empire.'

She grabbed my shoulders and gazed at me. 'If you walk in there and tell Druin and his boys, that's what could still happen.'

I closed my eyes. 'I can see that,' I said, 'but I'm more concerned about the power Fergal, or someone like him, might have.'

'Open your eyes,' Merrial said.

She was looking very serious. 'That thing, the AI, the planner, it can only do what people let it tell them to do. Fergal said there are no such people yet. What he should have said is, there are no such people *any more*. Your people, colha Gree, they are not the types to let themselves be ordered about by communists – because they have never been ordered about by anyone!'

'Ah!' I said, suddenly understanding. 'Because of the Deliverance, and the Deliverer!'

Merrial laughed.

'"No saviours from on high deliver",' she said wryly. 'Your people delivered themselves. That's another thing I saw, and I'll tell you about one day. If you're still with me.'

'Oh, yes,' I said. 'I'm still with you.'

'Good,' she said. 'We have a lot to do and a long time to do it in.'

She looked around pointedly. The square was jumping.

'So, colha Gree, are you going to ask me for a dance?'

'Of course,' I said. 'Would you do me the honour?'

For a second before we whirled away I stared at the scene before me, fixing it in my memory. Behind the statue Mars was rising, a blue-green dot in the East. Whatever became of the ship, whether it soared to a safe orbit or was blasted to smithereens, other ships would get out there somehow, on the sky road.

Whatever the truth about the Deliverer, she will remain in my mind as she was shown on that statue, and all the other statues and murals, songs and stories: riding, at the head of her own swift cavalry, with a growing migration behind her and a decadent, vulnerable, defenceless and rich continent ahead; and, floating bravely above her head and above her army, the black flag on which nothing is written.